Pride's Way

Pride's Way

By ROBERT MOLLOY

THE MACMILLAN COMPANY

New York   1945

To
Sylvia Chatfield Bates

Pride's Way

Part One

CHAPTER ONE

IT WAS A SUNDAY MORNING IN MAY, and the sun was blazing over Charleston. The sunlight poured its silver over the harbor and over the wharves, over the gleaming white spire of St. Michael's and the more sober spire of St. Philip's. It shone with entire impartiality on the stately old houses of the East Battery and on tasteless Mid-Victorian dwellings and gingerbread houses of the eighties and nineties, and on Negro shacks. Its warmth lay on tiled roofs, and slate roofs, tin roofs, roofs of tar paper. It struck the gleaming whitewashed walls of old houses, and the mellow bricks of others, and the plaster walls of various pastel hues, and the unpainted wooden houses, and somehow, like the Charleston legend, it beautified them all.

It shone on cobblestones, and on macadam, and on dirt streets. It streamed over live oaks, laurels, crape myrtles, sycamores, palmettoes, fig trees, azaleas a little past their prime, wistaria that clung to fences and gates and walls; on gardens hidden behind high fences, and on geraniums set in tomato cans on the window sills of Negro hovels. It glanced obliquely into the room in Henry O'Donnell's house on Tradd Street, where Miss Julie Gerard was preparing, for the second time that Sunday, to attend Mass.

Miss Julie Gerard: Officially she was Mrs. Andrew Sharp, but Charleston has a convention much older than the Lucy Stone League, and she would have been Mrs. Sharp only to strangers and to servants. She was a widow; she had been born in 1840, and therefore, in the year 1910, she was seventy. And since it was 1910 and not 1943, she felt seventy.

Miss Julie was short, just a bit over five feet two, and very plump. She was pink-skinned and blue-eyed, and she wore gold-rimmed spectacles with black silk thread wrapped around the bridge to protect her nose. She had a heavy, good-natured jaw, which, when she had her plate in, protruded slightly. She was dressed in heavy black silks, a little round widow's bonnet with a thick black crape veil, and heavy black high-topped shoes which fitted her loosely. "You'll never get to Heaven in tight shoes," was one of Miss Julie's maxims.

She was going to eleven o'clock Mass, and as it was exactly 10:11 as she stood there, making her final preparations, she felt there was no time to be lost.

"I'll put me beads in me pocketbook," she said. Miss Julie had a trick of muttering to herself and suiting the action to the word, or vice versa. She put the rosary into her bag, at the same time making sure that there were two nickels, one for each collection, handy in the change purse.

"Now, lemme see, have I forgotten anything?" she mumbled (rather loud, for she was hard of hearing). "The indulgences, that's what. . . . Well, too late now. I'll write them down when I come back." She ran them over in her mind: a plenary indulgence for receiving communion at seven o'clock Mass; three hundred days for saying "All for Thee, Sweet Jesus," as she awoke. Fixing them firmly in her memory, she descended the stairs.

As she came out the side door (which was really the front door, on the piazza, for the house was what in Charleston is called a single house, and turned its side to the street) Henry O'Donnell, her son-in-law, looked up from his *News and Courier*, which he was enjoying in the shade of the split bamboo screen. It was a hot day, but Henry wore his coat, in deference to ironclad custom. Some wit has rather unkindly described a Southern gentleman as a man who won't kick his wife downstairs while he is wearing his hat. He might have said, a man who never takes off his coat where anyone may see him. It is true that Henry O'Donnell did not belong to the *haut ton* of

Charleston society; but he had his own place to keep up, and he was punctilious to a degree about it.

"I'm going to eleven o'clock Mass at St. Mary's," Miss Julie said in her heavy deaf voice.

Henry nodded. Miss Julie couldn't resist saying:

"Henry, why don't you come with me? You know you ought to go to Mass on Sunday."

"Why should I go to Mass? You know I'm a saint. It would be a waste of time."

Miss Julie grunted disapprovingly, but she could not help smiling. Henry was a devil, she thought. Well, she was not responsible for his soul. She set him a good example, and she wasn't one to interfere.

James and George, the two little O'Donnell boys, had seen her from the back yard where they were squabbling. They came tearing through the garden and onto the piazza to tell her goodbye.

"Granny! Goodbye!" James shouted. He ran up to be kissed.

"Me first!" George, the younger boy, shouted. He tried to thrust James aside, and James promptly struck him squarely in the face.

"Boys! Don't fight," Miss Julie said. "Brothers should love each other. James, tell him you're sorry."

James sulkily complied, and Miss Julie kissed them both and went out. Henry tensed his big frame in anticipation of the slamming of the door. It slammed heartily, and he relaxed. Miss Julie was noisy; that was one of his grievances.

"Annette!" he called.

Annette came out of the passageway leading to the kitchen, where she had gone to speak to Jennie, the cook.

"What is it, Henry?"

"Miss Julie's gone to eleven o'clock Mass at St. Mary's. At a quarter past ten."

"Yes, I know."

"Isn't she a bit late?" he asked. "St. Mary's is every bit of fifteen minutes from here."

"You know how Ma is about being early."

"I should say I do," Henry retorted, for he was awakened at five every Sunday by Miss Julie's rising to attend seven o'clock Mass. He remarked upon it once more, as if for luck.

"That's Ma's way," Annette said peaceably. "She doesn't approve of low Mass on Sunday. She just goes for communion."

"I suppose when we move to the new house she'll get up at four-thirty."

"Probably."

Henry snarled under his breath, and Annette cautioned the children against noise on the Lord's Day and went back into the house, wondering where Sarah, the nurse, was.

Meanwhile, Miss Julie, looking very much like Queen Victoria, was proceeding at her bishop's walk along Tradd Street. She noted that it was a fine day, but did not dwell upon it; and that Mrs. Henry was sitting on her piazza, and wondered how Mrs. Henry's pains in the back were progressing. She walked past the fine old houses without giving them a thought. They were an old story to her. She knew a lot about the people who lived in them, too—which ones paid their servants promptly and which did not, and whose cook was fed butts meat, and who their ancestors were. But there were a number of other things on Miss Julie's mind.

She was thinking of the fact that they were going to have a ham for dinner; that she wished Henry would fulfill his religious duties; that her son Francis hadn't been near her for weeks and weeks, and that Emma and Josephine, her sisters in Chattanooga, were trying to persuade her to patch up her latest quarrel with Tessie.

A few people were straggling home from nine o'clock Mass at the Cathedral. "Father Schmidt was late today," Miss Julie thought. "Father Mellon will have to hurry with ten o'clock Mass."

She trudged on in the Sabbath stillness. A keener pair of ears would have noticed the rustle of the live oaks and palmettoes, and the far-away clip-clop of hoofs on the cobblestone streets; but to Miss Julie the calm was complete.

At Meeting Street she turned north toward St. Michael's, blazing white against the sky over pastel-hued walls and mellow brick and brilliant gardens. She did not give St. Michael's more than a glance, for the utilitarian purpose of telling the time. A gleam in the gutter caught her eye, and she stooped amid all this historical elegance to pick up a choice oblong of tinfoil for her collection. Calmly stuffing it into her purse, she went on.

A 1907 automobile, resplendent with brass and blue enamel, sputtered by like a motorboat, with a hoarse toot from the rubber-handled horn. A cyclist tinkled his bell. A few colored maumas in gay turbans were wheeling their charges to the Battery. A lone buzzard circled above the market to the northeast. The trolley car clanged.

The sun was almost oppressively warm now, and Miss Julie walked even more slowly, so that ten o'clock Mass was two-thirds over when she entered the little church. St. Mary's was not Miss Julie's parish, but it had a French tradition, and Miss Julie liked to go occasionally. Besides, Father Dodd was an impressive preacher, and did her soul good.

She knelt in the last pew, and with religious thrift opened her missal and followed the remainder of the Mass; and, as usual, it annoyed her when the congregation bustled out, with a whiff of sandalwood and cologne, the instant Father Murray left the altar. She sat in silent disapproval, nodding or smiling to acquaintances, until the church was once more empty, when she proceeded to the front pew and knelt to recite her rosary in the loud rumble which she imagined was a whisper. She felt quite peaceful now. Her troubles had almost faded out of her mind. Miss Julie was fundamentally a happy old woman. She wanted only peace of mind, enough to eat, and time for her quilting and churchgoing. Her grandchildren adored her, and her daughter and son-in-law were kind. If it hadn't been for that quarrel with Tessie there wouldn't have been any real cause for uneasiness in her mind, none whatever.

And now Miss Julie was seventy, and Miss Tessie sixty-eight, and they were both widows. Miss Tessie had been a widow for twenty years. Her children were all dead, and she was entirely alone. It would have been admirably right and fitting had she and Miss Julie maintained close relations, but the pity of it was that they had disagreed steadily ever since their childhood. They had quarreled over Julie's greater success in school and greater attraction for young men. They had quarreled over their children, and taken up the children's childish quarrels. They had done battle over fancied slights, and memories, and over commissions and omissions. And steadily the intervals between reconciliations had become longer.

It was all so foolish, Miss Julie thought. They had been sitting talking at the sodality meeting, and old Miss Georgie Peters had mentioned Miss Tessie's husband and his career in the war. Miss Julie loved a joke, and something had prompted her to say:

"Willie Fisher? Why, Willie was so nearsighted the Yankees came right up and took the sword out of his hand."

She had never known who repeated that to Tessie; but they hadn't spoken again, after the quarrel, until Pa died three years later, in 1903. . . . Well, Tessie had a kind heart, when all was said and done. She had made the overtures to her newly widowed sister, and they had edified their circle of acquaintances by being seen together for all of eighteen months. Until Lucien died.

Lucien, as the eldest, had come into possession of the daguerreotype of their father and mother, and on his deathbed he bequeathed it to Miss Julie. And then Tessie had come along and sworn that it had been promised to her. But Miss Julie had kept it. And now it was six years since they had spoken.

"She had no right to it," Miss Julie said aloud. And then she realized that she was in church, and hoped no one had heard her.

Miss Julie hadn't worried about that quarrel until lately. She said that as God was her judge she hadn't started any of the quarrels between her and Tessie, and that being on peaceful terms with her was just another occasion of sin anyway, for they were sure to quarrel again. "And I have enough occasion of sin as it is," Miss Julie said.

It was only when Emma and Josephine had decided that her seventieth birthday called for a reconciliation with Tessie, and had begun writing letters from Chattanooga trying to make peace, that the matter had really entered her mind again. First she had been indignant at the interference; then troubled; then penitent. She had almost reached the point of making up her mind to go and see her sister and put an end to the quarrel.

Kneeling there, she tried to thrust the matter out of her mind by meditation on the mysteries of the rosary, but it kept cropping up.

It was the purest coincidence that Miss Tessie was moved to go to St. Mary's that very Sunday, unless, as Miss Tessie afterwards did, one attributed it to the hand of Providence. But as the organist was beginning a prelude, Miss Tessie entered the little church and sat in a pew halfway up the center aisle.

Miss Tessie was pink-skinned and blue-eyed, too, but there the resemblance between her and Miss Julie ceased. She was short, also, but she was very slender. Her mouth drew down peevishly at the corners. Her eyes had great haws under them, like those of a St. Bernard dog, but she didn't in any way resemble a St. Bernard dog. She looked for all the world like an angry rabbit. Even her mourning, though complete, was different from Miss Julie's. Instead of the black silks she wore a broadcloth skirt and a shirtwaist of a black material like lawn, with a high collar and a frill. Her hat was not the little black widow's bonnet, but a hard black straw with a moire band, and her veil was transparent. A gold watch hung below her left shoulder from a gold brooch. Although she was myopic, she did not wear glasses, for she was vain about her eyesight. And thus she did not see Miss Julie.

Father Murray was never one to make haste with the divine service, and in the close heat of that Sunday morning he dawdled more than ever. Miss Julie approved this—she did not think it reverent to hurry through Mass, as some of the younger priests did—but she was relieved when Father Murray had finished the reading of the Gospel in Latin and Father Dodd clambered into the pulpit, paused dramatically, and read the announcements and the Gospel in English.

Father Dodd was a tall, cadaverous priest with a gentle face and a reputation for saintliness. It was generally believed that he disciplined himself very harshly; but he was the favorite confessor of the erring young. Nothing seemed to shock or surprise him, and his penances were light. For all his saintliness and gentleness, however, he was an unrelenting preacher, and he did not choose his texts because he thought they might please his hearers.

That day was no exception. It was the first Sunday following Memorial Day, which is May 10th in Charleston, and Father Dodd had made up his mind to preach on peace. As he announced the text, "Blessed are the peacemakers," the palm-leaf fans were still for a moment, and the congregation waited for its next breath. For Charleston in 1910 had neither forgiven nor forgotten, and peace, so close to Memorial Day, was a dangerous theme.

Father Dodd went about his subject in a general way. He spoke of the beauties of forgiveness and of Christian charity, and the binding up of wounds, and brotherhood; and old Dr. Dupont coughed, and Mrs. Pugno writhed in her cushioned pew, and everyone wondered what was going to come next; and several elderly gentlemen who had fought in the Civil War sat up just as straight and stiff as they could.

Of course, Father Dodd did not say outright that they must go and embrace the Yankees. He approved peace in more general terms, but his meaning was clear. Then he proceeded from generalities to the particular. He said that there were too many prejudices and differences and hatreds in Charleston—family feuds and the strife of brother against brother and of kin against kin. He described some of the more notorious family disagreements with a high degree of anonymous exactness, and if his congregation had acted upon his exhortations there would have been such a peacemaking as Charleston had never seen in its long life. But some of the auditors were merely uncomfortable, some turned a deaf ear, and the majority sniffed and thought that Father Dodd might do better to preach about religion and leave people's private affairs alone.

But Father Dodd's eloquence did not wholly fail of its effect. It moved at least two people profoundly. The instant he spoke of family dissension Miss Julie felt as if he were looking right into her soul.

"I'll go and see Tessie right away," she muttered. "God forgive me, I'll do the right thing if it kills me." And she really meant it.

Miss Tessie, whose imagery was more dramatic, said to herself that she would atone for her sin of pride by humbling herself to the uttermost.

And when Father Dodd mentioned "a case he had heard of," in which two branches of a family had been separated for almost a generation over a silver porringer, Miss Julie thought of the daguerreotype and was ashamed. She did not resolve then and there to cede it to Miss Tessie, but she felt ashamed, at least.

Miss Tessie thought then of the daguerreotype, too, and of how foolish she had been to make a fuss over it. Not that she wasn't properly entitled to it; it had been meant for her, and Julie had taken unfair advantage of poor Lucien in his last extremity. But then, one must forgive, and the more obvious the wrong done, the more merit in forgiveness.

All through the remainder of the Mass the sisters continued to make their good resolutions. Miss Julie felt like a different woman. She was so moved and excited that she inadvertently put ten cents into the plate at the second collection. Miss Tessie, who thought in terms of miracles, was certain that God had performed one in bringing her to hear just that sermon of Father Dodd's. She was so deeply impressed that she didn't even notice when the plate was passed.

Miss Julie's agitation was such that she did not stay to utter her thanks for the privilege of visiting God's house, but went out right after benediction and right down the aisle, full of the intention to visit Tessie and end the long quarrel. Miss Tessie left her pew determined to do the same thing. And Providence, who had brought the estranged sisters to hear the salutary sermon, now extended His hand further, and in the middle aisle, directly under the ceiling fresco of St. Jerome, He brought them face to face.

For a moment the old ladies stood, startled, each looking into the other's face for encouragement. Then, so weak is humanity, even when fortified by divine grace, that Miss Tessie, out of long habit, averted her head. Miss Julie sniffed. Miss Tessie said "Humph" in a particularly disagreeable way she had which made it rather like a hoot. Miss Julie, with a swish of black silks, turned her back.

Carefully avoiding each other, the sisters walked out. They left the church on opposite sides. Miss Julie turned toward King Street, and Miss Tessie, though that would have been a shorter way for her, turned toward Meeting.

Neither had received quite enough grace for the deed she had resolved to perform. After all, Charleston had not forgotten the War in forty-five years. Their quarrel had lasted only six.

Miss Tessie walked home with her usual brisk step. At first she was full of indignation with Julie for refusing her advances, which she was certain must have been evident from her expression; then she wondered if she had been to blame; and finally she very nearly decided that she had.

At first, Miss Julie was certain that Miss Tessie had deliberately insulted her. Then she began to wonder if she shouldn't have spoken first. Finally, she blamed herself completely. But she didn't turn around and go toward Miss Tessie's house. Nor did Miss Tessie retrace her steps to catch up with Miss Julie.

Miss Julie was further troubled by the problem of her indulgence book. In view of what she had just done, should she consider the morning's gains forfeited? It was a nice point, and she gave it a good turning over in her mind.

[10]

Finally, on the principle that the just man falleth seven times a day, she decided to make the day's entry.

As soon as she had taken off her gloves and hat, she got the little copybook out of the bureau drawer and entered the day's total of indulgences. She had been keeping the account for years, and there were hundreds of plenary indulgences and whole centuries of lesser ones. Like most Catholics, she was not very clear on the subject, and she preferred to continue gaining new remissions of sin from day to day. To put it bluntly, she was not sure that all her indulgences were valid.

She put the little book away, and humming "The Bonnie Blue Flag," which the school children had sung as always on Memorial Day, she took a glass jar from the bureau top and shook out a peppermint, which she sucked with noisy relish.

This time on Sunday, that blessed interval between high Mass and Sunday dinner, was usually the most contented part of Miss Julie's entire week, a period of spiritual satisfaction blended with the anticipations of a keen appetite. But today the thought of how she had rejected the promptings of God's grace just a few minutes earlier disturbed her customary Sunday mood. It would have been so easy to get the thing over with then and there. Now it was all ahead of her.

She sat in a rocker on the piazza, inhaling the aroma of the baking ham and the tomato pilau and gazing out upon the river. On Jones' wharf she could see a pair of boys, and she recognized Joe, her eldest grandson, and his friend Walter Greene. They were climbing to the top of a clump of piles at the very end of the pier.

"If he falls off that wharf in his good Sunday suit his father will skin him," Miss Julie thought. Her heart was in her mouth until the boys finally got down and walked off the wharf. Sometimes she wondered how it was that any children ever lived to grow up.

Now if Tessie would only . . .

The gate of the high wooden fence on the side of the garden opened, and Sarah entered the yard with James and George.

[11]

They looked very cunning in their white sailor suits and wide-brimmed straw hats.

The sight of the little ones made Miss Julie happy again. She called to them ("Henry won't like that much, on Sunday," she thought with a chuckle) and they waved back. Miss Julie could tell by their gestures that they were informing Sarah of their intention to come upstairs to her, and she could see from the way Sarah glanced up and said something to them that she was in doubt about whether to let them or not. "She's just trying to keep them away from me," Miss Julie muttered jealously. She didn't care much for Sarah; she was jealous of the children's affection for the little black woman. She had tried to persuade Annette that a big child like George, four years old, didn't need a nurse any longer. But the children were so attached to Sarah: that was Annette's excuse, and besides, Sarah acted as maid. She took trouble off Annette's hands, that was the real reason for keeping her. Well, if people had two dollars and a half a week to waste on an extra servant, that was none of her business.

The little boys came running out to the piazza and clung to Miss Julie.

"Well, boysies," she said, "did you have a good time?"

"We saw a sailboat," James said. "Just like a real one. On the pond. Two sailboats. Didn't we, George?"

"I want a sailboat," George said. "Like that boy's."

"You do, eh?" Miss Julie said, squeezing him. "Well, then, you'll have to learn to build one."

"They came from the store," James said.

"When my brother Joe was a little boy," Miss Julie said, "my father built him a sailboat. It was a beautiful one, all rigged and everything."

"Did he make the sails, too?" James inquired, fascinated by this piece of history.

"Certainly. My father could make anything. He made my little altar, too, you remember."

"Maybe Papa will make me a sailboat," James said. Miss Julie could see that he was giving the matter thought. "I'm afraid he's too busy, though," he added.

Miss Julie chuckled. "James, you've got a long head." She couldn't imagine Henry building a sailboat. He was too busy reading the *Wall Street Journal* and those agricultural magazines. People were always in a hurry nowadays. They couldn't spare time for things like building boats for their children. Her father had managed a business and a farm besides, and he'd always had leisure to amuse his children.

"I guess we'll have to buy one," James said.

"A red one?" George asked.

"You can get any color."

"Maybe Santa Claus will bring you one," Miss Julie said.

George brightened. "Tomorrow?"

"Well, no, Bubber, not tomorrow. Christmas is a long way off yet."

"One hundred hours?" George asked.

"Longer than that."

"Christmas is in the winter," James said. "Ain't it, Granny?"

"Yes, in the winter."

"I wish it was winter," James said.

"Winter will come soon enough," Miss Julie said. " 'The north wind doth blow, And we shall have snow, And what will poor Robin do then, poor thing? He'll hide in the barn, and keep himself warm, And tuck his head under his wing, poor thing.' But you can't sail your boat in the winter."

James thought for a moment. He was a tenacious child. George had already forgotten about the question of the boat and was busy shifting the blades of one of the green shutters. "Maybe I can get one now," James said.

"But you're going away to the mountains, soon," Miss Julie said. "You won't be able to sail your boat this summer, either."

James sighed, as if it were all too much for him.

"Are you going too, Granny?"

"I suppose so. I always have."

She didn't care greatly for the country. In fact, it suddenly occurred to her that she hated it; hated the boarding house in which she always had to be well dressed, and the North Carolina "crackers" with their twangy speech, and the lack of fish and crabs and the absence of a church. Her conscience had hurt her, each summer, for going to a place where she couldn't hear Mass, but she had taken the attitude that after all she had no other place to go. That wasn't really true. She could have stayed in the city with Henry or gone to Chattanooga.

George climbed up into her lap, and she rocked him and sang "Frère Jacques" in very bad provincial French. James stood staring over the banisters, one foot in the space between two of them and his hands grasping the rail. "'Frère Jacques,'" Miss Julie explained, "is 'Brother James' in French." She cuddled George and chuckled at him. "What are you thinking of, Boysie?" she asked James.

He took his foot off the banisters and turned. He looked very serious as he explained what was on his mind:

"When I'm a big man and rich I'm gonna have a hundred sailboats. And Christmas every day, and automobiles, and a box of mints as big as that." He pointed up to show her how big. "I'm gonna have everything I want," he said vehemently.

Miss Julie smiled, but she felt a little troubled.

"That's not the way to be happy," she said gently. "The way to be happy is not to want anything very much."

"I want a lot of things," James said obstinately.

She let the struggling George slip out of her lap.

"I wanta play with the buttons, Granny," he said.

"All right, Bubber. Come in, and let's get the can of buttons."

James went back to the banisters and stared again at the nearby wharf. Miss Julie, while George was scattering the buttons out of the baking powder can, looked through the open windows at James.

"Poor little fellow," she murmured. "Just like his father. Never satisfied. And Tessie . . ."

She thought suddenly of Tessie, almost sixty years earlier,

shedding floods of tears because their father had given them silver watches while the girl next door had a gold one. ("I think ours are prettier, Tessie," she had said. But Tessie refused to be comforted.)

"Well, she has a gold watch now," Miss Julie thought ruefully. "But not much more time to tell from it."

There was no more time to be lost. She must go to see Tessie.

James slipped out of the room and went into his mother's. Annette was busy winding her hair over a transformation, which in those days was known colloquially as a "rat."

"Mamma, can I have a sailboat?" he asked.

"You've got a sailboat." Annette took a strand of hair out of her mouth. "The one you and George sail in the bathtub."

"I mean a big one that will sail across the pond."

"You're too little for that," Annette said.

"No, I'm not."

"Don't bother me now. Run out and play."

James, who was sensitive, left the room with a hurt look on his face which his mother didn't notice. There were a great many things she didn't notice. He went downstairs, where his father was sitting on the piazza with a magazine.

"Papa," he said.

Henry O'Donnell looked up. "What is it, my son?"

"I want a sailboat."

Henry looked at him, and as always when one of his children made a request, his first thought was of his own poverty-stricken childhood. It tempted him to grant every request. Then he recalled that it was not good for children to have everything they asked for.

"Not for the present," he said.

"When?" James insisted.

"Never, if you worry me about it."

"Please, Papa."

"You have too many things already as it is."

"No, I haven't."

"I said you had!" Henry exploded. "Now that settles it. You can't have any sailboat."

James stood there, and the tears came into his eyes.

"Go away, and let me read," his father said irritably.

The boy ran up the stairs. There was just one refuge, Sarah being too busy helping with dinner, and that was Miss Julie. He sobbed out his disappointment in her arms, and she tried to comfort him.

"Look at George," she said finally. "He isn't crying about a sailboat."

James wrenched himself loose from her.

"George never wants anything," he said angrily.

Miss Julie thought again of the silver watches.

CHAPTER TWO

On monday miss julie awoke at her usual hour, before it was very light, and this in spite of the fact that she had not got to sleep as early as usual in her troubled state of mind.

"All for Thee, Sweet Jesus, all for Thee!" she murmured hoarsely. Thrusting off the light counterpane, she swung her feet out of bed, touched them to the floor, and sat up, wide awake and brisk.

Her clothes, when she took them from the chair beside the bed, felt slightly damp. "Foggy," she thought, sniffing the air. "Hot day." She began to recite a prayer that was designed to be said while dressing, and had finished it by the time she began to get into her corset. She said it over again for good measure while she put on her petticoat and apron and pulled on her stockings and gaiters.

There was enough light for her to arrange her hair by, and she jabbed a few hairpins and a comb briskly into place, washed quickly at the washstand, trying not to make a noise for fear of waking Henry, and went to the bathroom.

Miss Julie's next move was toward the wooden altar in the inner corner of the room. That was the altar her father had built for her with his own hands. It was surmounted by a little tabernacle, in front of which was a white linen cloth. On the altar stood two white china candlesticks with blessed candles in them, plaster statues of the holy family, a sprig of palm, and a small votive lamp which Miss Julie proceeded to light, throwing a feeble gleam on the Botticelli Madonna and the Raphael on the wall and the portrait of the Christ with transparent eyelids which seemed to open its eyes if you looked fixedly at it.

Miss Julie dipped her fingers into the little holy water font hung on the wall beside the altar and made the sign of the cross. She recited the Lord's Prayer and the Hail Mary and the Creed and the Acts of Faith, Hope, and Contrition. After that, she prayed for her husband, her father and mother, her grand-parents, her dead brothers and her dead son Samuel; for her three sisters, her son Charles who was in California, her son Francis who was in Charleston but might as well have been in California for all she saw of him, for Annette, for Henry, with special note aimed at his being brought to a proper attitude to-ward his religious duties, and for her grandchildren and nephews. Then, since it was the month of May, she read the Litany of the Blessed Virgin. She added a plea for steadfastness in her purpose to make up her quarrel with Tessie, blessed her-self once more with holy water, and arose.

Having entered the day's total of indulgences gained to the already impressive total in the little black memorandum book, she spread her bedding on the window sill to air and sat out on the piazza for a few minutes to enjoy the morning and improve her appetite. The reconciliation with Tessie faded for a while from her thoughts, and she felt remarkably lighthearted. She sat happily there until she saw Sarah come in through the back gate, and concluded that it was time to dress the children. This duty gave her a chance to oversee their prayers.

James and George slept in a cubicle off their parents' bedroom, a small red-carpeted room with a crib and a child's bed and nothing else in it save a framed print of the infant Jesus which Miss Julie had placed there for their edification. When Miss Julie entered, both boys were awake. James was lying on his back, muttering something to himself which she could not hear but which seemed to give him immense satisfaction, for he was laughing at each repetition. George was bouncing in the out-grown crib and grinning as usual.

"Say 'All for Thee, Sweet Jesus,'" Miss Julie told James.

"'All for Thee, Sweet Jesus,'" James repeated hastily as he went out to the bathroom.

"That's a good boy. Now, George, you say 'All for Thee, Sweet Jesus,' like James."

"'All for Thee, Sweet Jesus,'" George said, still grinning. "Raw swimp!" he added in imitation of the vender who bawled his way past the house every morning.

Miss Julie was amused at the juxtaposition. "You rascal! Here, get into these rompers."

George, with the entire day before him, was in no hurry. He deliberately put one foot into the wrong leg of the rompers.

"That's not right," she said patiently. "Stop teasing Granny, and do this right."

George put the other foot into the rompers in such a way as to snatch them right out of her hand. Miss Julie seized them and, grasping his ankles one after the other, inserted his legs properly.

"Now come and get your face and hands washed," she com-manded. "James," she added, "put on your rompers and come into my room to get washed up."

James stood at the window listening to the fish vender who was passing, filling the air with his cry of "Shark steak, don' need no gravy! Shark steak, don' need no gravy!"

He repeated it himself at the top of his lungs, three, four, five times. At the fifth repetition his father's head appeared around the corner of the door. His face was full of lather.

"James!" he barked. "Stop that racket. Papa's shaving. You don't want to make him cut himself, do you?"

"No, Papa," James said. He threw off his nightgown and

slipped on his underwaist, blouse, and pants and then went in for his grandmother to button them.

Miss Julie scrubbed the struggling boys' faces with a cold washcloth, saw to it that they used their toothbrushes, and then gave George a ball of tinfoil to play with while she led James to the little altar and superintended his recitation of the Lord's Prayer and the Hail Mary. Then she sent them down to Sarah, tidied the top of her bureau, and went downstairs to wait for breakfast.

She walked through the garden, enjoying the sweet damp smell of the earth and the fragrance of the opening garden flowers. She fingered a rose or two on the bushes Pa had planted just before his last illness, looked at the fig trees to see how they were coming along, and went back to the porch to gather up the paper and steal a look at the obituaries before Henry got what she called his death grip on it. But there was no one dead whom she knew, and she put the paper aside.

She poked her head into the kitchen where Jennie was stirring the hominy pot.

"How long before breakfast, Jennie?" she asked the fat yellow cook.

"Good mornin', Mis' Sharp. All ready," Jennie said.

Miss Julie went over to the dresser, where the cold shrimp, just out of the icebox, were waiting to be served. She picked up one or two and popped them into her mouth.

"Just to help keep body and soul together," she muttered to Jennie. "I feel weak sometimes before breakfast."

"Yes'm," Jennie said. "Ain't it the truth!"

Miss Julie sniffed.

"Biscuits or muffins?" she inquired.

"Biscuits, muh."

"Tell Sarah not to forget the molasses," Miss Julie said. "I'll take a cracker out to Polly. He must be hungry too. Here, get out of my way, Beauty," she addressed the tomcat, who was stretched across the sill, and who, when she prodded him delicately, shifted a few inches to allow her to pass out to the piazza.

The crusty old parrot cackled out his desire for a cracker, and took the one Miss Julie held out to him. He looked sleepily at her and gnawed at the hors d'œuvre clutched in his talons. She poked a finger into the cage, and he promptly snapped at it.

"Poor Polly," Miss Julie murmured. "He's getting old and queer." But Polly had always been a snappy bird. She recalled with a smile the day he escaped and Pa climbed up the persimmon tree after him and was nipped. Pa could certainly turn the air blue. Poor fellow!

And then, by association of ideas, she thought of his death, and Tessie coming to make peace with her, and of the peace she now had to make with Tessie; and on an empty stomach it made her gloomy.

"Confound it," Miss Julie muttered half to herself with truly Christian emotion. Something seemed wrong with the world of late. She couldn't seem to feel peaceful, the way she used to. She stood there lost in thought for some minutes.

The call to breakfast interrupted her meditations, and she called to James and George, who were prowling around the back yard, and waited for them to come onto the piazza before she went in.

Annette was seated, and Henry was standing behind his chair with a look of impatience. Miss Julie greeted them and took her seat, and Henry pulled his chair up to the table and began to eat his sliced bananas. He took a few mouthfuls and then stopped and put down his spoon.

"Why aren't Betsy and Joe here?" he demanded.

"They're coming right along," Annette said. "Here, James, you and George hurry and get into your places."

"I don't like this business of coming late to the table," Henry grumbled. He looked out at the hallway, as if that would bring the laggards down a little sooner.

He frowned when Betsy came in. She was a fair, snub-nosed girl of ten, the apple of Henry's eye, the reason for all his ambitions. He did not scold her. He reserved that for Joe, who came sleepily in a moment later, with all the insouciance of thirteen.

"Why are you late to breakfast, sir?" Henry demanded.

"I couldn't help it, Papa," Joe declared. "I popped my shoe-string, and I had to stop and find another one."

Henry grunted. "Pop your shoestrings before you go to bed," he said with entire unreason.

Joe grinned and slid into his chair. "Let's go!" he said.

"Aren't you forgetting your manners?" his father demanded.

The irrepressible Joe said that he was sorry, and the meal proceeded.

Miss Julie was fairly content now. She loved her meals, and she loved the big dining room, with its French windows letting in the sun. It was not an aristocratic room. In place of the old mahogany you might have found in the houses of the old families, or in the houses of such as hadn't been forced to sell their heirlooms to collectors, here all was Victorian, of a sort to tell the connoisseur of Charleston that the O'Donnells were on the way up. The chairs and sideboard were of reddish oak; the walls were paneled waist-high in the same wood, and hung above that with dark red wallpaper. An ornate clock stood on the mantel, flanked by two enormous vases. Over the clock was a game piece, with various dead and bleeding birds, and over the china closet a companion picture in which a red lobster consorted with sea foods in a raw state. Game dishes stood upright in the china closet, and a great bowl of cut glass was placed in the center of the sideboard.

But what chiefly interested Miss Julie was what stood on the table—the great dish of hominy, the pile of pink shrimp, the radishes, the hot biscuits, the pitcher of molasses. She filled her plate to the brim with the fiery hot hominy, melted and stirred in a huge lump of butter, and heaped the ice-cold shrimp to one side. Then, methodically, she took the shrimp one at a time on her fork and plunged each into the hot cereal.

There was never very much conversation at the O'Donnell breakfast table. The children were discouraged from talking at meals; Annette was not likely to say very much in the morning, and Miss Julie was too busy eating. Usually the dialogue was between Henry and James or George, when either rattled his fork absently or kicked his heels against the rung of the chair. As both were barefoot in the spring and summer, this annoyance was not in evidence.

When coffee was served, Henry took up the paper; and during his perusal of it, as during his shaving, it was understood that there was to be entire silence except in case of necessity.

Miss Julie, after a few casual words to Annette about the state of the fig trees and rosebushes, paid strict attention to her food. As she didn't hear casual comment very well, she made it a rule not to puzzle herself or to spoil her enjoyment of the food by overmuch trying to listen to it. She finished her coffee, asked to be excused even before the children rose, and went upstairs to her room.

She intended to visit Tessie "that morning, or afternoon," and as she meant to be forehanded about it she set promptly to work on her room, examining the mattress for bugs, making the bed, and straightening the washstand and dresser. "A lick and a promise," Miss Julie muttered, "and then I'll sew on me quilt." She smoothed the linen dresser cover, opened the capacious bottom drawer, and took out the materials of her handiwork.

Henry had now gone off to the office, the older children to school. Save for visits from the baker, the iceman, and the grocer there would be quiet for hours, with only the children around. Annette usually went visiting or shopping in the morning. Miss Julie sighed contentedly as she began to sew.

Miss Julie's quilts, of which she had made dozens without number, had a sort of tile pattern. First she would carefully cut out, with great accuracy, little hexagons of crisp smooth paper, such as magazine covers were made of, and something over an inch in diameter. Over these she sewed bits of cloth from various sources; then she joined a number of them to form a center, and each varicolored center was imposed on a square of maroon or dark blue cloth. The dark blue and red squares were alternated, stitched together, provided with a gingham backing, and the whole was quilted.

The occupation was one admirably fitted for the using up of time, and permitted entirely free use of the mind. Miss Julie worked away, her thoughts shuttling from Tessie to James and his wish for a sailboat, and then back again, and then to Francis and Charles, and then back to Tessie. It was on the latter that they dwelt most, and she murmured many times, "I'll get me hat on and go to see her," without doing it. And so the morning wore on.

Miss Tessie, meanwhile, was having her own struggles of conscience, and had been having them since yesterday's meeting with Miss Julie in St. Mary's. Alone in her neat room in the great crumbling house in Archdale Street, she had wrestled with her pride. Sunday afternoon she had almost succeeded in carrying out her determination to visit Julie and be friends with her— but not quite. Then she had prayed long at night and gone to bed fortified with a firm resolve. "Right after breakfast," she said to herself. "After all, it was God's own command, and I must obey it. To err is human, to forgive divine."

But right after breakfast she had discovered that her room really must have a cleaning before the day became too warm. And with Miss Tessie, cleaning a room was none of your licks and promises such as were entirely satisfactory to Miss Julie. When she cleaned, she cleaned in the manner of a Philadelphia housewife, and woe betide any speck of dust that stood in her way.

She even washed the glass over the picture of Theodora, which stood on an easel, and changed the water in which the flowers under the picture stood. "Pray for me, daughter," she murmured. She was convinced that Theodora was a saint—she had once had a vision of her in long white robes—and the easel was a sort of shrine to her.

By about ten o'clock, however, this excuse for delay had been exhausted, and Miss Tessie put on her best clothes and her hat. She got only as far as the landing outside her door, and then her heart failed her. She could not bear the idea of humbling herself, and she dreaded a rebuff.

"The spirit is willing, but the flesh is weak," Miss Tessie said, putting her hat back in the wardrobe and sitting restlessly and uneasily down. But not for long. She was a woman of energy and action, and not one to sit and mope. She rose, put on her hat once more, and this time actually went down the steps and out the front door and in the general direction of the O'Donnells' house. Her impetus took her as far as the farthest corner of the block on which their house stood; then she retraced her steps and circumnavigated the block like a timid child.

It was an action apparently betokening indecision, irresolution, and timidity, none of which qualities Miss Tessie possessed in the slightest degree. Along with her belligerency, however, went a pride so exquisitely sensitive as to make her, in the present case, precisely like a fearful person. She felt that she could not face that first moment of surrender. She went back toward home, but when she arrived at the Cathedral she decided to go in. She knelt before the side altar dedicated to the Blessed Mother and prayed. She was especially devoted to the Blessed Mother.

Likewise agitated, but not to the point of dressing to go out, Miss Julie finally put aside her quilt and got up. She took, from a bag on the window sill, a black and oozy banana and thrust it into the pocket of her apron.

"I'll go down in the gyarden and sit awhile," she muttered.

James and George were playing in the shade of the bamboo screen when she reached the downstairs piazza, George piling blocks into a crazy structure and James playing with his crayons and a coloring book.

"Look, Granny," James said to her. "Ain't I coloring this fine?"

Miss Julie was too greatly preoccupied to do more than grunt absently.

"Yes, Bubber," she said, without looking at his handiwork, and went down the steps.

James looked surprised at her lack of interest, and went ruefully back to his task of coloring a sailboat bright red and yellow, there being no white crayon for the sail. "I'm gonna get a sail-boat," he said to George.

Miss Julie ambled across the path among the flower beds to a great rice drum painted green that was set under the crape myrtle, sat down heavily with a sigh, and took the banana from her pocket, brushing off a few crumbs that adhered to the end of it. Meditatively she removed the skin from one end and began to eat.

The sun was so bright by now that the brown house with its red tin roof glared like the picture on a postcard, and the shade in which Miss Julie sat was blue-black by comparison. The marshy smell from the near-by river at low tide hung heavy over the neighborhood. Flies and yellowjackets buzzed among the morning-glories and sweet peas and nasturtiums; a little green lizard sunned itself on the brick side wall. The roses looked wilted in the heat.

Miss Julie threw the banana skin into the hole in the center of the rice drum and crossed her hands. "Sooner or later I'll have to do it," she thought. She felt drowsy.

A vagrant colored boy went by, rattling a stick against the iron fence rails. A wagon passed over the cobblestones. A faint breeze stirred the persimmon tree close to the back-yard fence. Miss Julie closed her eyes and nodded a little, recovering her balance with a jerk.

She was suddenly aware that someone was coming through the garden towards her.

"My heavenly fathers!" Miss Julie ejaculated, nearly toppling off the drum. For there, only a few yards away, was Miss Tessie.

Miss Tessie strode purposefully over to the crape myrtle. Miss Julie, who hated scenes, felt that there would now be a dramatic one, right in public, and shrank inwardly as she arose to greet her sister. "What on earth can I say to her?" she wondered, with a feeling that was strangely like dread. She sensed trouble. But it was too late.

"Good morning, Julie," Miss Tessie said, as casually as if they had parted on the best of terms just the day before. "How are you?"

[25]

"She's lost her mind," Miss Julie thought, and responded with wary politeness that she was quite well. "And how are you, Tessie?"

"Very well."

"Sit down here," Miss Julie said. "It's so warm."

The two old ladies perched side by side on the green drum, like two black beetles on a leaf. Miss Tessie mopped the beads of perspiration from her forehead and opened her fan. They sat awhile in a somewhat embarrassed silence.

Sarah saw them from the kitchen window, out of which she had peered to see who was coming in the gate.

"Jennie," she said to the fat yellow cook, who was picking rice, "do for Gawd's sake look hyuh."

Putting down the pan of rice, Jennie went to the window.

"Do, Jesus!" she exclaimed. "Miss Tessie talkin' to Miss Julie!"

"Bible say de lion lay down wid de lamb," Sarah remarked.

Jennie wagged her turbaned head.

"How come dey always so quarrelsome?" she asked.

"Gawd knows, chil'. Miss Annette say they been like that befo' she born."

"Buckra is funny," Jennie declared. "Mo' people een Charleston don' talk to each other than does."

"Ain't it!" Sarah said. "Think o' them po' ol' souls feazin' and frettin' fuh six 'ears all over a fool picture de junkman wouldn't trouble to pick up."

"Ain't I always tell yuh dat comet t'ing bring bad luck?" Jennie asked. "Well, it done bring bad luck to Miss Julie."

"It's de truth," Sarah said.

The two Negresses looked at each other with shining eyes, and rocked with silent laughter. There was nothing funnier than the doings of old people, particularly old white people.

"I had a letter from sister Emma on Saturday," Miss Tessie said finally. Her voice, when she raised it for Miss Julie's benefit, was croupy and had a break in it, and the two boys stood at the edge of the porch to listen more intently.

"I had a letter too," Miss Julie replied in her husky baritone.

"I was sorry to hear about poor John. They asked me to come to Chattanooga and stay for a while."

Miss Tessie's face fell slightly. "They didn't ask me; but perhaps they knew I shouldn't care to go, anyway. Chattanooga! Hoo! I've had enough of that backwoods settlement!"

"I suppose they thought you wouldn't want to be away from your work," Miss Julie said kindly. Ask Tessie? She remembered Tessie's last trip to Chattanooga. "It's nice that you're having a bit of rest from nursing, though," she added.

"I expect to be called any moment," Miss Tessie said.

Miss Julie knew very well that her cases were becoming longer and longer separated, and wished she hadn't said that.

"It's these nigger nurses," Miss Tessie went on. "Everybody wants to hire them now. And I ought to have a telephone, too."

Miss Julie hated telephones, and had never, after her first trial or two, consented to use one. She had been known to tell her daughter: "The phone rang when you were out, Nettie, and Sarah was gone somewhere with the children, and it was Jennie's afternoon off, so I didn't find out who it was."

"I don't like telephones," she said. "I'm always afraid of getting a shock from them."

"Shock! Nonsense," said Miss Tessie dogmatically. "They're perfectly safe. Especially if you stand on a mat. That catches the sparks, Brother Joe told me."

Miss Julie shook her head. "Anyway I don't care for all these newfangled grandeurs."

"It's very nice here," Miss Tessie said, rather aimlessly, like one unable to think of something better.

"It's a nice gyarden," Miss Julie agreed. "The Spanish bayonet isn't doing very well. Henry put some fertilizer on it last month, but it don't look healthy."

"Annette sent me some sweet peas," Miss Tessie said. "She certainly has lovely ones. I kept them under my dear Theodora's picture."

"Annette is very kind. She's a good daughter," Miss Julie said proudly.

There was another silence, and then Miss Tessie cleared her throat uneasily.

"Julie, I came here today to—"

By this time the boys, devoured by curiosity and possibly by ennui, had evidently deemed it safe to come down from the protection of the porch. They trotted over and stood fidgeting and staring at their grandmother and at their less familiar great-aunt.

"James, say 'How do you do' to your Aunt Tessie," Miss Julie ordered.

"How do you do, Aunt Tessie," James said obediently, but without warmth. "Is she going to live here?" he asked his grandmother.

The old ladies smiled, Miss Julie fondly, Miss Tessie rather coolly, for she was no great hand with children. George, not to be outdone, smiled too.

"Aunt Tessie has her own home, thank you," replied that lady sharply.

"I was there yesterday," George said. "She has a lot of funny pictures."

"Yesterday means any past time to George," Miss Julie explained, hoping to soften this rather tactless remark about Tessie's cherished family photographs.

"He certainly favors his father," said Miss Tessie with obvious distaste.

"All the children favor Henry," Miss Julie conceded. "Sometimes he jokes and says they take after the doctor. Henry is full of fun."

Here Sarah came to the rescue.

"James! George!" she called. "Want a taste?" She held up a spoon, and the children trotted off in her direction.

"Francis! Charles!" the old parrot squawked.

"Polly is jealous," Miss Julie said. "He's never called a single one of Annette's children. He keeps on calling mine. Strange, isn't it?"

Miss Tessie nodded, and returned immediately to her interrupted beginning.

"Julie," she said, hesitating a little, "I came today—to ask you to forgive me." Miss Julie's deafness made it necessary to utter such intimacies rather loudly, and Miss Tessie looked around as she uttered them.

Miss Julie took off her glasses and held them in her left hand on her knee.

"I was going to do the same thing," she said.

"There's never been a Christmas or a New Year's but I've always made up my mind to come and see you. But it was always my foolish and sinful pride that got in the way."

Miss Julie nodded, comprehendingly.

"So I never did," Miss Tessie continued. "And yesterday, the Lord Himself must have guided me to hear Father Dodd. I knew right away what I must do, and I meant to do it right after Mass. But when I saw you the Devil tempted me. I went home, and I thought and thought about it. I thought I would write, but that didn't seem to be the way to do it. And yet I was afraid of a rebuff."

Miss Julie patted her sister's bony, twisted hand.

"This morning," Miss Tessie said, "I put on my hat to come, and I put it back in the wardrobe. And then I put it on again, and walked over the whole way to Tradd Street, and then went around the block. And then I went back to the Cathedral, and I prayed, and God gave me the strength and grace, and here I am."

Miss Julie chuckled, and this disconcerted Miss Tessie.

"I said to myself, 'My sister and I are old and lonely, and need each other, and it's time to stop this foolish quarreling,'" Miss Tessie continued earnestly, her chin quivering just a little.

"Quite right, sister," said Miss Julie, calmly.

"You're very cool about it," Miss Tessie almost snapped. "I should think that when your old sister, who is alone in the world, came to patch things up after six long years, and humbled herself, you'd show a little more pleasure."

"I've never been happier in my life than I am to have you here," Miss Julie said.

Miss Tessie, for all her pride, began to cry. "Nobody needs me; I'm so terribly alone, and everybody avoids me."

"Tessie, Tessie, don't cry. You've always been your own worst enemy, child," Miss Julie said with blunt kindness. "But let's forget all about that. I've never held the slightest hard feelings against you." She thought, a little guiltily, of the daguerreotype, but something within her closed over that thought like a shell. "Don't say any more about what has happened," she urged.

Miss Tessie didn't feel entirely satisfied, but she wiped her eyes and tried to smile.

"We'll see each other and talk over old times and enjoy these last years in peace," Miss Julie added, with a comfortable complacency. She felt happy, happier than she had felt in years, it seemed to her. "Two old ones like us have better things to do than quarrel," she said.

Miss Tessie, overcome with emotion, took her sister's hand impulsively. "I want you to come and live with me."

Miss Julie was startled. "Oh, I can't leave here. I'm too used to it."

"We are not going to live much longer," Miss Tessie said. "Let's make the best of the few years we have left, as you say."

Having her own words come back to her slightly twisted like that was not precisely pleasing to Miss Julie. She had her own ideas about her possible longevity and the best use of her last years. But she couldn't think of an argument, except the rude one that she didn't want to do any such thing. What, move again? Never!

"I'll have to think about it, sister."

Miss Tessie did not pursue the point. She arose, put both hands behind her neck, and stretched. "It's to keep my rheumatism from stiffening me too much," she explained.

"You ought to take salts."

As a rule Miss Tessie did not take kindly to presumptuous lay advice, but this was her day for humility.

"Salts are very good sometimes," she admitted.

"They helped Tante Eulalie," Miss Julie recalled.

"Yes, I remember."

"Sloan's liniment is fine too."

"But it smells so strong." Miss Tessie was fastidious.

"I've always been a great believer in red flannel."

Miss Tessie, though she considered red flannel the purest nonsense, did not argue about that either on this red-letter day of humility.

"I do exercises every night and morning. And I move my fingers like this." She held up one twisted hand and demonstrated. "Of course, I don't forget my prayer to St. James every day."

"Rheumatism don't bother me, thank God," Miss Julie said. "But if it did I'd take salts."

"I can't afford to be run off when I may be called on a case," Miss Tessie objected.

"No, of course."

"But how is your own health, Julie?"

"Very good, thank the Lord. I'm getting a little hard of hearing these last few months, though you may not have noticed it. That's the only thing that worries me. I've tried ear oil, but I don't think it's done me any good."

Miss Tessie, whose hearing was very keen indeed, glanced at that moment toward the house, where a commotion arose following the clang of the front-door bell. She saw Annette come onto the piazza, and go into the hall, and heard the children's voices, and with them the graver tones of her niece and Sarah. She was always absurdly self-conscious, and she reddened, just as if she had heard them talking about her.

Annette came tripping down the stairs, carrying her wide-brimmed flower-laden straw hat and swinging a silver card-case.

"Aunt Tessie! It's so nice to see you!"

She was a handsome, somewhat overdressed small woman of forty. She had her mother's clear blue eyes, but her features were more decided.

"Good day, Annette."

"I've just come from a visit to Kate Garrison's. Have the children been good, Ma?"

"I've hardly even seen them," Miss Julie said. She could detect a gleam of amusement in Annette's eyes, and she frowned to indicate that this was a very delicate situation, indeed.

"You must stay to dinner, Aunt Tessie." Annette made the invitation sound as casual as she could. "We're going to have hopping-john."

"I don't want to put anybody out," Miss Tessie demurred.

"Nonsense, Aunt Tessie. One more is nothing. Do stay for dinner. We'd love to have you."

"Very well then. Thank you. I will." Miss Tessie spoke with the air of a sovereign acceding to a subject's plea. "But I must go home first and fetch my coffeepot."

She would never drink coffee made in any pot but her own. As she had cherished this peculiarity for years and years, neither her sister nor her niece showed any surprise.

"Betsy can go for it when she comes from school."

"No, thank you," Miss Tessie replied. "I'm perfectly able to go for myself."

"Just as you like, Aunt Tessie," Annette said pacifically, and without remonstrance she and Miss Julie accompanied Miss Tessie to the garden gate and waited in silence until she was around the corner.

"Will wonders never cease!" Annette exploded. "What's got into her?"

"Tessie has a good heart, poor thing," Miss Julie said. "Don't be too hard on old people, child." She was at the point of telling about the sermon and her meeting with Tessie, but she refrained.

"Well, I can't imagine what brought her here all of a sudden," Annette said; "but I'm glad this foolish quarrel is over with. It's a scandal, and you know it very well, Ma."

"I suppose so. I don't know, though, just how happy I am about it. I knew that comet would bring something. They say that's all superstition, but it never fails. The last time it appeared, Tante Philippine fell down the cistern and had to be hauled out. Or at least that's what they said." Miss Julie put on her glasses. "Tessie hasn't changed much," she said with one of her frequent chuckles. "She and her precious coffeepot! You know why she insisted on going for it herself? So she could eat something to keep her from seeming hungry at the dinner table. Tessie's false pride will kill her some day."

"That's Charleston all over," Annette said.

"Did I ever tell you about the time she got the chicken in Chattanooga?" Miss Julie went on as they returned to the porch. "Well, she had a room near Emma's that time, and one day Emma sent little Edmond around with a nice chicken for Tessie. Tessie said her best thanks and gave him a sugarplum, and he went out. Well, just as he was in the street, he felt something go whizzing past his head. And what do you suppose it was? The chicken."

Miss Julie laughed merrily at the recollection. Annette, who had heard the story dozens of times, forced a polite little laugh.

"Poor thing. Her troubles have gone to her brain."

Miss Julie shook her head vigorously in denial.

"She was always like that. . . . Well, Georgie Porgie, how are you, eh?"

"Granny," George said. He grinned and stood up.

"Come to Granny!" she said, picking him up.

James, envious of this attention to his younger brother, caught hold of her skirt.

"You rascal," Miss Julie said, patting George. "Do you know what this little limb of the Old Boy said? He said Tessie's house was full of funny pictures."

"She'll never forget it."

"She never had any use for any children but her own. They were perfection," Miss Julie said. "Well," she added with a sigh, "God didn't let her keep any of them long enough to learn better."

Annette looked at her sharply.

"Gracious peace, I don't mean you, child!" Miss Julie said.

"God knows you've been kind to me, poor old soul that I am."
And then because she was old, and the morning's events had
upset her, her eyes filled up, and she put George down and took
out her handkerchief to blow her nose with a great show of energy.

CHAPTER THREE

"She's a torn-down devil, that's what she is," Miss Julie said.

"God don't love ugly," said Miss Tessie ominously.

The sisters were up in Miss Julie's room, discussing their
brother Joseph's wife, to whom, for perfectly good reasons, no
one of the family ever spoke. Miss Julie was about to add a bit
for good measure when the dinner bell rang.

At that welcome interruption, she rose from her rocker.
"Henry comes in at five to two," she said, "and the bell rings at
two sharp. He can't stand anything being a minute off sched-
ule."

Miss Tessie rose too, reluctantly abandoning the discussion.
"It's a great pity about Henry O'Donnell," she said, following
Miss Julie down the stairs.

The object of this remark was standing in the doorway of the
dining room as the two old ladies entered. He was a massive
man, and in the light-colored spring suit he was wearing he appeared even larger. For all his strong, stern, heavy face with the
big nose, the knobby head fringed with reddish hair, and fierce
mustaches of the same color that did not suit his features and
looked false, his bright blue eyes had a twinkle that told you he
was a genial man, and his expression, as he welcomed Miss Tessie, was geniality itself.

"Well, it's certainly a pleasure and a privilege to see you, Mrs.
Fisher," he said enthusiastically, the mode of address showing,
however, that he did not feel very intimate with his wife's aunt.
He took her hand and squeezed it.

"Thank you, Henry. I'm very glad to see you," Miss Tessie said coolly.

"And how are you, ma'am? You look as young as ever and just as pretty."

Miss Tessie's opinion of Henry had been too frequently expressed for him, or anyone, not to be aware how she felt towards him, but there was a charm in his hearty manner that was very taking, and Miss Tessie nearly smiled in spite of herself.

"Oh, go along, Henry. You and your flattery! I'm too old a bird for that."

Henry smiled gayly. "And here's my big girl," he said as Betsy came in, followed by the little boys and Annette. "Say good afternoon to your Aunt Tessie, Betsy."

Betsy obeyed prettily, and Miss Tessie kissed her with frigid restraint. Then, after a brief delay while James was settled and it was explained to George that his place was changed for the occasion, Henry prepared to carve.

"Joe is late as usual, I see," he said frowningly. "Kept in, no doubt." He glared.

Miss Julie, not hearing this, was staring with pleased anticipation at the respectable remains of Sunday's ham, the great dish of hopping-john, the baked sweet potatoes, beets, greens, the mound of bread and the dish of piccalilli. Miss Tessie was telling Annette of the illness of her adopted brother John, as if Annette didn't already know all about it, and Annette was listening politely with a vacant look in her wide-spaced eyes.

Henry, as usual, found the knife not very keen; but he sliced the meat and served rapidly ("Very little for me, please," Miss Tessie said), and the great English dishes were soon filled. By the time he laid down the carving set and passed his own plate for helpings, everyone was ready to eat. Hearty appetites were a tradition in the Gerard and O'Donnell families. Annette, who took after her father, had the meager appetite of the Sharps and was a light eater; Miss Tessie was putting on a show of delicacy.

At this moment Joe appeared from the kitchen, where he had stopped to wash his hands.

"Hello, Aunt Tessie," he said nonchalantly.

"'Hello' is for sailors," Miss Tessie replied.

"Joe!" Henry said.

"I was kept in, Papa," Joe hastened to explain. "It wasn't my fault. It was—"

"Never mind that," Henry said sternly. "What about your manners? Speak properly to your Aunt Tessie."

Joe, with a puzzled look at his escape from a scolding on account of tardiness, said, "How do you do, Aunt Tessie," sat down, and pinched Betsy, who screamed. "What? Ham again?" he inquired jocularly.

"If you don't care for what is provided, you may leave the table," Henry said. "That's the rule of this house."

"I was just joking, Papa."

"That will do." Henry was grieved that his son should humiliate him before Miss Tessie. He shook off his frown, and turned to Miss Tessie, who sat at his right. "I suppose Miss Julie has told you we're going to move?"

"No, she hasn't."

"Miss Julie," Henry asked, raising his voice, "you haven't told Mrs. Fisher about our new house?"

Miss Julie looked startled. She put down her fork. "What new house?" she demanded, looking from one to the other. "I don't know what you mean."

Henry frowned again, and made a noise in his throat.

"Why, the Lafontaines' house," he said, very loud. "We've been talking about it for weeks."

"Well, this is the very first thing I've heard about it." Miss Julie suddenly felt peevish. "Nobody ever tells me anything," she declared.

"Why, of course we told you about it." Henry reddened with annoyance.

"Why, of course we did, Ma," Annette told her.

Miss Julie shook her head obstinately. "I'm not as deaf as all that," she stated in a tone of dogged insistence.

Henry sat back in his chair and let out his breath in a puff, as if to say he gave up.

"I've bought it," he said proudly. "I'm going to move in when the others go to the country, and Sarah and I will have it all ready when they come back."

Miss Tessie said, "Indeed?" but betrayed neither surprise nor approval. It was no affair of hers if Henry O'Donnell had bought the City Hall and the Customhouse into the bargain.

Miss Julie found it difficult to take in the news. New house? The suddenness of it stunned her. New house? Why, this one they were living in was the second Henry had moved to since his marriage. People ought to stay in the houses they were born in. That was the proper way.

"Grandeur," she thought disdainfully. That was the trouble with Henry. He was never satisfied to leave well enough alone. And there were those rosebushes Pa had planted, too. She was not going to have them left behind for some stranger to enjoy— or, worse, to neglect.

She was suddenly aware that the others were still talking.

"What are you going to do with Pa's roses?" she demanded.

"I've arranged to have them moved," Henry said. He wanted to impress Miss Julie with the significance of the change. "We really need more room, and it's about time we left this sleepy old street," he added.

"Tradd Street has some of the most distinguished houses in Charleston," Miss Tessie said.

"This isn't one of them," Henry replied, drily. "It hasn't any conveniences, and it's an eyesore. The new house is a fine place, right near the lake, and with hardwood floors, and a big garden and back yard for the boys to play in. The Lafontaines spent a lot of money on it, and they built it just like one of the old Charleston houses. Only an expert could tell them apart."

"They didn't have any right to spend it," Miss Tessie said. "The money wasn't theirs. It was their old grandmother's, and they took it and built that house without telling her a word about it. When she found out about it, she was going to sue Henry

Lafontaine; but they hushed it up for the sake of family pride. Though what family pride they meant, I'm not able to say."

"The Lafontaines always thought a lot of themselves," Miss Julie said; "but they weren't any great cracks, I can tell you."

"You can't tell me anything about the Lafontaines or their house," Miss Tessie said. "I nursed the old man, and I know all about them. Why, the first one of them that came to this country was a barber. They call him a surgeon, but I know better—my mother and father told me all about that. Surgeon! Hoo! He was a barber in New Orleans, that's what he was. It makes me sick, the way some people put on airs. Our family had their carriages and servants when old Lafontaine was cutting hair for a living."

"Well, they've done well for themselves," Henry said.

"No wonder," Miss Tessie retorted. "They were so mean they fed the servants butts meat, and when I was there I saw old Jeanne Lafontaine weigh the sugar in the barrel once a week to make sure the darkies weren't stealing it. The Lafontaines! Hoo!"

"You know," Annette said, "Jeanne's son Robert thought he saw a burglar in the parlor and threw a bottle of ink at him, and it splashed on one wall. And she never would have that spot papered over, because it was a memorial to Robert's bravery."

"The idea!" Miss Julie said.

"They're touched, every one of them," Annette said.

Henry did not particularly care for these *chroniques scandaleuses,* and sat through them in an offended silence.

"Some of them were very dark, too," Miss Tessie said. "I've always suspected their blood. They're very swarthy for white people, even with French blood."

"Oh, go on, Tessie," Miss Julie protested.

"There's more than one changeling in many a family tree," Miss Tessie said darkly.

"That's dangerous talk, you know, Mrs. Fisher," Henry said.

"I don't care whether it's dangerous or not," Miss Tessie snapped. "I'm entitled to my opinion."

"What will you do with the cow and Princess?" Miss Julie asked. She wanted to get the matter all straightened out in her mind, despite the fact that she felt irritated about it all.

"We'll have to give them up," Henry said. "The cow is unsanitary and there are going to be new regulations about milk. The Board of Health is going to be very strict about it. I met Dr. White, and he told me so."

"Harry White?" Miss Julie inquired, not altogether sure she had heard correctly, although the conversation was now becoming loud enough for her to follow it with pleasure. "Well, he's got a sight of gall interfering with other people. Why, his old father poisoned half of Charleston with rotten meat for years. I remember how we used to hold our noses when we ran past his butcher store and yell, 'Buzzards!'"

"And now he puts on airs and tells the rest of us how to live," Miss Tessie said contemptuously. "'Dr.' White, indeed! I wouldn't call him to put a dog out of its misery."

"Anyway," Henry said, "we'll have to give up the cow." He looked challengingly around. "And the horse, too. Joe and Betsy don't care for driving her any more, and I'm good and tired of trying to persuade her to pull the cart. It's been months since it was out of the stable, and all Princess does is eat and get fat."

"Will we get an automobile?" Betsy asked eagerly.

"No, my girl," Henry said. "We have troubles enough as it is. But—"

"Henry Lafontaine was another peculiarity," Miss Julie said. "I can see him now, with his telescope, looking at the sky and telling everyone that came near about Venus and Jupiter and such nonsense."

"He married a woman from Orangeburg," Miss Tessie reminded her. "They said she—" She glanced at Betsy and said no more.

"It seems that we're moving into a house with a lot of traditions," Henry said drily. "I hope we'll live up to them. Anyway, I want a house where I can entertain friends once in a while in a proper manner."

"Will Santa Claus find his way to the new house?" James inquired, struck by a sudden doubt. "Will Santa Claus find his way to the new house? Will Santa Claus—"

"Not if you aren't a good boy," Annette said. "Now stop shouting, James, and finish your dinner."

"I'll have the house painted and papered, you see," Henry said. "Miss Tessie, let me cut you a slice of ham."

Miss Tessie, who had eaten almost nothing, refused, but Miss Julie was not averse to accepting the suggestion when it was made to her. She glanced at the untouched heap of hopping-john on her sister's plate.

"Does hoppin'-john make you flatulent, sister?" she asked, intending to whisper but bringing out the words with considerable volume.

Betsy laughed delightedly, and Joe guffawed.

Henry frowned furiously. "Joe! Betsy!" he scolded. He saw that Annette was barely restraining a smile. Miss Tessie did not seem to have heard. Henry glowered at Miss Julie, and then Miss Tessie smiled ever so slightly; but it was not a smile of amusement.

To change the conversation, he asked Betsy how she had got along in school that day, and listened absently to a long recital of minor events at Miss Low's. Tessie and Annette and Miss Julie, relieved of paying particular attention to him, returned to the Lafontaine family and had it thoroughly in its place by the time dessert was served.

Miss Julie ate a tremendous dish of bread pudding, and put her spoon down with a sigh. "I feel as if I would pop," she said to her sister.

Henry shuddered. Then Sarah took the little boys away, Betsy and Joe asked to be excused, and the others sat and drank their coffee.

Henry retired to the parlor for his siesta, and the two old ladies returned to their rockers on the upstairs piazza.

"I must say," Miss Tessie offered, "that it was very humiliating for you not to have been told about this new house."

[40]

"They both say they told me. I don't doubt their words, but I'm sure they never said a word about it."

"Hoo! Of course they didn't. When they get ready to do anything they just pick up and do it, without so much as a by-your-leave."

Well, thought Miss Julie as she settled with a grunt into her chair, they didn't have to have her permission to change residences. Of course, they might have asked her advice, or at least told her right away. Her pride had been deeply wounded, and she couldn't help showing it. To be treated as she had been made her feel useless and old. Yet she did not want to admit that feeling to Tessie. To do that would have been to confess that she had been slighted; and in the Southern code, to be slighted without resenting it and showing that resentment was to lose face.

"Well, I suppose they must have told me," she said unconvincingly. She felt a strong urge to justify her position in the O'Donnells' house as an honored and privileged one. "Anyways, I haven't got any cause to complain. Henry couldn't have treated his own mother any better than he's treated me. Anything I do is perfectly all right for him."

She could recall exceptions, but she did not mention them.

"Henry O'Donnell is an Irish upstart," Miss Tessie said in as low a voice as she thought Miss Julie could hear. "I know it sounds ungrateful, after I've enjoyed his hospitality—though it was really yours I was accepting—but he makes me gag sometimes. He and his notions! Why, we had our big house and our servants and carriage when his grandfather was driving a dray for a living."

This was an exaggeration. Henry's grandfather had been in the trucking business, but he hadn't driven a dray. In fact, the O'Donnells even then had been recognized as thoroughly worthy people. But Miss Julie was too full of dinner for an argument, and she was not going to risk a quarrel over such a trifle. Loyalty, however, compelled her to say:

"Henry is an ambitious young man. He's worked hard, and he deserves anything he gets."

"That's no reason for putting on airs," Miss Tessie said sourly.

Miss Julie was silent for a moment. She could not suppress the feeling that Henry *was* putting on airs. She belonged to a generation that could understand and condone a descent from a higher estate. That had been the fate of many a Charleston family, including her own: but when you descended in the world it made no real difference. You were entitled to retain your notions of yourself. Rising in the world, though, did not carry with it the same privileges; you had no right to be pretentious.

"Henry wants his children to have all the things he never had," she explained, thinking of the poverty-stricken childhood he had struggled against.

"Humph!" Miss Tessie hooted. "I have no objection to Henry getting prosperous. It's his social climbing that I can't stomach. I suppose he thinks he'll get into the St. Cecilia Society, now. He'll come down off his high horse when he tries." Ordinarily she despised the St. Cecilia Society with all her heart, but she admired it for keeping upstarts in their places.

" 'Kind hearts are more than coronets,' you know," Miss Julie said. "There never was a more generous man than Henry. Nobody ever wants for anything if he finds out about it. I could tell you lots of things he's done for people. And he has been good to me."

"It's a fine thing to be easily pleased. I don't care to be beholden to anybody: I like to lead my own life and be my own boss." Miss Tessie stood up and stretched. "I must go along, Julie. There are some things I have to attend to, and 'never put off' is my motto."

"Well, if you must, you must," Miss Julie said with relief. Tessie was strong medicine, and a small dose was enough. Besides, she was sleepy and felt she must have a nap. "I'll get Sarah to wrap up your coffeepot." She went to the back of the porch and leaned over. "Sarah!" she roared.

Sarah put her head out of the kitchen window.

"Yessum."

"Wrap up Mrs. Fisher's coffeepot, please. She's going home."

"Yessum."

"That Sarah has a saucy manner," said Miss Tessie. "Annette spoils all her niggers."

"Darkies are not what they used to be."

Miss Tessie grunted. "Nothing is the way it used to be." She went in and put on her hat and veil and gloves.

"Annette!" Miss Julie shouted. "Aunt Tessie's going home."

Annette came out of her room and accompanied them down the stairs. At the foot of the steps Sarah stood with the precious coffeepot wrapped and ready. Miss Tessie took it tenderly.

"I did without coffee for three months after my old pot wore out," she said, "until I found this one."

Miss Julie and Annette nodded to show how well they understood the difficulty of procuring a satisfactory coffeepot.

"Henry!" Annette said. "Aunt Tessie is going."

Henry sat up with a start and then rose. He came out into the hall.

"I'm sorry you're going so soon, Mrs. Fisher."

"I don't wear out my welcome," Miss Tessie said.

"We hope you'll come again soon."

"Oh, you don't have to invite me to dinner," Miss Tessie replied. "Goodbye. Come to see me, Julie."

"I will," Miss Julie promised.

"I'm all alone, you know."

Miss Tessie managed to look pathetic as she said it, and Miss Julie's heart ached for her. She stood with Annette watching the brisk little figure trot away, head up in defiance of the entire world.

"Poor Tessie," said Miss Julie.

"Poor soul," Annette said.

She brought it all on herself, Henry thought as he went upstairs to spruce himself up for the return to the office. He felt very peevish with both Miss Julie and Miss Tessie. It was damned mortifying to have Miss Tessie think that they hadn't said anything to Miss Julie about their new house; and he resented the way they received the news of the move, which, after all, was a big turning point in his career.

"Poor soul indeed," Miss Julie murmured, thinking how worn Tessie looked. "Although she's a good two years younger than I am," she reflected, and felt quite brisk for a moment at the thought of Tessie's poor state of preservation. She followed her daughter up the stairs at a rate unusual for her, and wound up painfully out of breath.

"Ma," Annette said, "I can't understand how you didn't hear us talking about the new house."

"I don't pry into any of your affairs," Miss Julie said stiffly. "You don't have to tell me anything. When you're old and dependent, you just go where people take you, that's all."

"Now, Ma, don't carry on. We were sure you understood all about it."

"I don't see how that can be," Miss Julie argued. "Anyway, you don't have to worry about me. Tessie wants me to go and live with her. She don't let any grass grow under her feet," she added, more good-humoredly.

"Ma, don't you be foolish. You know you couldn't keep it up. We all wanted you to make up with Aunt Tessie, but nobody could wish you the trouble of living with her. Why, Our Lord and Savior Himself couldn't do it. Don't let her put that in your head."

"I don't need anyone to make decisions for me," said Miss Julie.

"Well, don't you be foolish. If you start listening to Aunt Tessie you'll go crazy." She swept into her room, and Miss Julie went into hers.

"Henry," Annette said. "Ma's feelings are hurt. She doesn't believe we told her about the house."

Her husband gave a last touch of the comb to the few strands of hair on the top of his head. "I don't care what she believes. She's mortified me, I know that."

"Aunt Tessie has already put a bee in her bonnet. She's asked Ma to come and live with her. I'm afraid she's going to upset Ma."

"There's no fool like an old fool," Henry said.

Miss Julie, meanwhile, was loosening her corset and easing off her gaiters. "A good nap will do me good," she muttered. "It's been quite a day. And this is only the beginning. Tessie will never let me alone until I go to live with her. That's the way she is."

With a heavy sigh she stretched herself on the bed. But she didn't, as usual, go to sleep right away. She lay there on her back, staring at the canopy and the tucked-up mosquito netting, and thought of her humiliation in the affair of the new house. The idea of their trying to say she hadn't heard them when they told her about it! Ridiculous!

They just hadn't bothered. They thought it was none of her business; they'd just move her around like a piece of furniture, without telling her a word in advance. They could deny it until the Cooper River ran dry, but she was convinced.

Maybe, as far as that went, they just didn't want her. Maybe that was why they were so glad for her to have made up with Tessie, even though Annette had just said she couldn't live with her. Maybe that was just to cover up her real intentions.

She could have stood it if Tessie hadn't been right there to see how she was treated.

Miss Julie felt pretty miserable.

"I guess nobody cares very much for me," she murmured, with her mood at its blackest. She shut her eyes and tried to sleep.

She felt something bounce the bed, opened them, and saw James.

"Hello, Bubber."

"Can I lay down by you, Granny?" James asked.

"You bet you can."

"I'll be very quiet."

He snuggled up to her and put his arms around her neck.

[45]

"Where's George?" Miss Julie inquired.

"He's sleeping in Mamma's room. But I like to come in and sleep in your bed."

"That's right. You love your poor old Granny, don't you, Jamesy?"

"I love you best of all," James said.

Miss Julie was touched and comforted. "You must love everybody the same," she protested.

James did not reply for a moment. He snuggled up closer to her. Then he rolled over on his back.

"How long will it be before I'm a man?" he demanded.

"A long time."

"A hundred years?"

"No, not a hundred years. About fifteen years."

"And then I'll have little boys, like me and George?"

"Probably. You rascal!" She tickled him.

"When I'm a man," James said, "and have little boys, I'm gonna give them everything they want."

Miss Julie chuckled.

"I'm gonna give them sailboats," he added.

Miss Julie did not reply.

"I wish I had a sailboat," James continued.

"You'll be going to the country in a little while," she told him once more. "You won't have any place to sail your sailboat."

"I don't care. I want one."

The longing in his eyes was more than Miss Julie could bear, and the urge to satisfy that wish of his heart for a sailboat was stronger than her thrift.

"He's only going to be a child once," Miss Julie reflected. "I'll buy him a sailboat."

"You let Granny sleep awhile now," she said, "and in the morning, when I go out, I'll take you and we'll buy a sailboat like the one you saw on the pond."

"Couldn't you buy it this afternoon?"

"No, Bubber, I'm very tired and it's too hot to go out."

"Well, then, I guess tomorrow will do," James said.

CHAPTER FOUR

HENRY CAME IN TO SUPPER TIRED AND HOT, and the two little boys raced to see him. Rather wearily he tossed them into the air and put them down.

"Papa! Granny's gonna buy me a sailboat!" James announced.

The look of paternal affection vanished from Henry's face.

"But I said you were not to have a sailboat, my son."

"Well, Granny's gonna buy me one." James was suddenly conscious of a threat in the atmosphere. "It won't cost you anything."

Henry frowned. "I said you were not to have a sailboat. It doesn't matter what it's going to cost. I don't want you to have one. You have too many toys already. Understand?"

"Granny can buy it for me, can't she?" James insisted, while George stood by open-mouthed.

Henry lost his none too secure patience.

"Damn it, I said no!"

Annette, coming downstairs to see what was the matter, found James dissolved in tears.

"What's he done?" she inquired.

"Oh, to hell with it!" Henry snorted, going up the stairs.

"What's the matter, James?" she asked the boy.

"Papa says I can't have a sailboat, and Granny promised to buy me one," James sobbed.

"Well, then, I suppose you can't have it."

"But Granny said she would buy it," James protested through his sobs.

"Your father knows best. Come, now, don't cry. You wouldn't cry like that if I was dead."

George put his arm around James. "Don't cry, Bubber," he pleaded, bursting into tears himself and doing rather well at it.

James was a high-strung child, and his crying became more

and more violent. He was nearly in hysterics by the time Miss Julie descended the stairs.

"What's the matter, Bubber?" she immediately inquired.

"Papa says I can't have a sailboat," James yelled. "I want a sailboat, and he says I can't have any."

"Well, I suppose your Pa knows best," Miss Julie said. "Though I can't see why he doesn't want the child to have a toy he's set his heart on and that I promised him," she told Annette.

Miss Julie's voice, at its softest, was carrying. Henry came hastily down the stairs, and his face was like a thundercloud.

"Let's get this settled." He slapped one hand into the other for emphasis. "I told James he was not to have a sailboat because I thought he had too many toys already. That settles it."

"Of course," Miss Julie said stiffly. She didn't like Henry's tone at all. "I have no intention of interfering. But I promised the child I'd buy him a sailboat."

"I told him yesterday he was not to have one," Henry said angrily. "He deliberately went to you behind my back and asked you for one. That in itself would be enough for me to forbid him ever to have one. I don't like sneakiness. And I won't have it."

"Well, of course I didn't know anything about that," Miss Julie said. "I didn't know it was because you didn't *want* him to have one."

"Why else should I refuse him?" he demanded. "I'm able to provide anything my children want, as long as it's reasonable."

"I'm very sorry, Henry. I didn't understand that."

"I suppose you want the child to think I'm just being stingy about it," he growled.

"I never meant to suggest anything so ridiculous," Miss Julie retorted, reddening. "I declare, Henry, I'm surprised at you for saying such a thing."

Henry was about to reply; but he made a noise in his throat, and that was all. He never could be really outspokenly rude to Miss Julie, who was old and was a permanent guest in his house.

"I'm sorry, Miss Julie." He patted her shoulder. "I know

you're fond of the children and want them to be happy. But it's a matter of principle. I've told James he can't have a sailboat, and I'll have to let that stand. He can't be allowed to think I will change my mind over it for no reason at all, and he had no right to go to you after I had forbidden him."

James, completely unappreciative of the values of all this ethical discussion, continued to cry over his disappointment. Miss Julie's honor was satisfied, but she was grieved and angry. She put an arm around him.

"Never mind, Bubber," she said. "Try to be a big boy now, and don't cry any more about it. We have to do what your Pa says, you know. He understands what's best for you." But she cast a wrathful glance at Henry that belied her words.

"Of course James understands," Henry said. He patted the boy. "Don't you, son?"

James was silent. He snatched his head away and turned his back.

"Very well," Henry said, with a heavy heart. "If that's the way you want to act, all right." He had to keep his dignity; but he had never developed a thick skin where his children were concerned, and this bitterness on the boy's part hurt him. "When you're ready, we can have supper," he announced.

"I don't know why Joe and Betsy aren't here," Annette said. "They know it's suppertime."

"Damn it, I'm not going to have these children coming late to meals," Henry blustered. "What are they doing out at this hour, anyway? I won't have it."

"Well, it isn't my fault," Annette replied defensively. "I don't tell them to come late for supper, if that's what you mean."

"Oh, for Christ's sake!" Henry said wearily.

Annette took James and George out to the kitchen to freshen them up after their bout of crying, and Henry and Miss Julie sat down.

"It's been very hot," Henry remarked, to show that he was perfectly calm now.

"Yes," Miss Julie replied.

[49]

"I thought Mrs. Fisher looked rather affected by the heat."

"Tessie is rather frail-looking these days."

"I suppose it's hard for her to be all alone, the way she's been all these years."

Miss Julie could feel herself flushing. It sounded very much like a hint. The thought returned that perhaps they didn't want her.

"She prefers it," she replied noncommittally.

Henry might have added something that would have indicated more clearly what he meant; but Annette came back with the children, and as the dishes were passed he dropped the thread of his remarks, and Miss Julie remained offended and doubtful. Both of them looked at James's reddened eyes and woebegone expression.

"It's an outrage to upset a child like that," Miss Julie thought, more indignant than before. "And to make a fool of me, too. What will the child think when I promise him something and then they forbid me to keep my promise, just as if I was a child myself."

Henry felt considerable compunction, too. "It's a small matter to make such a fuss about," he thought, and was half tempted to say, "Go ahead and get your sailboat, if your heart's so set on it." But he really felt that the children were overindulged, and the fact that he had already taken a stand made the thing a matter of pride. He could not reverse himself. He sighed, and tried to banish the affair from his mind. He turned to the lateness of Joe and Betsy for diversion.

"Where do you suppose those two have gone?" he asked.

"Why, I know very well where they've gone. Betsy went to the Browns, and Joe went to play ball on West End."

"Call up the Browns," Henry said.

Annette, with a sigh, rose to do as he asked, and had just asked for the number when Betsy, hot and bedraggled, entered from the piazza. Annette hung up the receiver and returned to the dining room, plainly angry at having gone to all the trouble for nothing.

"Betsy, what do you mean by staying out so late?" she scolded. "I didn't know it was so late."

"Didn't know? I suppose you waited until they were ready to have supper?"

"Well, I didn't know it was so late," the girl repeated.

Annette made a little sound of disapproval. "It's very mortifying to have you children hang around until people think you're hinting for an invitation. Try to have a little pride. I declare, I try to bring you up to be a lady, and you act like a child from the Borough."

Betsy felt the disgrace she had brought upon her family. There were tears in her eyes as she went upstairs to wash her face and hands. This annoyed Henry, for Betsy was his especial favorite.

"Weren't you a little hard on her?" he asked.

Annette was not accustomed to arguing with Henry, however she might feel. But she had been upset about James's fit of crying, and angry at Henry for having caused it, as she felt, unnecessarily.

"You don't like me to interfere when you correct the children," she snapped. "Why do you meddle when I do it?"

There was a moment of profound silence.

Henry's eyes narrowed disagreeably. "Damn it, I asked you a civil question," he said. "If you don't want to answer the same way, don't answer at all."

"You're always spoiling Betsy. She's enough of a tomboy as it is. I want her to be a little lady."

"I know what constitutes ladylike behavior as well as you do," Henry replied. "Or don't you think I do?"

Annette discreetly said no more, and there was silence, amid which Betsy took her seat at the table. Everyone being unhappy, nothing was said beyond requests for the passing of dishes until Joe came blithely in.

"Gee, supper's early," he remarked, stowing his bat and glove in the most convenient corner and pulling out his chair.

"No, it isn't," Henry said. "You're late. As usual. . . . Wait a minute. Do you think you're going to sit here with us before you wash your hands and face? Go upstairs, and be quick about it."

"Aye, aye, sir." Joe marched out singing, "Who put that pair of overalls in Mrs. Murphy's chowder."

"Damn that boy, he's incorrigible," Henry fumed; and then the absurdity of it struck him and he smiled.

"Joe is a case," Miss Julie said, to be affable. "He's well named after his uncle."

Henry finished his scrambled eggs and ate another muffin. "I don't know what parents do with a real old-fashioned houseful of them," he remarked, with a shake of the head. "How did your father manage with his seven, Miss Julie?"

"What's that?"

"I said, I don't know what people do with a lot of children. How did your father manage?"

"He never had any trouble."

"Remarkable," Henry declared with a touch of sarcasm.

"Children were different in those days," Miss Julie reminisced, "though I don't mean any criticism. These little rascals are good, too. But we were brought up with a rod." She was a little puzzled about it all; she disapproved of seeing her grandchildren disciplined, yet she had been severe enough with her own—it was customary; and her father had been a good-natured martinet.

Joe, looking like a drowned rat, took his seat. "I'm starving," he said. "We played thirteen innings. I pitched the last six, and I hit six home runs."

"So that explains the time you come in to supper," Henry said.

"I couldn't leave while the game was going on, could I? You can't walk out on a game."

"I suppose not." Henry considered the social implications of this. "It must have been quite a big score, if you hit all those home runs all by yourself. Did you win, or was the game called on account of darkness?"

"We won—21 to 20."

Henry laughed. "There must have been a lot of base running. Well, don't let it happen again; and get through with your supper. You've got to work on your arithmetic tonight. I don't want any failure. Remember, this is your last chance to graduate."

"Oh, I'll come out all right," Joe said.

"You didn't come out all right on your last report card."

"He got 50," Betsy said.

"You shut up and mind your own business!"

"Joe! I won't have you speaking to your sister that way."

"Well, she hasn't got any right to criticize me," Joe grumbled.

"Betsy, you'd better tend to your own affairs," Henry said, gently. "Joe, hurry up with your supper now, and get to work on your lessons. I'll look them over when you're done. And don't talk under your breath. I don't want any of your impertinence."

Sarah, who had been keeping Jennie posted on all these developments, put a pile of plates in the sink, and murmured:

"They's trouble ahead."

"What all them children needs is a good fannin'," Jennie said.

"Miss Julie ain't like it none about James and the sailboat. Sometimes Miss Julie is very haughty. And 'e feelin's is hurt. Tha's the second time today." Sarah laughed. "My Lawd, I hear 'em all talkin' about the new house over and over, and Miss Julie say 'e ain't hear a thing about it." She clapped her hands in merriment. "Old peoples is funny. Miss Julie ain't so deaf when anybody say anything about somethin' to eat."

" 'E sure can stuff 'eself."

"Goin' ta kill 'em some day," Sarah said, going back with the tray. She looked at them all: Mr. O'Donnell looking sad, and Miss Nettie too, and Miss Julie staring off into space; James subdued, and Betsy pouting, Joe sulkily quiet. Only little George, half asleep in his outgrown high chair, seemed unaffected by the commotion.

Miss Julie was first to leave the table. She made her excuses, crossed over to James and George and gave them each a hug, and went upstairs. She thought she would go early to bed. The day had been a strain, and she needed solitude to restore her.

She was still indignant at Henry about the sailboat, and about the new house.

"Mortifying, that's what it is," she muttered. She got a mint out of her dresser and sat out on the porch in the twilight to enjoy it. She belched heartily. "Nothing like mint to bring up the gas," Miss Julie murmured.

She watched the stars appear, and that made her think of the comet. "The darkies said it was bad luck," she thought. "Almost seems as if they were right." For there was something wrong with the world, all of a sudden.

She said long prayers before she let down the mosquito net and lay down to sleep.

CHAPTER FIVE

NEXT DAY MISS JULIE AWOKE feeling more like her old self, and quite ready to forget about the indignities she had suffered. She dressed rapidly, abbreviated her prayers, bustled the children down to breakfast, ate cheerfully of *bouillie salade*—marinated boiled beef—and hastened to get her room in order. Then she put on her street clothes and started out for a visit to Tessie, who would be deeply offended if her call weren't immediately repaid. She told Annette, who was also getting ready to go calling early, where she was going.

"You and Aunt Tessie are going to be hand in glove now, I see," Annette said.

Miss Julie chuckled. "I may as well do this right. Tessie will have a duck fit if I don't go right away to see her. She'll think she's been slighted. It just goes to show how hard she is to get along with."

"I hope you'll remember that when she tries to talk you into going to live with her."

Miss Julie grunted. "Child, I haven't got any idea of doing anything so foolish. Indeed not!"

She trudged down the stairs and out into the street, where the sun was already bright and hot. Old Mr. Carroll, the next-door neighbor, was strolling through his garden as she went by, poking at the cannas with his cane, and smoking a newly lighted cigar.

"Good morning, Miss Julie," he said, sweeping off his faded Panama. "How are you, ma'am, and all the family?"

"Good morning, Mr. Carroll." Miss Julie drew up at the fence. "We're all very well, thank you. And how is Miss Sally?"

"Just as usual, thank you."

Mr. Carroll took his hat into the same hand that held the cane, and threw down his cigar as he realized that Miss Julie was going to stop and talk. She would have urged him not to; but she recollected that he could afford only one cigar a day, and to have urged him to save it would therefore have been insulting. Mrs. Carroll, as everyone knew, was mad and was confined to a single room; it was simply a polite fiction to refer to her illness as something ordinary and subject to fluctuation.

"I'm sorry to hear it," Miss Julie said. "Your gyarden looks fine."

"I'm worried about it," Mr. Carroll confessed, his bony face bobbing as he spoke. "I wish Mr. Sharp was here now. He'd be able to give me a lot of help."

"Yes, Andrew was a great gyardener," she agreed, with pride. "He had a green thumb."

"He certainly did. I hear you're leaving Tradd Street, Miss Julie."

"Yes. Henry has bought the Lafontaine house."

"Fine young man," said Mr. Carroll. "Fine young man."

The Carrolls were among the "old" families, and Miss Julie wondered if there were some slight condescension in the remark.

"We'll hate to see you go," he added, poking again at the cannas with his stick. "Can't tell who we'll have in next, nowadays.

Charleston is changing so. This new Boulevard business and all."

"I suppose that's true. Henry didn't mention who'd bought the house, or even if he's sold it. Well, goodbye, Mr. Carroll. I must be going on."

He bowed and replaced his hat, and Miss Julie ambled on. She was very sorry about his cigar. The Carrolls were terribly poor now, and the servants reported that they had meat only two or three times a week. When she reached the high wall of the next house she stood out of sight and peered to see if the old gentleman would recover his cigar. After a moment he stooped and picked it up. Miss Julie was amused and pleased by this bit of hypocrisy. Gallantry was a thing she had been brought up to expect, and it was sacred to her; but somehow she rejoiced that Mr. Carroll had transgressed the code. The waste of that cigar would have hurt her French sense of thrift.

She supposed he was reproaching Henry for moving and leaving the house for a possibly undesirable family. People ought to stay where they are; she half agreed with him.

She listened sympathetically while Mr. Bell, the street cleaner, leaned on his brush and complained about his feet. She nodded to Winters, the colored policeman, as he touched his buff helmet to her. Winters was a good darky, and kept his place even in the most difficult circumstances. Not like some of the uppity ones that thought they were just as good as white people.

Passing through Logan Street, she encountered Miss Susan Williams, who was hobbling slowly along on her stick. They greeted each other warmly.

"I heard your adopted brother had been under the doctor," Miss Susan bleated, after the usual exchange of symptoms.

"I'm afraid he's not long for this world," Miss Julie responded with pious regret.

Miss Susan sighed and said they were all growing old. "I don't feel any older, Julie; but I see everything going to rack and ruin, and it makes me feel real bad. Nothing seems to be right any more."

Miss Julie said it was so.

"I hear the Peters girl has taken a job as stenographer," Miss Susan said.

"These are new days," Miss Julie replied. "It wasn't so in our time. Ladies didn't work then."

They shook their heads over it.

"The Grants have taken in boarders," Miss Susan continued. She was always a mine of information.

"You don't say."

"It's a terrible comedown for them."

"Yes, indeed," Miss Julie said, forgetting that she had once had a boarder when things were going bad for Pa.

"Rich people from the North. An old lady and her son. He's a writer, and he's going to write some things about Charleston. They want to be introduced to some of the old families so they can putter around the houses." Miss Susan's voice quivered a little. "They think Charleston is quaint. That's what they said."

"The idea! I suppose they think because they've got a little money that they can come here and be lords of the manor." Miss Julie shook her head at the audacity of it. "By the way, we're moving," she said, feeling that she ought to tell the faintly shameful fact before she was asked about it. "My son-in-law has bought the Lafontaine house."

"Is that so? He must be doing very well." Miss Susan implied disapproval.

"Young people are restless nowadays," Miss Julie said.

Shaking their heads, they parted, each with some fresh news.

No other encounters delayed Miss Julie's progress to the run-down street behind the cathedral where her sister lived, next door to several houses full of Negroes. The tall, stately house in which Miss Tessie had her room had its side to the street, and its front door opened onto the piazza. It had once been a residence, but now it was broken down and almost beyond the need of anything but demolition. A shutter on the first floor hung by a single hinge; the bolts on the rods that had been put in after the earthquake to steady the building were rusted and had

[57]

streaked all the street side. There were great patches of naked brick where the plaster had peeled off. A plank was missing from the high wooden fence, and weeds poked through it. The whole was trimmed with wood that had once been white and gray but was now weathered and virtually bare of any covering.

A slatternly landlady with red hair opened the door for Miss Julie. Inside on the piazza the air of decay was even more pronounced. Weeds grew lushly around the edge of the piazza and through the cracks and missing boards. The wall of the house next door showed great patches of moss, and there was a rank smell of earth and vegetation. Miss Julie wondered how on earth Tessie could live in such a place.

She puffed up the musty stairway to the second floor and knocked. Miss Tessie opened the door.

"Good morning, sister," she said. "I'm glad to see you."

Miss Julie still felt a bit strange with Tessie. "I'm glad I found you in."

"I never go out until I've put the room in order," Miss Tessie explained.

The room was as neat as a pin, everything in place, the pictures all straight and the glass in front of them shiny, the flowers fresh before the picture of Theodora that stood on the easel.

Miss Julie wanted to talk about something, but she did not like to mention the Peters girl going to work, for after all Tessie had worked as a nurse these many years.

"The Grants are going to take in boarders," she said.

"Well, well! How have the mighty fallen!"

"A gentleman and his mother from the North." Miss Julie explained. "I met Miss Susan Williams today, and she told me about it."

"Hoo!" Miss Tessie's lip curled. "I suppose Susan Williams thinks she's somebody. Her father was only the tax collector."

"The gentleman is going to write about Charleston. They say Charleston is 'quaint.'"

"What's quaint about it?" Miss Tessie snapped. "They have

[58]

sight of unmitigated gall coming down here and telling us our city is quaint! They must be trash that never had anything."

"They sound very ordinary," said Miss Julie.

"All Yankees are. Why do they allow such people to come here? There's the root of the whole trouble."

This was treading on Miss Julie's toes, for her husband had been the son of Northerners. She disliked the word Yankee, too. Nice people didn't use it.

"Well, Tessie, you and I aren't used to all the changes that are coming over things. We belong to another generation. We'll just have to get used to it."

"It's people like Henry O'Donnell that are responsible for ruining Charleston," Miss Tessie said.

Miss Julie sighed. She didn't feel energetic enough to take up the defense of her son-in-law.

"I thought we might go to Mass together Sunday," she suggested.

"Very well," said Miss Tessie. "Why don't you stay and have dinner with me?"

"I couldn't disappoint Annette and Henry, and they'd be worried about me."

"Isn't your life your own?" Miss Tessie demanded.

"Why, yes, it is, but I can't run away and not go back to dinner without letting them know about it."

"I suppose you're afraid of offending your high and mighty son-in-law."

"I can do anything I like," Miss Julie said doggedly. ("Does Tessie expect me to be ill-mannered just to show my independence? Really, she's as peculiar as she can be," she reflected.)

"I don't like to be answerable for my comings and goings," Miss Tessie said. "You ought to come and live with me, Julie. Then we could both do just as we pleased."

"Tessie, I am doing just as I please. I've been very happy with Henry and Annette, all these years, and I owe them a debt."

("Really," Miss Julie said to herself, "if she keeps up this begging me to come and live with her, I'll begin to wish we'd never made up.")

"I never could bear people who put on airs," Miss Tessie said. "Of course, you're your own mistress, or so you say, and I don't believe in interfering with people."

("Oh, no, you don't," Miss Julie thought.)

"I'll make you a promise, Tessie. Any time I feel unhappy with Annette and Henry, I'll tell you about it, and then I'll move in with you." That, she thought, ought to stop her sister for a while. She rose. "I'll be getting along. I just came in for a very short visit. We'll meet at eleven o'clock Mass, then, on Sunday. In Henry's pew."

She got out as quickly as she possibly could. "Really, Tessie is a gadfly," she murmured. "She won't rest until she gets me out of the O'Donnells' house."

She thought, though, that it might be nice to be answerable to nobody for what you did.

She went over to King Street and stopped in at the little French candy shop to buy a bag of peppermints from old Mr. Leduc, who made the best stick candy in Charleston, or in the South, or in the world.

Mr. Leduc too was rather down in the mouth that day. He told Miss Julie how the big manufacturers were making it hard for the smaller ones, and she was properly sympathetic. She had known him since his boyhood. She remembered him as a soldier in the War. "My, how old we're all of us getting!" she thought, depressed again.

The ten-cent store was her next objective, and she puttered around from counter to counter without buying anything. The things offered for sale were not what they used to be.

She did not cheer up until she found two choice specimens of tinfoil outside the tobacconist's on Wentworth Street. This comforted her a little. But she was cast down again when she passed the toy shop and saw the sailboats in the window, and all yesterday's unpleasantness came back to her. She went home in a pensive mood.

At dinner she asked Henry to whom he had sold the house.

"I haven't sold it yet," he said. "I'm going to offer it for rent. Values will go up when the Boulevard is built."

"Mr. Carroll was wondering if he'd have nice neighbors."

Henry snorted. "Anybody who can pay the rent and take decent care of the house will suit me. I'm not responsible to the Carrolls or anybody else. Let them buy the house if they want to keep up the neighborhood."

Miss Julie was a little shocked at this. She remarked: "We always felt we had to look out for people like ourselves."

"That's what's the matter with Charleston. They'd rather starve than have somebody buy their house without showing a coat of arms. Your ancestors don't pay your taxes."

She said no more about it. She didn't even mention her news about the Peters girl and the Grants' boarders, for she didn't want to start Henry off on another argument. "Buying that new house has not been good for Henry," she thought.

Even Annette did not respond to her point of view when she told her the items she had collected from Miss Susan Williams.

"Well, people can't starve. I'm surprised at you, Ma, having all that false pride."

That was the New England in her, Miss Julie thought. It was the Sharp blood.

"We had a boarder once, when we needed money," Annette reminded her; and that was unanswerable. "And Aunt Tessie has worked at nursing all these years. I don't like the idea of girls shut in offices with men, I admit."

"They ought to get husbands," Miss Julie said.

"But all the young men are going away to other places to work. There aren't any husbands for a lot of them, and they haven't much chance to meet what men there are. Why, Ma, Charlie had to go away to find something to do—your own son. And Francis hasn't done any too well here."

"Well, I don't know that it's any of my business," Miss Julie said. "I just hate to see everything going to pieces."

("I mustn't let myself get old and discontented," she told

herself as she sat working on her quilt. "It's none of my affair. We've had our day.")

After supper, when they went into the old-fashioned parlor for music, and Annette played Leybach's "Fifth Nocturne" and Lange's "Flower Song"—Joe's piece, Miss Julie called it, because it was the one thing Joe had learned in his ill-fated piano lessons —and then "Too Much Mustard," and some other new things, Miss Julie felt again that life was pleasant. She was glad they had given Annette piano lessons, even if she had been obliged to practice on a neighbor's piano.

"Henry, you sing," Miss Julie suggested. And Henry set his quavery parlor baritone to "Silver Threads Among the Gold" and "The Bedouin Love Song," and one of Miss Julie's great favorites, "Dear Old Girl."

That song always brought tears to her eyes. In this pleasantly melancholy mood she went up to bed, her content with her lot restored.

But when, next day, after all the fuss he had made, Henry bought a sailboat for James, she was furious.

"It was just to hurt my feelings," she muttered wrathfully.

CHAPTER SIX

"My heavenly fathers, how the time flies!" Miss Julie murmured, stuffing the letter into her apron pocket and pushing her spectacles up onto her forehead.

It had been every bit of sixty years ago, that crisp Sunday afternoon. . . . The big carriage spanked along, with the usual orphan sitting among the Gerard children. The one that Sunday was a curly-haired chap with black eyes, very cute in spite of his homely uniform. He was enjoying himself thoroughly.

But when they came within striking distance of the orphanage, he began to cry. He threw himself into Mamma's lap and begged her not to take him back to the orphan house.

"François, stop the carriage a moment," Mamma said. And Papa had told the driver to pull up and had looked in through the window to see what was the matter.

"We can't take this boy back when he's crying like this," Mamma said. "They'll think we've done something to him."

"What's the matter, son?"

"I don't want to go back there," the little fellow sobbed. "I want to go to your house."

"Poor fellow," Papa said. He didn't think twice about it. "Do you think you'll be a good boy if I take you to my house?"

The little fellow said he would; and Papa looked at Mamma, and said: "We've got seven. One more won't make any difference." And Mamma said it was a lot easier to get them that way than the regular way, and laughed, although she was a little overcome by the suddenness of it.

Well, that had been long ago. . . . It was strange to think of John as old and sick and not likely to get well now. So many of the others had gone: René, and Lucien, and Louis, and Charles, and Augustus. There were only herself and Tessie, Emma, Josephine, and Joe, and John; and now John was likely to go too. Strange that John had been the only one to do anything for himself. Miss Julie couldn't help thinking of the money he was going to leave her, in spite of her grief . . .

She went in to tell Annette about it.

"Your Uncle John's very ill," she said. "I just had a letter from Emma, and they just heard about it."

Annette had seen very little of her Uncle John. She clucked sympathetically, though she didn't feel the news very much.

"Well, I suppose you'll come into your money," she said.

"Don't talk like that, child," Miss Julie said sharply, not without a feeling of guilt. "I'm not thinking about the poor fellow's money. I'm surprised at you. Besides, I never intended to use the money for myself if I did get any of it. I always meant to save it for Francis and Charlie. . . . But it would be nice for Tessie."

"I wouldn't spend it if I were you," Annette said. "Uncle John has had these spells before and fooled everybody."

[63]

Miss Julie was offended at this flippant sort of talk and went back to her room. She knelt at the little altar and said a prayer for John's recovery or grace for a happy death. "I wonder if he's kept up his duties," she thought.

She consulted the gold hunting-case watch that had been Samuel's, and saw that it was time for her to be off to her sodality meeting. Dressing took her mind more or less off John's illness; but she thought of it all the way to the convent, not without some pleasurable anticipation of the legacy.

"Lord have mercy on my soul, I must be getting avaricious," she muttered. "It must be the Old Boy putting such things into my head."

The ladies of the Sodality of the Blessed Virgin Mary were very congratulatory. They thought it wonderful that Miss Julie had become reconciled with her sister after so many years of estrangement. The Misses Perry—the "Perry girls"—were particularly happy about it.

"I wouldn't know what to do without *my* dear sister," said Miss Margaret, who was tall and thin, patting the hand of the short, plump Miss Frances. "A good sister is a great blessing," said Miss Frances.

Miss Annie Mitchell, who was known to have a bad tongue, came up looking for scraps of gossip.

"Of course, I don't know anything about your quarrels," she said to Miss Julie; "but most family quarrels begin in such silly ways."

"The old hypocrite," Miss Julie thought indignantly. "As if she didn't know every bug in every bed in Charleston." She said aloud:

"Tessie was most Christian about it. She was the one who remembered her duty and set about patching things up."

"That," she thought, "ought to stop her right now from going and telling Tessie anything I said."

Miss Annie looked crestfallen, and remarked on how nice it was to make peace.

"They all make me sick sometimes," Miss Julie thought disgustedly, as she strolled homeward. "Gossip, gossip, gossip—backbiting and scandal. And they have the gall to go to the sacraments." But that was uncharitable, and she regretted thinking it.

When she got to Tradd Street, she thought she would go down to see Mrs. Angelotti and at the same time see if Mr. Angelotti had any very ripe bananas at a good price. She trudged down to the foot of the street and went into the store.

Mr. Angelotti, a little fat Italian who always wore a blue striped shirt and a black felt hat, was sitting on a stool just inside the door and looking as usual as if he hoped nobody would come in to buy anything and disturb him. He rose lazily as Miss Julie entered.

"I want a dozen good ripe bananas," Miss Julie said.

Mr. Angelotti rummaged in the bin of loose bananas and counted out some that were black and almost liquid.

"How much?" Miss Julie asked.

"For you," Mr. Angelotti said, "ten cents a dozen."

Miss Julie started out the door. "You must think I'm rich," she said. She stopped at the door, though, and opened her pocketbook, from which she removed a nickel and three coppers, and held them out to Mr. Angelotti, who immediately began to put the bananas back into the bin.

"I losa money," he said.

Miss Julie shook her head and started for the door again.

"Nine cent'," Mr. Angelotti said.

"Too much," said Miss Julie.

Mr. Angelotti put another runny banana into the bag.

"Put in a pod of garlic," Miss Julie said, "for lagniappe."

"You put-a me out of business," Mr. Angelotti grunted, including the pod of garlic, and putting the nine cents in a cloth bag he kept in his trousers pocket. Miss Julie took the bananas and stalked out in triumph. She could hardly wait to eat one of them; and the garlic would be good for her blood pressure.

She sat out in the garden and ate three of the bananas, giving the bag to Jennie to put in the icebox for her.

"Take one yourself," she urged.

Jennie thanked her and laid one of the nearly liquid bananas on the dresser. When Miss Julie went upstairs, Jennie quietly put the piece of fruit in the garbage pail. She was particular.

On Sunday, after her usual attendance at low Mass, Miss Julie met Miss Tessie outside the Cathedral, and they marched together up to the O'Donnell pew. Miss Tessie sat in an agony of self-consciousness while Miss Julie said her rosary in the usual loud groaning whisper. It was grotesque, and she was half tempted to speak about it. However, she refrained and endured it. Julie, after all, was old and peculiar. Very peculiar. Miss Tessie shrugged it off and concentrated on her prayers. She had a lot of people to pray for.

They came out into the hot midday, and Miss Julie, after commenting on the sermon, asked Miss Tessie to come to dinner.

"Annette wants you to come to dinner," she said. "They're going to have a leg of lamb."

"I am never on the lookout for what people have," Miss Tessie said primly. "Hospitality is hospitality to me. And I never eat much, as you know very well."

"They set a very good table," Miss Julie said. "Good morning, Miss Thompson."

"Hoo!" said Miss Tessie. "Our darkies wouldn't have sat down to what white families serve nowadays."

"We'll go over and get your coffeepot," Miss Julie said.

"Well, for your sake I'll go to dinner with you," Miss Tessie said, and Miss Julie, nodding briskly to this and that one, turned with her and went along the side of the church to Archdale Street, conscious of numerous wondering glances. "We certainly attracted enough attention," she chuckled. "People must think the end of the world is coming."

Miss Tessie forbade her to climb the stairs. "You sit here on the piazza and I'll go up and get the coffeepot," she said.

"She wants to grab a bite again, so she won't seem to be hungry," Miss Julie thought with amusement. "Dear me!"

Miss Tessie was gone only a few minutes, however, and Miss Julie couldn't be sure whether she'd eaten or not. They talked of old times, which both agreed had been incomparably better than the present, until they reached the house; and then they sat on the drum out in the garden and looked at the flowers and discussed symptoms and the children until it was time for dinner.

Promptly at two o'clock they entered the dining room, and were followed by Joe, who was always last, even on Sunday.

"Hello, Aunt Tessie," Joe said, offhand.

"'Hello' is for sailors," replied Miss Tessie, as usual.

"Joe," said his mother coming in at that moment, "you ought to say 'Good afternoon' or 'How do you do.'"

Not in the least abashed, Joe substituted a politer phrase, to which Miss Tessie responded, and took his place at the table. "Let's go!" he said.

His father glared at him. "Aren't you forgetting yourself!" he demanded, with a tremendous frown.

"Sorry, Pop," Joe said gayly.

With this brief interruption, dinner went on smoothly. The dishes were all to Henry's taste, and he was full of enthusiasm for the new house and found time to talk to Joe about the baseball prospects for that year. Miss Tessie appeared to enjoy herself, and Miss Julie ate with her customary lack of moderation. She had applied for a third helping of lamb when Annette saw fit to caution her.

"Now, Ma," she said, "remember, lamb doesn't agree with you."

Miss Julie flushed. "Nonsense," she said, passing her plate. "I'm not a child, I know what's good for me and what isn't."

She was offended, and sulked for the rest of the meal; and afterwards Miss Tessie took occasion to rub it in.

"I never heard of anything like it!" she fumed. "The idea of telling you what to eat and what not to eat!"

"I suppose they think I'm getting old and foolish," Miss Julie said resentfully.

"I don't see how you stand such superintending," Miss Tessie said.

"Nothing like that has ever happened before," Miss Julie declared. "You don't suppose I'd put up with it day after day, do you?"

Miss Tessie refused to be convinced.

"Thank God I can do as I like," she said. "Nobody can tell me to have more of this or less of that, or what to do at any time. To think of my own sister being treated like a child just makes me boil."

She had worked Miss Julie up to a considerable fit of indignation by the time she took her leave.

Now, Miss Julie had always been notable for a calm disposition. "I've been through the War and the earthquake," she said when people admired her easy-going ways. "I'm not going to let little things upset me," was another of her favorite phrases. She had always prided herself on being easy to get along with and easy to please and extremely hard to offend. Perhaps it had been the presence of Tessie that had made it so hard to bear Annette's presumptuousness; and Tessie's triumph afterwards had made it harder. Miss Julie was puzzled at herself.

"Either I'm getting old and foolish and don't know it and have to be treated like a child," she thought, "or there's something the matter." Of course, she could recall, there had been little run-ins with Annette and Henry from time to time over the years, but she had always managed to forget them. Most of all, she had not permitted them to humiliate her. But just this week! "I must be getting thin-skinned," she reflected with annoyance. "Maybe I'm catching it from Tessie."

She resolved to be very careful, and not to take offense at little things.

But the very next day she had new cause for annoyance. They were at dinner, and something was said which Miss Julie understood to mean that a certain piece of cheese was missing.

"I ate it this morning for lunch," she said.

Everyone laughed heartily; and somehow, even after it was

explained to her that Sarah had caught a rat with a piece of cheese meant for a mouse, and that her answer had come after Betsy had said, "I wonder what Sarah did with it," meaning the rat—even after this Miss Julie was offended. She frowned, and muttered something about respect for age. She refused a second helping of chicken, a thing almost unheard of, to show that her feelings had been injured. Afterwards she told herself that she was being a foolish old woman, and that no harm had been meant. But when she thought of the incident her face flushed.

She was still smarting a little on the day following when Tessie came to visit her and renewed her attack.

They sat out in the garden and got around to discussing Emma and Josephine. They had reached the point of concluding, rather aimlessly, that Emma was a wonderful manager.

"It's lovely for Josephine to be with them," Miss Tessie said.

Miss Julie brushed a small caterpillar off her black apron and assented.

"Julie," Miss Tessie said, "why don't you make up your mind to come and live with me?" There was an imploring expression in her eyes; with the haws under them, they reminded her sister of a faithful dog's eyes.

Miss Julie had been expecting this, and still she didn't quite know what to say.

"Why, Tessie," she said, "I've been here so long. I'd miss the children terribly. And I think they'd miss me."

"They have Sarah to look out for them," said Miss Tessie, skillfully touching on that tender spot, Miss Julie's jealousy of the children's affection for their black nurse.

"Yes, they have," Miss Julie said. She winced, ever so slightly. "Well, Tessie, I don't know. I think Henry would be offended, and I think Annette would hate to see me go, if I do say it. She's been a very good child to me, the youngest and spoiled as she was."

"Julie," Miss Tessie said, "I've been up against the world a lot more than you. When you get old, young people don't really want you. They don't need you. And as you get older and older, they'll want you less and less. Especially now that Henry has the society bee in his bonnet. He'll think you're too plain for his great friends. And besides," she added, "look at the way they treat you. Now, don't deny it—I saw it with my own eyes and heard it with my own ears. That's not proper for a woman of your family and at your time of life."

Miss Julie was Frenchwoman enough to see things objectively, and she had to admit, unwillingly, that what Tessie said about Henry's attitude might be true; but her pride and her sense of her daughter's affection struggled against the admission that they were anything but perfect to her.

"I've never had anything but kindness from either of them," she replied. "I don't think you're right, Tessie. Not in this case."

"The old," said Miss Tessie, "should stay with the old. 'Crabbed age and youth'—wasn't that what Mr. Timrod said?"

Miss Tessie attributed all poetical quotations to the South Carolina poet.

"It wasn't Mr. Timrod," Miss Julie corrected. "It was Shakespeare."

"Well, Shakespeare," said Miss Tessie, as though Mr. Timrod, in her opinion, had been the one who should have said it. "But it was true then, and it's still true."

"I'll have to see about it." Miss Julie felt that she must avert this crisis. It had long been a saying in the family that, once Tessie got an idea into her head, there was no getting it out. And she had a will of iron.

"You just notice, sister, some of the little things," Miss Tessie pursued. "Such as Annette telling you you'd had enough to eat. Then ask yourself, without any prejudice, if you wouldn't be happier with your old lonely sister, and if you wouldn't do better to throw in your lot with her."

"H'm," said Miss Julie.

"If it's the expense," Miss Tessie said, "I'll take care of that. I earn enough from time to time to take care of us both. And I have my little pension."

She had struck another tender spot. Miss Julie lived absolutely free and clear with the O'Donnells, and nursed her nest egg with true French thrift.

"Oh, that has nothing to do with it," Miss Julie said quickly. "But of course I couldn't think of letting you support me. I'm not so stingy as all that, whatever people may think." Really, Tessie was a holy terror when she got started.

"Of course," Miss Tessie said, adopting her characteristic tone of injured pride, "I won't force my company on you." She closed her jaws with a snap, and looked aggrieved, and said no more on the subject.

However, she had got her dart into the flesh, and Miss Julie, though she pooh-poohed Tessie's insinuations, began to feel the tiniest bit less comfortable. That business about the cheese and the sailboat—well, perhaps it showed how things were.

It is not difficult, when you are old and especially when you have begun to grow deaf, to find slights. Heretofore Miss Julie, secure of her position, had not done so. Now, she said to herself, just to see if Tessie was right or wrong, she'd watch a little more carefully.

The next morning she asked Sarah where she was going to take the children, and Sarah replied:

"Miss Annette tell me to take 'em down to the Batt'ry."

"I didn't ask you who told you to take them," Miss Julie said, just a trifle huffily.

"I beg your pardon, ma'am," Sarah said. "I jist meant I was goin' to take 'em to the Batt'ry."

Miss Julie was pacified, but she did not like Sarah, and was convinced that the little black woman was trying to be sassy. "She resents my having anything to do with the children," she thought unhappily.

These little things began to make her think that Tessie had been right. Another event was sufficient to convince her.

Miss Julie had a liking for certain exotic dishes. One of these was a sort of chowder of crabs' claws, shrimp, diced fish, okra, tomatoes, salt mackerel, garlic, and curry, which she called "bouillabaisse"; and on Friday morning she busied herself with getting the ingredients, mixing them carefully, and cooking the dish. She meant it for a surprise dinner.

It chanced that Henry O'Donnell was in a rather bad humor that day. When the dish was placed before Miss Julie he stared at the greenish, high-smelling chowder and asked Sarah, "What's that concoction?"

"That Mis' Sharp dish," Sarah said.

"Well, it doesn't look fit to eat. I wish she would be satisfied with the food we have," he added crossly to Annette.

Miss Julie heard his comment, and saw that he was saying something disagreeable to Annette. She pushed back her chair and arose, white and shaken, and marched out of the dining room. She had not been upstairs two minutes when Henry, penitent and ashamed of his ill humor, knocked on her door and entered.

She was seated in her rocker, full of wrath and almost ready to put on her hat and leave the house forever.

"Miss Julie," Henry said, "I beg your pardon, ma'am. I was very rude, and I apologize. Please come downstairs again."

"No, I won't. My feelings have been hurt." Poor Miss Julie wiped her eyes. "I'm old, and nobody wants me."

"Miss Julie, you know that's all nonsense," Henry said. "I've had some annoyances today, and I was ill tempered and ill mannered. Please don't be cross about it. You can do anything you please here, and you know it."

Miss Julie stood up, still wiping her eyes. She felt it would be silly to insist upon taking offense, and said that she would come down. They descended the stairs and went into the dining room arm in arm. It was an embarrassing entrance. Annette had been upset, and her eyes were red; and Betsy looked uneasy. Even little James appeared unhappy.

Miss Julie sat down again before the dish of chowder, and Henry humbled himself still further.

"Sarah, just wait a moment," he said. He cleared his throat. "I was very rude to Miss Julie awhile ago," he said, "and I want to apologize to her before everyone."

("The Cap'n sure has a good heart," Sarah said to Jennie when she returned to the kitchen. "Miss Julie is gittin' very haughty all of a sudden," she added.)

Miss Julie was touched by Henry's self-abasement. "Oh, it's all right, Henry," she said. "I really have no right to put dishes on the table. It was only that I meant it as a surprise."

"It was very kind of you," Henry said, and the thoroughly disorganized meal proceeded in a funereal silence. He gallantly ate a portion of the chowder and made the others try it; but that did no good.

Even Miss Julie didn't enjoy the chowder after all the pains she had taken. And though Annette tried to console her afterwards, pointing out that Henry was terribly busy and tired and strained, she was doleful for the rest of the day: she had been grossly humiliated, and it hurt her deeply.

This time Miss Julie, forgiving as she had always tried to be, could not down the feeling that she had been wronged. It ate at her spirit like a canker. At supper she had a sensation of acute embarrassment, as though she were in a strange place, stared at by everyone.

Worst of all, perhaps she had been in the wrong—had committed an offense against hospitality, like bringing food to a friend's house when you were asked to dinner. It actually interfered with her digestion, and she went to bed early with a heavy heart and a heavy stomach, and awoke next morning on rather bad terms with the world. She was actually sharp to the children when she dressed them, and grumbled aloud that she was getting too old for such tasks.

"Ma," said Annette, who had overheard, "you don't have to dress them if you don't want to."

"I know I don't have to," Miss Julie snapped. "I do it because I choose to. But I won't if you object."

Annette looked searchingly at her and went out of the room. Miss Julie finished dressing the little boys and took James in to be washed and to say his prayers.

"And ask God to take good care of you when you're old," she instructed him, somewhat spitefully.

James was also in a contrary mood that morning.

"I don't wanta say prayers," he protested.

"All right, then, don't," Miss Julie said crossly. "Grow up to be a heathen, like your Pa that never goes to church." She sucked her teeth.

The boy stared at her, round-eyed. "Heathen," he repeated, fascinated by the word. "Heathen. Is Mamma a heathen, too?" he inquired.

"Go along downstairs to your Sarah," said the unhappy old lady, half pushing him out of the room. "Georgie will be my boy after this." She picked up the smaller boy and hugged him. "James will miss Granny when she's gone," she told the little fellow.

George said "Granny," and patted her cheek. That made her feel better, but she was still offended at James's apostasy. She ate breakfast hurriedly; the food seemed to stick in her throat; and she went promptly upstairs to straighten up her room.

"There's no place for me here any longer," Miss Julie thought unhappily. "Everything comes to an end sooner or later, I suppose. Once everybody was lovely to me. Now they laugh at me and tell me what to eat and never say anything about their plans to me, just as if I was an outsider. Probably I won't live very long to plague them."

She wiped her eyes.

"Even the little ones turn against me," her thoughts ran on. "They think more of their nigger nurse than they do of me."

And working on her quilt failed to make her feel better.

"I'll go over and talk to Tessie," she said. "It was God's blessing that we made up when we did, I suppose, just when I really needed somebody."

Tessie, just finishing her midmorning coffee, was full of the usual apologies about not being ready for visitors, although her room was as neat as ever.

"Never mind," Miss Julie said. "I just wanted to come over

and spend a few minutes with you, and I came early, because I thought you might go out."

Miss Tessie drew a rickety chair up to the little oilcloth-covered table and got a fragile cup and saucer from the cupboard.

"Now, don't make any fuss, Tessie," Miss Julie said with a protesting wave of the hand.

"I'm not making any fuss. I'm just going to pour you a cup of coffee."

"Thank you," Miss Julie said. "I've had breakfast." But she took the cup with a shaky hand and filled a spoon with condensed milk which she stirred in.

"Well, what has happened?" Miss Tessie asked. "I can see in your face that there's something wrong."

Miss Julie flushed. She had come to pour out her dissatisfactions, and now she felt that she didn't really want to.

"Oh, nothing unusual, Tessie." She stared down at her spoon and cup, very uncomfortable.

"What have they done now to insult you?"

"Well, I don't think they meant to insult me. It was just thoughtlessness, and I was partly to blame." Miss Julie told all about the affair of the chowder.

Miss Tessie's eyes blazed as she listened.

"I don't know where your pride can be, Julie," she said. "It seems to me you've had enough of that kind of treatment to make it impossible for you to stay there any longer. The very idea of a Gerard being treated like that makes my blood boil. Who does Henry O'Donnell think he is, I wonder."

"I can't understand it," Miss Julie said. "It's all happened in the last couple of weeks. Before that everything was perfect."

"Nonsense," said Miss Tessie. "You just haven't been aware of it because you haven't had anybody to talk to about it, and you begin to realize it now."

Miss Julie had the feeling that she was being sucked into a whirlpool and couldn't draw back. "I don't know just what I can do," she said.

[75]

"You'd better do what I suggested to you: come and live with me."

"How much would it cost if we shared this room?"

"Oh, we couldn't live here," Miss Tessie said. "It would be too crowded for the two of us, and besides, I don't like this woman here. She's too nosey, and she doesn't know her place: you ought to hear the questions she has the gall to ask. And I don't like the looks of what goes on up the street. After all, gentlewomen have to be careful; and no breath of scandal has ever touched a Gerard."

Despite her bad mood Miss Julie smiled at this absurdity.

"I'm not worried about scandal at my age," she said with something of her old lighthearted manner. "But if it's not pleasant otherwise, I suppose it wouldn't do. However, I'd like to be near the church." That, she realized, meant that she had given her consent to the plan.

"Of course. So would I. I think I'll look on Franklin or Queen Street. We really ought to have the whole floor to ourselves."

"They are going to the country the first week in June," Miss Julie said, "and that's the time I'll move. So you'd better start looking. But don't go too high on the amount of rent, you know."

Miss Tessie thought twenty dollars a month would be enough. Miss Julie thought she could afford her share of that, and after they had discussed a few other necessary details she said goodbye and left.

She half regretted the step she had taken, but it was too late to back out now without making herself ridiculous. And Tessie would never forgive her again. That would be the end.

She couldn't help feeling, however, like a child who has paid his last pennies for a toy and then thought of the other things he might have bought.

And how she dreaded breaking the news to Henry and Annette!

"Really, life is getting too troublesome," Miss Julie said to herself. "Nothing's as simple as it used to be."

CHAPTER SEVEN

IT WAS SUNDAY AGAIN, and they were all at dinner, where the dramas in the O'Donnell family usually had their setting. Henry had just served the fried chicken from the heaping platter, and when he put down the serving fork he said:

"Well, this is one of the last dishes of chicken we'll have together in this house. It's the end of May, and school will be out next week. I'm going to write to Mrs. Flint at Brevard tomorrow."

"Can I go to camp at Hendersonville, Papa?" Joe asked.

"I've arranged for you to have a month there. Then you can join your mother and the others."

"Only one month? What am I going to do at Flint's all the rest of the summer?"

"You'll do as I say," Henry answered sharply. "Don't get beyond yourself."

"There's nothing but old people there," Joe protested.

"You know that's nonsense," his father said. "Now let's not have any more discussion of it."

"Besides, you'll have Betsy to play with," Annette said, with serene misunderstanding.

Joe laughed scornfully. "That's rich! A ten-year-old girl to spend the summer with."

"You don't have to play with me," Betsy said, sticking out her tongue at him.

"Betsy!" Annette said.

"Now, that will do," Henry said. "We'll go two weeks from yesterday. That will give you time to get them all the things they need."

Annette had been thinking of that for weeks.

"I'm gonna put pins on the railroad tracks," James said. "Remember, George? You cross two pins and put them on the track and then the train comes—*choo-choo-choo!*—and it goes shooting past and—" He moved his arm to indicate the speed of the train, and knocked over his glass of milk.

"Now look what you've done!" Annette scolded.

Henry's frown made one of its frequent appearances. "That's what comes of ungentlemanly behavior at the table," he said sternly, while Sarah was mopping up the pool of milk.

"I jist wanted to show George how the train comes and mashes the pins," James said.

"Well, that's enough about it," Henry said.

Order being temporarily restored, he turned to Miss Julie. "Will you be ready to go with us Saturday after next?" he asked, to be polite, for he couldn't imagine any possible reason why she shouldn't.

Miss Julie had been listening intently, awaiting her cue. She had thought for days how to inform them of her decision without adopting any definite way. She had even thought of precipitating a quarrel so that she could walk out in a huff. This was a God-sent opportunity to tell them. She took a deep breath and laid down her fork.

"Please don't make any plans for me," she said.

"What do you mean by that, Miss Julie?"

"I'm not going to the country." Miss Julie tried to be casual about it, but her voice and hands shook.

"Why, Ma! Why?" Annette exclaimed. The children looked up, startled, and Henry drummed on the table with his fingers.

"Well," Miss Julie said, getting the whole explanation into one speech, "I really don't like the country very much, although I appreciate your kindness in taking me there every summer. But Tessie needs me"—that was the way to do it!—"and I've promised to go to live with her."

Henry became very pink and very haughty. "Do you mean you're not coming to the new house with us in the fall?" he demanded.

"No, I'm not, Henry," Miss Julie said, guiltily. "It's not that I'm ungrateful for all the kindness I've had from you. Far from it. But Tessie is old, and she shouldn't be alone at her age. The two of us will be able to take care of each other."

"Well!" he said, letting his breath out like air from a punctured balloon. "Miss Julie, I'm amazed. It was understood that our home was to be your home as long as you lived. I can't understand this sudden change."

Betsy got up and ran around to her grandmother and hugged her. "Granny," she said, "you're not going to leave us! Please don't!"

Although she was pleased by this display of affection, Miss Julie shook her head.

"I've made my decision," she said firmly, "and I've given my word. I can't take it back."

"But, Ma," Annette expostulated. "You've never been able to get along with Aunt Tessie, even at a distance. You haven't lived with her for almost fifty years. You'll never be able to stand it. You know what she is."

Henry did not approve of this attempt to persuade Miss Julie to remain.

"Let's not say any more about it, Annette," he said in a tone of injured pride. "Miss Julie is her own mistress, and if she doesn't want to share our house any longer, we have no right to ask her to."

Miss Julie understood perfectly from his tone that the matter was closed, and that she would never again be asked—by him at least—to live in his house again.

She was about to make further explanation, to smooth over the abruptness of her announcement; but Henry didn't give her the chance. He turned the conversation to their plans for the country, and for the new house, and kept it on that course with almost painful imperturbability, while Betsy pondered her grandmother's imminent departure, and Joe puzzled over it between plans for his month at camp, and the little fellows promptly forgot it.

Not until he and Annette were alone did Henry betray his feelings. He had a dramatic gift which he never failed to exercise on such occasions. He let his usually erect shoulders droop, and walked into the sitting room with a heavy tread, like a man who has seen his hopes perish. He sank into the Morris chair with a heavy sigh.

"I can't think what's come over Ma," Annette began in a fretful tone, not noticing these bits of theater.

Henry sighed deeply again.

"Aunt Tessie will drive her crazy in six weeks," Annette pursued. "To think of my poor old mother letting herself in for what she's going to go through. Isn't there some way we can stop her?"

"We have no control over her," Henry said heavily.

"We've got to think of some way to stop her," Annette said. "I can't let her do it. It'll be the ruin of her last few years."

"I thought so." Henry's manner was at once grieved and accusing. "No one thinks of me. I'm the last one to be counted."

Annette stared at him. "How is it going to affect you? After all, it's not your mother."

"How is it going to affect me?" Henry thundered. "Do you mean to stand there and tell me you don't know people are going to say that we put her out—and what's worse, that we aren't willing to take care of her in her old age, or that we aren't able to?"

"What do you care?" Annette said.

"I care a hell of a lot." Henry sat up in the Morris chair and thumped the right arm. "It means everything to me in my business to have people think well of us. They'll say we put her out, and that we're straining so to keep up that new house that we haven't got enough left to take care of my mother-in-law."

"Well, I don't give a sou marquee what people say about it," Annette retorted. "I'm thinking of the poor old soul's peace of mind. Why, she won't be able to call her life her own."

"Anyway, the damage is done." Henry settled back and prepared to take his nap. "We can't ask her to change her mind. I've got that much pride."

"You're so worried about what people will say about you, it's a wonder you wouldn't give in to that and ask her to stay."

"Well, I won't." Henry put his handkerchief over his face to keep the flies away.

Annette drew the shades down and left him. She had other ideas on the subject.

"I'm not going to have my mother leave my house and go to live with that old virago," she said to herself.

But the business must be handled with care. Urging would do no good: once any of the Gerards made up his mind to do anything, persuasion was useless. You couldn't move them with a crowbar. There might be some subtler way to do what she hoped to do, without Henry's knowing about it; but the time before they were to go away was so short.

"If I could only get Ma to the country, and work on her while we're there," she thought. However, that was almost impossible. Her mother hated the mountains, and she knew all the reasons for that.

She thought of having the children work on her mother's affection; but the old lady would be suspicious of protestations from any but James, and he was too small to be entrusted with so delicate a mission. If Uncle Joe could come over to talk to Ma, letting her inform him of her decision to go and live with Aunt Tessie, and could use his powers of ridicule . . . But he hardly ever came to see his sister, because of the family row, and her mother would be suspicious if he came just at this time. No, she would have to do it herself.

Gradually she evolved a plan.

She began by taking her mother to see the new house: "You're practical about these things, Ma. Maybe you can give me some advice."

"Child, you'd better do what you think best," Miss Julie said. "I never was one for interfering with other people, if I do say it."

"Well, come over and see how the painting is getting along." Annette always left such matters to Henry, but it seemed like a good excuse for going to look at the house.

"Well," Miss Julie said, "painting is something of a novelty in

Charleston, but I don't know that it's interesting to me at my time of life. You're the one to be satisfied."

But she yielded and went along.

Annette opened the front door of the house and waited for her mother to go in. Miss Julie entered and sniffed.

"There's been rats around here," she declared.

"How can you smell rats, Ma, with all that odor of paint everywhere?"

"Well, maybe it's mice," Miss Julie conceded. "Of course, there's rats or mice in every house in Charleston, so far as I know. And you'd better look out for bedbugs, too."

Annette nodded grimly. "This is the sitting room," she said, throwing open the double door.

"Hardwood floors? Somebody's going to break his neck on them," Miss Julie said. "It may be very stylish, but I'd rather have matting any day. And good cyarpets. I like something that gives underfoot."

Annette led the way into the dining room, which was paneled and had a great crystal chandelier.

"Grandeur," Miss Julie said. "I'd hate to have that come down on my head."

She was not impressed. She found the kitchen too big to keep clean, and the butler's pantry too showy for plain people. As for the rear wing, where Sarah and her husband were to live, she said it was too good for niggers.

They went upstairs, and Annette pointed out the room they had intended for her.

"It's pretty big," Miss Julie said dubiously, "and I don't think that fireplace will keep it warm on those cold days."

"Henry thinks he might put in furnace heat."

"I suppose Henry's thinking of putting in an elevator, too. Furnace heat! For mercy's sake!" Miss Julie laughed.

"I hope you're going to be happy, here, child," she said as they came out. She cast a critical glance up the street on either side. "Those automobiles will make a lot of noise. . . . The Archibalds' house is getting pretty run down. I wonder how their crazy sister is. . . . And there's old Lawyer Perry with the Panama hat he's had since the earthquake." She looked up at the big house on the corner fronting the lake. "I've forgotten who lives here now," she said. "It used to be the McDevitts' house. They live up the road now."

"It'll be nice for the children to be so near the pond," Annette said, "if they don't fall in. I'll have to tell Sarah to be very careful about letting them run out. It's nice to be so near it, though. It makes it cool on hot nights."

"Cool for who?" Miss Julie demanded. "You'll be in the mountains in another week or so."

"Well, Henry will sleep better."

"Precious little sleeping Henry'll do while you're away."

"That won't worry me. I'm not concerned about what I don't know about." But a worried look crossed Annette's face.

"Men are all alike," Miss Julie declared.

"She's actually getting like Aunt Tessie," Annette thought. "Oh, for goodness' sake, Ma!" she said. "Henry's forty-two."

"I don't mean to upset you," Miss Julie said, "but Charleston is a terrible place. People don't know half of what goes on. Why, right on Archdale Street, where Tessie lives, there are two or three houses of bad women." She chuckled. "That's one reason Tessie wants to move away from there. She's worried about her reputation."

"For God's sake," Annette said.

Miss Julie spied a piece of tinfoil in the gutter, picked it up and dusted it off, and thrust it into her bag.

"Tessie is a case," she said.

"She certainly is. Ma, don't you think you'd better go slow about moving in with her? You're going to regret it."

Miss Julie set her jaw and said that she'd already made up her mind.

"When I make up my mind to a thing, it's as good as done," she said. Unwilling to be drawn into argument and perhaps to reveal her real reasons for leaving the O'Donnell house—after all, you can't admit that your feelings have been hurt, not if you have any pride left—she changed the subject and told Annette a long and rambling story of a poor family some of the sodality ladies were planning to help.

The matter of Miss Julie's departure was never discussed again. When there were visitors the week before the O'Donnells' departure for the country, Annette informed them that her mother was going to live with her sister. Otherwise the subject was taboo in the house.

The breakup came nearer. The little horse was driven away, and Betsy cried bitterly; and the cow was led out. Tessie had found a flat on Queen Street, and Miss Julie had already prepared her things for the move. She was going to move out on the day the family left for the country.

The day came, and the children were bundled into the hack to go to the station. Miss Julie had her first moment of weakness when she watched them drive off, and went back into the lonely house. The desolation smote her.

But it was after the wagon came and took her own things away that she sat down in her empty room and had a good cry. She took a last look around, particularly in the little room where James and George had slept, then went to the kitchen to say goodbye to Sarah, and marched off to a new life.

Part Two

CHAPTER ONE

NEVER IN THOSE DAYS a city bursting with life and merriment, Charleston was settling heavily into its long, sticky summer. People who could afford it had, like the O'Donnells, left the city for the mountains or for the beach. Some of those left behind did the natural thing and cursed what they had to endure; a few die-hards protested that Charleston was one of the world's finest places to spend the summer in. Why, that southwest breeze every afternoon! That was why the houses were built with the piazzas facing south and west. Go away! Nonsense!

Miss Julie and Miss Tessie, as lightly clad as was compatible with dignity, were chatting after supper in their sitting room.

"It seems just like home," Miss Tessie said complacently, fanning herself briskly with her palm-leaf fan.

Miss Julie, who was also plying her fan without any effect upon the perspiration that stood out all over her and ran down her neck, was grateful that the lamplight wasn't very bright. She didn't want Tessie to see the expression on her face. Though they had now been moved for three weeks, she felt far from at home. Very far.

She looked around the room, and her gaze took in the old clock that had been an anniversary present and that now stood motionless and silent on the mantelpiece (it had pointed to half-past one ever since 1902), and the small cheap gilt clock that companioned it for practical purposes. On one side of the clocks was Miss Julie's Dresden shepherdess; on the other, the daguerreotype of her father and mother that had caused so much trouble. Her old wrought-iron candlesticks stood at either end of the mantel. She saw the frayed lace curtains; the grate polished with lampblack; the oil lamp with the flowered shade on the mahogany table; the spool whatnot in the corner; the easel with the picture of Theodora and the never-absent flowers; her pictures of Pa and the boys, and Miss Tessie's various photographs on the wall. Miss Julie sat in the Morris chair that she had contributed, an oak one with green and yellow velvet cushions; Miss Tessie, in her little mohair rocker that matched the worn and rickety sofa. Everything looked very strange, very shabby, and very poor, even to Miss Julie, whose tastes were simple indeed.

"I'll get used to it, I suppose," she said, wiping her forehead with a man's-sized handkerchief. Then she realized that the remark must have sounded very tactless. "You've made it look very nice, Tessie," she added.

Miss Tessie's glance swept the room, too, and her expression was smug.

"Any place is home for me. When you've knocked around for years as I have, with no one to keep you company"—her voice assumed a mournful note—"any place seems like home very soon. If I have the pictures of my sainted Theodora and my family and my coffeepot and bed and a good gas stove, I'm satisfied."

Miss Julie grunted. She abominated gas stoves. It was her firm conviction that food prepared on them was not properly cooked, and that anyone who ate it would pay for the privilege sooner or later. Right now her liver was beginning to be torpid again, after just three weeks of gas cookery. She resolved to take some salts.

"And speaking of gas stoves," Miss Tessie went on, "I'm not particularly satisfied with the one they've got here. I don't think I'm going to get along very well with it."

"Why not? What can be the matter with it?" Miss Julie asked. It did not seem possible to her that there could be various grades of excellence in such pernicious things as gas stoves.

However, Miss Tessie was certain there was something wrong.

Gas stoves were her hobby, and she was a perfectionist where they were concerned. "It just don't seem right," she said. "The holes are too small, or something. The flame don't look right to me."

"Oh, go on, Tessie. It must be all right, if it don't leak or explode."

"You'd better let me decide about that, sister. If there's one thing I really know about, it's gas stoves."

"Why, of course, Tessie." Miss Julie had been yielding to her sister like this ever since they had moved, first on one trifle and then on another. You had to, or—

"I really think we'll have to get a new one," Miss Tessie said.

Miss Julie shrank. Tessie's extravagances were the worst cross she had to bear—buying at the most expensive stores, and buying whatever she saw, if it took all the money she had in her purse. Miss Tessie had somehow missed the French frugality that Miss Julie had inherited from a long line of saving ancestors.

"How much would that cost, Tessie?" she inquired uneasily.

"I'll have to go over to Murray's and look. I suppose about thirty dollars."

Miss Julie winced, just as if a corn had throbbed. Her share of that would be fifteen. The income from the family legacy that had come to Andrew just before his death—the only money he had ever been able to keep—was just a trifle under fifteen dollars a month. Her pension as the widow of a Confederate officer was just thirty-five dollars a year. Out of that trifling total, seven dollars and a half a month went to pay their rent. This would mean breaking into her capital.

"Buy two," she suggested jocosely. "One might make you sick."

Miss Tessie frowned. "I wish you wouldn't joke about serious affairs, sister."

Miss Julie checked a retort and said it seemed like a heap of money.

"I'll pay for it."

Miss Julie had seen to it from the very first that expenses were accurately halved, thus making it impossible for Tessie to gain any moral ascendancy in that respect. She rose to the occasion again.

"No, you mustn't do any such thing. I'll carry out my part of the bargain. I wish we had a coal stove, though."

Miss Tessie sniffed. "Hoo! I suppose you'd really like to cook over a spit."

"Well, there's nothing better than a coal stove," Miss Julie said stoutly. "However, go ahead and get your gas stove. But be sure it's one you'll like."

Miss Tessie flounced out to the piazza.

"I'm glad her taste don't run to automobiles," Miss Julie grumbled. She took up her fan and whisked it back and forth vigorously. "She's going to end up by having both of us in the Confederate Home, that's what she's going to do.

"Wilful waste brings woeful want. . . .

"Buying groceries at Bettenkampf's!

"New gas stove. . . .

"She must think our father is still alive. . . .

"You could buy a house with what she throws away.

"Wrapping all her things in new tissue paper every week!

"Undressing behind a screen, as if there was a man looking at her!

"Five scapulars! Fanaticism, that's what it is.

"I never saw a human being with so many peculiarities.

"Shredded wheat for breakfast! They say it's made out of peanut shells.

"She'd like to rule me body and soul.

"Trying to get me to do those foolish calisthenics every morning!

"I wonder if I'm going to be able to stand this."

Miss Julie felt somewhat better after she had muttered this litany of dissatisfactions. "I'll read a little," she said to herself, moving over to the lamp and taking from the table a copy of "The Trail of the Lonesome Pine," a Christmas present from

Henry, which she had half finished. She tried to get on with it, but it tired her; and, besides, the setting reminded her of North Carolina and the children she wouldn't see again until late September. "I can't read any more about these country crackers," she muttered, and put the book down.

She missed the music and gayety of Henry O'Donnell's home, and the good meals she had had without the trouble of preparing them. She missed the children—oh, how she missed them, and the cat, and Polly! She even missed Henry; she even missed Sarah.

"Gas stove," she muttered wrathfully. "Tessie'll have one of those fireless cookers next."

Miss Tessie was still out on the porch, sulking, no doubt.

"Let her scratch her mad place," Miss Julie thought. "Drat that mosquito!" She slapped her arm. "Ought to have some citronella."

Francis might at least come to see her in her new home. He knew she had moved. She didn't stand on ceremony with her own children, but she certainly wasn't going to visit him. She had some pride left. As for that wife of his—if she lived to be a hundred Miss Julie would never forgive her. Telling her that she had spoiled Francis! Right to her face!

Samuel would have been different if he had only lived.

"Julie," Miss Tessie said, coming in from the porch.

Miss Julie looked up apprehensively.

"Tomorrow's my day for going to the cemetery to clean up my plot," Miss Tessie said. "You'd better come along with me."

"Very well." Miss Julie was relieved to find that the subject of the stove had been temporarily shelved, but a little startled that Tessie's thoughts about her dead had coincided with her own about Samuel. She never thought of Samuel, nor of any other deceased member of her family, without seeing the image of his grave.

"I'll give you some help with your own plot," Miss Tessie offered. "It looked very shabby week before last."

"I suppose so," Miss Julie said with a sigh. "But you don't

[89]

need to help, Tessie. You've got enough to do with your own."

"I keep mine in such good condition that it's very little trouble. I can easily help with yours."

"Well, you're very good," Miss Julie said politely. But she resented Tessie's attitude that she couldn't do anything for herself. "You'd think I was a mere child," she thought.

"It's the only thing we can do for our dead," Miss Tessie said, "except pray for them. . . . All my children, sister. Six of them, and my husband, too. What do you suppose I could have done to bring such sorrow upon myself?" Her eyes filled up.

"My God, she's going to start that to-do again," Miss Julie thought. She was alarmed. The last time—well, she had thought Tessie was gone clean out of her mind.

"My dear Tessie," she said, "God knows best. Maybe He saved them from something worse, like losing their faith, or something like that. We mustn't question His ways."

"But all my children, Julie! My beautiful Theodora, my only girl, and my five fine sons." Miss Tessie began to cry silently.

Miss Julie had a good mind to send for the doctor if her sister should have another one of those fits. She went over and eased her into a chair. "You mustn't brood, Tessie. It's unhealthy."

"I can't help it," Miss Tessie blubbered. "I don't know why God chose me for such punishment."

"If it's God's will, Tessie"—Miss Julie felt, in spite of her beliefs, like a sanctimonious hypocrite—"you have to accept it. After all, you're going to join them some day."

"I only hope it will be soon," said Miss Tessie, who took excellent care of herself.

"Don't talk like that, Tessie. God may take you at your word. Besides, it's sinful."

Miss Tessie was somewhat abashed, but she continued to weep loudly.

Miss Julie talked on, mechanically saying the same thing in as many ways as she could. And all the while she was thinking that her sister had brought much of her trouble on herself. If she hadn't been so headstrong about that typhoid fever that carried poor little Theodora off; and if she had only called the doctor sooner when Julien had his attack of malaria . . . But Tessie had always known better than the doctors.

"You go to bed now, Tessie," she urged finally. "You're overwrought. And all this heat is bad for you. . . . I'm glad Annette and the children are up in the mountains."

Mention of this appeared to restore Miss Tessie. She hooted vehemently.

"Mountains!" she sputtered. "We had our place on Edisto Island to go to every summer when Henry O'Donnell's father would have considered himself fortunate to have the price of a ferry ride to Mount Pleasant. And we could go to church on Sunday, too. We didn't have to risk our immortal souls just to show off."

"It's for the children's sake that Annette goes to the country," Miss Julie said.

"I don't know how she pacifies her conscience," Miss Tessie replied. "I really think you ought to talk to Annette about it."

"Annette has her own soul to save. And I've got my own doorstep to keep clean."

"It seems to me that you're responsible for the spiritual welfare of your own daughter," Miss Tessie argued.

"Live and let live. If Annette is satisfied that she's doing right, it's not my place to upset her. . . . I wish I could get Henry to go to church, though."

"You know what I think?" Miss Tessie said. "I think Henry is ashamed of being a Catholic. He'd rather be an Episcopalian because it's more stylish, and he'd like to be in the St. Cecilia Society. Henry O'Donnell is a climber."

Miss Julie didn't especially want to criticize Henry or to argue in his behalf, either, but she kept the subject going because it had diverted Tessie from her fit of self-pity.

"Oh, I don't think Henry feels that way."

"Henry O'Donnell is a snob." Miss Tessie was now fully restored and quite her bitter self. "First it was the Elks, and then he got too good for that and all his old friends. I know. I hear things. He's got the social bee in his bonnet. But he'll get his comb cut. You wait and see."

Miss Julie could think of nothing more pleasant than the society of Henry O'Donnell and his family, and she felt disloyal for not saying so; but she adhered to her policy of handling Tessie with gloves.

"I suppose he thinks it will be nice for the children, especially for Betsy."

"It would help the children a whole lot more if they were brought up with some manners," Miss Tessie retorted. "I can't stand the way they say 'Hello' to you in the street. '"Hello" is for sailors,' I always tell them."

This criticism of the children irritated Miss Julie.

"They're really very nice children," she said. "You do them an injustice."

"Hoo!" Miss Tessie ejaculated. "Not one of them has any more manners than the cat."

("Everything she says is an attack on somebody or something," her sister thought. "Really, you can't talk to her at all unless you want to hear people belittled. And she calls herself a Christian.")

"I'm afraid I must get to bed, Tessie."

"It's early yet." Miss Tessie was disappointed at this termination of their talk.

"The heat makes me sleepy."

"Well, go ahead," Miss Tessie said tolerantly, as if to an invalid. "I don't need as much sleep as you. And don't forget me in your prayers."

Miss Julie wasn't really sleepy, but she wanted to get off by herself and think about the mess she had got herself into. She lighted her oil lamp in the bedroom and sat down on the edge of the bed.

"Really, it's like living with a crazy person," she thought. "And you can't get away from her. There's no privacy whatever. She's so lonely she wants to be at my side every minute. I wish she'd get a nursing case. Then maybe I could get away from her long enough to break wind in peace."

Miss Tessie, left to herself, arose. She went over to the daguerreotype, took it from the mantelpiece, and caressed it.

"After she's gone it will be mine," she said fiercely; and then, as if horrified at herself, she replaced the daguerreotype and went over to the picture of Theodora.

"Theodora, ask God to forgive me," she murmured.

CHAPTER TWO

AFTER BREAKFAST MISS JULIE WENT DOWN to empty the slops, for there was no water closet nor bathroom in the house, and as she descended the musty dark stairway she thought again what a disheartening place it was that they had moved into. She felt hemmed in by the little back yard with the high board fence that cut off any view there might have been. There were a few bean vines straggling up the fence, and beside the privy a couple of small tomato plants. Maybe Mrs. What-you-may-call-it would let her have some ground to plant in. A few radishes and some carrots and squash might do well even now, and she could ask the street cleaner for manure. The vegetables in the O'Donnells' yard would be fine right now. She wondered if Jennie or Sarah had picked them.

Curiosity prompted her to look at the yard next door through a broken plank in the fence; but there was nothing to be seen there that was not visible from the back of the piazza—a pile of brickbats, a heap of rusted tin cans, and a broken barrel that had sunk partly into the ground. It was so typical a Charleston back yard that it was not even interesting.

"I wonder how long Tessie is going to be able to stand this," Miss Julie thought. "If it's too much for me, I don't see how a beau-nasty person like her can put up with it for a minute."

Mrs. Atmeyer, the landlady, put her frowzy head out of the kitchen window.

"Sho's hot again," she commented.

Miss Julie nodded pleasantly; but she was in no mood to start a conversation, and did not stop to ask about permission to have a garden. Besides, she might not stay long enough to get anything from it, and what was the use of wasting money for seeds and the effort to plant them? She tramped up the stairs and found Tessie well started on the breakfast dishes.

"Here, I'll help," Miss Julie said.

"Never mind. I can do it. There's the shrimp man you wanted me to listen for."

Miss Julie took a pan out to the front of the house. She hailed the shrimp man, a tall, thin fellow with a battered straw hat and a skin the color of cooking chocolate.

"How much?" she roared.

"Ten cent' a plate, ma'am," the vender said in rich Gullah.

"That's dear," she shouted.

He smiled blandly and waited respectfully to see if she would come downstairs. She decided to. "They want a cow and a calf for everything nowadays," she grumbled.

"Give me a plate, and don't put your hand in it, either," she said to the vender.

He heaped a pie plate with the small shrimp that the Charleston taste demands, poured them into Miss Julie's pan, knotted the dime she gave him in a blue bandanna handkerchief, and almost in one motion tipped his ancient hat, picked up the handles of his barrow, and trudged on, roaring "Raw swimp" in his peculiar, long-drawn fashion.

She took care of the shrimp while Tessie straightened up the house; and she had them in the boiling water and cooked and skinned before her sister began to dress.

"I'll be ready in two shakes of a lamb's tail," Miss Julie said.

"Take your time, take your time," Miss Tessie said. "I'll get the gyarden tools out and ready in the meanwhile."

But Miss Julie made it her business to be brisk, and they were ready to leave within a quarter of a hour. Miss Tessie carried a sunbonnet and a watering pot and a bag with a pair of gaiters and canvas gloves in it. Miss Julie bore the child's-size rake and hoe and the trowel, all held together with twine.

They had gone out the front door when Miss Tessie stopped short.

"I'll have to go up and see if that gas is properly turned off," she said.

"For heaven's sake, of course it's properly turned off."

"I'm going up to see," Miss Tessie said firmly.

Miss Julie had never been troubled with the *folie de doute*. She could have gone to California without giving anything in the house a second look; but Tessie—she shook her head. If there was not a cloud in the sky, Tessie wouldn't go as far as King Street without seeing that every window was shut tight.

Miss Tessie reappeared, and they started off toward Meeting Street, passing the Medical College and the Catholic orphanage and the convent and commenting on each. Miss Tessie walked just a little ahead, for she did not approve of Miss Julie's deliberate gait and wanted to show her impatience.

"Here comes Ellen Murphy," Miss Julie said.

Mrs. Murphy, a pleasant-looking middle-aged woman, said good morning, and Miss Julie halted a moment to exchange a few polite remarks.

"I hear you've moved together," Mrs. Murphy said.

"Indeed!" said Miss Tessie. "Yes, my sister and I have moved together, although I don't see what business it is of anyone else's."

Mrs. Murphy stared for just an instant, said goodbye to Miss Julie, and walked on.

"I guess that cut her comb," Miss Tessie said, triumphantly.

"I don't see why you have to be so disagreeable to people," her sister protested.

"Common thing!" Miss Tessie exclaimed. "Why can't people tend to their own affairs?"

"She's a good soul."

[95]

"I can't take up with every Tom, Dick, and Harry just because they're good souls. I have to remember who I am."

Miss Julie sighed heavily. She was fond of "ordinary" people. "If I go out many times with Tessie, I won't have any friends left," she thought. "I'll have to think up some excuse." She spotted a magnificent piece of tinfoil, and regretfully passed it. Tessie had been shocked the first (and last) time she had gathered such an addition to her collection when they were together.

"Drat her and her ideas," Miss Julie thought. She wished fervently that she hadn't come on this junket. The sun was beginning to blaze, and the streets shone like a stage under a spotlight. She was sweating, and her legs felt weak.

She recovered somewhat on the long ride up to the cemetery, which she spent looking out of the car window. Miss Tessie occupied herself with reading in a small volume of prayers for the dead. She was so nearsighted that she couldn't have seen anything much from the car anyway.

The sisters got awkwardly down the car steps at the end of the line and trudged the remainder of the way to the entrance gates, looking like the drawings in a child's book of two black beetles equipped with garden tools.

Miss Julie enjoyed the peace and restfulness of the place, the shade of the great oaks and the faint breeze. She would have liked to sit down and drink it all in; but Miss Tessie set briskly about her change of headgear and shoes.

"Now, Julie, there's a lot to do," she declared. "We'll go over the family plot first, and then we'll work on our own. I'll fill the watering pot, and you can begin by clearing up the leaves and things."

They worked busily for a while, pleasantly sad as they spoke of incidents in the lives of those who lay beneath, and then knelt together at the railing and said a prayer for all the dead: four generations of them, for this was the Gerard family plot, which Miss Tessie had always cared for in addition to her own. It was entirely full, and Miss Julie and Miss Tessie sometimes regretted this. They would have liked to be buried with their father and mother, had it been possible to have their own immediate families there too, instead of in the separate plots a dozen yards away.

When they moved over to their own, and Miss Julie saw the Sharp graves, her heart failed her. There were only three of them—Pa's and Samuel's and Alfred's—but the place was overgrown and disorderly, in shocking contrast to the neatness and propriety of Tessie's. She pottered about, raking a little here and there, and removing the rotted Confederate flag, there since Memorial Day, and the decayed wreaths. It made Miss Julie weary to see Tessie bustling about the carefully kept plot with five times the energy she was expending on her own disordered one. She straightened up with a groan and joined Miss Tessie.

Miss Tessie looked up at her with her eyes full of tears, and Miss Julie promptly forgot all the irritation she had been storing up. She stood there at the border of the plot and dropped a few tears herself.

"I am a mother of sorrows," Miss Tessie said, wiping her eyes.

"Well, Tessie—"

Miss Tessie pointed to the vacant space beside her husband's grave.

"Who'll care for all this when I'm laid there?" she asked. "I can't bear to think of it."

"Perhaps John will see to it that it gets perpetual care," Miss Julie said. "If he happens to go before us, you could take the bit he leaves you and set aside some of it for perpetual care." ("If you don't spend it for new gas stoves and things," she reflected.)

"John? Hoo! You'd better let me help you with your plot, now. It needs a lot of work."

"I've been very negligent," Miss Julie admitted. "But there's so much to do, and it's so hot. I think we'd better come another day. In this weather it'll just get ahead of me, no matter what we do. In the fall I'll clear it off thoroughly."

"Don't shirk," Miss Tessie said sharply. "Come now, let's clear away some of this mess. It's disgraceful."

She took the rake and set to work; and pride would not allow Miss Julie to do less for her own graves than another person. She took the little hoe and joined in the task, although she felt as if her back would break.

"It's a great improvement," she said when Miss Tessie indicated that they had done enough for the time being.

Miss Tessie smiled complacently. "You have to be resolute about these things. Now let's gather this stuff together and go. It's been too much for you."

"Nonsense! I'm perfectly all right. . . . I want to have a look at Annette's place."

"Well, go ahead." Miss Tessie's face hardened at the mere thought of anything, even a cemetery plot, that was connected with Henry O'Donnell. "It's no concern of mine. I'll wait for you here."

"I suppose she thinks it was very pretentious of Henry to have a cemetery plot for his family," Miss Julie thought. "I guess she thinks potter's field would be good enough for him." "Poor fellow," she murmured aloud, kneeling to say a short prayer beside the two tiny graves. She could remember with wretched clarity the deaths of those two infants and Henry's dreadful grief; and she remembered his agonies of anxiety whenever the other children showed the faintest indication of illness. And again, suddenly, there swept over her a flood of loneliness for them all. September was a long way off.

She rose and dusted her knees and went back to Tessie, and they boarded the car and rode home, both weary and silent.

"I'll start the rice for dinner," Miss Julie said.

"You'd better rest."

"Once and for all, Tessie, I'm going to do my share around here," Miss Julie snapped. She was tired, and that made Miss Tessie's solicitude harder to bear. "The shrimp are in the icebox, and I've got some cabbage. You can make the coffee if you like."

She picked the rice, washed it, and set it on to boil. Then she sat down in the porch rocker and closed her eyes peacefully. The children playing in the street out front made a faint outline of sound. She dozed.

When she awoke, the table was set and dinner was ready.

"Why didn't you wake me?" she demanded, crossly. "Now I won't sleep a wink tonight."

Miss Tessie looked triumphant. "I thought you must have needed a nap."

Miss Julie grunted. "I don't want you to do all the work. You can't stand it. You need to rest between nursing jobs."

"Indeed! Hoo! There are very few people, young or old, with my energy. Why, Dr. Trumbull told me once, a little while ago, that it was wonderful how I kept my energy and strength. Wonderful."

"It's just nervous energy," Miss Julie said. "Or maybe it's your blood pressure."

Miss Tessie hooted. "Blood pressure, your grandmother! With your weight, you'd better look after your own blood pressure." She gazed at the mound of rice and cabbage and the heap of shrimp her sister was demolishing.

"I eat plenty of garlic when I think my pressure's up."

"Julie, you know that's just a superstition, that business about garlic."

"Well, it helped Tante Octavie after the doctors had given her up. They told her she would have a stroke if she didn't get her pressure down. She never went near a doctor again. She just ate a pod of garlic every day, and you know how long she lived."

"I remember," Miss Tessie said grimly. "Nobody could go near her." She shuddered. "And then she got the idea that bathing opened the pores too much, you remember?" She looked at the food and shook her head.

"She was a dear old soul, even if she did get awful queer in her old age."

"You have to be on your guard against it," Miss Tessie said with entire gravity.

"Yes, you certainly do," Miss Julie agreed, also without the faintest smile.

They went on eating, each staring into the past, and saying little.

"I'll do the dishes," Miss Julie proposed as she drained her coffee cup.

"No, you sit and rest."

"I'll do nothing of the kind." Miss Julie got up and stacked the plates. "I didn't come here to be nursed."

"I don't think you're very careful about washing dishes."

Miss Julie refused to take offense. "Don't worry about your precious dishes. You can get mine out if you like. I've had them for twenty-five years or more."

"I don't mean breaking them. I don't think you get them clean enough."

"I haven't poisoned anybody yet," Miss Julie said with maddening calm, removing part of the pile of dishes.

Miss Tessie yielded to fatigue and sat by the window.

"Tessie is so cranky," Miss Julie said to herself. "I'm sure she doesn't feel well. She looks tired and frail. I mustn't mind her little ways. She's had so much trouble."

Later, when Miss Tessie determinedly went out to "see about getting a gas stove," Miss Julie worked on her quilt and went to sleep over that, awakening just before her sister returned with her arms full of packages.

"More money gone," Miss Julie thought. Tessie would buy out Louis Cohen's if something didn't stop her.

She looked inquiringly at the packages.

"Some cloth for a dress and some new pillowcases," Miss Tessie said. "I don't like to use my nice ones that Willie gave me. . . . Well, I got a nice stove. The man will be here to put it in day after tomorrow."

"And what did that cost?" Miss Julie asked, fearing the worst.

"Just what I said. Thirty dollars."

Miss Tessie gathered her packages and started toward the bedroom.

"Now," she said, "we can have some decent meals."

Miss Julie gazed after her. "I wonder," she thought, "if Tessie is altogether right in the head?"

CHAPTER THREE

LATE THAT AFTERNOON MISS TESSIE was summoned to a nursing case. She packed her things in great haste, as if the patient's life depended on her reaching the sickroom on the instant.

"Old Mrs. Atchison on the Battery," she informed Miss Julie, who had been in the kitchen when the colored boy came with the message.

Miss Julie ran rapidly through the Atchison family tree.

"She was one of the Calhouns," she remarked. "Her grandfather was old Judge Bennett. That will be a nice place to stay, Tessie."

"She wasn't one of *the* Calhouns," Miss Tessie corrected. "And you may think it's a nice place. Great airs, and the St. Cecilia Society, and a butler and two housemen, but you ought to hear the stories about the butts meat they feed the servants." She hooted. "And who are the Atchisons? When we were living in Trumbo Court they were starving because the old man was drinking up what little money they had left, and he had his nigger children to support besides. They don't impress me. Not at all."

"How long do you suppose you'll be gone, Tessie?"

"I can't say. Maybe until the Devil claims his own."

Miss Julie felt it her duty to protest against this unchristian sort of remark.

"You shouldn't speak so ill of people, Tessie."

"Ill? Hoo! I know enough about these self-styled aristocrats to fill a book. Well, you can't choose your masters when you work for a living. Send one of those little niggers from across the street if there's any mail that looks worth the trouble, and don't forget to turn off the gas stove. And if the new stove comes on time, you tell that man to be sure he hooks it up right or I'll do for him."

"I'll tell him," Miss Julie said.

"And keep some fresh flowers under my little Theodora's picture. I'd take it with me; but there are some people you don't want to have any more dealings with than you can help, and I'd hate to have the Atchisons say anything to me, for Dr. Smythe's sake. I'd very soon read their titles to them."

She paused again on the way out.

"Don't forget about the gas and the windows."

"I won't," Miss Julie promised.

Miss Tessie trotted down the stairs. Miss Julie drew a deep breath of relief.

"Now I'll have a little peace for a while," she muttered hopefully.

She pottered around agreeably for a half-hour or so, and had the remains of the shrimp and some fried rice for supper, which she ate on the piazza with the plate in her lap. For dessert she sucked a couple of fragments of peppermint sticks. She sat there until it began to grow dark and the mosquitoes annoyed her, and then she went inside and tried once more to get ahead with "The Trail of the Lonesome Pine." But she decided once more that it was stupid sentimental rubbish, and put it down. As she did so, there was a loud knock on the door.

"Come in!" she roared.

Her son Francis entered.

"Hello, Ma," he greeted her, putting his Panama on a chair.

Miss Julie looked him up and down.

"Well, Francis," she said haughtily, "it's a good thing you've finally decided to come and see your old mother. It's a long time since you remembered your duty."

"Well, now, Ma, you know I have to work late," he protested, sitting down and taking out his handkerchief to wipe his forehead.

"Do you work on Sunday, too?" she demanded.

Francis ignored the question. He took out a sack of Bull Durham and began to roll a cigarette.

"I can't get over you coming here to live with Auntie," he said.

Miss Julie shrugged and grimaced. She looked fixedly at her son, and even with a mother's partiality she had to acknowledge that he was not extremely prepossessing. He was about forty-five, shorter than average, broad-shouldered for his height, somewhat stooped, and thin. His face, not unlike Miss Julie's in contour, was sallow, and his heavy jaw gave him a sullen look. His eyes were gray, and his gaze was hard. He had crinkly hair like his father's, and it was becoming gray. He wore a white suit, a brilliant blue tie with a horseshoe stickpin, yellow button shoes and a flashy ring set with a large red stone. The fingers of his left hand were stained a deep yellow.

"Where is Auntie?" he asked.

"She's gone over to nurse old Mrs. Atchison on the Battery."

"I guess you're glad to get rid of her for a while, Ma."

"Tessie and I get along very well."

"Since when? You were always fighting like cat and dog ever since I can remember."

"All families quarrel," Miss Julie said.

"Not like ours. Well, never mind. How are you, Ma?"

"Very well, thank the Lord," Miss Julie responded. She forced herself to inquire about Francis's wife, and to make the inquiry sound cordial.

"She's all right," Francis said carelessly. "Annie has a happy disposition. Even if we haven't got much money, she seems to enjoy herself. Though how anybody can do that in Charleston I don't know."

"It's a good thing to be satisfied with little," Miss Julie said.

"I'm getting tired of doing it," Francis said. He drummed on the chair with the fingers of his right hand, and looked around at the obvious poverty of the room. "Why did you have to pick up and leave Annette's house?"

"Because Tessie is getting old, and I thought I ought to be with her."

"I guess Henry had something to do with it," Francis said.

"Henry had nothing to do with it. You know I have no criticism to make of Henry. He's been wonderful to me."

Francis looked skeptical. "Maybe so. . . . What do you hear from Charlie?"

"I haven't had a letter for some time. I judge he's well. He sends me money whenever he has a little to spare."

Francis squirmed. "Lucky fellow," he said uneasily. "That reminds me, Ma: I've got a chance to make some money. If I had a couple of thousand dollars, I could double it in six months on a stock deal I know about. Fellow tipped me off. He says you can't make a mistake. It's in a new automobile company they're starting in Detroit."

Miss Julie did not answer him. This, she thought with a pain at her heart, is the reason my boy has come to see me after all these months!

"Ma," Francis went on, "you could let me have that much, couldn't you? I'd be able to give it back in six months. And with what I make on the deal I could go on and make some more."

"Why, Francis," Miss Julie said, "I haven't got much more than that. What would happen to me if you lost it?"

"It's a sure thing, Ma."

"Sure or not, I can't take such a risk, son. I don't dare. I just can't."

Francis looked sulky. The wheedling smile disappeared. "That's the trouble with all of us!" he burst out. "Never take a chance. Always pinch every penny until the Indian whoops, and stay poor all your life."

"We never had any money to squander on stock gambling," Miss Julie said. "And the one time your Pa took what little money he had and put it into that business, look what happened."

"Pa wasn't a businessman. He didn't know how to make money."

"There's no use in discussing it, Francis. I can't let you have the money, so there. You'll have to save until another chance comes along."

"All right, then," Francis said harshly. "I'll have to go on being a clerk all the rest of my life, checking niggers in a damned stinking fertilizer plant. I've never had a chance."

"We did all we could for you," Miss Julie said. "It wasn't our fault that we were poor. Everybody was poor after the war. Of course you had to go to work early. But so did Henry O'Donnell, and look at him."

"Oh, don't talk to me about that big Irish ape," Francis retorted. "Why do you have to compare everybody with that windbag? He's just been lucky."

"Well, he's made a fortune for himself; and he didn't do it by sitting in the Poinciana drinking beer and playing pool."

"If you mean me," Francis said, "I have to have a little fun. . . . Well, don't let's discuss it any more, Ma. I thought that the little money Pa left was meant for all of us."

"You're young," Miss Julie said. "You still have a chance to provide for yourself. I've got myself and Tessie to look out for. When I'm gone you and Charlie will get what I leave. And maybe your Uncle John will leave you something."

"You think more of Aunt Tessie than you do of your own son," Francis said. "And anybody that counts on old John Gerard's money is a fool. Anyway, there's no use of my staying here any longer. I know when I'm not wanted."

He picked up his hat and flung out of the door.

Miss Julie's instinct was to jump up and call him back, to say, "Come back, son, and you can have the money." But she didn't. She sat there, alone with her wounded feelings and her pity for Francis. There wasn't much chance in Charleston for young men; that was why so many of them had gone away as soon as they could. Like Charlie, who had gone all the way to California.

What if this were a real chance for Francis to make some money and build a future? She would feel bad if she kept him from bettering himself. She reviewed the familiar pattern of a life in Charleston without money—work for a small salary, if you could get work; a small house that you owned, and a few extra dollars if you took in a roomer or a boarder. Genteel pretense that you didn't want the things you couldn't have. . . . She thought of Francis taking his first job at thirteen, and working long hours, not the easy ten hours or so that people worked nowadays, with half Saturday off. She tried to think of young Joe doing the same, and she couldn't. Yet at the time she hadn't felt really bad about it. The few extra coppers a week had been such a godsend.

The more she thought about the matter, the sorrier she felt for Francis. And although her pride had been terribly wounded when she thought that he had come to see her only to demand money, and although it wasn't the first time that had happened, either, and although her French sense of thrift was aroused and alert, she resolved to go to Henry's office next day and ask his advice. She half hoped, at the same time, that his advice would be against the investment.

CHAPTER FOUR

Next morning, after her breakfast of herring and hominy, Miss Julie gave the rooms a lick and a promise and started out on her visit to Henry's office.

She had put on her best mourning and her silk gloves; and, while she had done this chiefly for the sake of Henry's pride, she was glad she had done so. Being turned out in her very best made her feel more sure of herself. Of course, very best nowadays was not what very best used to be. Why, this black silk dress was only three years old, and it had already begun to show signs of wear!

As it was still early—not yet ten—Miss Julie decided to stop in at church and say a few prayers before she went on up Broad Street. She had acquired a new short prayer which carried with it an indulgence of three hundred days, each time, and she felt that saying it in church would perhaps give it added efficacy. In the cool and quiet of the bare white cathedral Miss Julie experienced as always a sense of comfort and peace. She recited her new ejaculation a great many times, mentally noted the number of days to be put down in her indulgence book, and then "made" her beads.

It was almost half an hour later that she climbed the stairs of the little white building with the cotton boll on its sign that represented the Edisto Cotton Company and told the office boy, Joseph, to announce her. Then she sat down in the glass-partitioned anteroom, and while she was waiting she spied a tinfoil tobacco package near the waste basket. She inched over on the bench, picked it up, and thrust it into her pocketbook.

"Right under Henry's nose," she chuckled.

Henry, she reflected with some pride, was a big man in the Edisto. To have become vice president of such a concern at the early age of forty-two, after a childhood of poverty and a struggle to educate himself, did him credit even in Miss Julie's eyes; and she was not one to be vastly impressed by success. She could see, through the partition, Henry's broad back in his white suit. With him was the president, Mr. Augustus Jenkinson, and she could perceive that they were arguing good-naturedly.

As a matter of fact, Henry was debating his favorite theme with the boss. This was that the city needed new industries, particularly the Navy Yard.

"Mr. Jenkinson," he said, in the rather pompous manner characteristic of so many businessmen of the time, "Mr. Jenkinson, don't forget, sir, that the total assessment of real and personal property in the city last year, according to the Mayor's annual report, was at a figure of only twelve millions of dollars. Why, think of it! A multimillionaire could have bought the entire city, lock, stock, and barrel."

"Ah, yes, Mr. O'Donnell," replied Mr. Jenkinson, stroking his goatee as softly as he spoke. "But you forget the intangibles. The intangibles. Can't buy Charleston's spirit and culture, you know. That's not to be bought at any price. They can't buy our gracious tradition."

Henry detested this argument and all it stood for. He belonged to the new generation of "businessmen."

"A devil of a lot its culture will amount to when there's not enough business in it to support the inhabitants," he snorted. "Where are all our young men going, and why? What's my son going to do in a few years' time? I tell you, we need that Navy Yard, and we ought to thank God for it and for any new industries we can get."

"They will only bring in an undesirable element," said Mr. Jenkinson softly.

"Well, I don't believe that will do much harm," Henry said. "These are different days, and we have to be forward-looking. This is the twentieth century, the age of the—the automobile and the airplane. Charleston has got to take chances and expand or be left hopelessly behind. Why, Savannah and Atlanta and Jacksonville will go on growing and developing, and Charleston —pretty soon there won't be enough business going on here to support the Negroes." He was pink with earnestness.

Mr. Jenkinson smiled an obstinate gentle smile, like one talking to a lunatic.

"There will always be mills to buy our cotton," he said. "And there'll always be enough railroad lines to ship it. I mustn't stand here talking, though, when you have a caller."

Henry touched a bell, and the office boy appeared.

"Show Mrs. Sharp in, please."

Miss Julie entered, and nodded to Mr. Jenkinson.

"Good morning, Mrs. Sharp," Mr. Jenkinson said. "How are you, ma'am?"

"Very well, thank you," said Miss Julie. "And how are Mrs. Jenkinson and the girls?"

Mr. Jenkinson replied that they were very fine, and bowed himself out.

Henry drew up a chair for Miss Julie and motioned to her to sit down. He beamed welcome upon her, for he was certain that she had come to ask him to receive her once more into his home.

Miss Julie sank heavily into the chair.

"How are Annette and the children, Henry?"

"They're having a good time," Henry said. "How are you and Miss Tessie, ma'am?" He smiled knowingly.

Miss Julie shrugged. "Tessie is away nursing old Mrs. Atchison on the Battery. We're both fine and getting along nicely."

Henry's face showed a trace of disappointment. He said, "That's good."

"And the new house?" Miss Julie asked.

"I'm moving in next week."

"Don't you forget about those rosebushes," Miss Julie cautioned.

"I've already arranged about them. Do you mind if I smoke, Miss Julie?"

"No, indeed," Miss Julie said. "Let joy be unconfined." Henry took out a box of Murads and lighted one. "Here, give me that silver paper," Miss Julie said, and Henry handed it over.

"What can I do for you, Miss Julie?"

"I've come to ask your advice on a matter of business, Henry."

"I don't know what my advice is worth," Henry replied, with a smirk of false modesty, "but you're welcome to it. What's the trouble?"

Miss Julie told him about Francis's request. Henry listened with the patient smile of the expert who hears an old story.

"I've had the same offer made to me," he said airily, "and by the same man, I think. I don't know anything about him, good or otherwise. But I do know there's nothing in this automobile business. It's a fad still. They are making a lot of them, but the market will soon be glutted. For one thing, the oil won't hold out forever. There's only a certain amount of it in the ground— and then the good cars are so expensive. This man Ford is putting out cheap cars; but that won't last either, and he's said to be a very poor businessman, with all sorts of ideas about paying big wages and so forth. And look at the horrible little rattletraps those Ford cars are."

His air became faintly pontifical.

"The roads we have are not suitable to the automobile," he continued. "People will get tired of the jolting and jarring. I myself wouldn't have one of my own accord, but Annette and Joe and Betsy are set on having a car; so I suppose sooner or later I'll have to give in. They cost a fortune to start with and another to run. To make a long story short, I don't think the automobile will ever be much more than it is now. There won't be enough people able to afford it."

"Then you think this is not a good thing?" Miss Julie inquired.

"By no means. Don't touch it. Miss Julie"—Henry leaned forward confidentially—"there's only one way to get rich, and that's to work hard and invest your money in a good business, or in 6 per cent bonds. Unless you have a margin that you can take a chance of losing. And while we're talking about money, Miss Julie, I wish you'd do what I suggested awhile back and take your money out of Herbert Moore's hands. I don't think you're doing a good thing to leave it there."

Miss Julie set her jaw.

"I have entire confidence in Herbert Moore," she said. "Why, he was one of Andrew's best friends, and he's always paid me 6 per cent on the money. Besides, I couldn't hurt his feelings."

"Just as you like," Henry said. "I won't say anything more about it. You know best."

Miss Julie was mollified.

"I do wish I could do something for Francis, though," she said.

"Miss Julie," Henry said, "Francis is his own worst enemy, you know. That's one reason he hasn't done well at his job. His mind is on sport."

In her heart of hearts, Miss Julie knew this was just. But she resented it, coming from Henry.

"Francis is a good steady fellow," she said stoutly. "He hasn't made opportunities for himself, maybe. But I have no fault to find with him."

"Perhaps I'll be able to do something for Francis, when things pick up a little," Henry said kindly. "If we expand a little, as I hope we are going to, we may need a good man, and I'll see about it when the time comes."

"I'm sure he'd appreciate it," Miss Julie said.

Henry rose from his chair. "You won't think about going to the country for a few weeks?" he asked.

"Thank you, Henry, but I think I'd better stay with Tessie," Miss Julie replied. "She's a poor unfortunate soul, and she needs someone to stay with her."

"I'd be glad to do something for Miss Tessie," Henry said, "but you know how she'd receive such an offer."

Miss Julie smiled. "You've always been kind and generous, Henry," she said. "You've done enough. Tessie wants to feel independent. God knows what will happen to her when she can't afford to be."

"Well, then, you hang on to your money," Henry said, "and don't go putting it into stocks." He patted her shoulder. "I'll have Jennie make you up a box of figs in the next few days and send them over to you."

He followed her out to the landing and waited politely until she had started down the stairs.

Miss Julie, greatly relieved by his advice, proceeded down and westward to King Street, where she had the good fortune to meet her old friend Miss Euterpe Greene, a sufferer from gas and heartburn. They strolled along, chatting animatedly about remedies and doctors.

Then Miss Julie went into the big stationery store and bought a picture book for James and George, and over to Louis Cohen's where she got some khaki cloth and some red muslin to make the Indian suits she had planned. It was extravagant, she knew, but she was so relieved over saving her bit of money that she felt she could afford this.

That afternoon she wrote to Francis, telling him what Henry had said.

"I just wanted you to know that I had not forgotten what you had asked me," she concluded. "I know Henry's advice is good, and I am sure you will be satisfied with that. When I am gone, you and Charlie will have my money, little as it is, and perhaps by that time you will be able to do something for yourself. They say these are years of opportunity. . . . And do try to come once in a while to see your old mother. I may not be around very long. It might be a good idea, I think, if you went to see Henry some time. He is so thoughtful and anxious to help people, and he seemed really anxious to do something for you."

But Francis did not trouble to answer her letter.

CHAPTER FIVE

"IT'S NONE OF MY BUSINESS, OF COURSE," Miss Tessie said, pulling her shawl a little more snugly around her shoulders, "but I'd let my daughter come to see me first. I'd have a little pride."

"I'm not going to stand on ceremony with my own daughter," Miss Julie replied, sharply. "Why don't you put the window down if you're cold?"

"I'm not cold. This is for my rheumatism. The wind always begins to get damp this late in September. Well, as I said, I have no business to interfere. Do just as you like."

"I'm going to." Then Miss Julie softened her tone: "The poor child is probably tired to death with all that vacation, and with that long trip yesterday. Besides, I want to see the children, and I want to see what they've done with that new house."

Miss Tessie hooted contemptuously.

"I suppose you'll stay to dinner."

"Probably." Miss Julie arose and picked up her plates and her cup and saucer. She was so eager to see her grandchildren that her hand trembled a little.

"What's the matter, sister? You're shaking like a leaf."

"You just imagine that, Tessie."

"No, I don't. You're not feeling well."

"Nonsense," Miss Julie retorted emphatically. This supervision of her health was her sister's latest quirk, and she was sick and tired of it. Tessie had been away for only three brief nursing jobs that summer, and Miss Julie felt oppressed by what she had been through.

"You're not planning to go back to Henry O'Donnell's to stay, are you?"

"No." Miss Julie took a fresh grip on the plates and moved

toward the kitchen. "Drat it," she grumbled under her breath, "Tessie is so jealous. I never in my life saw such a person."

Miss Tessie came bustling out with the rest of the breakfast dishes, and as usual protested against her sister's aid. This had become a daily struggle, and Miss Julie's way of winning it was simply to go ahead with her part of the task as if she weren't listening. She poured hot water from the old copper kettle into the dishpan and sloshed the china and silver around in it.

Miss Tessie, her jaw grimly set, put her dishes into the pan too and waited for Miss Julie to wash them. She did the drying at the end of each of these tussles of will. This gave her an occasional opportunity to pass a plate back for rewashing.

Luck was with her on this particular morning.

"Here," she said gruffly. "There's some hominy still stuck to this plate."

Miss Julie took the plate, scrutinized it, and removed the offending grains with a careful fingernail, dipping just the corner of the plate back into the water. She handed the finished product to Miss Tessie, who took it with a scowl. Miss Julie chuckled, with a pleasant feeling that she had been very annoying. She wondered how James and George were going to like their Indian suits. It had been shameful of her not to send those suits to the country, but she was selfish enough to want to see the boys put them on and get the first enjoyment out of them. . . .

"I beg your pardon, Tessie, I didn't hear what you were saying," she said.

"You're getting so very deaf, it's a wonder you hear anything."

"I'm not as deaf as you think," Miss Julie replied.

It seemed almost too good to believe that the summer was already over, and that the children were here, right in the city, this morning, and that she was going to see them.

"The rascals," she muttered.

She hurried through the few dishes and, leaving Tessie to her task of polishing them, went downstairs with the slops, and the coffee grounds which she had formed the habit of giving to the old colored woman in the next yard for use at second hand.

She emptied the slop pail and then knocked on the fence with it and called, "Corinne!"

Corinne hobbled from her little house in the back yard, managed a painful smile as she said good morning, took the already used coffee with a grateful remark that it would taste mighty good, and asked about Miss Julie's health.

"So-so," Miss Julie replied. "How are you today?"

"Po'ly," Corinne said.

That was usually the extent of their conversation, for as it was hard to understand Corinne's toothless mumbling, Miss Julie made no attempt to encourage the old woman. But today was a gala occasion. She stood at the place where the board was broken out of the fence and said:

"My grandchildren are home now. I'm going to see them to-day."

"God bless them!" Corinne said. "I got grandchillen myself. I got great-grandchillen."

"Is that so?" Miss Julie asked. "You know, your children and grandchildren ought to do something for you, Corinne."

"They gots enough to do for themselves," Corinne said, with a shrug.

Miss Julie wagged her head in sympathy and went back upstairs. She was accustomed to the spectacle of Negro poverty and fairly callous to it. Someone always seemed to help the Negroes, and they always got along somehow. "Suppose I was all alone and neglected like that," she thought.

She went to the mailbox and peered in. Nothing.

"No mail," she informed Miss Tessie.

Miss Tessie was disappointed. "It's a week since I sent for that mail-order catalogue," she said.

Was Tessie going to buy out the mail-order house now? Miss Julie hoped the catalogue would never come.

"Sometimes," she told her sister, "it takes a little while for such things to arrive." She shook her head despairingly and set about dressing.

Her sister was sweeping the matting when she left. "Making

a great show of doing all the work while I gad about visiting," Miss Julie thought.

"Well, I'm off, Tessie."

Miss Tessie studiously refrained from sending any message to her niece.

"I shan't expect you for dinner," she said.

"I'm sure Annette will ask me to stay. They miss me," Miss Julie said, not without malice.

She walked swiftly along, talking to herself. "Never thought I'd be visiting my grandchildren again," she muttered. "It seems like years since I lived with them. . . . Well, it's been a long summer.

"I didn't bargain for all this superintending, either.

"Tessie would like better than anything else to have me totally dependent on her.

"It isn't that she wants me there because I'm her sister. She wants someone she can feel superior to—somebody she can sacrifice for, so she can feel prouder of herself.

"Tessie has always wanted to be a hero to somebody. I wonder she hasn't taken to wearing a hair shirt.

"I've got to be careful what I say to Annette. I don't want her to think I regret what I've done, or that I admit I've made a mistake.

"I wonder if the boys really did miss me while they were away. I suppose they've got their Sarah back, and that's all they want."

Miss Julie felt a sinking sensation as she thought that maybe they wouldn't be glad to see her after all.

"I won't give them the Indian suits until I see," she muttered

She peered through the iron garden fence for a sign of the boys; but nothing was visible through the thick hedge that separated the garden from the back yard. There was nobody on the piazzas, either. Feeling very like a stranger, Miss Julie rang the front-door bell. It was answered by Sarah.

"How do you do, Mis' Sharp?" Sarah greeted her.

"How are you, Sarah?" Miss Julie responded, her gaze straying immediately to the back yard, where James and George were overseeing Stevens, Sarah's husband, in his task of building a new chicken coop. "Yoo-hoo! James! George!" she roared.

The boys paid no attention, and Miss Julie's heart was heavy. But she thought that maybe they hadn't heard her, and shouted again. They came running, scrambled up the rear steps of the piazza, and flung themselves upon her.

"My goodness!" Miss Julie exclaimed. "How they've grown! Why, they're men already."

"I've got a new tooth," James said, exposing a gap in his lower jaw and putting a grimy finger on the tiny spot of white that was struggling to fill the vacancy. "One came out."

"It did?" Miss Julie asked, feigning great astonishment. "Well, well! And did you put it under the pillow and did the angel bring you a nickel?"

"He left me a dime," James said. "I hope I'm gonna lose a lot of teeth soon."

"I'm gonna lose some teeth, too," George said.

Miss Julie chuckled happily, and Annette's first glance at her caught her in this happy mood.

"Ma!"

They embraced. It was the first time in years that they had done so. It gave Miss Julie an odd but pleased feeling.

"Come in and sit down, Ma, so we can have a long talk."

"Directly," Miss Julie said. "First I have some business to do." She indicated the package which she was still holding under her arm.

"Granny, have you got a mint?" George asked.

"Don't ask for things," James reprimanded him primly.

"What did you say, Bubber?" Miss Julie asked.

"Have you got a mint?" George repeated.

"Well, I shouldn't be surprised," Miss Julie said. She handed the package to Annette, fished in her bag, and took out two peppermints.

"Thank you," James said, and George repeated it. Then they both popped the candies into their mouths and crunched them like rock crushers, each with a look of painful concentration on the task.

"My, my," Miss Julie said. "I wish I had teeth like that. If I could chew like you boys, I'd eat everything, bones and all."

She surveyed the browned little fellows with a burst of delight.

"Where are the big ones?" she asked.

"Oh, they're off to see their friends," Annette said. "You'd think, with a new house to pry into, that they'd have stayed a little longer; but they were off right after breakfast. But how are you, Ma? You look just a little thinner."

"Well, child, it's been hot."

"And how is Aunt Tessie?"

"Oh, Tessie is fine." Miss Julie chuckled. "She didn't want me to come. She said you ought to come and visit me first. I said I wasn't going to stand on ceremony with my own daughter. . . . But here, we're going on talking and these little limbs of the Old Boy are waiting for their presents. Or maybe they don't want them?"

"Yes, we do," George said.

"We want them now!" James declared.

Miss Julie opened the package and took out the khaki Indian suits trimmed with red fringe, and hats with turkey feathers stuck in them. The boys pranced with excitement and raced off to get Sarah to help them put on the suits. Miss Julie stood smiling at the success of her presents.

"Come on in, Ma, and see the house."

"I've got to see Polly first," Miss Julie said, going down to the back of the porch and poking a finger into the old bird's cage. "Polly want a cracker?" she asked.

The sulky old bird struck at her finger and blinked.

"He remembers me," Miss Julie said, pleased at this demonstrativeness. "And here's Beauty! What have you been up to, you old rascal?" She prodded the sleepy cat, and he blinked. Miss Julie was pleased at that, too.

Then she consented to go in and look at the new furnishings.

She tossed her hat and veil onto a table in the hall, and followed Annette through the rooms, commenting only with a grunt except when she said of the mission furniture:

"It reminds me of coffins."

"Oh, for goodness' sake, Ma!" Annette protested. "It's the latest thing."

"Well, I don't like it, latest thing or not."

Miss Julie was shown the kitchen, which actually had an enameled sink, and she spoke to Jennie; then she trudged up the stairs and looked over the bedrooms. Finally they returned to Annette's big, airy bedroom and she sank into a rocker at the window.

"I've been on me feet since early this morning," she explained. "Well, it's certainly nice to see you again, child."

"I'm glad to be back," Annette said. "I got tired of the mountains, as usual. There's really nothing to do up there, except go for hay rides and see the falls, and once is enough. It gets pretty dull. But the children enjoyed it." She glanced out at the little ones, who were racing around in their Indian suits and whooping at the tops of their voices. "They certainly were pleased with those suits."

"I kept them so I could see the children get the pleasure out of having them on for the first time." Miss Julie peered out at the boys. "They look fine."

Annette took up her embroidery frame. "It's done them good," she observed. "Now tell me all about you and Aunt Tessie."

Miss Julie grimaced.

"It's a long story, as the man said about killing his wife. . . . Tessie is peculiar, and she's getting more peculiar every day, but we haven't flown at each other's throats yet."

"You probably will."

"Oh, I don't know. What happened to your bedroom furniture?"

"Henry gave it to Sarah. He wanted everything new."

"Henry is very freehanded."

"Entirely too much so," Annette agreed.

"Listen!" Miss Julie said. "Do I imagine it, or is that Jenkins' Band?"

"They're right outside," Annette said.

Miss Julie stood up and looked out the window. "I haven't heard them all summer."

They went out to the piazza to see better, and laughed when the tiny drum major, a coal-black child in a red uniform, swung his baton and the boys broke into another flood of brazen discord. One of the boys came to the front door, and Annette called Sarah and sent her down with a dime.

"Jenkins has done wonders for those children," she said. "Even if they sound awful."

"Yes, he's a good man." Miss Julie sniffed. "Is that tomato and okra soup?"

"It must be next door. We're not having it today. You'll stay for dinner, Ma, won't you?"

"Of course." Miss Julie sighed. "It will feel good to sit down and have a dinner served to me for a change."

Annette looked at her mother as if expecting her to say more; but she did not enlarge upon her statement.

"Ma, it was your own choosing."

"I'm not complaining."

"You can come back any time you like."

"I'm well off where I am," Miss Julie said obstinately. Did they think she was going to ask them to take her back? "This is all too grand for me, anyway."

Annette said nothing.

"There's one thing I do like, though, and that's the view," Miss Julie said. She stared out at the corner of the lake, and at a solitary vegetable wagon drawn by a gaunt mule and driven by a fat and aged Negress in a turban, who sat under a great canvas umbrella and from time to time sang out what might have been the names of vegetables. "Old Hannah," she remarked.

"I can remember her from the time I was no bigger than Betsy. She must be ninety."

"She always reminded me of my old mauma," Miss Julie said.

[119]

"The one John always loved so because she used to hide him whenever Papa was going to give him a licking. Poor John! I'm afraid he's not going to last much longer."

"He was still failing when you heard from Minnie?"

"Yes. He wasn't any better, anyway. . . . He was such a cute little fellow."

"I wish he'd give you some of his money now, and not keep you waiting for him to die," Annette said.

"What do you mean, Annette? I never was so unchristianlike as to wish for anybody's death." But Miss Julie felt hypocritical.

"Well, he's certainly held onto his money."

"Sometimes I wonder if a little thrift isn't a good thing," said Miss Julie. "Look at Tessie. . . . She can't resist a store window if she has ten cents in her pocketbook—or a beggar, or some poor devil selling packets of needles."

"Well, Ma, you knew that. You know she was always extravagant."

"What's that got to do with it? Anybody would think I was complaining to listen to you."

"I didn't say you were complaining." Annette bit off her thread. "But it oughtn't to be a surprise to you, after all these years, that Aunt Tessie can't keep a cent."

Miss Julie grunted. She stared out of the window. "Here comes the old groundnut cake woman. I'll have to get some. I haven't seen the old soul in months. Nobody ever comes to Queen Street."

"I'll get some," Annette said. She went to the piazza and leaned over the banisters. "Sarah!"

Sarah appeared in the garden.

"Get me a nickel's worth of groundnut cakes. The old woman is out in front now."

"Yessum."

A moment later they heard Sarah's whooping laugh.

"That old Clarissa is a devil," Miss Julie said. "She knows everybody's business."

"Stevens doesn't like Sarah to have anything to do with her. He says she's a 'wulgar ol' 'oman.' Sarah!"

Sarah broke off her interesting conversation with old Clarissa, and the ancient crone trudged off with her great tray of candy. Sarah appeared a moment later with the tough discs of molasses taffy and peanuts, each resting on a circular piece of butcher's paper, and Miss Julie grabbed one.

"You take one, Sarah, and give one to Jennie and one to the boys. What did Clarissa tell you?"

"Thank you, ma'am," Sarah said. "That Clarissa is something else," she added, slapping her thigh in her amusement. "She was tellin' me about her midwifin'. She say de gal was hollerin' and hollerin', and she tell 'em: 'Da's right! Yell! Go ahead and yell! You didn' yell like dat when you was gittin' 'em.'"

Annette blushed slightly, but she laughed, and Miss Julie shook with merriment. They could hear Sarah laughing in the kitchen as she communicated this edifying anecdote to Jennie, and Jennie's cries of "Do, Lawd!" They smiled tolerantly.

Miss Julie took her groundnut cake and stripped off the paper. Then she calmly removed her plate and put it on the window sill. "I have to chew these with me own teeth," she explained. "I'm glad Tessie can't see me doing this. She'd have a duck fit."

"Ma," Annette said, "you don't feel very well satisfied with Aunt Tessie, do you? Tell the truth and shame the devil."

Miss Julie waved her hands, unable to talk while she was chewing the taffy. Finally she got the words out: "Whatever put that into your head? I'm perfectly satisfied. Tessie is peculiar, but she's very good."

But she knew her protestations weren't very convincing. She was conscious that this was the first really happy morning she had spent since the O'Donnells went away. She reveled in the great airy room, and the view right down to the lake, and the garden on the side that looked just a little wild—for Stevens was not the most scrupulous of gardeners—but was nevertheless a tonic to the eye. She went down to the yard to watch the boys playing Indian, chasing each other around with blood-curdling screams and eating biscuits and molasses which James said were buffalo meat and grunting, "Ugh, heap good!" at each mouthful. She went into the garden to see how those rosebushes of Pa's were getting along; then she returned to Annette's room and begged some darning, and she and Annette worked and chatted pleasantly until Henry came home for dinner.

And then there were Betsy and Joe to hug and kiss and give her trifles to; and there was a merry dinner, for Henry was gay, and steak and rice and squash and sweet potatoes and ice cream, of which Miss Julie ate so immoderately that she felt just a bit uneasy. But she was content. "Better belly bust than good victuals spoil," she quoted to herself. She rocked George into his afternoon nap, singing silly songs like

> Buh Rabbit, whuh you fuh do dey?
> I duh pick oshtuh fuh young gal.
> Oshtuh duh bite off my finguh,
> An' young gal duh tek 'em fuh laugh at.

She was terribly reluctant to go home, and it was painful to enter the poverty-stricken flat. Her sister was just finishing a thorough job of housecleaning, pleased with her own house-wifeliness. "If she thinks I believe she's been cleaning house all day, she's buying rotten meat," Miss Julie said to herself. The bit of drama made her cross, and she limited herself to a brief description of the new house and its furnishings, which was nevertheless sufficient to inspire Miss Tessie to happy sneers.

Miss Julie ate scarcely any supper, which made Miss Tessie uneasy. She thought she had better call Dr. Edmonds. Miss Julie forbade that in no uncertain terms, and they were on the point of quarreling about it when the doorbell rang.

It was Francis. He entered with an air of sulky triumph.

"Hello, Aunt Tessie," he greeted his aunt. "How are things, old gal?"

She was offended at this familiarity.

"I am very well, thank you, Francis," she said haughtily. "And how are you and your wife?"

"All right," Francis said, ignoring the deliberate offensiveness of the "your wife." "No, I won't sit down, I'm not going to stay. Here's Ma. Well, Ma, I hope you're satisfied. I just came in to tell you that stock I had a chance to buy was way up. Maybe you won't be so glad to listen to Henry O'Donnell next time he wants to give advice."

He turned and went out, and Miss Julie could see that he swayed just a little. She stood thunderstruck.

"Well," Miss Tessie said. "Well." The monosyllable conveyed criticism of both Henry and Francis, or so Miss Julie fancied. She was about to retort bitterly, but thought better of it and flounced out of the room. She was glad afterwards that she had been speechless. There was no telling what she might have said under the circumstances.

"There must have been bad luck in that comet, just like people said," she muttered. Otherwise, how could everything have gone wrong the way it had ever since the beginning of summer?

She was angry not only with Francis, but with Henry and Tessie and herself; and the day that had begun so pleasantly was spoiled.

CHAPTER SIX

Miss julie was a frequent visitor at the O'Donnells' after that. In fact, her place was set so often at their table that she might as well have lived there and been done with it. This did nothing to relieve the growing tension with her sister, who saw in these frequent visits signs of defection.

"I've tried to save your pride for you," Miss Tessie said, "but if you want to keep on being insulted and humiliated go right ahead. I can't do any more about it."

"Why, Tessie, you talk like a rag baby."

"All right, go on," Miss Tessie said. "Get yourself insulted again. I saved you from it once, remember, and it's your own doing if you want it to happen again."

This was getting to be a perfect mania with her, Miss Julie thought. She crossed her arms on her breast and looked fixedly at her sister. "Once and for all, Tessie, I came to live with you because you wanted me to. You wanted someone to live with you, and you thought it was proper because we were both getting old and ought to spend our last years together. It wasn't for my sake at all."

"Well, Julie, your memory is certainly failing. I persuaded you to come and live with me because I wanted to save you from humiliation. If your pride doesn't matter to you—"

"Well, don't let's argue about it." Miss Julie suddenly felt sure that she was dealing with someone not quite rational. "We came to live together, and we'll make the best of it, and the least said the better. But I'm going to see my daughter and her children whenever I get good and ready to, and I don't care how corn sells."

It was just jealousy, she said to herself, after they had both become calmer.

She persuaded Annette, without any difficulty, to ask Tessie to come to dinner every Sunday.

"I don't need their charity," Miss Tessie said.

"Now, don't be foolish. They have a big family, and it's nice for you to be there once in a while with the children. It'll do you good."

"Brats!" Miss Tessie said. "Henry O'Donnell's children! . . . I suppose they think I'm not getting enough to eat."

"Why, they don't think anything of the kind, Tessie. They just thought it would be nice for us to enjoy dinner without having any work to do."

"I must have coffee made in my own pot."

"That's nothing new. Nobody's going to object to that."

"That Jennie is a breaker. I hate to trust her with it," Miss Tessie demurred. But she decided to take the risk. And so, on Sunday, Miss Julie, Miss Tessie, and Miss Tessie's coffeepot went to the O'Donnells'. And each Sunday afternoon, when they returned home, Miss Tessie poured into her sister's ears a lengthy criticism of everything Annette, Henry, the children, and the servants did.

This arrangement lasted about six weeks, or until the middle of November.

James was now at school, and afternoons and Saturday mornings were the only times Miss Julie could see him. She was particularly interested in James at this time, for he was to make his first communion the next spring, and she wanted to see that he was properly prepared for it. Whenever she could, she inquired if he remembered to repeat, "All for Thee, Sweet Jesus," every morning, and if he continued to say the prayers she had taught him; for she had a conviction that Henry's laxness was certain to infect the children.

To keep a closer eye on James, she persuaded him to come over on Saturday mornings with George.

This was a great privilege for James, whose trip to school with Betsy prevented his showing independence and going alone. He guided George through the streets and protected him from the meager traffic, and deposited him safely at the door of the flat with the air of a retriever delivering a bird. This delighted his grandmother.

"I brought George," was his invariable announcement on these occasions.

"Well, what big boys!" Miss Julie exclaimed just as invariably.

Miss Tessie kept to herself most of the time when the children were there. She said that their hands were dirty, and that they got into things. And unfailingly at least once per visit she told James, whose posture was faulty:

"Straighten your shoulders! Do you want to grow up to look like a fishhook?"

But when she wasn't there, George and James had a lively morning with Miss Julie's tinfoil balls, and buttons, and such other treasures as her glass paperweight, the little vial of colored sand collected after the earthquake, and the enameled jumping-jack stickpin that had belonged to Andrew Sharp.

At first they were very slightly in awe of their aunt; but this

wore off quickly, and one day, when they were playing boisterously around the sitting room, George was so unfortunate as to
bump against the easel that supported the picture of the beloved
Theodora. The easel tottered, and for an instant seemed about
to crash to the floor; but it righted itself and stood level again.

Miss Tessie turned white with anger.

"Why don't you look where you're going?" she shrieked at
George, who, being too small to have an answer ready, merely
stood there and grinned at her.

"Haven't you been taught any manners?" she shouted at him.
"Answer when you're spoken to!"

"Don't be cross to the child, Tessie," Miss Julie remonstrated.
"He's only an infant, after all, and he didn't mean to do it."

"Why does he go running around like a wild animal, then?"
Miss Tessie straightened the flowers under the picture and set
the little vase in place again. "My poor little daughter's picture!"

"Why, because he's little and wants to be active," Miss Julie
said. "You can't expect a child of that age to keep quiet, you
know."

"My children were quiet in the house, no matter what age
they were."

"Oh, pshaw, your children were marvels."

Miss Julie intended to be jocular, but merely angered Miss
Tessie further: her eyes blazed, and she charged right up to Miss
Julie.

"Don't you ever mention my children in that tone of levity
again," she said, quivering. "I won't have their memory profaned
by your coarse talk—do you understand that?"

The boys watched this interesting exhibition with keen appreciation.

"Tessie, you're forgetting yourself. Don't forget these children
are here."

"I suppose you think Henry O'Donnell's Irish brats are too
nice for my conversation? They'd never know the difference.
Their father never had any bringing up, and I don't suppose
they'll ever have any, either."

"My father is just as good as you are," James said, angrily.

"You see?" Miss Tessie said. "There's manners for you!" She shook her finger at James and then at George. "Don't either of you come here again if you can't be polite."

The children merely stared.

Miss Julie was angry but helpless. If she really fought this out with Tessie, they would have to part; and if she left, she would have to live somewhere by herself, which she couldn't afford to do. She patted James and George but said nothing.

"I think we'd better go," James said to George. He was only six, but he had already learned the Southern code.

Miss Julie got their coats and went down the stairs with them.

"You mustn't mind your Aunt Tessie. She's nervous. Now go straight home, and be good boys."

The little fellows walked along for a block or so without saying a word to each other. Then James spoke.

"Don't say anything about this to Papa," he cautioned. "It'll get him mad."

"I ain' care nuttin' fuh da' 'oman," George said, lapsing, under stress, into Gullah.

"Well, don't you say anything about it, that's all," James insisted. George was hard to impress.

They went home along the lake, picking up acorns and polishing them and taking a long time about it; and then they stood and watched the roller skaters. Among these was Joe, who ordered them several times to go home, but was ignored.

It was late in the morning when they straggled into the house.

"My," Annette said, "have you been all this time at Granny's?"

"No, we've been playing down on the pond."

James's face became very red as he told her that, and Annette looked at him sharply.

"What have you boys been up to?"

"Nothing."

"Well, then, it must have been George. George, what did you do?"

"I bumped against the picture," George said.

"What picture?"

"The picture that stands up on the ladder."

"Oh! The picture that stands up on the ladder. And then what happened?"

"She yelled at me."

James, who had been making threatening faces at George, trying to head off this confession, now threw in his testimony. "Aunt Tessie said we didn't have any manners," he said hotly. "She was yelling at Granny, and Granny said to remember we were there, and Aunt Tessie said how would we know the difference, our own father didn't have any bringing up. And I told her Papa was just as good as she was, and she said never to come there again if we couldn't be polite."

"Well, now, that settles it," Annette said. "Don't go there again. If your Granny wants to see you she can come here. I won't have you scolded like that."

James and George started to leave the room. Annette turned and said to them:

"Don't say anything about this to your father."

Henry was in a bad mood; he felt that the neighbors had snubbed them by refusing an invitation to supper, and Annette did not want to have him crossed.

"We won't say anything," James promised. "Remember, George, don't say anything to Papa, now."

"I won't. I won't tell him about that old bitch."

However, that day, at dinner, Henry inquired what his little men had done that morning.

"We went to Granny's," George said.

"Sh-h-h!" James nudged him to remind him not to say anything about what had happened.

The gesture aroused Henry's suspicions, and he was instantly on the alert. He had a chronic certainty that things were kept from him, and in his present irritation this was too much.

"What happened?" he demanded.

"Nothing." James reddened.

"Why did you shush George, then?" Henry asked, like a Grand Inquisitor.

"Oh, it was nothing. They had a little run-in with Aunt Tessie," Annette said.

Henry wasn't satisfied. His detective fever was up.

"What happened?" he asked again. "I want to know about it."

Annette had to tell him. Henry was furious.

"All right," he said. "Now listen to what I say." He cupped his left hand and pounded the right into it for emphasis. "I don't want any of you to go to your Aunt Tessie's again and take the chance of being insulted. No one." He glared at the little boys as if it had been their fault.

"I've already told them they are not to go there." Annette fingered her napkin ring.

"I mean you, too," Henry said, "and Betsy and Joe. If Miss Julie wants to see any of you, she can come here."

That, it was understood, settled the matter. It wasn't a good plan to disobey Henry, especially where his pride was concerned.

Meanwhile, despite her pacifistic resolutions, Miss Julie had reproached her sister bitterly. "You're going to get me to fall out with my daughter and grandchildren if you keep up this sort of thing," she said, finally.

Miss Tessie grinned triumphantly.

That was the end of their Sunday dinners together at the O'Donnells'. Miss Julie, however, continued to go as often as ever to Annette's house, Sundays included.

"It's none of my affair," she said. She was sorry that the children weren't allowed to come to see her any more, but she understood. Although she was thoroughly disgusted with Tessie there was nothing she could do about it.

"Confound her mean ways," Miss Julie muttered.

She took to complaining more and more about their life together, and Annette began to hope that they would quarrel and her mother would return to their home. But the time was not ripe for that.

CHAPTER SEVEN

ON A SATURDAY MORNING IN DECEMBER Miss Julie left the house particularly early and bustled over to Annette's. She had a very important task to perform. She was going to mix the Christmas cake.

She had a recipe for fruit cake beside which all other fruit cake recipes were mere evasions, and she had mixed one for the O'Donnells every Christmas since they had been married.

Accepting only a cup of coffee—it was just after breakfast time —she put on an apron, rolled up her sleeves, and hastened out to the kitchen. For this was a very serious undertaking.

She examined the materials piled high on the dresser in the great gloomy room—currants, raisins, citron, dried figs, shelled walnuts, dried orange peel, dates, flour, rose water, brandy, and spices.

"Seems to be all there," she remarked.

James and George entered.

"Granny, can we watch?" James asked.

"If you're very good."

"We won't do anything," James promised.

Miss Julie began her ritual, admonishing herself in the usual way as she took each step.

"I'll pick me raisins apart. . . . I'll roll them in the flour. . . . Now the currants." Then came the chopped figs and dates and the nuts, and the orange peel and the citron; and then all was mixed and dusted with cinnamon and nutmeg and allspice. Next Miss Julie added a minimum of flour—she despised cakes made with more than just enough flour to hold them together— and poured in the rose water and stirred and kneaded the whole in a great wooden washtub. She became coated to the elbows during this process with sticky brown batter, which she calmly scraped off into the tub. Sarah and Jennie lined the great baking pans with butcher's paper heavily coated with butter; and the pint of brandy was poured on and stirred, and the cakes were popped into the oven. By the time Miss Julie had removed her apron and rolled down her sleeves and composed herself, a heavenly smell began to penetrate the entire house. To Miss Julie it was like incense. She sniffed joyfully.

James and George were deeply impressed by this undertaking, since it set a seal on the Christmas anticipations they had begun to harbor. As soon as the first grocery shops and seed stores and fruiterers had begun to display firecrackers and Roman candles and skyrockets and spitfires, they had begun to discuss Santa Claus. By the time the cake was mixed they had reached a high pitch of excitement, with several weeks to go. Miss Julie had recited "The Night Before Christmas" and "Santa Claus Was a Funny Old Man" endless times and had conspired with them to send innumerable notes up the chimney to Santa Claus. And James had a daily conference with George.

James had a problem. He could not decide which he wanted the more, an express wagon or a hook-and-ladder truck; and as he was big enough to realize that he mustn't make too long a list, he compromised by trying to inspire George with the desire for the things he felt would unduly lengthen it.

Miss Julie overheard one of these discussions:

"Now," James said, after pinning down George's attention by telling him that they were going to talk about Christmas, "what is Santa Claus goin' ta bring you, George?"

"A fireman hat," George said.

George was what the Negroes called fickle-minded. He could not remember more than one thing he wanted at a time. This inability to make the most of a good opportunity was very trying to James.

"And a fire hook-and-ladder truck," he reminded George.

"Yes, a fire hook-and-ladder truck."

"And what else?" James asked.

[131]

"A fire hook-and-ladder truck."

"A fire hook-and-ladder truck and a fireman's hat," James prompted. "And what else besides?"

"A fire hook-and-ladder truck and a fireman hat."

James sighed.

"And a wind-up train," he reminded George. "Remember the great big trains in the mountains when we went down and put pins on the track? Well, a little train like that, that runs on a track."

But George could remember now only the train that wound up.

"George," James said, "you don't deserve anything."

"I declare," Miss Julie muttered, "that James is a case."

Once or twice she took the two boys to see the stores on King Street, avoiding the ten-cent store where the Christmas tree ornaments were displayed. "How can they keep on believing in Santa Claus when they see all these things for sale?" she wanted to know.

She went to the ten-cent store alone to buy a few trifles for each of them. Tessie, of course, was going to buy presents for them, with her usual contradictoriness. "She's so mad with all of them you'd think she wouldn't bother about Christmas," Miss Julie thought. But Miss Tessie went to the department stores, and to Legerton's, and spent more than she had a right to.

"As if Henry wasn't extravagant enough about Christmas," said Miss Julie.

Henry's way of buying Christmas presents was to do it all at the last moment. He always became gloomy when Christmas approached, and his temper became more unreliable than ever. Miss Julie and the others knew the reason for this.

There had been one particularly tragic Christmas in Henry's boyhood, and he had never forgotten it. It was after his father's death, when Henry and his older brother had been obliged to work to support their mother and their younger brother and sister. It had been a hard pull, and there had been one Christmas Day on which the dinner dish was stew, and not very much of that. Henry and his older brother had stinted themselves so that the little ones might have enough.

This dark thread in his spiritual tapestry unraveled every December in gloomy predictions that it would be a very poor Christmas that year. But it never was, and the children were always confident that they would get all they wanted. Henry's gloom was nothing to them.

The excitement and the impatience mounted, until, at last, it was the day before Christmas. Miss Julie spent the whole of Christmas Eve with the O'Donnells, tucking the excited little boys into bed and warning them to be very quiet, and watching Annette and Henry trim the great tree after Betsy and Joe were also out of the way. When the trimming and the inevitable argument that accompanied it were over, Henry escorted her to Queen Street. As he was leaving her at the door he put an envelope into her hand. "Don't say anything about this," he told her. "And share it with Miss Tessie."

"Thank you, Henry," Miss Julie said, with that gracious air the Gerards used to express recognition of a favor.

She did not open the envelope until she had talked to Tessie, who was very sulky about being left all alone.

"Henry gave me a present for the two of us," Miss Julie finally told her, holding up the envelope.

"Present? Hoo! I like his impudence."

"Don't be silly, sister." Miss Julie tore open the envelope and took out a pair of crisp new twenty-dollar bills, one of which she held out to Miss Tessie.

"I really wouldn't take it," Miss Tessie explained, "except that I don't want to be rude at Christmas time. Henry is just trying to show off. I hate purse-proud people."

Miss Julie checked the temptation to reply. After all, it *was* Christmas Eve.

In the morning, Miss Julie arose at a quarter to four. Miss Tessie got up shortly afterward, and they dressed carefully and went through the dark streets to the cathedral and sat in Henry's pew up near the front. Miss Julie began as always to pray in her stage whisper, and Miss Tessie, since it was Christmas, smiled sourly and tried to ignore it.

Annette came in shortly afterward with the children, who were naturally restless and inattentive; they had already heard the first boomings of giant crackers set off by impatient merry-makers, and had snatched a look at the dark room where the tree stood banked by toys, the glass ornaments dimly gleaming. Miss Julie had to speak quite sharply to Joe and James, telling them to kneel up and asking if that was all their mother had taught them.

It was a lovely Mass, she thought; the choir sang loud and clear, and Father Mellon's sermon was not too long and was very charming. Some of it she could not hear; but she could fairly well imagine what the parts she missed were about. And she was pleased to find Betsy's deportment so good, especially at communion.

James gave more trouble. Halfway through Mass he began to ask in loud whispers when it would be time to go home; and, despairing of ever getting there, he began to employ such traditional time-passing devices as kicking the pew in front, squinting through hands cupped to form binoculars, and riffling the pages of a prayerbook. But at last it was over.

Everyone swarmed out of the church, and there were dozens of people to wish a Merry Christmas to, while James tugged at his mother and at Miss Julie and asked when they were going home, and Joe and Betsy tried in vain to pull away.

Miss Julie was going to breakfast with the O'Donnells. Miss Tessie had consented to come to dinner, but had refused to go to breakfast besides. She felt that was too much of a concession.

"It's too bad about Tessie. It makes me feel bad to see her going off to breakfast by herself," Miss Julie said.

"Well, I'm not going to worry about Aunt Tessie," Annette said. "I'm not going to let her spoil my day—you can bet your bottom dollar on that."

Miss Julie sighed and fell into step.

Firecrackers were banging everywhere now, and some boys passed by on new bicycles, and Joe shouted to them, and was reproved mildly for this breach of decorum. In the O'Donnells' back yard Stevens was firing off three-inch salutes in an empty barrel, producing a series of deep hollow booms that delighted George, who stood at a safe distance with Sarah and jumped up and down with excitement.

The children were permitted one look at the Christmas tree and at the pile of presents, and then they were herded in to breakfast and compelled to eat a minimum. Miss Julie and Henry, undisturbed by the anxiety that was upsetting the young, ate a solid meal of fruit and *bouillie salade* and hominy, topped off with waffles. Annette, a small eater, soon finished. Joe and Betsy and the little ones ate scarcely anything. And when the meal was over there was such a crashing and banging as had not been heard since the preceding Christmas.

Miss Julie, always a little apprehensive about fireworks, muttered darkly about lockjaw, giving a few histories to add to the cheer of the occasion; but she went out and watched Joe and Betsy and James shoot off their firecrackers and torpedoes and capsticks and spitfires, because she felt that everyone should share in the children's pleasures. She exclaimed with delight over the express wagon and the hook-and-ladder truck, laughed at the monkey on a string and the clown in the little cart that backed up so suddenly, and gave her own poor presents with chuckles. Tessie's gifts were more elegant, but Miss Julie thought the children really liked hers better.

It was a wild morning, and Miss Julie was tired—and hungry —by the time the dinner guests began to arrive. Christmas dinner was always a big event at the O'Donnells'. Tessie came in good season, and then old Colonel Beauchamp, and Mr. Bennet, the lawyer, and Captain Davis, who had only one arm (about which George inquired); Henry's Aunt Mary, a stiff elderly lady, and old Mr. White who claimed to be a hundred years old, and who had been almost too old to fight in the Civil War, and Henry Lemay and his sister Zoe, Miss Julie's second cousins. It was quite a gathering, and there was someone for each one to talk to.

Henry was in his glory as master of ceremonies for this big party. He carved with his best flourishes, told jokes one after another, pressed everyone to eat heartily of the turkey and ham, and in general dispensed old-fashioned hospitality with a lavish hand.

James and George, almost too weary and excited to eat, were at a separate small table, where they kept as quiet as could be expected, although Sarah had to restrain George from throwing raisins at his brother. The talk welled up into a small roar as the wine went around, and everyone ate tremendously right down to the mince pie. After all the labor she had expended on it, Miss Julie's cake wasn't even cut. But she was accustomed to that; nearly every Christmas the cake had to wait until suppertime.

Finally, the ladies went out to the sitting room, and Henry and the gentlemen lighted cigars and talked business and politics before joining them; Betsy and Joe went to visit friends, and Miss Tessie went home. Sarah took the little boys out for a walk, and after the last guest had been sped there was a blessed interval of quiet.

Miss Julie felt a bit heavy. She had eaten liberally of all the meats and vegetables and trimmings, with special attention to the turkey stuffing, and had put away a large wedge of mince pie in addition. She took a brief nap before suppertime, and awoke ready to begin all over again. At supper, however, she contented herself with some sliced turkey and ham, a few biscuits, a large chunk of cake (just to see if it was good), and the remnants of the olives and celery. She felt a bit uneasy, but not to the point of distress, and went out wrapped in her shawl to see "Henry's fireworks."

It was now Henry's Christmas. The others waited in the back yard, where Stevens had put chairs for Annette and Miss Julie; Stevens had dragged out the packing case full of fireworks, and with many exclamations of admiration nailed up the pin wheels and other displays. Then he lighted a Greek torch for Henry, which colored everything a deep red, and Henry, after a preliminary warning to everybody to watch out for sparks, set to work.

First there were a few skyrockets; then came paper balloons, particularly a large one made in the shape of a fish, and Roman candles, which the children were allowed to handle, with the result that George got a spark in his ear and had to be comforted before the proceedings resumed. Then there were aerial bombs, and more skyrockets, and finally several fountains and two enormous and brilliantly colored pinwheels; and Stevens added his bit by setting off a half-dozen cannon crackers, to which Henry at first objected, consenting only when Stevens agreed to take them to the rear end of the back yard.

Miss Julie, who was very uncomfortable now, observed that the crackers were not as loud as they used to be—a comment she made every Christmas; and Henry put the last official touch to the day by making his annual remark, "That's a fine way to burn up money," as Stevens carted away the combustibles reserved for New Year's Eve. But Henry had enjoyed it.

Miss Julie, when she was getting ready to go, confessed, "Something seems to have disagreed with me," and Joe was told off to go home with her.

"I'll tell you what disagreed with her," Henry said. "It was just half of the dinner she ate."

"Ma loves her stomach," Annette said, and gave no more thought to it.

Miss Julie, plodding homeward with Joe, asked him what he had done that day, and if he had remembered to offer up his communion that morning for a good intention. Joe replied evasively; and then she began to feel so utterly miserable that she stopped trying to make conversation.

At the first sight of Miss Julie's face, Miss Tessie was triumphant.

"I knew it," she said. "You don't need to tell me you feel sick. I watched what you ate at dinner, and it was enough for three people. I knew you were going to bring this on yourself."

"Oh, be quiet, Tessie," Miss Julie said miserably. "You go home, now, Joe, and tell your ma not to worry. I think I just have a little indigestion."

Miss Tessie prepared some camomile tea and saw her sister to bed, where she pitched and tossed awhile, very wretched indeed. About midnight she went off to sleep, but early in the morning she was seized with violent cramps.

"No wonder," Miss Tessie said, refusing to comfort her. "What that stomach of yours has stood all these years! I'll get you a good dose of salts."

"Never mind 'bout medicine," Miss Julie groaned. "It's too late for that sort of thing now. I want you to send for Father Mellon and ask him to come and give me extreme unction."

"Priest! Extreme unction! Hoo! What you need a priest for is to confess the sin of gluttony to him, that's what."

"Very well," Miss Julie said with pained dignity. "If I die without making my confession, it'll be on your conscience."

She recalled with terror that Tessie had once refused to summon the doctor for her own son Julien, and that it was too late when she finally consented to do so.

"Tessie, you'd better send for Father Mellon," she pleaded.

"I'll do nothing of the sort."

"Please, for God's sake, Tessie! And for Mr. Bennet. I want to make my will."

"Ipecac is what you need," Miss Tessie said firmly, and proceeded to supply it.

"I want to leave my money to Charlie and Francis," Miss Julie went on, as soon as she could speak again, hoping that mere insistence would cause her sister to relent. "There'll be a little bit for you, too, Tessie."

"I don't want your money."

"And the daguerreotype is to be yours, of course."

"Hoo! You don't say! To be mine, indeed!"

"I want Annette to have me earrings and me wedding ring. The watch, I think I'll give to little Joe. He'll soon be big enough to trust with it. . . . Betsy will have the little pearl pin and the gold clutch pencil. It don't work any more, but it's pretty."

"If you're finished talking all that foolishness, I'll go back to bed," Miss Tessie said callously.

Miss Julie groaned. "You think it's all a joke," she said. "All right, go to sleep, and in the morning when you find me lying cold and stiff you'll regret it."

"I'll take the responsibility," Miss Tessie said. "Call me if you need me and I'm asleep."

Miss Julie was terribly sorry for herself, and moaned for a while about being allowed by her own sister to die like a dog. But the combined effects of the camomile tea and the ipecac and salts gave her relief, and she dozed a little. When she awoke, she insisted that a message be sent to Annette, and Miss Tessie enlisted a small colored boy from the house across the street for the errand.

The O'Donnells were having breakfast in the gray atmosphere that always characterizes the day after Christmas when Sarah brought the little Negro into the dining room. The child was frightened in the strange white folks' house. His eyes were like little butter plates, and he stood there with his mouth open, too awed to speak.

"Go 'head, tell the lady and gentleman what you gots to say," Sarah prodded him.

"Mis' Fisher say 'e sistuh sick and wants you to come fuh see 'em," the boy said.

Annette thought instantly of Tante Leonie, who had died of acute indigestion after eating cheese late at night. "My God!" she exclaimed, and leapt up.

"Wait a minute," Henry said. "Let's find out what's the matter before we get excited." He put his hand into his pocket and took out a dime. "Here, boy," he said. "What else did Mrs. Fisher tell you?"

"Da's all, suh. 'E say 'e sistuh want ev'ybody fuh come fuh see 'em." He looked at the dime and blinked. As if he wanted to give a full measure of news in order to earn it, he added: "She dyin'."

[139]

"Good God Almighty!" Henry roared. He leapt up, too. "Sarah, take this boy out to the kitchen and give him some breakfast. Joe, get a package of firecrackers for him, too." He ran out to get his hat and overcoat.

Leaving James and George as too young for the harrowing experience of being present at a deathbed, Annette and Henry took Betsy and Joe along with them and fairly flew to the house on Queen Street.

Miss Tessie, still in her wrapper, received them and led them in to see Miss Julie, who was very white and weak. Annette ran over and clutched her mother's hand and begged her to speak to her, and Miss Julie groaned a heart-rending groan.

"Don't be frightened, Annette," Miss Tessie said coolly. "She thinks she's worse than she is. It's just plain gluttony."

Miss Julie groaned even more piteously.

"But that boy said she was dying," Henry said, finally understanding what Miss Tessie meant.

"Dying!" Miss Tessie sneered. "I told that fool little nigger boy to say that she *thought* she was dying, but that she wasn't doing anything of the kind. I told him particularly to say that she wanted to see you and I thought you'd better come, but that she wasn't in any danger. Though it's God's mercy she isn't."

"Well, of course they never get messages straight," Henry said.

He went over to Miss Julie, patted her hand, and said she must cheer up. Under his breath he cursed fluently. He muttered that his breakfast had been ruined, and all for the foolishness of a couple of God-damned old women, and that it beat all hell what a lot of mischief a couple of old fools could get into when they didn't have somebody to watch over everything they did. Miss Tessie did not retort. She saw him out without a word and went back to the sickbed.

Miss Julie was still very sorry for herself, and was talking in her deathbed vein and sending messages and bestowing forgiveness right and left.

"Now, sister, stop that," Miss Tessie said. "You're getting yourself excited over nothing. All you need is a good sleep, and you'll be just as well as you've ever been. . . . But her diet will need watching after this," she said to Annette.

"Never mind talking about diet," Miss Julie pleaded. "I'll probably never eat again. You're very callous about my last illness."

"Oh, don't talk that way, Ma," Annette said. "You've just had a little indigestion."

Miss Julie, irritated by their making light of her condition, turned away wrathfully, and Annette, after a few words to Miss Tessie, said goodbye and took the children away.

"Now, you get yourself some sleep," Miss Tessie ordered, "and later on I'll give you a good purging."

"Let me die," Miss Julie groaned. "You're trying to kill me! Then let me die in peace, at least."

"Stop that roaring," Miss Tessie commanded. "Do you want to have the police in here?"

By afternoon, when Annette came to see how she was, Miss Julie was much better. She was able to laugh a little at herself and at the fright she had given Annette and Henry.

" 'Better belly bust than good victuals spoil,' " she quoted.

After Annette was gone, she pleaded for something to eat.

"You can have some weak tea and toast bread," Miss Tessie said.

"One soft-boiled egg," Miss Julie begged. "How will I ever get me strength back?"

Miss Tessie was adamant, and Miss Julie had to content herself with the thin toast and weak tea. As she swallowed them she thought of all the delicacies she would enjoy later—blood pudding and herring and hominy, fried whiting, crab stew, root beer, bananas, cowpeas, hopping-john, tomato pilau . . .

"I'll put a stop to this diet business," she determined.

CHAPTER EIGHT

WITH THAT ATTACK OF ILLNESS, Miss Julie had signed away her freedom.

Her sister ruled out the things she liked best to eat, with a convincing earnestness that frightened her and kept her from bursting out and declaring her independence; and meals at the house in Queen Street became a perpetual Lent. Even at the O'Donnells' table Miss Julie tried to obey the rules laid down for her.

She complained bitterly of Tessie's tyranny.

"It was your own doing," Annette said. "You weren't satisfied until you had your flat with Aunt Tessie, and now you've either got to like it or come back here."

Miss Julie set her jaw and said she had no intention of doing anything of the kind. But she did speculate upon taking a room for herself. That came to nothing, for she had now come to the point of being proud of her success in "getting along" with Tessie, which everyone had said would be impossible.

She had finally admitted to herself that she was not happy, but she was determined to stick it out. As it was, when the winter days brought more sickness and Miss Tessie was busy nursing, Miss Julie spent most of her time at Annette's. She slept in Queen Street, and had breakfast there; but, except when she went shopping or visiting or to church or sodality, she was to be found at the O'Donnells' big house. Sarah regularly set a place for her, and if she wanted a nap during the early part of the afternoon she lay down in Joe's room or Betsy's. In fact, she lived there except for sleeping; that reservation was sufficient for her pride's sake.

Miss Tessie nagged her and nagged her about what she could and couldn't eat; yet, as her fright about the Christmas attack wore off, Miss Julie began to think of returning to her old ways. But by that time it was almost Lent.

A week before Ash Wednesday, Miss Julie, having prepared an elaborate list of abstentions and religious activities, discussed them with Miss Tessie:

"Of course I'm not expected to fast. I'm old enough to be excused from that. But I'm going to abstain from meat except on Sundays, and I'm going to give up sweets, and eating between meals, and I'm going to Mass every day, and stations every Friday."

"Hoo! Why don't you plan one thing and stick to it, instead of making a lot of resolutions you know you're not going to keep, like all the ones you made at New Year's?"

"I intend to keep all of these," Miss Julie said, stiffly.

"Well, you never have. I never saw anyone as able to fool herself as you, Julie."

"Is that so? That's fine, coming from you, I must say! You've lived on self-deception."

"I refuse to discuss it," Miss Tessie said.

"What are *you* going to do for Lent?" Miss Julie challenged her.

"All the things a good Catholic should do. I'm going to give up dessert, and meat except on Sunday, and I'm going to Mass every morning and to stations on Friday. I never eat between meals, so I haven't got to worry about that. And on Friday I intend to eat just bread and tea."

"I'll do all that too," Miss Julie declared, relieved that Tessie had not thought up anything radically different from her own plans.

Miss Tessie sniffed, and said they would see.

Miss Julie began well, after devoting Shrove Tuesday to preparatory fortification. On that day she ate the remaining candies in her closet, had some parched peanuts when she went over to Annette's, and put away a fine dinner with an extra helping of dessert. "It will help to remove temptation," she explained.

She foresaw that having dinner regularly at the O'Donnells'

was going to be a source of difficulty. They were going to observe the Wednesday and Friday abstinence from meat; but after all, Annette said, Henry was a working man and needed meat at dinner, and the children were growing, and three of them at school, and they needed meat too. Miss Julie resolved that she could content herself with the other dishes and do without the meat. If the dishes happened to be cooked with meat, well, that was only flavor, and while she wouldn't think of eating such a dish on Friday. . . .

"Lent is very easy now," she remarked, to give herself courage. "When we were younger, we didn't even have milk or eggs or cheese on Friday. And every grown-up had to fast and abstain strictly. These are easy days."

After she had received ashes on Ash Wednesday, Miss Julie went over to Annette's and sewed and darned. Toward eleven o'clock she felt terribly hungry, but thrust aside the temptation and managed to survive until dinnertime. At that meal she contented herself with a single helping, bravely refused dessert, and drank her coffee without sugar. She felt positively empty afterwards, and looked with dread on the seven weeks that lay ahead.

She kept to her intention to hear Mass every day, and went with Tessie. She attended stations on Friday night and heard an excellent sermon, which partially consoled her for having gone all day on bread and tea. But she was snappish, and felt that she couldn't wait until Sunday came around and she had a square meal. By Saturday evening all she could think of was food, when she should have had her mind on communion.

Miss Tessie was in one of her most fussy and domineering moods that night. She insisted on helping her sister to food so that she wouldn't overeat, and then complained of the way she did the dishes.

"I'm doing them the way I like," Miss Julie said. "Now don't aggravate me, Tessie, and spoil my chances of going to communion in the morning. Just leave me alone."

"I'm not to blame if you lose your temper. I'm just pointing out that you're not getting these dishes clean."

"I've never poisoned anybody yet." Miss Julie fell back on a stock witticism which she knew her sister hated.

"I suppose you'll gorge yourself tomorrow," Miss Tessie said, changing the subject.

"I expect to eat substantially. I need it. I've always been used to good food," Miss Julie replied with malice.

"You've got a bad tongue, that's what's the matter with you."

Content with success in this skirmish, Miss Julie began to sing a hymn. This assumption of triumph was too much for her sister.

"I suppose you mean that my family was never used to anything. Well, that's a lie, and you know it, Julie. When your husband was obliged to send his boys to work so that you could all have something to eat, my Willie—"

"Yes, your Willie was a big man in Charleston. He owned three or four banks." Miss Julie laughed a scornful and irritating laugh; she remembered the story of Willie Fisher working as a bookkeeper and getting his accounts so muddled that they had to call in someone to help him straighten them up every year's end. She mentioned this recollection in considerable detail.

"I won't have you talk that way about my sainted husband because his sight was poor." Miss Tessie became very pink.

"Well, I won't have you disparaging Pa," said Miss Julie, joining battle. "Pa was impractical—everybody knew that; but he did his best."

"He was a fool. A pluperfect ass."

"'He that calleth his brother a fool,'" Miss Julie quoted. "I suppose your conscience is perfectly clear about going to communion tomorrow, with all the speaking ill of the dead you've done tonight."

"You provoked me to it," Miss Tessie said. "It's you that ought to worry about your conscience."

"I provoked you?" Miss Julie asked dramatically. "Well, you certainly are crazier than people say you are, Tessie."

"No doubt you go around to your fine daughter's house talking about me and listening to all sorts of scandal and gossip," Miss Tessie shouted. "I want to tell you right here and now that

I don't give a sou marquee for what people like that say about me. I despise them."

"You despise everybody, because you're jealous of them."

"I'm not going to argue with you," said Miss Tessie. "You're deliberately trying to make it impossible for me to receive communion tomorrow, but I won't let you succeed."

"Argue? You can't argue with me," Miss Julie replied. "In the first place, I win all the arguments, and the minute you see you're losing you make some excuse for not going on."

"I'll pray for you," Miss Tessie said, going out of the room.

Miss Julie's fighting blood was aroused, but she conquered it. She stayed in the kitchen and finished the dish drying. Then she said to herself that to forgive was divine, and sat down by the grate in the sitting room to say her rosary.

Next morning Miss Tessie sought Father Schmidt before Mass and made a new confession—a thing she had often done before because of an affliction known as the scruples. But she did not seem to hold it against Miss Julie, and they sat through Mass and breakfast quite peaceably. Miss Julie went alone to eleven o'clock Mass and then to Annette's, where she ate a dinner that virtually made up for what she had missed during the week.

"After all, I'm an old woman and I've got to keep up me strength," she reasoned.

Miss Tessie had two brief turns of nursing during Lent, and Miss Julie was free of her society at least that much. She suddenly found that Tessie's little ways were annoying her all the time: such things as wrapping all her various small belongings in new tissue paper every week, going over Miss Julie's cleaning, and fussing about the way she washed the dishes. But they avoided another real quarrel until Holy Week.

On the day before Holy Thursday Miss Julie felt so energetic that she started to clean up the house right after breakfast, so that when Tessie returned at noontime from her current case she would have no ground for complaint about the appearance of the rooms. She was in the midst of this task when Miss Georgie Peters came in. Miss Julie left things more or less as they were, and she and Miss Georgie (who was also rather deaf) sat and shouted at each other for an hour and a half.

After her visitor had gone Miss Julie, hastening to set things right, committed a bad blunder.

Miss Tessie came in, and Miss Julie was expecting to hear a little praise of the way the house looked although she should have known better. Her sister took one look, and saw the portrait of Theodora facing the wall. She walked over and pointed to it.

"What is the meaning of this desecration?" she shouted.

Miss Julie did not catch the word but saw what Miss Tessie meant. "Oh, that," she said calmly. "I was just straightening things up, and Miss Georgie Peters came in for a little while, and I didn't notice that." She went over and moved the easel back into position, setting it down with a bang.

"I forbid you to sling the picture of my daughter around like that!" Miss Tessie screamed.

"Why, Tessie, there's no need to make such a fuss about it."

"I will make a fuss about it! I won't have the sacred picture of my sainted daughter flung around like a piece of paper! It's a holy relic to me!"

"Why, that's sinful, Tessie. It's idolatry, pure idolatry!"

Miss Tessie dropped her hat to the floor. "Who are you to judge?" she shrieked. "My daughter is a saint, and you have no right to touch her picture! You ought to be satisfied with the privilege of looking at it!"

"Tessie, you're beside yourself. The idea of your having the presumption to say that Theodora is a saint! I never saw anything saintly about her, I must say."

Miss Tessie shook her fist. "You'd better confess that blasphemy," she shouted. "God will punish you for it."

Miss Julie burst into tears. She was sure Tessie would have to be put away, and the thought of that disgrace was more than she could bear. Miss Tessie, taking the tears for repentance, became gentler.

"You may think it's presumption," she explained, "because I don't tell all my business to everybody. . . . But, if you want to know, I had a vision once, and I saw Theodora wearing a crown and dressed in long robes, and I knew that she had become a saint."

"It was probably a dream," said Miss Julie, not so tearful that she could not be tactless.

Miss Tessie smiled the enigmatic smile of one who knows a secret. "I know better," she said, gazing fixedly at Miss Julie. "I could tell you lots of remarkable things."

Miss Julie shrank.

"Another time, Tessie," she said placatingly. "I have to get dressed to go out now."

Miss Tessie nodded. "By the way, sister, I think we ought to take some sulphur and molasses," she said. "It's just the season when the blood gets sluggish. Remind me to buy some. I don't like to take it in Lent, because of the molasses."

"I don't think sulphur and molasses is any treat," said Miss Julie, pleased to see Miss Tessie restored to normal.

"Still, it's sweet."

Miss Julie went in to dress. "Really, I'm sure she's crazy," she said to herself. "I wonder if it's safe to live with her. She might do something to me in one of those fits of temper."

On the way to Annette's, she turned over and over in her mind the advisability of telling about Tessie's peculiar behavior that morning—"just like Dr. Jekyll and Mr. Hyde," she said to herself. But she was afraid to do it. If it turned out that Miss Tessie was not crazy, people would say that she, Julie, was the crazy one; crazy people always had the idea that all the rest of the world was mad.

She was glad she had said nothing about it. Miss Tessie was quite normal and ordinary the rest of that week. The sisters went together to the churches on Holy Thursday, went to Tenebrae, shared their bread and tea on Friday. They went to confession together on Saturday, bought some sweets for the children's Easter baskets, and attended two Masses on Sunday. They even took their sulphur and molasses in concert.

"Everyone has these little tiffs," Miss Julie concluded, trying to convince herself that everything would be all right.

CHAPTER NINE

Soon it began to be really warm. The tourists came with the bloom of the magnolias and azaleas, bringing a faint stir of activity in the city, and when they departed the fleet came in to upset the calm for a short while. May approached, and James made his first communion, to the immense gratification of Miss Julie, who gave him a mother-of-pearl rosary and a prayer book bound in white celluloid; and then school ended and it was time for the family to go away to the mountains again, and she was left alone with Miss Tessie.

The worst of that was that it meant hunger, for she was no longer able to go to Annette's for meals and Miss Tessie kept her on a tight rein.

"It's worse than Lent," she grumbled. But she had come so under the spell of Miss Tessie's warnings that it was with a feeling of guilt that she sneaked out to the Negro cook shop where fried fish were sold cheap.

But she had lived exactly a year with Tessie, and she considered that as a feather in her cap.

"If she only gets enough nursing to keep her away from here for part of the time," Miss Julie said to herself, "I think I can stand it. She's been much more sensible lately."

Just that morning, Miss Tessie had gone to nurse someone on Legare Street, making the usual fuss about taking her uniforms and her "infallible" thermometer and her coffeepot, and warning Miss Julie at least a dozen times about turning off the gas, closing the windows, shutting off the faucet, and otherwise indulging her *folie de doute*. Miss Julie, having nowhere to go, sat quilting, and rejoicing in her temporary freedom.

She took a nap in the afternoon, ate just the things she liked for supper, and after writing to Annette went to bed early.

Next morning she was finishing a leisurely breakfast and reading half aloud a letter from Emma, when the door burst open and Miss Tessie entered, very red with haste, heat, and temper.

"What's the matter, Tessie? You sick?"

Her face must have expressed her dismay, for Miss Tessie glowered at her.

"I've no doubt you're sorry to see me back so soon," she said angrily. "But here I am. I've had all I can bear."

"What happened?"

"I've nursed some of the best people in Charleston, these many years." Tears came into Miss Tessie's eyes. "But never yet have I been treated the way I was this time."

"It's a shame," Miss Julie sympathized.

"The idea! The idea of giving a gentlewoman her supper alone, like a servant! And not even silver to eat with, but some sort of cheap knives and forks that they must have got with soap coupons."

"Why, that's an outrage, Tessie," Miss Julie said. "Well, sister, you see how it is. People want colored nurses nowadays, because they don't require to be treated except as servants."

She meant to be tactful and comforting, but her words had the opposite effect.

"Well!" said Miss Tessie in a sepulchral tone. "Well!" she repeated, as if unable to believe what she had heard. "My own sister tells me that I belong to a servant class! Indeed!"

"Why, Tessie, I never said anything of the sort."

"You did!" Miss Tessie shouted. "You did! How can you sit there in the presence of your God and tell a lie like that? Very well, then. I'm a servant—"

"I never said anything of the sort," Miss Julie repeated. "You're overtaxed and excited, and you're imagining all sorts of things. I said people wanted colored nurses nowadays because—"

Miss Tessie laughed shrilly.

"Never mind what you said! You've managed to be insulting and that's all you want! I come home insulted by outsiders, and looking for a little understanding, and what do I get but more insults! My own sister tells me that I'm no better than a nigger! That's all I ought to expect from such a person."

"You're forgetting yourself." Miss Julie drew herself up with great dignity. "It wouldn't do you a bit of harm to think once in a while before you began to abuse people."

"I'll never forgive this as long as I live!" Miss Tessie was now quite beside herself, striding up and down. "It's all very well for you, that haven't any pride and are willing to be kept by Henry O'Donnell out of charity, to talk about other people being servants, but I'm not the one to stand for it. I've always had my self-respect, and I never went crawling to any of my relatives to ask them to support me."

This was going to be the end, Miss Julie said to herself. She took a deep breath and stood up, going behind her chair and putting both hands on the back of it for support.

"No, of course you didn't," she said. "You preferred to make a martyr of yourself, and to go around insulting everybody that tried to do anything for you, to show what a wonderful brave woman you were and how independent you could be. That's your way of being happy and independent."

"At least I've never been under obligations to anyone. I've stood on my own feet."

"Oh, no, you were independent." Miss Julie's voice was rich with scorn. "All you did was to go and look pathetic to every doctor in town and tell him that you were poor and had to have nursing to do, and get his help that way. Do you think people don't talk, and that everybody don't know these things? Nurse! All you do is give the patients medicine and wash their faces, and then when there's any work to be done you call for the housemaids. And God knows how many patients you've hurried to their graves with your evil disposition."

Miss Tessie was purple.

[151]

"How dare you tell me I'm not a good nurse?" she shrieked. "Don't you dare try to smirch my professional reputation! I'll have you taken to jail! What do you know about it, indeed? You don't even know how to take care of yourself."

"At least I didn't pretend that I knew better than the doctors, and let my children waste away because I was so proud of my own knowledge," Miss Julie said cruelly. "At least I haven't got that on my conscience."

Miss Tessie clenched both fists. "Get out of my house!" she yelled. "Never speak to me again!"

"I'll do just that," Miss Julie said promptly. A great weight seemed to fall off her shoulders. "I'll get out, and quickly, and you needn't worry about my ever speaking to you again or even giving you a thought. I'll know better. Where you belong is in the crazy house, and the sooner the better!"

With trembling hands she begin to pick up the little things around the house that belonged to her.

"I suppose you'll steal that daguerreotype again," Miss Tessie shouted.

"You bet your sweet life I will," Miss Julie retorted, grabbing the daguerreotype from the mantel. "It was left to me, and you'll never see it again to your dying day."

She went into the bedroom and placed the daguerreotype in her pocketbook. She threw a number of her possessions into her valise, dressed hastily, and without saying a word to Miss Tessie, who sat white and brooding in a corner of the sitting room, she took the pen and ink and wrote on a piece of paper:

"I'll come tomorrow to see about taking my things."

Without a backward look, she left the house.

When she reached the street, she felt a bit shaky, and had to get a colored boy to carry her bag.

"I'll give you a nickel to take this for me to Ashley Avenue," she said to him.

"Sho, muh. I take 'em," the boy said, eagerly. He seized the valise and shuffled alongside.

Miss Julie wondered if she ought to leave her sister alone. She took out her handkerchief and mopped her forehead. "She's raving crazy, that's what she is!" But she did not go back. She kept on walking, faster than usual, becoming more and more short of breath. "I'll leave me things with Sarah," she said to herself, "and spend the night there if I have to, and then arrange about moving to that room I saw for rent in Franklin Street."

For after what had happened, and after Tessie's taunts, she couldn't possibly think of going to Henry's to live; at least, she couldn't ask Henry. Of course, if Henry really urged it upon her . . . In her heart, the poor old soul hoped that he would.

She paid the boy his nickel and rang the bell.

Sarah answered. "Good mornin', Mis' Sharp," she said, as though the arrival of Miss Julie with her valise were the most ordinary thing in the world.

"I've just come to put up here for the night, Sarah. I suppose you'll have enough dinner for both Mr. Henry and me."

"You come in, ma'am," Sarah said. "The boss away on a trip, but we got somethin' in the kitchen."

"Don't go to any trouble."

"Me and Stevens don't stint none when the boss away," Sarah said. "We got some chicken and some rice, and we'll git you some figs and coffee, and I got some sweet muffins."

Miss Julie's mouth watered at this list.

"Thank you, Sarah. And I'll sleep in the boys' room. It'll be less trouble for you to make up."

Sarah took the valise and accompanied Miss Julie upstairs to see if she wanted anything. She promised to come up later to get the bed made.

"Since Henry isn't here, I won't bother looking for a place until tomorrow morning," Miss Julie soliloquized. "If he was here, I'd have to tell him that I already have a place. But now I can put it off." She removed her hat and veil and coat and sat out on the piazza, remaining there over an hour.

"Miss Julie hyuh. Ol' ladies must 'a' bus' up," Sarah said to Stevens, who came to sit in the kitchen and watch her work.

"Uh, uh," Stevens said. "Ain't it."

"I never think they kin live together a whole year," Sarah said, laughing softly. "Miss Julie must 'a' broke Mis' Fisher coffee-pot."

"Maybe 'e turn dat picture de wrong way again."

Sarah chuckled. "My Lawd," she sniggered. "Anything could make dem two fight. Once 'e ain't speak for years because Miss Julie say Mr. Fisher was so shortsighted the Yankee take the flag right out of 'e hand."

"I wonder is Mis' Sharp goin' ta live here regular?" Stevens murmured.

"'E say 'e goin' ta stay overnight," Sarah replied. "But 'e might as well stay all de time. 'E come every day God send when Miss Annette hyuh, don't 'e? But dat don' count. 'E can't live hyuh unless the Cap'n ask 'em, because 'e too stiff, and can't admit 'e made a mistake."

Stevens shook his head. These points of honor were too much for him.

"Buckra is funny," he declared.

"Ain't it," Sarah said. "Well, now, ol' man, you better be gittin' nex' do'. Don't fuhgit you gots them jobs to do for ol' Miss Becky."

"I ain' fuhgit 'bout 'em."

"Well, git along, den. You ain' goin' ta git 'em done settin' hyuh in the kitchen. And I gots to see about gittin' some dinner for Mis' Sharp."

Sarah was picking rice for dinner when Miss Julie, weary of being alone, came into the kitchen, after stopping to greet the parrot and the old cat. She was somewhat red about the eyes, and Sarah knew that she had been crying.

"I wonder if there's a little coffee on the back of the stove," Miss Julie said, reaching for the coffeepot as she said it.

"They's a little," Sarah said.

"I'll just put a little water on the grounds and heat it up a little," Miss Julie said. "I feel as if I ought to have a sip of coffee."

Sarah fetched a cup and saucer and some sugar and condensed

milk, and Miss Julie poured water on the grounds and sloshed the pot around in silence. It was not until she had poured the coffee that she saw fit to make an explanation of her presence.

"My sister and I have decided to part company, Sarah," she said.

Sarah, who knew that Miss Julie didn't particularly like her, was very guarded in her reply.

"Tha's too bad, muh."

"It was a trifle that we quarreled about. I won't even mention it, it was so silly." Miss Julie could not tell Sarah the exact cause of the quarrel: it would hurt her feelings. "However, it was just the result of a lot of little disagreements. . . . I can't stay there with her any longer, and I'm going to find a room somewhere in the neighborhood as soon as I can get out tomorrow to look for it." She took a sip of the coffee and put down the cup. "I'm afraid I made a great mistake," she admitted.

Sarah clucked in sympathy.

"I'm an old woman," Miss Julie said, "and you're a fairly young one. Let me tell you that pride is one of the worst things in the world. It makes more trouble than anything else I know— and it's been the curse of my family and a lot of other families I know. Everyone would be better off without it."

"It sho goes befo' a fall," Sarah said.

"There's many a family in this city," Miss Julie went on, "that could have been happy and contented if someone hadn't got mad about some nonsense or other and broken the family up—and many a one that could have been happy if they'd admitted that one or another of them was ready to be put away somewhere, like these old ladies next door and their crazy sister that ought to be in the asylum instead of being locked in that room upstairs."

Sarah grinned. She had had many an entertaining talk about the mad old lady next door with the cook of the family, and she could have told Miss Julie some remarkable facts; but she kept them to herself.

" 'E sho is mighty peculiar," she said.

Miss Julie put down her coffee cup and rose. "Thank you,

Sarah. That did me a lot of good. I've been feeling a bit upset."

She pottered around the garden for a while, and then sat on a bench and gave way to her worries. For it was going to be difficult, living by herself; difficult, and expensive, even though she would be free of the burden of Tessie's extravagance. And there wasn't so much of her money left, after all. It wouldn't last very long, and even if it held out until she died, she liked to think that there would be enough to bury her.

That was only one side of her concern. The other was a matter of embarrassment. Everyone would say once more that the Gerards were quarrelsome, and that she and Tessie had only done what was to be expected. She could see heads nodding all over Charleston, and she was going to hate facing friends and admitting that her attempt to get along with her sister had been a dismal failure.

For the rest, she was worried about Miss Tessie. Maybe it was her duty to stay with Tessie and see that she didn't come to any harm. . . . Perhaps even this minute she was in need of attention. Miss Julie considered returning that afternoon and trying to smooth things over. But that would mean a possible rebuff, and she wouldn't care to answer for her own actions if Tessie became insulting again.

She fancied, with particular irritation, that Henry would be triumphant. She could hear him saying to Annette that he had known it all along but there was nothing he could do about it, and that if people would take a little thought once in a while they could keep out of a lot of trouble. She thought of the thoroughly bad advice he had given her about that automobile investment, and longed for the privilege of casting that in his teeth.

Sarah fed her a good early dinner, and that cheered her, although she felt strange and lost, sitting alone in the great room while she ate it. Despite the morning's disagreeable event, she ate double helpings.

"I've got to keep up me strength," she told herself, as usual.

After dinner there was a nap, and then Miss Julie went for a stroll all the way to the Battery. She met an old friend or two and had a little gossip. She did not tell them that she had parted from Miss Tessie.

That night she sat on the piazza looking out at the lights, and hearing faintly the laughter and songs of the boaters on the lake, and watching the infrequent streetcars over on Rutledge Avenue, that looked like the toy cars the children made out of dry-goods boxes, with tissue-paper windows and stubs of candles inside for light. . . . It was already late for her when she undressed in the boys' room. She glanced at the pathetic playthings they had left—a shabby drum that belonged to George, and his fireman's hat, and James's cardboard soldiers and popgun. She wished she had the little rascals here right now.

She turned out the light. Electric light was a great convenience. It was all very well to sneer at modern luxuries, but some of them were good.

At first, after she had crawled under the mosquito canopy, she could not get to sleep; but then she slept right through until morning and woke up cheerful and ambitious after the shock of finding herself in a strange room.

"All for Thee, Sweet Jesus, All for Thee," she croaked.

She was determined to go and see Tessie that morning and make up again. After all, blood was thicker than water.

"I mustn't be foolish," she murmured. "I'll be a Christian and make up with her."

But she did nothing of the kind. She ate breakfast, read the single obituary that was in the paper, dressed in her best things, and went over to Franklin Street to engage the room in the house where she had seen the sign.

It was a rather poor room, but it was extremely cheap, the family was a respectable if shabby one, and there was a gas burner, so that she would not have to use the kitchen for preparing her meals. Miss Julie would not have dreamed of boarding. That was too expensive, and besides, she was sure she wouldn't be able to eat the food. She had been used to plenty and variety, and she could not bear to think of okra and tomato soup three times a week, gummy rice, poor meat, weak coffee, and all the other horrors of a poor family's diet.

She arranged to move in immediately. She hired the colored expressman with the tumble-down wagon who had moved her things before, and met him at the door of the house on Queen Street.

"Go upstairs," Miss Julie said to him, "to the second floor, and tell Mrs. Fisher that her sister is here to take her things."

The expressman returned with a puzzled look on his shiny black face and reported that the coast was clear.

Miss Julie led him and his assistant up to the flat and directed the dismantling and packing of her things. All the while Miss Tessie sat on the piazza, and neither sister made any attempt to speak.

Miss Julie left one cracked dish and a worn saucepan. All the other things were standing in the street ready to be piled into the wagon, and Miss Julie was about to leave the scene, when the plate and the worn saucepan came clattering down to the pavement.

Miss Julie's mortification was extreme; she felt that all Queen Street was observing the incident, and with a hasty word or two to the drayman she fled.

She spent the rest of the morning tidying up—everything was in confusion, and the space was scarcely enough for her furniture—and then had dinner at Henry O'Donnell's. Before she left, she pressed a quarter into Sarah's hand, for she felt that the service and kindness she had received were worth it.

After she had gone, Sarah flung the coin into the yard. She had her pride too.

CHAPTER TEN

WHEN HENRY O'DONNELL LEARNED FROM SARAH that Miss Julie had moved to the room in Franklin Street, he had one of his fits of fuming, and, without Annette to calm him down, the fit lasted until Sarah began to be worried.

He wrote angrily to Annette, complaining that no one had any regard for his feelings, and that here was her mother gone off to a rooming house, and giving people the opportunity to say that he was too mean to take care of her. He added that Miss Julie could easily come and ask him to take her back again, if it were not for her foolish pride.

Annette wrote that perhaps he could put his own pride in his pocket, and go and ask Miss Julie to return. After all, she was an old woman and deserved consideration. To which Henry replied that he would be damned if he'd do any such thing: Miss Julie had left his home of her own accord, and she could not return to it until she asked her way back.

Miss Julie, interrogated by letter about the breakup, wrote furious complaints to Annette, saying that Tessie ought to be put into an institution, that it was not safe to trust her around sane people, and that trouble would surely come of allowing her to roam at large; and she added that if they hadn't been so anxious to get her out of their house she wouldn't have had to go and live with Tessie.

Annette replied, after her anger had cooled down, that she herself had asked her mother not to make the move, over a year ago; that she had constantly urged her to return to their home, and that she was urging her now. She said that Henry had been hurt when Miss Julie had decided to move, and that his pride would not allow him to ask her to return, but that if she went and asked him, he would be more than delighted to have her come back. To which Miss Julie replied that she would do nothing of the sort, and that they would both whistle for the time when they'd see her in their house again. And so everyone was thoroughly unhappy.

The miserable little room was even more uncomfortable than she had anticipated. Within a day or two she hated everything about it: the evil-smelling gas rings on which she had to do her bit of cooking; the window sash that fell without warning, sometimes in the middle of the night; the cracks in the calcimined walls and ceiling; the roaches and the occasional bedbugs. The children's diapers hanging in the downstairs piazza, the poverty-stricken family and the good-for-nothing husband chronically out of work irritated her. She refused to speak to the other roomers—a man who worked in the Customhouse, and a decayed gentlewoman who did sewing and smelled strong of liquor.

Her stinginess and her desire for rudimentary comfort were at war for a week or two, with the latter gaining the advantage, when the blow fell. She had a letter from Henry, which she believed was an invitation to return to his house, and opened with shaking fingers:

It informed her that Herbert Moore had failed and absconded —only a couple of hundred dollars of her money was left— securities that happened to be in her name.

At first reading of the letter, Miss Julie was stunned, and could hardly realize what had happened. Then she read it again, and her loss seemed more real.

"I'm a pauper," she thought with a shock. "Even this will be more than I can really afford now." Two hundred dollars and her tiny pension, and the occasional small check from Charlie, who could not afford to give much away. She could not afford, with the utmost economy, to live by herself more than a year.

"And then it will be the Confederate Home," Miss Julie thought. "And that will just about kill Henry.

"It will serve him right. That will take his pride down. He won't be so high and mighty then.

"It's all his fault anyway. Didn't he tell me not to let Francis invest my money?

"If Francis had done that, I would have it still, and maybe more.

"It's Henry with his big head, and his idea that he knows better than anyone else, that's to blame for this.

"I'll tell him what I think of him."

And she wrote him a letter and did; and she sent a similar letter to Annette, upbraiding her for neglect, for turning the children against her, and for other things at the prompting of her poor old mind.

With that, to which Annette replied with cold courtesy, she was alone. And she had absolutely no one to whom she could tell her troubles. Such things were personal and sacred. She could have discussed them with Emma, perhaps, or Josephine; but that would have meant that they would have to ask her to live with them, and now, with her money all gone, she shrank from accepting anything from people. She began to understand how Tessie had felt about assistance and even kindness.

From this time on Miss Julie was driven in upon herself, and led a queer life not uncommon to old ladies in her condition. She had jeered at Tessie for false pride, but she began to keep more to herself. She ceased to attend sodality meetings, and learned the trick of avoiding people she did not wish to talk to—walking around corners or at such a pace that they could not catch up to her, pretending to be deafer than she really was so that she might appear not to hear when addressed from the distance of a few feet. No one ever called out to anyone else in Charleston—no lady or gentleman, that is; and a person you did not see across the street might for all practical purposes have been in the next state.

There were practical difficulties in this mode of life. Miss Julie had been accustomed to begging rags for her quilts from all her friends. Now she had no one to supply them, and she exhausted her materials within a week or two. She tried crocheting, but her fingers had grown a trifle awkward, and she found it difficult, anyway, to follow the directions.

And as she no longer went out except when she was obliged to, for shopping and to attend Mass, her collection of silver paper and string remained almost at a standstill.

She was reduced to buying clippings of cloth from the dry-goods stores for her quilts, but found that expensive—her money would permit only the miserable meals she managed to get together.

Her economies in food were remarkable. Twice a week she

bought, from the little bakery around the corner, a stale loaf of caraway-seed bread which cost her a total of six cents. Half a dozen cracked eggs per week, and an occasional nickel's worth of herring or a ready-fried fish purchased from the Negro cookshop at the foot of Tradd Street, represented her flesh foods. Every two weeks she purchased a half-pound of second-grade butter, which the landlady kept in the icebox for her, and a half-pound of cheap coffee. She limited herself to one cup a day, at breakfast, boiled and boiled until it was strong enough to be palatable. Rice and hominy, which were the cheapest of all foods, were her staples, and from time to time a half-dozen half-rotten bananas, bought from Angelotti's at a half-cent each, eked out the coarse molasses which was her only source of sweets except the condensed milk she put sparingly into her morning coffee.

After a month of this Miss Julie did not feel very well or very energetic, and began to spend the major part of her time in the Morris chair, dozing when her thoughts and memories became too monotonous to keep her interested and awake.

Out of sheer inability to find anything else to do, she finished reading "The Trail of the Lonesome Pine," which depressed her, and which she thought, moreover, was nonsense. She reread "The Faith of Our Fathers" and her tattered prayer books and the little Douay Bible in small type; but this made her sleepy, for the print strained her eyes.

It was in one of her dozes that her glasses, which she had had for about ten years, fell out of her lap and onto the floor. When she awoke and stood up she stepped on them and ground them to bits.

"My last pair," Miss Julie murmured in despair. "What am I going to do now?"

She bought a pair which she picked off the counter at the ten-cent store; but they did not really fit her, and she realized that she would have to have the old ones duplicated. She had thrown away the pieces, and it was unlikely that the prescription was still at the optician's.

He was obliged to examine her eyes again, and the examination and new lenses cost her ten dollars. She scolded him thoroughly for not having kept a record of her prescription, but it did no good. He would not come down one penny in his price.

Only Miss Julie's fear of blindness made it possible for her to part with that ten dollars.

She had just enough money to carry her to the next spring, if she bought no new clothes and had no unusual expenses, such as doctor's bills. After that, the Confederate Home, or—

"I may be dead and gone by that time," Miss Julie thought.

She had a note from her brother John, saying that he was better.

"Confound him!" she exclaimed.

Annette wrote that she and the children would be home within a week. But they'd have to come to see her, Miss Julie resolved: she was not going to enter Henry O'Donnell's house, or his yard, even.

Of course, it would be possible to stand outside the garden fence and talk to the children.

"But why should I demean myself?" Miss Julie thought. "Let them come to see me. I'm their grandmother and their mother's mother. They owe me that much respect. Tessie was right. I had no call to go rushing there to see them. The idea! What do they take me for, I'd like to know."

She was quite indignant at Annette and the children for presuming to think it was her place to come to see them.

CHAPTER ELEVEN

THE MORNING AFTER HER RETURN FROM THE COUNTRY, Annette put on her hat, took her cardcase and parasol, and started out to see her mother.

She pulled the bell of the shabby little frame house on Franklin Street for fully three minutes before anyone answered. During this time she was aware that someone was peering out of the shutters on the first floor; immediately following the click of the shutters, the front door was opened and a bedraggled woman with no teeth in front asked what she wanted.

"I've come to see Mrs. Sharp. I'm Mrs. O'Donnell, her daughter."

"Go right up," the woman said. "Right at the top of the stairs, there, on the second floor."

Annette, not liking the looks of things at all (she was sure the woman was expecting the bill collector), hurried up the stairs and knocked. There was no response. Alarmed, she knocked harder.

"Come in," said the heavy voice of Miss Julie.

She pushed open the door and entered.

"Ma! What is the matter?"

Miss Julie surveyed her coldly. "What do you mean—what is the matter?" she demanded.

"Why—" Annette stammered.

The room was so cluttered with Miss Julie's things that there was hardly more than room to stand. It was dusty and unkempt, and the air was bad. It was like a junkshop; and there in the tattered Morris chair was her mother, changed unbelievably. Miss Julie was considerably thinner, and less smart in her appearance, and she looked pale and feeble.

"Ma, what are you doing in a place like this?" Annette almost shouted.

Miss Julie's once good-natured face darkened.

"If it's good enough for me, it's good enough for you."

Annette had all she could do to keep from crying. "Ma, what is the matter?" she repeated.

Miss Julie again refused to understand. "There's nothing the matter. I'm flattered to have you come to call on me. It was more than I expected."

She sounded just like Aunt Tessie. So that was what living with that old devil had done for her!

"I can't understand why you should talk to me like this, Ma."

Miss Julie grunted. "I suppose you think I should have come running to see you right after breakfast," she said. "You don't seem to think that it's your place to come and see me. I suppose Henry doesn't want you to do that."

"Ma, you're not acting like yourself," Annette replied, in a calm voice. "You were never this way. You must be sick."

The old lady stared coldly at her.

"I'm perfectly well. I'm poor, that's all, and this is the best I can afford, and I'm not asking anyone for sympathy or help. I'll get along."

"But what has Henry got to do with it?"

"What has Henry got to do with it?" Miss Julie mocked. "Hasn't Henry O'Donnell given me bad advice, and made me lose my money, and insulted me? Didn't he move to that big house, without asking me whether I wanted to go or not? Didn't he buy it, without saying a word to me for weeks, and then mortify me by telling Tessie as soon as he told me, and making me look like a fool for not knowing about it? Don't talk to me about Henry O'Donnell. I don't want anything to do with him."

"Ma, you're beside yourself. You must be, or you wouldn't act like this. If you were"—Annette hesitated—"if you were in your right mind, you wouldn't be in such a place and carrying on the way you are."

Miss Julie sulkily kept silent and she shook off Annette's hand.

"I'm old, and I have nobody to care for me, and I can just die this way," she complained.

"Why don't you come over to dinner?"

"I don't want your dinner. I can feed myself. And I don't intend to set foot in your house again. I've had enough of Henry O'Donnell. He's done for me, and he ought to be satisfied."

Annette sat down on a chair which she pulled up close, and looked earnestly at her mother. Henry had not told her about the investment, and she did not understand Miss Julie's allusions.

"I don't know what all this is about, Ma, and I won't ask you if you don't want to tell me. It all sounds like nonsense to me. But, however you feel about Henry, you can't go on living in a place like this. I won't have it."

"I didn't ask you to tell me what I ought to do. I'm able to mind my own affairs, and all I ask is for other people to attend to theirs and leave me alone."

"You don't need to take out your ill feeling on the children. James and George have talked for weeks about coming home to see you, and now you say you'll never step into my house again. What am I going to tell them?"

Miss Julie hesitated—the mention of the children affected her more than she cared to admit; but she had taken a stand, and out of sheer perversity she stuck to it.

"If the children want to see me, they're welcome. I'll be glad to have them at any time."

"Ma, why don't you come to dinner? Why don't you get off this high horse and act like a person of sense?"

"I don't propose to let you insult me," Miss Julie retorted. "You seem to forget that I'm your mother."

Annette lost her temper. "You seem to forget it. I think you're out of your mind, Ma—that's what I think. Why, that old lady next door to us is no queerer than you are."

"Very well," Miss Julie replied icily. "I'm crazy. Your mother is crazy. Thank you. Thank you very much." She sat up very straight. "I never thought my own daughter would come to my house and tell her own mother that she was crazy; but I should have known better than to expect anything but insults nowadays."

Annette got up. "Very well, Ma," she said. "You've quarreled with me, although I haven't done anything to cause it, and I can't do anything more. I'll just have to wait until you're acting like yourself."

"Goodbye," said Miss Julie, coldly. "When you come to my deathbed, remember the things you said to me today."

Annette went straight to her husband's office—a place she usually avoided, for Henry did not like mixing family and business, and often lectured about the women who went to their husband's places of work for no reason at all. But she had to talk to him immediately.

It was like talking to another person, to discuss anything with Henry in his office. His home personality was likely to make him break out into argument or sarcasm; surrounded by the atmosphere of business, he changed completely. He listened to Annette's recital of her morning's experience as a lawyer might have listened to a client.

"I'll tell you just what she means," he said finally. "Last summer, after she moved, your mother came to ask me about letting your brother Francis have her money to invest in an automobile company, and I advised her against it. It turned out better than I expected—better than anybody expected; and that's what she was referring to. I meant to do my best for her. I advised her, as you know well, to take her money out of that fellow Moore's hands."

"Well, we've got to get her out of that room," Annette said, with unusual positiveness. "Somehow or other, we've got to get her to our house. I know," she went on, as Henry frowned, "you said she could never come again unless she asked of her own accord. But this isn't a time to be foolish about that sort of thing. After all, she's old, and old people are silly sometimes. Living with Aunt Tessie has put the devil into her, and she hardly knows what she's doing. If she stays in that place much longer, I feel perfectly sure that she'll go crazy altogether."

Henry considered. He had to admit to himself that it was foolish to stand upon the code with such an old woman, and he was a little ashamed of having stood upon it so long. Furthermore, it was better to give in and ask her to come back to his house now, than to have her lose her mind. That would be harder to bear, in Charleston. He foresaw the social ignominy—the children taunted by their playmates for having a mad grandmother, the hundreds and hundreds of conversations all over the city as the servants told other servants all they knew.

"I'll ask her to come back," he said. "I suppose it's the only thing to do, now that she's so down and out. And anyway, the children do miss her. I even miss having her get up at five every Sunday morning." He smiled.

Annette sighed.

"I'll write her a letter," he promised, and she left, content.

The children were mystified by Miss Julie's failure to come to see them and to bring them something, and Annette had a difficult time explaining. She made rather a mess of it.

"Your father is going to ask Granny to come back here to live," she said. "Maybe she'll be here in a few days."

Miss Julie read Henry's letter with mixed feelings; but she was still certain that he had wronged her, and she finished it just as resentful as ever.

Nevertheless, she was triumphant. Henry had humbled himself, had got off his high horse and admitted that he had been wrong, and this gave her a tremendous satisfaction.

Whether to answer the letter was a matter for deliberation. If she did not answer it, that would be a direct insult; if she did, Henry might think that she was just angling for another letter to satisfy her own feelings, and she knew that he was not one to go far in his compromises.

But she was determined to stay right where she was. She was through with Henry O'Donnell. He had done her enough harm already.

"If I go to the poorhouse," she thought, with a chuckle, "that will serve him right. I wonder how he'll like having Charleston say that his mother-in-law is in the poorhouse."

She didn't answer the letter. And she did not go to see the children, and they did not come to see her.

Henry was no less distressed than Annette, though for different reasons. He had been fond of Miss Julie, in spite of the fact that she often irritated him and there were times when it bothered him to have an old and eccentric mother-in-law around his house. But he had fulfilled—more than fulfilled—all his obligations toward her, and the debt was all on her side. That, however, didn't trouble him. What did annoy him was the thought of the consequences to him, socially, of all this: the gossip, the backbiting, the sneers.

"There's nothing more we can do," he said. "I've asked her to come back, and she hasn't even answered my letter. I'm sure the old lady's troubles have affected her mind, and I'd do anything reasonable to help her; but there you are."

"God, I wish we'd never tried to persuade her to make up with Aunt Tessie!"

"It's always best to let well enough alone," Henry said smugly. "That was my advice at the time, you remember."

"Oh, you're always right about everything," Annette retorted. "Of course, you never make a mistake. You were right about the automobile stock, too, weren't you?"

"My business judgment is usually good. I certainly could have saved her from losing her money, anyway, if she'd listened. Now the old fool can take care of herself. I'm through with it." Henry was angry and flushed.

"I really think you're glad to be rid of Ma. You were glad to get rid of her, and now you're happy that she's hard up and miserable and has nobody to do anything for her. I'd like to see that letter. You must have said something to humiliate her and keep her from even answering it."

"She just hasn't any manners," Henry said. "None of the Gerards ever had any decency about them. They talk a whole lot about their family, but every one of them acts like a savage. Why, look at the way they all quarrel."

Annette rose and swished out of the room, and Henry put on his hat and left early for his office, shutting the door with a tremendous bang. The Gerards, he said to himself, had broken up their own family with quarrels, and now the curse was threatening to break up his.

He was not on speaking terms with his own brother. But one forgets consistency in the heat of temper.

"They're always talking about the Irish being quarrelsome," Henry said to himself, "but the French can do just as well or better. Damn the old bitch! She's going to break up my home, that's what she's going to do."

CHAPTER TWELVE

THAT OCTOBER THE TAIL END of a West Indian hurricane struck Charleston with more than usual force. The storm signals were flying, and St. Michael's tolled the warning at two o'clock of a Wednesday afternoon. However, it was nearly eight o'clock when the full fury of the storm struck. The wind roared over the city, rolling up tin roofs like so much paper, and raising a tide that swept over the low land and up through the sewers to flood first floors and ruin furniture and matting and carpets with mud and salt. Some Negro shacks were washed away, and there was damage to boats and wharves and gardens and the water supply; but this was a puny affair to a place that had seen the earthquake of 1886, and the people took it calmly.

Miss Julie, who was still conducting her feud with Henry, was marooned for a day or two, and felt very hungry, for she had been caught with only a minimum of food on hand and would not have considered asking any of her landlady; she determined to go over to the cookshop at the foot of Tradd Street, when the streets were dry and entirely navigable, and get herself a fried fish. She felt that a good, crisply fried whiting would do her more good than anything else, and did not delay in starting out, just before dinnertime, to get it.

To the foot of Tradd Street was not by any means a long walk; but Miss Julie was weak from long inactivity and from her two days' confinement and her months of meager diet. By the time she had reached the old house—which gave her a pang as she thought of all the happy times she had had there—she began to wonder if she could get as far as the shop without stopping to rest.

She pushed on, however, very slowly, somewhat alarmed by waves of faintness that came over her. She was accustomed to feeling well, and as usual, any disturbance of her equilibrium frightened her more than it would have frightened a valetudinarian. The idea of her last will and testament came into her head, although she had little now to leave, but suddenly she felt better and kept going until she reached the little shop.

There a disappointment awaited her: the shop was closed. There was no indication of a reason for this disappearance from active commerce, and Miss Julie walked away disappointed, and indignant at this slight to her patronage. "Just like niggers," she muttered.

She took out a mint and sucked it, and it seemed to give her strength. Common sense dictated that she go home as rapidly as her feet would take her, but her streak of obstinacy came to the fore. She would go to the other cookshop, Jerry's, at the foot of Beaufain Street, and get her fried fish there, though it wasn't as good.

She retreated to Broad Street and crossed the foot of the Lake to Ashley Avenue, past the lumberyard; and there she suddenly felt that she could not go a step farther.

Miss Julie was terrified now. She sat down on the low coping that separated the sidewalk from the dirt roadway of Ashley Avenue. Beads of sweat popped out on her forehead. She was sick at her stomach, and every muscle of her body was quivering.

It would be mortifying to die here in public. She said a short prayer for aid, and then, not feeling any better, she judged it discreet to say an Act of Contrition. "If I could only stretch out for a while, I'd feel all right," she muttered, as the sensation of weakness again passed and the dizziness left her for a moment.

"I've got to get home somehow," Miss Julie muttered. She stood up, took a step, and fell heavily on her right arm.

"Help!" she bellowed, sick with pain and fear and the knowledge that her voice would not carry above the noise of the lumberyard.

She lay there for several minutes, and no one came to her aid. The pain in her injured arm was mounting, and she was certain that it was broken and she would have blood poisoning if she didn't get help soon. She struggled to get to her feet and was completely unable to do so.

Miss Julie closed her eyes and said a prayer for help. Then she waited for the succor she was certain would not fail.

It arrived in the form of a Negro workman, who came out of the gate of the lumberyard with a pair of planks under his arm. He dropped the planks and rushed over.

"What's the trouble, ma'am?" he asked.

"I've fallen and hurt me arm. I'm Mrs. Sharp—Mr. Henry O'Donnell's mother-in-law." Miss Julie knew that the name of Henry O'Donnell was likely to have some effect. Many a Negro in Charleston had worked for him at one time or another.

"Yassum, I knows Mr. Henry," the man said. "He live in the big house nex' do' to Wentfoot Street."

"Well, you take me there," Miss Julie said, "and I'll be much obliged to you."

The Negro looked doubtful. He was afraid she would not be able to go that far.

"Maybe I bettuh git a wagon," he said.

"Nonsense," said Miss Julie energetically. "You get me to my feet and let me lean on your arm, and I'll get there all right. Be careful of my arm, now," she added, as the man seized her beneath her armpits and hauled her first to her knees and then to standing position. Feeling very weak and sick and yet somewhat ridiculous, she stumbled ahead, leaning on the Negro's arm, and muttering prayers as she went along. She hoped not too many people would see her as they went along Ashley Avenue.

When they reached Beaufain Street she was obliged to sit down and rest on one of the benches that surrounded the Lake. The colored man waited patiently, not without an eye on the planks he had dropped.

Finally, they reached the gate of the house. The man rang the bell, and Sarah came, her eyes popping at the sight of Miss Julie on the arm of a strange Negro.

"Sarah," Miss Julie said faintly, "don't ask any questions.

Take me bag and give this man a quarter. He helped me home. I'm feeling a little weak."

Sarah fished out the coin and gave it to the man, who departed with his curiosity unsatisfied and with something to tell about for some time to come.

"I fell down," Miss Julie said weakly, sitting on the lowest step. "And I think I've broken me arm."

"You set there a minute," Sarah said. She rushed up the piazza to the door and called up the stairs.

"Miss Nettie! Come quick, ma'am! Miss Julie hyuh, and 'e sick!"

Jennie came rushing out of the kitchen, and Annette down the stairs, and they surrounded her in an instant.

"Ma! What on earth is the matter?" Annette leaned over and put a hand on her forehead.

"Nothing, child. I just felt a little gone after I got a short ways from home, and I fell and hurt me arm. Just let me lay down awhile, and I'll be all right."

"Call Stevens," Annette said to Sarah. "We've got to get her upstairs and to bed."

"Oh, I don't need to go upstairs. Just let me lay on the couch downstairs."

Sarah returned with Stevens, and, disregarding Miss Julie's protests, they prepared to move her upstairs.

"Jennie, you take Mis' Sharp under the right arm. Stevens, you take 'em under the left. I'll come up behind," Sarah ordered.

"Mind now, I'm heavy," Miss Julie said.

And she was heavy; but with many grunts they hoisted her up the stairs, and Annette put her to bed.

"I'm going to send for Cyril," Annette said.

"Oh, I don't need any doctor," Miss Julie groaned. "Don't make any fuss, child. Just let me rest."

But Annette was already at the telephone. Sarah had the smelling salts and was making Miss Julie sniff it. Jennie appeared with a glass of water and whisky, and Miss Julie had a swallow of that and felt better.

"I hope I'm not going to spend the rest of my days in bed like this," she said weakly.

"My Lawd, Mis' Sharp, they ain't nothin' the matter with you," Sarah said. "You jis wo'n out with all the trouble and worriation, that's all."

"I'm getting gay in my old age, though," Miss Julie said. "Coming home on the arm of a strange man."

Sarah whooped discreetly. "He sho would have liked to know more," she said.

"Cyril will be here in a few minutes," Annette said, as she came in.

Miss Julie nodded. Her arm was paining her severely again, and she cried a little.

"What's Granny crying for?" George asked, coming into the room.

"Sh! Granny's not feeling very well," Annette said.

"Come in, Bubber," Miss Julie said. She reached her good arm over and patted him.

"Are you going to stay with us, Granny?" George asked.

"We'll see about it," Miss Julie said. She had not seen the children since they had returned from the country, and she cursed herself for a fool.

"Dinner will be ready soon," Annette said, "and I'll keep yours until after Cyril has been here. It's better not to eat until he says you can have something."

"I feel all right," Miss Julie said, "except that this arm of mine hurts so."

"Can you move it?" Annette asked.

"Just a little." Miss Julie lifted the arm and groaned mightily.

"Then I guess it's not broken. Just what did you do, Ma?"

"I was taking a walk," Miss Julie said, "and when I got over to the other side of Ashley Avenue, I felt so weak all of a sudden that I had to sit down on the coping. Then, when I got up, I fell down."

"What were you doing on the other side of the Lake?" Annette demanded. "That's not much of a place to be walking."

"Oh, I just wanted to have a stroll," Miss Julie said, reddening.

Annette knew very well where her mother had been going. She said no more about it. "But where did you get those glasses, Ma? You had the old pair the last time I saw you."

"I stepped on me old ones and broke them. It cost me ten dollars to get new ones. I had these on when you came to see me."

"I didn't notice," Annette said.

"Child, I've had a bad time," Miss Julie said, beginning to sniffle.

"There, never mind," Annette said, patting her shoulder. "Let's not talk about it. You're here now, and you're going to stay here."

"Henry won't want me to stay," Miss Julie protested.

"Oh, don't be so foolish, Ma. Of course Henry wants you to stay. Didn't he write and ask you? You didn't answer his letter, and you couldn't expect him to go on writing letters after that, could you?"

"No, I suppose not."

"We never wanted you to go to live with Aunt Tessie, you know that. You did it of your own free will."

Miss Julie was silent, but she looked reproachfully at her daughter. It wasn't right to taunt her with her mistakes.

"That must be Cyril," Annette said, as the bell sounded. She walked out to the landing, and reappeared with Dr. Forbes.

"Well, now," Dr. Forbes said. He was a tall, thin man, with a gentle bleating voice and a pleasant smile. "What have you done to yourself, Mrs. Sharp?"

"I feel sort of weak," Miss Julie said. "And I fell down and hurt me arm."

"Mmm-m. Let me see your tongue."

He examined it. He took her pulse. He took out his stethoscope and listened to her heart and lungs. He asked about her bowels, a subject always interesting to Miss Julie, who provided him with considerable information.

"How long have you been feeling this way?" he asked.

"Oh, just today, really. I haven't had much to eat since the storm."

"H'm-m. Now let's see that arm." He rolled up the sleeve of the flannel nightgown Annette had put on her, and as he felt of the swollen forearm and wrist Miss Julie winced. "It's not broken," he said. "Just a sprain, and the same for the wrist. Lucky you didn't break both of them, and your hip too."

"My Tante Eulalie broke her hip," Miss Julie recalled. "She slipped on a piece of watermelon rind. She was in bed for weeks and weeks."

"What you need is a tonic," Dr. Forbes said, taking out his prescription blank. "I'll write out a couple of prescriptions for you. This fall has been a shock for you. You stay in bed a few days. I'll see you then, and probably you'll be as good as new."

"Is the tonic very nasty?"

"It's pretty unpleasant."

Miss Julie sighed contentedly. "I never had any faith in sweet medicines," she declared. "Can I have some dinner?"

"All you want."

Miss Julie sighed again. "What have you got, Annette?"

"Chicken and okra and rice with giblets and some yams."

Dr. Forbes rose. "Paint that arm and wrist with some iodine, Annette," he said, "and rub it with some witch hazel if it's very painful." He put the stethoscope away and snapped his bag shut. "Goodbye."

"Goodbye," Miss Julie said.

She wondered what that tonic was going to taste like, and smacked her lips over the idea of a good hot dinner; and she was concentrating on these two pleasures when Henry entered.

"How are you, Miss Julie?" he asked.

"I'm just old and foolish, Henry. But I'm all right."

He beamed benevolently. "Well, that's good. Better make up your mind to stay, now. We want you here."

"You're very good, Henry," Miss Julie said, her voice breaking.

"Anything special you want?" Henry ignored her thanks.

"No, son, I can't think of anything in the world I want. Where's James? He hasn't been in to see me."

"He's coming right up. He was late coming home from school because he stopped to see a dead horse." Henry shuddered.

Miss Julie laughed. *"Chacun à son gout,"* she remarked.

"I hear him running up the steps now," Henry said.

James rushed in.

"Why, how you've grown!" Miss Julie exclaimed, kissing him. "I wouldn't have known you, you're such a man!"

"I'm glad you came back to our house, Granny. I missed you the most of all."

"You rascal," Miss Julie said.

"You're going to stay, aren't you, Granny?"

"Until I'm put out."

James was satisfied. He accepted the situation as settled and returned to his own interests.

"I saw a dead horse," he told her.

Part Three

CHAPTER ONE

PERHAPS, MISS JULIE THOUGHT, tasting her content at being back with her daughter and grandchildren, this was the way life was intended to be—a series of ups and downs, an alternation of light and shadow. There were troubled periods, and then you reached a kind of resting place; and if God permitted you stayed there. There had been, for instance, the War and all the suffering and anxiety and acute poverty; and then had come her marriage, and the children; times of care, but happy, for she had not wanted much and had been too busy to fret. And then the departure of Charlie for the West—it was five years since she had seen the boy—and Samuel's death, and then, finally, Pa's. But that had been followed by the six years of ease and happiness in Henry's home, which she had been too foolish to appreciate. Yet, after that strange year with Tessie, and the two months of isolation she had forced upon herself, here she was, in a big luxurious house, with the children and Annette and no responsibilities whatever, and a small but regular allowance from Charlie, who had had a turn of luck.

Furthermore, her conscience was now entirely clear on the subject of Tessie. She had done her best, had made the trial, and had failed through no fault of her own. People were guarded in their references to the matter, but she sensed that everyone sympathized with her, and considered the incident closed. She harbored no ill feeling, but she knew now, beyond a doubt, that she and Tessie were better apart. If Tessie spoke to her, she was resolved to answer; but intimacy there could not be.

It just seemed too good to be true, Miss Julie thought, pushing up her glasses and putting the quilt aside. Here it was mid-March, and she had a fire, though it wasn't absolutely necessary. In an hour or so the children would be home from school, and there would be a good dinner; and in the afternoon she would take a stroll around King Street to look in the shop windows, and come home to do what she pleased, and have a pleasant supper; and then they would sit around the big table in the sitting room and sew and talk. And on fine days she could sit out in the sun in the garden, or talk over the low fence to the old ladies who kept the boarding house next door. Or she could read and sing to George, who was almost six now and would soon be at school himself—one of the few regrets she had.

It was too bad that children grew up so fast. Here was little Joe in high school, though not doing so very well at his studies, and Betsy ready for it, and James in the second year at private school and a communicant. And for that matter, Betsy would be confirmed that spring. How time flew!

But the only changes were those time enforced. Every day Miss Julie went through the old routine she had observed before she moved (as she described her departure to live with Tessie). She awoke with the usual prayer, superintended the children's dressing, saw to their prayers, and pottered around before breakfast. On Sundays she arose at five, and Henry grumbled as usual; and at ten o'clock she set out for her second Mass of the day, frequently urging Henry to go with her and getting the invariable joking answer. The weekly sodality meeting, an occasional funeral (it was odd how all the old group were dying regularly now), confession on Saturday, regular entries in the indulgence book, visits to cronies—that was how life went along.

And so, almost before Miss Julie knew it, Christmas time had come, and she had to bake her cake; and then came the great day with all its excitement and good food—she was more careful this time about how she indulged—and the first of the year, and resolutions that were not kept, and her seventy-second birthday, on which Henry gave her a brand-new sewing machine of her own ("I won't live to wear this one out," Miss Julie said); and now she was waiting for Lent to be over. Those months had been uneventful indeed, and just the way Miss Julie liked them to be. For that, she realized, was what happiness meant to her.

Even the *Titanic* disaster, which set the world to talking in tones of horror, failed to rouse Miss Julie beyond saying:

"They defied God, didn't they? They said the ship couldn't sink, and He showed them."

But she did say a prayer for the victims, in spite of feeling their fate was deserved.

One Saturday afternoon of late April, when Miss Julie and Annette were sitting on the piazza, a great red automobile drove up and stopped just at the gate. It was a huge car, with high wheels and enough brass trimming to make a day's work for whoever had to polish it. George and James, who were automobile-mad, rushed out to examine the wonderful machine, from which Henry O'Donnell alighted with a satisfied grin.

"Come on down," he called. "We're going for a ride."

James and George were on the running board by that time, ready to hop in just as they were; but Annette had other ideas.

"Come back here," she commanded. She descended to the street and hauled the little boys back into the house. "Do you think you're going out in the automobile looking like a couple of children from the Borough? Here, Sarah. See that they get their faces and hands clean. . . . Wait until I put on a veil," she told Henry. "Come on, Ma. Get your hat and veil on."

Miss Julie smiled indulgently. "My time is past for that sort of gallivanting. I'm not going to have my kidneys shaken out or my ears blown off in any automobile. The trolley car is good enough for me."

When the others were in the car, Sarah included, Henry tried to persuade Miss Julie to come along.

She repeated her remark about ears and kidneys, which Henry didn't like. He snorted and said, "Very well, then," and the car moved off with a roar and a grinding of gears.

"Grandeur," Miss Julie thought disdainfully.

Meanwhile, as the car rushed up the macadam of Ashley

Avenue, the little boys wild with delight, Henry told Annette that he had bought the machine.

"Mercy!"

"Well, you enjoyed riding in the Garrisons' car so much, I thought we might as well have one," he explained. "You and Betsy and Joe have been after me for years to buy one."

"Gee, Papa, won't Betsy and Joe be mad that they missed coming with us!" James shouted. "We've got a car!"

Mr. Bell, who had sold Henry the car, was trying to make clear, as he drove, the workings of the clutch and gears and accelerator. He stepped lightly on the latter, and the car shot forward and over the wooden planks of the Ashley River Bridge with a rattle like a volley of musketry.

"Ask Mr. Bell not to go so fast, Henry," Annette said, clutching at her hat and motioning James and George to sit quiet and not get so near the side.

"We're only going thirty-five miles an hour." Henry clutched his own hat as he turned around to answer. "That isn't any speed at all."

"It makes me dizzy," Annette said.

Mr. Bell slowed down to a more moderate pace, and it rolled past cabbage fields and rows of cabins, on the porches of which small colored children leaped up and down as they saw the big red car.

They turned around after going some ten miles into the country, and Mr. Bell suggested that Henry might like to try driving for a while.

"Henry," Annette said, "not today. Wait until you've got the car by yourself."

"Nonsense," Henry said. "It's perfectly safe."

"Henry, if you drive this automobile, or even try to drive it, I'm going to get right out with these children and walk home. I'm not ready to meet my God so soon."

"Well, all right." Henry was mortified; he frowned heavily and didn't say another word until they got home, and Stevens opened the gates, and the car rolled into the yard.

[181]

"I'm going to keep it in the old carriage stable," Henry said. "Now, you boys stay out, you understand? I'm not going to have the paint all scratched up and the upholstery ruined. There's fine leather on those seats, and the first footmark I find on it, there's going to be trouble."

Mr. Bell got out to walk home, and Henry went back into the house fuming.

"I suppose you're satisfied," he said to Annette. "You've made me a laughingstock, kicking up all that fuss before Mr. Bell. What will people think of us? Everybody is beginning to drive a car now."

"I'm sorry your feelings were hurt," Annette answered, "but I've got my life to think about. I don't want to go into a ditch, or into a telephone pole. And that's the very first thing that will happen when you try driving that car without someone showing you over and over."

But Henry did take lessons, and got a license, and drove the car without any mishap, except that it broke down one day just outside the city. He promptly hunted around for a mechanic and chauffeur, and found a huge black man named Wallace, with two gold teeth and a perpetual smile to expose them to view. Henry bought him a black broadcloth suit and a cap with a patent leather visor; the boys made him their constant companion, and Jennie complained that he ate twice as much food as any human being she had ever seen before.

Miss Julie consented finally to try a ride in the car; but she was determined not to like it, and she didn't. She said it made her teeth rattle, and she was sure it was not good for her insides to be shaken up like that.

"God never meant people to go tearing around in those things," she said. "If he had, he'd have let someone invent them sooner."

"Did God mean people to go rattling around in streetcars, Miss Julie?" Henry retorted.

"That's different," Miss Julie said, as if there could be no argument on the subject.

She blamed that single ride in the car for the "lumbago" (as she diagnosed the pain in her back) that attacked her several days later; and she resorted to her sovereign remedy for the ills of the flesh, Epsom salts, taking a half-pound in fairly stiff doses. Still the griping pains persisted.

She tried hot-water bags and very hot baths, but the pain did not diminish.

"You had better see Cyril about that," Annette told her.

"Nonsense. What do I want a doctor for, with a little pain in the back?"

"How do you know there isn't something wrong with your kidneys?"

Miss Julie looked startled, and then began to nod her head slowly in agreement.

"You're right, child," she said, in a tone of deep satisfaction. "That's exactly what it is. I knew I was right about riding in that car. You'd better sell it before you all have kidney trouble."

She put down her darning and stood up. "I'm going over to the druggist to get some of those kidney pills I read about in the paper."

She took half a box of the pills, and the pain went away.

"I ought to write them a testimonial," she said.

She broadcast the virtues of the kidney pills, and finished the box for good luck, while Henry and Annette worried.

"How can I go away and leave Ma sick, or liable to be sick?" Annette demanded.

"Well, Sarah and I will be here," Henry said.

"That's not the same thing."

"I can always send for Mrs. Fisher."

Annette grunted her lack of appreciation of this joke. "It's very serious," she said. "Ma's seventy-two, and there's no telling what might be the matter with her. I ought to be here."

"A lot of help you'd be if the poor old thing got sick."

"I wish you wouldn't belittle everything I do."

Henry patted her. "I was just joking," he explained.

Annette told Miss Julie they were worried about letting her

stay alone. "Why," she asked, "don't you change your mind and come to the country with us?"

"That godless place, with no church?" Miss Julie replied. "You must think I want to trifle with my eternal salvation. I've got little enough time as it is to enjoy going to Mass and to save my soul, and I'm not going to risk everlasting torment for a few weeks in the mountains. Besides, I don't like the way they cook things. There's not enough pepper in them."

"Still, I'm going to be worried about you," Annette declared.

"You go away, and don't worry about me. I know how to take care of myself." Miss Julie stopped, and a wry look came over her face. "There's that pain again," she said, clapping a hand to her back.

"Is it very bad?" Annette was alarmed.

"It's pretty bad. I think I'll go up to bed. Get me a couple of hot-water bottles."

Miss Julie hurriedly undressed and stretched out under the sheet; but neither the hot-water bottles nor the mustard plaster she insisted upon trying gave her any relief. She was alone when the pain suddenly became unendurable. It gripped her like a giant's clutch.

"Annette!" she roared.

Annette came running.

"Quick!" Miss Julie shouted. She felt as if her insides were being twisted right out of her. "Get the doctor. Quick! Don't stand there!"

All the while Annette was at the telephone, her mother kept calling to her to hurry. She knew she couldn't stand that pain much longer.

Dr. Forbes, coming as fast as his poor old horse would pull his buggy, found Miss Julie writhing, her face contorted. He questioned her, and prodded her and poked her, and then he said:

"It's kidney stone. No doubt about it."

"Oh, my God!" Miss Julie moaned. She had heard horrible stories of operation for "the stone." "Give me something to kill me right now. I'd never live through an operation. Let me die

Annette, send for Father Mellon right away. There's no time to be lost! And get Mr. Bennet. No, don't bother about Mr. Bennet. I haven't got anything to make a will about."

"I'll give you something to stop that pain," Dr. Forbes said. "Just try to stand it for a few minutes. Annette, you sit here with her. I'll be right back."

Sarah was standing just outside the door. "You put some water on to boil," he ordered.

He prepared the morphine and gave Miss Julie an injection. She immediately began to feel less miserable and to be sleepy.

"Will she have to be operated on?" Annette asked in unnecessarily low tones.

"Maybe. It all depends on whether she passes the stones or not. You'll have to watch for them and save a few to be analyzed."

Annette wrung her hands distractedly. "She'll never live through an operation. She's so terrified of the knife, too."

"Well, wait and see. I'll do the best I can. You want to see that she drinks plenty of water as soon as she comes to. And give her tea and toast tonight, if she wants it, but nothing else. I'll be around later to see if she needs another injection."

Annette telephoned Henry at the office and sat at Miss Julie's bedside until she awoke, which was not until suppertime.

"The pain is all gone," she whispered.

"You go back to sleep. That may be the drug still working."

"No, I feel as if the pain is really gone," Miss Julie insisted. "I feel stupid, but a good supper is all I need."

"Cyril said you could have some tea and toast."

Miss Julie groaned. "Have I got to go through all of that again?" But she accepted the tea and toast and obeyed the directions to drink a lot of water, and slept through the night.

Next day she began to think that she would live, after all. The pains did not recur, and she had a grand time hunting for and recovering the kidney stones, though she was aghast when, after having them analyzed, Dr. Forbes forbade her pepper, spices, more than a cup of coffee per day, kidneys, liver, and chicken giblets. She grieved over the restrictions, but enjoyed describing her interesting illness to the old ladies who came to see her. When Miss Georgie Peters claimed to have had kidney stones once, she put it down to jealousy and the wish to attract attention.

Still Miss Julie grumbled to her daughter about Dr. Forbes' rules: "What am I going to live on?"

"You'd better do as the doctor says," Annette replied.

"I declare, it's hardly worth living when you get old and your insides go back on you, and you have to give up eating good food."

"Well, you have to take care of yourself. Those are just the things that gave you that pain."

Miss Julie sighed.

"You'd better decide to come to the country with us," Annette went on. "You've got to have somebody to watch you."

"No, child. If there's anything really the matter with me, I want to be close to the cemetery. I'd hate to think of my poor body coming down on that hot Carolina Special."

"I guess you're pretty well if you talk that way. You wanted the priest and you wanted to make your will just the other afternoon."

Miss Julie laughed. Always afterward, those moments of weakness were irresistibly funny. "I wasn't far gone enough to send for Tessie," she declared. "When I do that, you can really know for sure that I'm going."

"All right, Ma, have your way. But if you get sick this summer with me away, for pity's sake don't hide it from Henry. Let him send for me at once."

"He will anyway. Don't worry, child. If there should be anything sudden, there's always the infirmary."

Annette decided, not without misgivings, that it would be all right to go away and leave her mother.

The problem was solved in an unexpected manner: a letter came from Chattanooga which Miss Julie read without a word, and passed over to Annette.

Annette's Aunt Emma had suffered a stroke, and they wanted Miss Julie to come immediately. The stroke was not a bad one, and all Emma needed was rest and recuperation; but they thought having Miss Julie there would be a comfort.

"I'll have to go," Miss Julie said. "They talk very lightly about a stroke being nothing at all, but I know better. I'm afraid this is going to be the end of poor Emma, and I want to see her before she dies. Poor thing! She's only sixty-five—seven years younger than I am. I always knew something like this was going to happen to her, though."

"Why do you say a thing like that, Ma?"

"Why," Miss Julie said, "her immoderate habits! She always ate too much. I've told her for years, ever since she was a young woman, that she couldn't keep on loading her stomach that way and expect to make old bones."

Annette repressed a smile. Afterward she said to Henry: "Wouldn't it lay you out to hear Ma say that Aunt Emma has eaten too much all her life? She's always eaten enough for two herself."

"They'll be horrible examples to each other," Henry said.

And so it was that Miss Julie, after less than a year of the peace and contentment of Henry's house, was once more uprooted and had to pack herself off to protect her younger sister against the dangers of overindulgence in food. She was upset about going, but she comforted herself by predicting that she would return before long.

"I don't think the poor child will outlive the fall," she said a number of times.

She would not ride to the depot in the new car.

"I've had enough kidney trouble already," she said. "Get me a good old-fashioned hack."

As the train moved out, she had a premonition she couldn't account for, that something would go wrong during her absence: that Fate was conspiring against her having a long period of peace and quiet ever again.

CHAPTER TWO

MISS JULIE FOUND THINGS VERY PEACEFUL in Chattanooga, and her sister not dangerously ill. But she had so long wanted some sense of importance—the one thing lacking to her entire happiness at Henry's house—that she began to consider her presence very necessary to Emma; and as much as she missed the children she wrote to Annette that she would stay on for a while. To make this seem more necessary, she implied that her sister might have another stroke at any moment.

Henry was relieved, but not for long. He was on the piazza one Sunday afternoon after dinner, trying to make up his mind whether to sleep the afternoon away or have Wallace drive him out into the country, when Annette's Uncle Joe appeared at the gate.

Joseph Gerard was the male counterpart of Miss Julie. He was short, round, pink-cheeked, and blue-eyed; he had the Gerard jaw, too. There was something indefinably sad about his face, despite his reputation as a joker.

Henry liked his uncle-in-law, whom he saw very rarely. He raised a hand in greeting, and Joseph Gerard came up the steps.

"Well, Mr. Joe, this is a pleasure," Henry said. "Sit down, sir, and I'll get you something cool to drink."

"Now, Harry, you know I don't touch anything," Joseph said with a smile. He put his tattered Panama under the chair and sat with his feet on the banisters. His shoes were shabby.

"Just this once," Henry said, and fetched the whisky.

As they sipped their whisky and ice, Henry said:

"How's everybody in the family, Mr. Joe?"

"Very well, thank you, Harry. And how are all of you?"

"Doing nicely. The children and Nettie are fine."

"So Julie has gone to Chattanooga to see Emma."

"Yes. She had a little attack, you know. She's all right now, but Miss Julie's going to stay there a little while."

Joseph Gerard nodded.

"Lovely place you've got here, Henry."

"Yes, it's a nice house. I thought, for the children's sake, we ought to live over here, near the Lake. That Tradd Street house was getting shabby."

"Sold it yet?"

"No." That was a sore point. Expecting the construction of the Boulevard to run values up, Henry had been disappointed. He changed the subject. "How are things in the stationery business?"

"Fair, just fair. I manage to keep body and soul together, you know. And how's cotton?"

"We're doing well this year," Henry said. "The mills have placed some very nice orders."

"Glad to hear it," Joseph Gerard said heartily. He took out a cigar case. "Have one, Harry?"

"No, thank you, Mr. Joe. I still smoke cigarettes. One box a day, that's all."

They lighted up and puffed in silence for a few minutes.

"Harry," his uncle-in-law said finally, "have you seen Tessie lately?"

"No, I haven't. She doesn't communicate with me very often. I'm not in her good books, you know."

"Poor old Tessie!" Joseph Gerard smiled faintly. "She is sort of queer, all right. Too bad she couldn't be more like Julie. Well, as a matter of fact, Harry, I came to see you about Tessie."

"If there's anything I can do— She's not sick, is she?"

"No. But she's not doing very well. I found that out in a very peculiar way." The older man drummed on the arm of the rocker. "I'm not in a position to do anything for her; and, besides, she probably wouldn't let me. But I thought you and Nettie— Harry, do you know what she's doing? She's selling magazine subscriptions!"

"Why, the poor old thing! She must be hard up, all right. That's a difficult way to make a living." Henry felt quite sorry for her. And then he wondered what people would say about them with Annette's aunt peddling magazines, and declared angrily, "We'll have to put a stop to that." He would be disgraced!

"Well, I don't think you can stop Tessie from doing anything," his uncle-in-law said. Although his eyes twinkled, his tone was worried. "But she won't keep it up long. The question is, what to do when she gives it up. You know how proud she is. She'll sit right in that room of hers, if she has enough money to pay for a room, and sell everything she has until there's not a chair to sit on, and then she'll starve. You mark my words."

"Yes, that's exactly what she will do," Henry said. "If she'd only be reasonable, you know, I could offer to help her. But I wouldn't dare to do it."

"Maybe Annette could talk her round."

"I don't think Annette has ever seen her since she and Miss Julie had their latest quarrel."

"My God, what a fool Julie was to go to live with Tessie!" the older man said. "I never knew her to do anything so silly in her life."

"Miss Julie is getting very old. There's more than one old lady in Charleston who's done something foolish, for the matter of that."

"Yes, you're right, Harry. . . . Well, I didn't come to stay very long. I knew you'd be anxious to help Tessie if you could."

"I'll write to Annette about it."

"For God's sake don't let Tessie find out I told you."

"No, I won't."

Joseph Gerard stood up and pulled his coat down in the back, reached under the chair for his hat and put it on.

"Henry, you've been mighty good to my old sister. You know I appreciate it, my boy. I wish you had had the poor old thing's money in your charge. Then that dirty dog Herbert Moore wouldn't have been able to steal it."

"I tried to persuade her to let me take care of it. But she said she had to be loyal to her husband's old associate."

"Uh-huh. Well, Harry, thank you very much, boy." Joseph

held out his hand. "This family was mighty lucky to have you marry into it."

"It was an honor," Henry said. He walked with his wife's uncle to the gate. "Come again, Mr. Joe. You're always welcome."

Joseph Gerard waved and marched away with the slightly pompous dignity that Henry associated with all the Gerards. He felt very kindly toward his uncle-in-law. Never had he had from the Gerards so much as a suggestion that Annette had not stooped very low indeed to marry him.

"Poor old chap," he murmured, returning to the piazza. Then he felt angry again. "That damned fool old woman!" he grumbled.

The hopelessness of the situation oppressed Henry. Miss Tessie was not a person you could help. An offer of money was a deadly insult to her; food sent to her house anonymously, she would refuse to receive, making you look like a fool indeed. He sought in vain some possible subterfuge or stratagem. He couldn't even ask Miss Tessie to come and share his house—that would reflect upon her ability to take care of herself.

"I might get sick, if I had the time, and have Cyril send for her to nurse me," he thought with a grim smile.

He went into the little office and wrote a letter to Annette. Then, to make sure of its delivery he took the streetcar to the post office.

Annette was just as little able to suggest a solution. Blaming her for the whole thing—wasn't Miss Tessie her aunt?—Henry felt considerably annoyed. He would have to wait until he went to the mountains for his two weeks. Perhaps, on the spot, he could impress Annette with the serious social consequences of her aunt's sally into commerce. But he realized, with a feeling of desperate irritation, that she wouldn't care about that part of it, not one bit. She would be worried about the old lady's being in difficulties, but she wouldn't give a damn about what people thought. Her mother could pick up string and silver paper and pins, and buy food from cookshops, and discuss her bowels with other old ladies right across King Street, and Annette wouldn't care a bit. In fact—he writhed—Annette would be more than likely to think it funny.

Miss Tessie's operations in the magazine field were based on a peculiar ethic, if one looked at it from the standpoint of, say, an insurance salesman, who makes friends in order to have someone to sell policies to. She would not ask anyone she knew for a subscription, but limited her approaches to strangers.

In a city where, as she was able to say, she knew everyone of any consequence (though she didn't necessarily consider all she knew as really consequential) she was compelled to do her soliciting among the less cultivated members of society—"Navy Yard people," and shopkeepers, and mechanics. This was a handicap, for she naturally shrank from association with strangers and from asking anybody for anything.

Miss Tessie had another handicap fatal to a saleswoman—she was inclined to consider refusal of a subscription as a personal affront, and unwilling or grudging acceptance as patronage; and many of her interviews ended with her delivering a frank opinion of the social standing, general intelligence, and breeding of people she had called to their front doors as possible customers.

Henry's concern for the reflections that might be cast upon him by his aunt-in-law's doings did not last very long. Miss Susan Williams, that fountain of personal information, had kept Miss Julie posted on her sister's activities and in August, just as he was about to leave for his two weeks' holiday with his family, he was relieved to hear of Miss Tessie's admission of failure.

He did not know how she was now keeping body and soul together, but he could wait until he returned to the city, or until Annette returned, to find out about that.

Being a man of resource, and not without a boyish humor, he toyed with various schemes for aiding Miss Tessie in a completely anonymous fashion. One of these he broached to Annette.

"Do you suppose," he asked, when they were discussing the eternal theme of Miss Tessie's troubles, "I could get somebody

[192]

to frame a story about discovering an old investment of Mr. Fisher's and paying her the dividends? She doesn't know a thing about such affairs, and I could get Charlie Morgan or some other lawyer to think it up and write her a letter enclosing a check."

Annette knew her aunt's peculiarities better than Henry.

"That might do," she said, "except that you couldn't count on her using it for living expenses. Aunt Tessie is extravagant, you know, and a check for a hundred dollars or so wouldn't last her very long. She'd buy a new gas stove, or put a new headstone on one of the graves in her cemetery plot. No, the money would be just wasted, not to speak of all the trouble."

"It's damned hard to help some people," Henry growled.

"Well, Aunt Tessie's like that. That's her pride."

Henry had heard the expression so many times that he was heartily sick of it. "Damn her pride!"

He abandoned his ingenious idea. Old Willie Fisher had never put his money into anything good, anyway, he was certain. He hadn't had enough sense.

"If she decides to go into the Confederate Home, I'll just have to face it," he told himself, and tried not to worry.

CHAPTER THREE

THERE WAS ALWAYS, IT SEEMED TO ANNETTE, some trouble waiting when she returned from the country.

The morning after her arrival she went to visit her aunt, with a balsam pillow and a bottle of Miss Tessie's favorite toilet water as peace offerings. She was afraid they would come hurtling out of the window as she departed, and not at all certain that she would get out alive herself.

Miss Tessie had moved to a single room again, in a house on King Street whose occupants needed the money in order to keep it. "Thank God she's at least living in a place with decent people," Annette murmured as she walked up to the neat and respectable dwelling. An elderly lady of unexceptionable manners answered the bell—"a real Charleston lady," dressed in black silks with a high collar and a golden brooch.

"I am Mrs. O'Donnell, Mrs. Fisher's niece," Annette told her. "Is she at home?"

"I think so. I'll go up and see." She didn't look at all as if she relished inquiring.

She returned in a moment. "Mrs. Fisher asks, Won't you come up? I'll show you the room."

Annette mounted the stairs and knocked at the door that was pointed out.

"Come in," said the bleating voice of her aunt.

Miss Tessie was seated at a table piled with envelopes. She had a pen in her hand, and there was an open ink bottle beside her. She laid down the pen and rose, smoothing her apron and adjusting her little widow's cap.

"Well," she said in the mocking tone she used so skillfully. "Well! This is an honor indeed, for you to come and visit your aunt."

"How are you, Aunt Tessie?" Annette ignored the sarcasm.

"Very well, indeed," Miss Tessie replied, looking suspiciously at her.

"I had a balsam pillow for you that I brought from the mountains," Annette explained, "and I thought I'd come with it myself. I got you a bottle of cologne, too," she added, handing over the package.

"Thank you." Miss Tessie's sniff was not intended to sample the odor of either the balsam pillow or the cologne. "You're very kind, Annette."

"You look a bit as if the heat had affected you this summer, Aunt Tessie."

It was a tactless remark, which Annette regretted.

"Indeed! I haven't lost my mind, if that's what you mean."

Annette flushed. "Of course I didn't mean anything of the kind. I meant that you looked as if you'd had a hard summer." But that, unfortunately, was equally tactless.

"I am very well," Miss Tessie said. "Charleston is good enough for me, summer or winter. I don't need to run off to some godless place, with no church to go to on Sundays, in order to keep my health."

Annette's reply was peaceful.

"You know we worry about you, Aunt Tessie."

"I don't need anyone to worry about me."

"Don't you think it's the Christian duty of a niece to worry about her aunt?"

"I don't feel that you're under any obligations to me. And I don't care to be under any to you, Annette." She hooted. "And I'm quite well provided for. I suppose you'd like to know what I'm doing with all these things."

Annette flushed again. "I'm not inquiring into your private affairs."

"Well, for your satisfaction, I'm addressing envelopes," Miss Tessie told her. "It's not a very good way to make a living, perhaps, compared with others, but I expect to make enough at it to pay for my rent and food."

"But how about your rheumatism?" Annette asked.

"That does bother me a little," Miss Tessie answered, softening; "but I manage. And while I haven't had many nursing cases lately, on account of the nigger nurses that are taking all the work, I imagine that sooner or later I'll have one."

"But can you keep this up?" Annette inquired.

"Certainly I can," Miss Tessie said with pride.

"If there's anything we can do, to tide you over—"

"Thank you. I don't need any help. I suppose the children are well?"

"Everyone is fine, thank you." Annette rose. "I mustn't keep you from your work."

Miss Tessie did not deny that she was losing time.

"Please don't be foolishly proud, Aunt Tessie," Annette pleaded as a last word.

"Foolishly proud, indeed!" Miss Tessie retorted. "Hoo! I'm glad someone has some pride left."

"I hope you'll come to see us, and come to dinner anytime you feel like it," Annette said at the door.

"Don't let the food get cold waiting for me," said Miss Tessie.

Annette reached the street feeling, as she always did after a visit to her aunt, like a schoolgirl who had been scolded.

"Really, she's impossible," she grumbled to Henry.

"I suppose that settles it," he said. "We'll have to wait now until she gets sick. Then maybe she'll let us do something to help her."

"How much money do you think she can earn addressing envelopes?"

"I think they pay about a dollar a thousand. You just try addressing a thousand some time, and see how much money you could make at it. Even if she addressed a thousand a day, I don't think the poor old soul could keep it up long enough to make a regular thing of it. And I don't see how, at her age, she can write that fast."

"Her handwriting is very stiff," Annette said.

"Then they probably won't keep sending the work to her," Henry said. "The thing may be a swindle, anyway. They may charge her a deposit for the envelopes and then not pay her for doing them on the pretext that the addressing is not good enough. I'd like to know where she's getting the money to live on."

This was to be George's first year at school, and in the preparations for his entrance to school—which both parents regretted as signifying the end of childhood for their youngest offspring—Miss Tessie's troubles took a subordinate position in their minds. Curiously enough, it was through George that they got the next news of her, quite by accident.

George was not a very communicative child, and it was at least two weeks after he began at Miss Low's school that his mother and father were able to get anything out of him about his impressions. Then he confided that he had a friend.

"His name is Arthur," George said.

"Arthur what?"

"Oh, just Arthur."

"James," Henry said, appealing to a veteran, "what's Arthur's last name?"

"I don't know, Papa."

The matter seemed unimportant, and Henry and Annette laughed over the innocence of small boys, who don't realize that anyone else has a last name, and teased George about it.

"How's Arthur Anonymous?" Henry liked to ask.

"He's fine," George would reply.

One day, however, he confided that he had stopped on the way home to see Arthur's train.

"You didn't stay very long," Henry remarked. "You weren't late to dinner."

"The old lady told me to get out of their house," George said.

Henry, always alert for insults, was instantly attentive.

"Who told you?"

"The old lady," George repeated. "The old lady with only one eye."

"Well, for God's sake," Annette said, exchanging glances with Henry. "Where does this Arthur live?"

"On New Street."

"Well, he's your cousin, Arthur Morse. The old lady is your Uncle Joe's wife."

"Don't you ever go to that house again," Henry said.

"If Ma could hear about this!" Annette stifled a laugh. "It would kill her."

"I yelled 'one eye' at her," George said.

"Well, you mustn't do that," his father objected. "Never ridicule anyone for a misfortune, no matter how disagreeable that person may be. But you remember what I've told you, and never go into that yard again. And perhaps it would be just as well if you didn't have too much to do with that Arthur, either."

"The idea of that woman insulting a child just out of her dirty spite," Annette said. "I've a good mind to write to Uncle Joe about it."

"Oh, don't make any more trouble for the poor chap," Henry

said. "He's had enough misery on account of that woman already. Let's consider this the last of it."

But that was not the last of it. The next day's mail included a postal card addressed to Annette, who reddened angrily when she read it, and passed it without a word to Henry.

There was no salutation to the message, which read:

Please keep your children out of our yard. I do not wish my grandson to associate with such people. Especially when they spend their time in pawnshops.   E. G.

"Well, she certainly is low," he said.

"She's a devil incarnate," Annette said. "I'd like to read her title to her."

"Well, of course we can't do anything like that without descending to her level. But do you realize what the pawnshop part means? It means that your aunt has been pawning her things. That's where she's got whatever money she has now."

"She hasn't got much to pawn."

"But that's not all," Henry said darkly.

Annette nodded. The pawnshop was a place no decent person entered if he could help it. It was the last resort, and something of a disgrace even then.

"I hope she isn't trying to pawn the picture of Theodora." Henry smiled, though he thought it no laughing matter. "We've got to do something. The old lady will starve to death, in the first place; and if she doesn't, there's no telling where these carryings-on of hers will end up."

"There's only one thing left for her to do," Annette said. "That's to enter the Confederate Home. Or perhaps the poorhouse."

"Good God Almighty!" Henry was horrified. "She couldn't do that!" And yet that was exactly the sort of thing Miss Tessie's overweening pride would lead her to do—humiliate herself thoroughly. "She ought to have a little more feeling for her family."

Annette shrugged.

"You know when people get old there's no making them listen to reason, Henry. Nothing on earth could change Aunt Tessie's mind if she was determined to do it."

Henry stared. His imagination had often been busy with the effects of having his wife's aunt enter a charitable home—not that the Confederate Home was any disgrace, but the idea that he, the well-to-do nephew-in-law, had permitted the old lady to enter it. The imminence of the possibility made it more awful than before.

"God, it's frightful!" he groaned. (He could see the children being taunted by their schoolfellows: "Your aunt's in the poorhouse! Your aunt's in the poorhouse." Whispers. Pointing of fingers. "Oh, the O'Donnells? Well, they've always seemed to be nice people, but there's one very odd thing. Do you know that Annette O'Donnell's own aunt is in the Home?" Head-shakings. "You'd think with all the money he's supposed to be making that Henry O'Donnell would make her an allowance." "Well, maybe he isn't making as much as he likes people to think. I guess that big house on Ashley Avenue was too much for him. . . .")

"We've got to ask her to come here," Henry said, finally. "I'd rather have a wild tiger in the house than that old lady, but there's nothing else to be done."

"Do you think for a minute that she'll come?" Annette asked scornfully. "How are you going to persuade her?"

"I'll have to do some thinking about it," he agreed. "There must be some way to appeal to her."

"It will be a miracle if you can get her to come here."

"Mamma," Betsy asked, going beyond the bounds of well drilled discretion, "is Aunt Tessie going to come to live with us?"

"You attend to your own affairs," Annette.told her. She felt like cursing—an outlet forbidden to Southern ladies.

CHAPTER FOUR

NOT UNTIL SEVERAL DAYS LATER did a single idea come to Henry. But this one, he thought, was good.

"I'll tell her we feel that the children need a good old-fashioned influence," he said.

"Do you think Aunt Tessie will be fooled by that?" Annette asked. "She'd see through that in a minute."

"Damn it, you're always throwing a wet blanket over any idea I have."

"I don't want you to make a fool of yourself."

"Thank you. Of course I go around making a fool of myself."

"You'll have to think of something better than that," Annette persisted.

They were sitting at the table after dinner, as they often did for purposes of discussion.

Annette rolled her napkin and unrolled it, thoughtfully; Henry's only response to her criticism was to drum on the table-cloth with the fingers of his right hand, *rat-a-tat-tat-tat-tat! rat-a-tat-tat-tat-tat!* Both continued these aids to thought for a long interval. They had been talking about the problem of Aunt Tessie for several days, and each day's discussion had ended with Henry finally saying, "Well, I've got to get back to the office."

Now there was complete silence, interrupted by the rattle of plates in the kitchen, and a crash which indicated that Jennie had caused another breakage. But they were so involved with their problem that they hardly noticed.

Suddenly Henry slammed his hand down on the table, as he did when he won at solitaire. The table teetered, and Annette looked up startled.

"I've got it!" he proclaimed. "I'll make her think she's doing me a favor."

His wife looked skeptical.

"This will really do it," he said. "It's this way. You know your Aunt Tessie's generous; I've often heard you and Miss Julie say so. Now, I'll tell her that we're being hurt by people saying that we are too mean to help her (I know, it will have to be done delicately), and I'll ask her, out of kindness, to protect me from being injured socially and in business—by accepting our invitation to come here and live."

"Well, you can try it. Maybe, if your plan works, you could persuade her to let us help her out without having her move here."

"I don't think she would accept money," he said. "That's why I don't even consider that side of it."

"I suppose not."

Henry was a man of action. "I'll go right over on my way to the office," he said. "Call up Mrs. Fuller, and tell her that I may be a little late."

Within two minutes he was on his way.

In the shelter of his own home, he had felt hopeful about his strategy: on the way to put it to the test, he quailed at the thought of the diminutive Miss Tessie's penetrating eye and tongue.

He found her finishing a meal of tea and bread. She was astonished to see him and was immediately on the defensive.

"Well, Mrs. Fisher," he said, cautiously resting his two hundred pounds on a slender chair, "Annette has been telling me that you weren't looking very well, and I thought I ought to come to see you."

Miss Tessie regarded him with cold unbelief.

"Hoo!" she said.

"And I've come to ask you to do me a favor."

She became more gracious. "I'll do anything I can," she said loftily.

"It's a rather hard thing to explain," Henry continued. "Charleston is a very strange place, ma'am. In some ways, that is. People always put the worst construction on everything."

"They'd do a heap better to mind their own business," Miss Tessie said sourly.

"But they won't. Now here's the way the thing stands. I've managed to make a place for myself in Charleston. I'm considered well-to-do—a little more well-to-do than I really am."

She gave a noncommittal nod.

"It's expected," Henry said, "that I should take care of those who are in any way connected with me."

"I'm not," Miss Tessie said, bristling.

"Well, not except by marriage." Henry smiled, to show that he did not presume to think himself one of the Gerards. "Now I don't like to say this, Mrs. Fisher, and I hope you'll pardon it, but you've—er—well—had a little difficulty lately. Your clients haven't given you sufficient engagements, and you find yourself temporarily embarrassed." He paused uneasily.

Miss Tessie quivered. "I don't thank any well-intentioned busybody for telling you that," she snapped.

"We've been worried about you."

"Hoo!"

He took his handkerchief and wiped his forehead.

"Now, then," he went on, "what happens? You find it necessary to look for other ways of earning a living, because you're too proud to be dependent, which is a fine thing. But they don't work out very well, and you find yourself—er—temporarily embarrassed."

"Well, you've said that twice," Miss Tessie said. "If you've come here to tell me that I haven't any money, you've wasted your time. I know it very well, and I don't want to discuss it with you or anyone else."

"I'm very sorry—I wouldn't injure your feelings for the world, ma'am." Henry felt angry. She made him feel impertinent. However, he went on with his story. "Now you see, ma'am, family pride works two ways. It isn't helping your niece and your grandniece and your nephews for people to say that your nephew-in-law is too mean to do something for you. In fact, it discredits your entire family. And, to put the matter on a personal plane, it's not good for a man who's trying to make his living. He needs all the good opinion he can get."

"What right has anybody to suppose that I'm to be supported by you?" Miss Tessie demanded. "I'll thank them to attend to their own affairs."

"Mrs. Fisher, that's the way of the world. Now, I wouldn't dream of offering to help you, ordinarily. Not that I wouldn't be glad to, but I know just how you feel about it. But my reputation will suffer if you don't allow me to, and I'm going to ask you, out of kindness to your own niece and out of feeling for your family, to do me a great favor. Come and stay with us until things are better with you."

Miss Tessie did not reply immediately, and Henry thought he could see a gleam of mockery in her eye; but she was discouraged and worried, and she was hungry. She could not deny that Henry was kind, both in offering her a home and in finding a loophole for her pride. She was inclined to give in.

"But what about Julie? You know that she has insulted me, and that we can't be there together."

"I think it will be some time before Miss Julie comes back from Chattanooga. I'm sure by that time you'll be on your feet again."

"You're very kind, Henry."

"Not at all." He persisted in his fiction. "You are doing us a favor. You are the one who is kind."

"Well, I'm going to accept your offer," Miss Tessie said.

"Annette and the children will be delighted to have you," Henry told her. "And the children need a good old-fashioned influence, you know."

"Perhaps so," Miss Tessie replied, drily. "I was about to say, Henry, that you will have to let me make my own conditions. For the sake of my own self-respect, I must pay my board—some of it, as much as I'm able—say five dollars a month."

"I don't like to accept it," Henry protested. "I've asked you to do us a favor."

Five dollars a month!

"Nobody will know it," Miss Tessie said. "It's just for my own satisfaction."

"Just as you please." Henry was delighted with his success, and was impatient to get away and tell Annette about it.

"I also want it understood that, whenever my sister wants to come back, you will tell me, so that I can go. Even Charleston won't expect you to take care of the two of us."

"Of course you'll do just as you please, Mrs. Fisher," he agreed. "Now about the arrangements: I'll have the drayman call whenever you wish it."

Miss Tessie thought the following Saturday would do, and Henry left to return to his office.

"She's coming," he told Annette by telephone, "—Saturday."

"God help us all," she said.

Henry felt that way, too; but the triumph of his strategy was gratifying.

Annette went promptly to the kitchen and had a talk with Jennie and Sarah.

"Mrs. Fisher is going to come to stay with us for a while," she announced.

Jennie drew a long breath. "Yes, muh," she said.

Sarah received the news calmly, but she looked sidewise at the mistress.

"I know you'll both have to put up with some trouble," Annette told them. "It may not be for very long, and I want you to be patient. If anything goes wrong, don't get huffy and walk out, that's all. I want to keep both of you as long as I can. I know you're satisfied here."

Jennie and Sarah promised to do their best and to remain faithful.

When their mistress had gone, Sarah laughed one of her quieter laughs.

"O-oh, Lawd!" She slapped her thigh. "This goin' ta be jis' like 1886 all over again. Miss Tessie is a earthquake all by 'eself. Gawd help you, chil'. You goin' ta have to wash that coffeepot three times every day Gawd send, and you better be careful, or we goin' ta have to pick you up in little pieces."

Jennie sucked her teeth.

"Miss Tessie Fisher can' get haughty with me," she boasted.

"You talk big," Sarah said. "Miss Tessie is a haughty ol' lady."

"Ain' none o' my concerns," Jennie insisted.

Miss Tessie, after Henry had left, sat down to think things over. She was bewildered by the suddenness of her own consent to the arrangement, and wondered if she had done the right thing. But there was a good deal of truth in what Henry had said. She *was* doing them a favor, and it *was* a privilege for them to have her in their house. That was undeniable. Of course, they *would* be difficult to get along with. They were a quarrelsome lot, and those nigger women would be just looking for a chance to show her that they didn't care to have her around. She would have to put the children in their place, promptly: they hadn't a particle of manners among the four of them.

Annette, with misgivings about the children, thoroughly warned them against actions that might annoy or humiliate their great-aunt. She gave them all the time-honored recommendations: to remember that it was a privilege to have a guest in one's house, that nothing must be done to make that guest uncomfortable, and that old age deserved special consideration. And they must behave particularly well while their Aunt Tessie was there, impressing her with the fact that she was welcome, and making their father proud of them.

Joe, who was fifteen and ready to fancy himself a man, said that he would keep out of the old lady's way as much as he could. Betsy, who was a bit of a prig, said that of course she would do everything she could to make Aunt Tessie feel welcome. James and George promised to be good.

Annette had Miss Julie's things moved from the extra bedroom into the storeroom at the back, and by Friday afternoon everything had been made ready for Miss Tessie's arrival.

Then there was nothing to do but wait. So Annette thought, until late in the afternoon a boy brought a special delivery letter. It was from Miss Julie.

When Annette had recovered from the shock she rushed to the telephone.

"Henry!" she fairly screamed into the mouthpiece. "Ma wants to come home next week."

Her husband's reply was brief and forceful.

"I just got the letter. She says Aunt Emma is much better, and she's going to leave Sunday. What can we do?"

"Well, we can't be made fools of," Henry said. "It would be enough to make us a laughingstock for the rest of our lives if we had to tell Miss Tessie that after all she couldn't come. And we'd have her to worry about all over again. Telegraph the old lady, and tell her just how things are. Ask her to stay there a little while longer, and tell her if it's not convenient for her to stay with the family any longer we'll be glad to send her enough money to rent a little place for herself."

"Ma will never forgive us," Annette twittered.

"What else can we do? Go ahead, send her the telegram, and we'll talk about it tonight."

Annette wrung her hands and wailed. She went to her usual recourse in difficult moments.

"Sarah, here's more trouble. Mrs. Sharp wants to come home right away."

"Do, Lawd!"

"Mr. O'Donnell says to telegraph her and tell her how things are, and ask her if she won't stay awhile longer in Chattanooga."

"She ain't goin' ta like that," Sarah said.

"That's just the point. What am I going to tell her so as to keep from hurting her feelings?"

"Her feelin's is very tender."

"I should say so," Annette exploded. "No matter what I do, there's bound to be trouble. But you know we can't ask Mrs. Fisher not to come, now that we've made all the arrangements. Her feelings are tender, too."

"It sho is a mess," Sarah declared.

"Can't you think of anything to say?"

"No, ma'am. This clean got me beat."

"Well, then, I'll have to put my mind to it." Annette was irritated.

She sat down at her desk and wrote a number of messages before she had one she thought brief and explicit enough, and yet tactful. Then she called Henry again.

"How does this sound?" she asked him. "'Aunt Tessie not well. Has come to stay with us until things are better. Can you stay in Chattanooga a bit longer? Love from all.'"

"That will have to do," Henry said.

She called the telegraph company, finally made the operator understand the address, the message itself, and the signature, and after notifying Sarah that the children were in her charge now, lay down and tried to sleep.

The situation was ridiculous, but that didn't make it any less painful; and Annette, who loved her mother, was distressed.

Especially in view of her mother's age, she hated to have any unpleasantness with her. By the time this situation ended, the poor thing might be on her deathbed. What was she going to do?

Of course, she could let Henry and his pride go to the devil, tell her mother to come, and let her Aunt Tessie take the consequences if she persisted in being foolish. But it was not so simple as all that. Annette was perhaps not very perceptive, but she could see on that troubled afternoon that the case had its paradoxical side: Miss Julie, of the two sisters, was the better fortified against the world, and Miss Tessie, with all her arrogance and hauteur, was relatively defenseless.

It was hard to choose between mother and aunt, but Annette made the decision.

If they were only sensible, and could get along, Henry might even be able to stand them both at once for a while. But as it was, it would have to be Aunt Tessie. Ma would just have to put up with it.

CHAPTER FIVE

BETSY AND THE LITTLE BOYS WERE EXCITED at having Miss Tessie come to live with them. They might have preferred their grandmother, but they had had her for years; now that she was away, having their mother's aunt was something new and untried.

Miss Julie had come to their new house under dramatic circumstances, but she had made little fuss about settling. She had gone to see about her things, packed her trunk and suitcase, and had them piled with the furniture on the wagon. When the wagon arrived, she let the men settle the furniture, and then she had unpacked the trunk and suitcase, put on her apron, and sat down on the piazza as if she had been there all her life.

Miss Tessie, however, stayed to see each single bit of furniture packed on the wagon, and then walked to the house ahead of it, carrying her coffeepot and her nursing kit. James and George were hopping up and down the piazza with impatience, and the instant they saw her, a block away, they shouted that she was coming.

Annette came downstairs and stood on the piazza; the boys raced down the street, expecting that their aunt would bend over and hug them the way their grandmother always had. But Miss Tessie didn't make any move of the kind.

"Good morning," she said. "Careful, now, don't bump into my bag. My thermometer is in it."

"We're glad you're coming to our house, Aunt Tessie," James said.

"Hoo! Very nice of you. I trust you won't regret it."

The boys looked a trifle puzzled by that.

"Aunt Tessie," George inquired, strolling along beside her, "have you got any silver paper?"

"No, indeed. I don't go round picking things up off the street, like a scavenger."

George looked disappointed, and said no more, and he and James marched a little ahead of Miss Tessie, rather like a brass band welcoming a returning hero, and much to her annoyance.

Annette was waiting at the street door.

"Well, Aunt Tessie, I'm so glad you've come." She put her arms around her aunt and kissed her cheek.

"Well, I've come, for better or worse."

"I hope you didn't mind the escort."

Miss Tessie grunted, and followed her niece up the piazza.

"Good morning, Aunt Tessie," Betsy greeted her.

"Good morning, Elizabeth," Miss Tessie said, looking her up and down from head to foot.

Sarah came up, smiling her pleasantest, and offered to take Miss Tessie's kit and coffeepot.

"No, thank you," Miss Tessie told her, with a stare.

"You can take your things off in my room," Annette said.

She led the way to the upper floor, where Miss Tessie put down her things. She removed her hat and put it on the sewing machine, took off her jacket and placed it on the back of a chair, and went to the mirror and straightened her hair. Then she stopped and stared at the two boys, who had followed them.

Annette, taking the hint, said, "Now, you boys go downstairs."

James and George obeyed. They went down the stairs very slowly, conscious that something was wrong.

"She didn't bring us anything," George said.

James considered the matter. "Maybe she has something in her trunk," he suggested, without conviction. "Let's go out and wait for the wagon."

Soon they saw the wagon coming at a snail's pace down Wentworth Street, and ran down the block to meet it. They could easily keep up with the wagon, and talk to the driver and Stevens, who was perched beside him.

"Why don't you drive faster?" James asked.

The drayman glanced humorously at him. "Ol' missus tell me to walk de horse," he said, "so her things wouldn' git shook up."

"We gots to do this with a lot of ceremony," Stevens said, grinning. "Don't you boys walk too heavy 'longside, now, or you'll shake things up." He guffawed, and the drayman joined him.

The wagon made a stately progress into the back yard, and Stevens and the driver dismounted, while the boys ran to tell Miss Tessie.

For the first time she regarded them with something like interest.

"Go right down and tell them not to touch a thing until I come," she commanded.

The little fellows clattered down the stairs and breathlessly repeated the orders.

"All right, boss," the drayman said. "Us'll wait. Stevens and me ain't got nothin' to do."

The little boys in the yard that backed up on the O'Donnells' mounted the fence and looked searchingly at the wagonload of furniture.

"Hey, James," Willie Robertson said. "Whatcha doin'?"

"Helping unload my Aunt Tessie's furniture."

Miss Tessie bustled out, followed by Annette.

"Hoo! Nothing like an audience," she remarked, staring at the Robertson boys, who quite impolitely stared back. She turned to the drayman. "Now, I want you to be just as careful moving my things in as you were moving them out. Just as I told you, I'm not going to have any rough handling of my furniture. Bring that dresser up first"—she pointed—"and I'll show you just where to put it."

She watched the men take the piece out of the wagon and hoist it to the piazza, and then preceded them up the stairs and showed them exactly where to place it. She supervised the moving in of the wardrobe, and of the bed, with the same care.

"You stay upstairs, Aunt Tessie, and let me watch them down here," Annette suggested.

"No, indeed," said her aunt. "I intend to watch every move they make. I know what they do to people's furniture when no one is looking."

"All right. I just thought it would save you some trouble. That's an awful lot of stair climbing."

"It's nothing for me." Miss Tessie was firm. "I never shirk any task that I consider necessary."

Annette yielded. She sat in a rocker while Miss Tessie directed the disposition of her treasures, and James and George rushed about, getting in the way, and Willie Robertson and his brother Ned stood by the wagon, announcing each new piece that was taken from the dray.

"That's the washstand," Willie said.

"There goes the rocking chair," he added as Stevens took it from the wagon and set it gingerly on the piazza, preparatory to moving it upstairs.

"There goes the mirror!" Ned shouted.

Miss Tessie went on with her superintending in pained dignity. Only when it came to her private chinaware did she lose her temper.

"There goes the slop jar!" Ned announced. "And the pot!"

The other children giggled, and the kitchen exploded.

Miss Tessie stopped short.

"Get away from here and mind your own affairs, you little ruffians!" she screamed. "You nasty little poor-white trash!"

A Negro voice, struggling against laughter, came from behind shutters, "Willie, Ned—you come back where you belong!" and the visitors unwillingly departed, scrambling over the fence.

"It's outrageous," Miss Tessie stormed. "And I'm amazed at you, Annette, smiling at such low vulgarity."

"They're only children. Don't pay any attention, Aunt Tessie."

Under other circumstances, Miss Tessie would probably have made a greater fuss—she did not like to let things hang in midair; but she was busy, and she returned to her task wrathfully muttering about low people who didn't keep their children in check.

Meanwhile Stevens and the drayman, each time they passed the kitchen, rolled their eyes at the women within, and Sarah and Jennie kept laughing silently in agony, while Annette was forced to look solemn.

At last the precious cargo was emptied from the wagon, and Miss Tessie had only the easel and the picture of Theodora to worry about.

"Those are to go in the front hall on the second floor," she told Stevens. "I'll trust you to put them down carefully."

"Yes'm, I'll be careful, Mis' Fisher." Stevens took them up in his arms with prodigious tenderness.

Miss Tessie went to the drayman. "You said two dollars was your charge." She handed him the money in small change.

"Thank you, missie."

Stevens reappeared.

"And here is a dollar for you," Miss Tessie said.

Stevens had not expected a payment; but in saying this he would have given the suggestion of presuming to do a favor. Torn between his sense of propriety and his awareness that it would be an insult to a white lady to refuse, he glanced at the mistress of the house to see if he should take the money.

Miss Tessie noticed the tiny delay in the holding out of his hand. "You needn't be high and mighty about it," she said. "I'm accustomed to paying for anything I ask to have done."

"Thank you very much, ma'am," Stevens said, bowing.

He walked into the kitchen with offended dignity to have a cup of coffee along with the drayman.

Annette sighed. Life with Aunt Tessie was not going to be a bed of roses. Miss Julie would have given Stevens a quarter or a half-dollar, and there would have been no misunderstanding whatever—Stevens comprehending that she took pleasure (however grudging) in rewarding him for the performance of an extra task, and Miss Julie understanding his hesitation and pooh-poohing it.

"She'll have the three of them ready to leave in a month," Annette reflected.

Miss Tessie said that she would go up and put her room in order.

"Wait a few minutes, Aunt Tessie, and rest yourself."

"Rest? Indeed! I don't need any rest, thank you."

"Let Sarah come up and help you."

"Thank you, I intend to take care of my room from the very beginning," said Miss Tessie with finality.

She went into the house, and the boys started toward the door too.

"Where are you going?" Annette asked.

"We're going up to see Aunt Tessie unpack her trunk," James said.

"You come right back here and stay with me. Or go back into the yard and play."

They hesitated.

"Come here," Annette told them. "Now, listen. You and George are not to go into your Aunt Tessie's room unless she calls you in. You hear me?"

George and James exchanged glances. This was not going to be the same as having Granny. Disconsolately, they went back to the yard, scuffing the dirt, their heads down.

"Maybe she'll bring the things down with her," James said. But he had lost belief in those presents.

Miss Tessie spent an hour or more arranging things to her taste before she went down to the kitchen to talk to Jennie on the proper care of her coffeepot and the correct way of boiling coffee in it, and then she returned to her room. The boys, whose hopes were not entirely dead, stood for a while at the foot of the stairs, waiting in case she should call them to get the things she had brought. But the wait was in vain. They heard Miss Tessie's footsteps for a few moments, and then the door was closed.

"Nothing doing," James said.

"Maybe she's gonna surprise us at dinnertime," George said. His father sometimes did.

"I don't know about that," James said.

"What are you boys doing here?" their mother asked.

"We thought maybe Aunt Tessie was going to call us," James said, embarrassed.

"Now, look here. You mustn't bother Aunt Tessie. Wait until she gets settled."

George finally broke down. "Didn't she bring us anything?"

"I don't know," Annette said. "People don't have to bring you things, you know."

"Granny always did."

"Well, Granny was different. Granny has always been with you; but your Aunt Tessie doesn't know you very well, and she hasn't always lived right with you, like Granny, and she doesn't understand about little boys. Now, run along and play."

The brothers wandered out once more, and sat on the joggling board.

"Maybe after she gets settled things will be different," James said. "Hoo!" He was pleased with his imitation, and repeated it; and George took it up. They leapt up and down on the joggling board at each repetition, until their mother heard and told them threateningly that she didn't want any mocking of their Aunt Tessie.

"And remember," she said, "Aunt Tessie is not deaf, like Granny. You don't want her to hear you, do you? That would hurt her feelings."

She was beginning to feel worn already.

At dinnertime, when Henry came down the street, James and George ran out to tell him that Miss Tessie had arrived.

"That's fine," their father said. "Is she all right?"

"She didn't bring us anything."

"She isn't settled yet," James said.

"That may take a little time." Henry was grave. "She's never lived with us before, you know."

"I guess she don't know about people, living by herself all the time like that."

"Very likely," Henry agreed.

Out in the kitchen, where the boys went to wash their hands before dinner, they received more advice.

"Wash 'em good," Sarah said. "Your Aunt Tessie ain' goin' ta stand for no dirty hands. You boys better toe the mark from now on."

George and James hurried to the table, and were in their seats by the time Henry had reached the dining-room door, where he stood to wait for Annette and Miss Tessie and Betsy.

"Maybe she's got them now," James said.

"I wonder what they'll be?" George said.

The others entered the dining room, Henry telling Miss Tessie how glad they were to have her, and standing behind her chair to show her that she was a very special guest.

"We're all very glad to have Aunt Tessie with us, aren't we?" he asked, looking around the table.

The three children (for Joe was late, as usual) said yes, they were. But the two little boys were disappointed over the presents that had failed to appear, and didn't feel half as happy about her arrival as in the morning.

"Maybe she isn't settled *yet*," James whispered.

"I don't like her," said George, who had abandoned all hope.

CHAPTER SIX

THE WEEK END WENT BY PEACEABLY ENOUGH, with the children behaving well and Miss Tessie seemingly satisfied with everything that was done for her; and Annette could have been content had it not been for the thought of Miss Julie.

Promptly Monday morning Miss Julie's letter came. With Miss Tessie present at breakfast, Annette couldn't in politeness read it, and she hardly knew what she was eating. She rushed out as soon as she decently could and opened the letter in the presence of Henry, who had delayed his departure until the worst could be known.

Without a word Annette handed him the note—the handwriting sloped more than was usual, indicating that Miss Julie had written under the pressure of strong feeling:

DEAR ANNETTE:

I got your telegram, and I am amazed, after all that has happened, that you could treat me in this fashion. I have been very much put out, telling them here that I have to stay on after all & for God knows how long. After all, they are not rich like you and Henry and it is a strain on them to have anyone else to feed, even if her wants are simple. I give them my allowance from Charlie, or most of it, which they are very unwilling to accept, but I have insisted.

I am not getting any younger, although God has spared me beyond threescore years and ten, and I had hoped to get back to Charleston to see my friends and grandchildren once more, at least for a little while before the end, whenever that may be. But I am *welcome* here, and will stay. I am not willing to come anywhere where my presence is liable to be *embarrassing*. I shall pray each night and morning for you to be happy with Tessie.

My love to you and Henry, and to my poor little grandchildren whom I may never see again.

YOUR MOTHER.

"Well, that's that," Henry said.

Annette wiped her eyes.

"I can't help it," Henry said. "Write to her and try to make her feel better. Explain to her that we'd be glad to get a place for her here in Charleston, but that that would mean that Miss Tessie would move out immediately, and we can't permit that to happen. And I'll write a letter to Howard and tell him that I insist on paying board for Miss Julie."

And there the matter rested.

Fortunately, Miss Tessie proved to be fairly easy to live with. She stayed in her room most of the time. James and George, prowling around softly in the hall, could hear her from time to time opening and shutting the drawers of the bureau, and wondered what on earth she could be doing. After three days, emboldened by growing familiarity, they knocked on the door.

"What do you want?" Miss Tessie asked, opening it.

"We want to come in and see you," James said.

"Hoo! Curiosity killed the cat. Well, come in if you like and see if everything suits you."

The boys accepted the invitation literally and stood there taking everything in: the articles lying on the bed, some wrapped in white tissue paper and others waiting to be wrapped; the neatness of everything, with not a single object out of place; and the almost complete emptiness of the top of the bureau, in contrast to Miss Julie's, which had always been heaped with a marvelous miscellany. It was a decidedly uninteresting room.

"Have you got a button bag?" George asked.

"Yes, I have. But I don't allow anyone to play with it."

"Granny always let us play with hers."

"I suppose you miss your Granny."

"She had mints," George said.

"I know she spoiled both of you," Miss Tessie answered. "Well, go on out now, since you've finished inspecting my room, and let me finish my wrapping."

Annette saw them coming out of the door.

"What were you doing?" she demanded.

"We were in Aunt Tessie's room," James said.

"Did she ask you to come in?"

"No, but we knocked first."

"Haven't I told you not to bother your Aunt Tessie?" Annette scolded. "Now, you leave her alone. Don't you ask her again to let you come in."

"When is Granny coming back?" George asked.

"I don't know. She's going to stay in Chattanooga awhile," Annette said grimly.

As indeed she was. Her next letter was plaintive, but dignified and offended too; she made no reference to coming back, as if that were a closed issue. And Emma's husband, with some protest, accepted Henry's offer.

"Thank God there's some sense in the Gerard family, even if it got in by marriage," Henry said.

Miss Tessie happened to be just outside the door when he said that. She came in challengingly.

Henry was embarrassed. He said, "I didn't mean anything personal, Mrs. Fisher. You know I've always admired the Gerards. And I apologize if I've hurt your feelings."

Miss Tessie looked straight at him.

"I'll accept your apology, *considering*," she said loftily, and swept out of the room.

Henry was pained and angry, but he smiled ruefully.

"I guess she's settled now," he said.

Little by little, Miss Tessie made a definite place for herself in the family. Accepting her place as a guest, she really outdid herself to get along with Henry and Annette and the children; and she made her occasional criticisms in an almost deferential manner. She appeared to enjoy her meals, and sitting out in the sun on any winter day that was fine. It was as if, having no occasion to take the upper hand in anything, she was quite willing to relinquish it.

She went to church by herself, did her chores at the cemetery regularly—finally accepting the suggestion that she go in the car with Wallace—and, as before, spent most of her time in her own room with the door closed.

And the only allusion she ever made to her circumstances was when she remarked that she ought to be getting some work soon so that she would be able to "do for herself."

Henry came to the conclusion that they had misjudged the old lady.

"Why, she's just like Miss Julie, except that she doesn't make so much racket. I can't understand where she got her reputation."

"Don't you go fooling yourself. You just remember the quarrel she had with Ma. Well, she's carried on like that all her life. You wait until something happens, and see."

Thanksgiving passed, and Christmas—Miss Tessie even consented to come down and watch the fireworks, although she declared that fireworks were not as good as they had been when she was younger—and still nothing happened to disturb the peace. Miss Julie was still in Chattanooga, smarting under the injury she had received, while Annette worried about her; but all else was serene. Only the coffeepot stood between them and complete security.

Now, Jennie was a good cook and a reliable woman, who always arrived promptly and did all her work and never gave any trouble. But she did have the fault of being a great breaker. It was a rare week in which those at the table did not hear something tinkle or crash in the kitchen. Henry and Annette had always put up with it, although Henry said sometimes that the china they bought to replace what Jennie broke would keep a kiln busy full time.

The coffeepot, therefore, gave Annette anxiety whenever she happened to think of it. Miss Tessie inspected the precious vessel regularly, to see that it was being properly cared for and that it had been well cleaned out. It was her theory that even a speck of brown in the pot would ruin the coffee.

"It's on my mind," Annette said to Henry.

"Why don't you look around and find some exactly like it?" Henry suggested. "Then, if anything happens, you can just substitute one. The old lady won't know the difference. Her sight's not very good."

Annette thought this might be a good idea. She and Sarah toured the stores trying to find a pot exactly like Miss Tessie's, but they failed; and there was no distinguishing mark on the white enamel which would have made it possible to trace the manufacturer.

Jennie complained that Sarah and Stevens teased her about the coffeepot and made her nervous about it.

And finally, one day late in January, she scorched the bottom of it.

She confessed the damage.

"Can't you scour it off?" Annette asked.

Jennie shook her head. "I done tried," she said mournfully.

"Well, then, I'll have to tell her about it. Jennie, I wish you'd be more careful." There was a trace of annoyance in Annette's voice, and she frowned.

"Coffeepots don't last fuhever," Jennie remonstrated.

"I suppose not." Annette looked at the brown shadow on the bottom of the pot, and shook her head.

"I can't understand how it burned," she said.

"The top of the stove git red-hot," Jennie explained.

Annette went wearily up the stairs to break the news. She knocked at her aunt's door.

"Come in," said Miss Tessie. She sounded cross.

Annette found her repacking her nurse's bag.

"Just in case there should be a call. I'm getting worried about that. It's those nigger nurses."

Annette clucked sympathetically and said nothing, remembering the trouble Miss Julie's remark had caused.

"It's taking the bread out of white nurses' mouths," Miss Tessie said fretfully. "And I can't for the life of me see what anybody wants with a colored nurse. Did you ever know one of them, nowadays, to do anything right?"

This was a bad atmosphere for the imparting of such news as Annette had, and she knew it.

"Well, they're just like children," she said. "Now there's Jennie. There never was a better darky. She's clean, and she's honest, and you can count on her to the last ditch. The only times she's ever had to stay away were because she was sick, and each time she sent somebody else to take her place. But even Jennie's far from perfect. She's a terrible breaker."

Miss Tessie started. "You don't mean she's cracked the enamel off my coffeepot?"

"Oh, no—nothing like that!" Annette tried to smile, as if there were something ridiculous in what had happened. "But I'm afraid it's not quite as white as it was when it was new. She's scorched a spot on the bottom of it."

Miss Tessie sighed. "You can't trust them with anything," she said. "Think of the trouble I had finding that coffeepot. The months I spent to get a proper one that would make coffee that was fit to drink. . . . Well, there's no use crying over spilt milk, I suppose."

"I'm sorry it happened, Aunt Tessie."

"That doesn't help any." There was a return of the old ungracious manner.

"If you can find a new one, I'll be glad to pay for it."

"That has nothing to do with it," Miss Tessie snapped. "It's the time and trouble."

Annette edged her way out of the room. The interview hadn't been as bad as she had expected. She would speak to Jennie again.

She did; and whether that had anything to do with the matter or not (that and the scolding Miss Tessie gave by indirection when she went to the kitchen) it was not a week later that Jennie dropped the pot and chipped several large flakes of enamel off it.

This time there was no softening the blow. Annette marched right in and told Miss Tessie about it.

Miss Tessie was at first sarcastically gracious about the accident. "Thank God it was no worse," she said. "Thank God it wasn't some of your precious china, instead of just a coffeepot of mine."

Annette was not in one of her more tactful moods that day.

"Well, after all, Aunt Tessie, don't you set more store by the coffeepots you pick out than is really necessary?" she asked. "After all, there really isn't such a difference, is there?"

"Well! Well! And now," Miss Tessie said to an imaginary audience, "now I'm told that I don't know good coffee from bad, and that I'm just a silly old woman making a fuss about my coffeepot! I must say, Annette, I like your impertinence."

"I didn't say anything of the kind, Aunt Tessie."

Miss Tessie drew herself up. "I'll thank you not to call me a liar," she said coldly. "It's bad enough to let your cook smash my coffeepot that I spent months to find, without coming into my room and abusing me. After all, I'm an old lady, and I deserve a little respect."

"Aunt Tessie, you're making a fuss about nothing. I came in to tell you that your coffeepot had been damaged, and nothing else. I'm sorry about it, and I wish it had never happened. God knows I worried enough about it. If it had been a sick child I couldn't have been more concerned."

"Well, don't say anything more about it," Miss Tessie snapped. "It's all very well. I know that I have nothing to do, and that I'm not working for my own living, and that my time is worth nothing. Of course, as you say, I can go around for months until I find the coffeepot I want. You don't have to tell me that I'm dependent on your hospitality."

"I never once suggested such a thing." Annette was almost maddened by the way her aunt twisted things about to suit herself. "I've never made you feel anything but welcome here, and everyone has tried to please you and to make you happy. I'm surprised that you should turn on me like this."

Miss Tessie was angry enough, but some of the fire had gone out of her. She was like a lioness grown old.

"Let's not discuss it any more," she said. "I'll try to find a new one."

Annette left her; but as she was closing the door she heard Miss Tessie burst into sobs. She returned.

"Aunt Tessie, you mustn't go on like this," she said. "It's terribly distressing."

Miss Tessie continued to sob. "No one cares whether I live or die," she wailed. "It doesn't matter to anyone that I'm a poor widow, with all my children dead and no one to comfort me, and everybody going around smashing my things right and left."

Annette stood there silent, unable to speak a word in her amazement. Why, her aunt was in her second childhood: she was acting just like a three-year-old.

"It won't last long," Miss Tessie continued. "God isn't going to let me go on very long. He'll take me away from all this. Thy will be done!" she ejaculated fervently.

"Aunt Tessie, you must calm yourself."

The older woman paid no attention, but went on crying. "Everything is a conspiracy to humiliate me," she sobbed. "Just because I'm alone in the world, with no one to defend me, everyone tries to take advantage of my good nature."

Annette wondered how her mother had stood it for a year. She tried once more:

"Aunt Tessie, you're overwrought about something. Try to calm down now, and you'll feel better."

"I didn't ask you to come in here! Get out of my room and leave me alone," Miss Tessie shouted.

Annette fled. "She's raving crazy! What am I going to do now?" she thought.

Miss Tessie recovered from her fit, however, and came down to supper that night quite cheerful. No one dared to mention the coffeepot, and as tea was served, there was no occasion to bring up the subject. Next morning Henry took his life in his hands and told her that she might buy all the coffeepots she wanted to try and charge them to him.

"You think money can do everything," Miss Tessie said.

"You can't do anything without it," Henry replied.

Miss Tessie said she didn't intend to be insulted, and went upstairs.

"There's trouble coming from that quarter," Henry said, cheerlessly.

However, Miss Tessie searched around and finally found a coffeepot that would do. She said she wasn't going to trust it to any servant; she was going to get out her little gas ring and rubber tubing and make her own coffee up in her room, where she could be sure it was properly done. And thus the first crisis in her life with the O'Donnells was passed.

The second crisis came right upon the heels of the first.

Every day, as she had done for years, Miss Tessie put something fresh and green—flowers, or twigs—before the picture of

Theodora, which stood by the window in the second-floor hall, and stood before it to say a prayer. Annette said it was idolatry, but Henry said it was pathetic. It had annoyed him at first to have the ugly ungainly easel and the picture in such full view, but he had become used to it and hadn't intended to make any fuss about it anyway. You had to stand some things.

Usually Miss Tessie stopped to perform her rite just before she came down to breakfast. It was on St. Valentine's Day that she came down to the table in a fury.

"Henry," she said, "I don't intend to stand for this."

"For what, Mrs. Fisher?"

"Desecration!" Miss Tessie shouted. She began to weep out of sheer helpless rage.

"What in the devil has happened?" Henry threw down his napkin and sprang to his feet. "Tell us what it is!"

Joe turned very red.

"I did it, Papa," he said. "It was only a joke. I didn't mean any harm."

"What did you do?" Henry demanded.

Miss Tessie continued to sob.

Joe tried to bring off a smile but couldn't.

"I pasted a valentine over the picture of Theodora in the hall," he confessed.

"A vile, disgusting, ugly picture!" Miss Tessie sobbed. "A disgusting comic valentine over the picture of my sainted daughter!"

"Joe, come upstairs," Henry said.

Joe followed him, and the younger children held their breaths.

"I'm terribly sorry, Aunt Tessie," Annette said. "Joe will be properly punished."

Stricken, Miss Tessie sat weeping, and her hands shook. Even the children felt terribly sorry for her, and George got out of his chair and went around and put his arms around her thin old body.

"Children don't think when they do these cruel things," Annette said. "Joe will never do such a thing again."

Henry returned to the table, looking pale and upset, and tried to continue eating his breakfast.

"Miss Tessie, I think we all owe you an apology," he said. "This is disgraceful, and we are all sorry for it."

Miss Tessie's feelings were too strong for her. She rose from the table and went upstairs.

"I told Joe that when he had apologized to his aunt, he could leave his room and come downstairs," Henry said. "I gave him a good tanning. He really deserved it, you know. It was a brutal thing to do."

"Yes, he deserved it," Annette agreed.

"It's a terrible thing to have to whip a boy as big as that," Henry said.

Joe came downstairs looking very subdued.

"Did you do as I told you?" his father asked.

"Yes, sir, I did."

"Well, then, sit down and eat some breakfast."

The boy slunk into his chair.

"Now, I'm not going to mention this again," Henry said. "But I hope you realize, Joe, that you've been a coward and a fool. You've wounded the feelings of an old lady by defacing the picture of a dead child. I hope you'll never do anything as contemptible as that again as long as you live."

Joe said, of course, that he wouldn't, and that he hadn't realized that Aunt Tessie would be so deeply hurt. But the damage had been done. It was a week before Miss Tessie would come downstairs to meals.

CHAPTER SEVEN

MISS TESSIE INSISTED ON A STRICT FAST DURING LENT, and followed her rigorous program with her peculiar tenacity. This did not improve her disposition generally; but she kept a good deal to herself, and gave little trouble aside from occasional grumblings at the noise of the children and her usual belittling remarks whenever anything or anybody was spoken of at the table.

"Maybe," Henry said, "a big family was what she needed. It sort of swallows her up."

But Miss Tessie had her problems. There was, for instance, the little gas burner that she used in her room. She could never be certain that she had put it out properly, and would make two or even three trips back to her room to make sure that she had. Sometimes these trips interrupted dinner.

Another thing of which the family knew nothing troubled Miss Tessie. She had devised a certain order in which to place the carefully wrapped articles in her bureau drawers, and she was never easy if she was in any doubt as to whether she had left them in that order. As there were many of these trifles, great and small, it sometimes required a good deal of time to unwrap similar-looking bundles in order to make sure that they were correctly arranged.

This was one of the reasons she was so constantly in her own room.

And then there was the matter of confession.

Miss Tessie had always been punctilious about her confessions. She regularly went over the commandments and the preparation for confessions printed in one of her prayer books, and examined her conscience down to the proverbial jot and tittle. But even then she was dissatisfied. For years she had been disturbed by scruples, which would cause her to return to the confessional, sometimes at the end of the very line she had stood in before—a thing that had brought her scoldings from the priest and had irritated Miss Julie, who was satisfied if she had done her best to remember everything.

In that first winter at the O'Donnells', Miss Tessie had become more scrupulous than ever. Fearing she would be scolded if she returned to the same confessor, she relieved her uneasiness by going to another confessor at another church, so that some Saturday afternoons she spent hours getting herself shriven. The worst of this was that she did not dare to tell how short a time it had been since her last confession, and she was doubly disturbed by the thought that this untruth had invalidated the confession that she had just made. When she was unable to convince herself that she had really made one proper confession out of all three or four, she refrained from going to communion the next morning, and was unhappy over that.

With all these varieties of the *folie de doute,* Miss Tessie's life was one of disquiet, and she commenced during her long Lenten rigors to look as thin and pallid as before she had come to the O'Donnells. And she noticed with alarm that her fingers were becoming even stiffer. The prayers to St. James and the daily flexings (which were torture now) did no good, and her attempts at sewing and darning brought her acute agony.

She was too busy with all these concealments and worries to be bothered by anything else, and this made the family conclude that her disposition had improved. She gave no evidence of feeble health, except that she wore her shawl more faithfully, and kept as close to the stove or the fireplace as she could.

In addition to her other activities, she went regularly every two weeks to tend her cemetery plot, attended by the good-natured Wallace. He would return punctually at the end of an hour, or two hours, or whatever period of time Miss Tessie commanded, and he never paid the slightest attention to her complaints about rough roads, or to the brusqueness with which she put aside all his attempts to be helpful.

It was just by chance that her visit on a particular day in April came after she had, for the first time in months, lost her temper and been difficult. The old laundress, Aurelia, had scorched one of her pillowcases—a birthday gift from her late husband. They were patched and mended and thin, but Miss Tessie cherished them dearly, and when she came across that brown mark in the telltale shape of the iron, she charged into Annette's room.

"Look at this!" she demanded, her eyes flaming.

Annette, who knew the history of the pillowcases, said that it was too bad.

This maddening understatement was all Miss Tessie needed.

"Too bad!" she bleated. "Too bad! Yes, indeed, it is too bad when no one takes the slightest care of anything! I never saw such a shiftless lot of people in my life! I want you to remember that these pillowcases are sacred! Yes, sacred! They were given to me by my blessed husband before he died. And you let a common nigger washwoman burn my sacred relics as if they were any old rags!"

"Why, Aunt Tessie, you don't think I encouraged her to do it, do you?"

"How do I know you didn't? Everyone tries to make me as miserable as possible, breaking all my coffeepots and pasting vulgar pictures over the picture of my daughter!"

Annette had no more idea of how to deal with this third tantrum than she had with the others. She repeated that she was sorry, and added that Miss Tessie was overwrought and did not know what she was saying.

"You might as well say what you mean," Miss Tessie shouted. "Go ahead, say I'm crazy! That's what you tell all your friends, and the children and the servants! I hear you laughing at me! You think I'm deaf, perhaps, but I'm not. No, indeed! I hear all the gibes and jokes, every one of them!"

The fit ended as usual, with Annette leaving abruptly and Miss Tessie bursting into sobs, and being very subdued that evening at supper.

Next morning, as though nothing had happened, she came down to breakfast. When she had finished she went up to her room, spent an hour rewrapping her possessions in tissue paper, and brushed her clothes. Then she got ready for her trip to the cemetery. She got out her gaiters, a coarse dress and her sunbonnet, and took her canvas work gloves. Then she fetched the tools from the storeroom, somewhat ostentatiously indicating that she intended to take the streetcar, as she had formerly done.

"Aunt Tessie, you're not going to ride in the trolley when Wallace is right here with the car?" Annette asked.

"I don't want anybody put out for me," said Miss Tessie, nursing her pride.

"Of course, you'll go in the car. Sarah!"

Sarah bustled in.

"Tell Wallace to bring the car around to take Mrs. Fisher to the cemetery."

"Yessum."

Miss Tessie was relieved. She had not intended to humble herself by asking for the use of their car, after they had let the laundress burn her precious pillowcase; but it was difficult to carry all those garden tools in the trolley. Besides, she ought to remember that she had to husband her energy for her work. She could never tell when she would be called on a nursing case.

Wallace had the big Rambler out front as she reached the piazza. In his most deferential manner, he installed her in the tonneau, and they were off.

He drove swiftly and smoothly, and it took only a few minutes to reach the gates of the cemetery. When they entered, he got out without even stopping to mop his forehead and helped Miss Tessie out of the car. He fished the tools from the front, followed her to her lot, opened the little iron wicket, and stacked the tools neatly inside the fence. Then he went to fill the watering pot, returned with it, and waited respectfully for instructions. He had learned from experience just how to get along with Miss Tessie.

"Thank you, Wallace," the old lady said in her hooting voice. "Call for me at twelve. That will be just an hour and a half."

Wallace lifted his cap and got into the car and drove off.

Miss Tessie, after putting on her sunbonnet and gaiters, said her usual long prayers beside the graves. She didn't really pray for her husband and children, for she was absolutely certain that all were in heaven. She prayed to them to intercede for her. And then she set to work. There was such a lot to be done.

After pottering about briskly for half an hour, she realized that she did not feel entirely well. Strange that she should become so tired after a few minutes' work. . . . She put down the tools and sat on the coping of her husband's grave, leaning against one of the ornamental urns.

[229]

The day was particularly beautiful. The sky was full of tumbling white clouds. The breeze was gentle; it just tinkled the dry leaves of the great live oaks, and swayed the Spanish moss ever so gently. Flies and wasps buzzed lazily. The gardener had been at work trimming the grass, and it smelled fresh and springlike and sweet. The air of spring brought back to Miss Tessie many, many remembered things.

The stillness, the peace, her memories and her fatigue brought the tears to her eyes. After a while she dried them and said a brief prayer to the Blessed Mother. She nodded a bit . . .

All at once she was aware that a tall, black-robed figure was standing over her—a lady. And the tall lady looked steadily at her. There was something uncanny about that stare. Then she said in a soft, sweet voice:

"Daughter, why are you crying?"

Miss Tessie regarded her haughtily. "That doesn't concern you, does it? Go away and leave me to mourn my dead."

The tall lady in black ignored her rudeness, and smiled a kind, sweet smile; a flashing smile.

"Don't cry, my daughter," she urged.

Miss Tessie looked again, and the serene lovely face made her ashamed of her ill nature and bad manners. She stared, and the lovely face became even more gentle and compassionate.

"I understand your sorrow," said the beautiful stranger, "because I, too, am a mother of sorrows."

Her face and her tone of voice made a strange impression upon Miss Tessie. And then, more wonderful still, the unknown lady drew aside the folds of her black robe and pointed to the left side of her breast. Miss Tessie gave a little cry.

The lady touched her softly on the shoulder and said, "Be gentle and kind." And with that she vanished.

As the vision faded, Miss Tessie saw the tall figure of Wallace standing beside her, cap in hand, waiting, with a curious look on his shiny face that was almost as black as his broadcloth uniform. At first she couldn't speak. Her tongue felt heavy and thick, and she couldn't seem to get up. She had to motion to him to help her. He raised her to her feet, and almost carrying her, got her into the car. Then he went to get her a drink of water from the faucet. He gathered up her tools and her shoes and hat and stowed them in the front.

If Wallace had been less in awe of the old lady he would have offered to take her to the doctor. All he dared do was drive home as rapidly as the streets would permit.

Miss Tessie lay back against the cushions. She felt terribly weak and shaken and confused. When they reached the front gate, she was trembling a bit still. She insisted that she was all right, gave Wallace the usual dime, declared that she could mount the stairs herself, and dismissed him. Then she tottered up to her room.

Wallace left the car where it was: he had to call for his mistress within half an hour. He went to the kitchen to get a drink of water and to tell Sarah and Jennie about what he had seen. Sarah was not there; he had to content himself with an audience of one. But he didn't blurt it all out. He knew the value of a story better than that. He took a drink of water and asked Jennie how she was.

"So-so," Jennie answered.

"I jis' bring Mis' Fisher back from the graveya'd," Wallace said.

"You all in one piece?"

Wallace grinned. "Me and Mis' Fisher git along all right," he boasted. "I ain' have no trouble with 'em."

"You talk big," Jennie said. "Mis' Fisher goin' ta slap you down when you ain' lookin'."

"Mis' Fisher don' look to me like 'e goin' ta slap anybody down. 'E sick."

"Where you put 'em?"

"'E go upstairs," Wallace said. "'E ain't very sick, but 'e act funny."

He could see that Jennie's curiosity was at the bursting point, and he waited a moment for greater effect.

"I leave 'em at the cemetery," he went on, "and then I go back at twelve o'clock. 'E sittin' on the edge of the grave, leanin' back against one them little jardeeneers. I see 'e ain't done no work on the graves. 'E sleepin'. I wait there for a minute or two, and then 'e open 'e eyes. An' 'e can't git up. I have to help 'em."

" 'E musta have a fit," Jennie said.

"I'll tell Miss Annette when I goes to fetch 'em."

"You better be careful what you say. Mis' Fisher is haughty."

"I ain' forgit that; but I got to tell Miss Annette—'e be mad if I don't."

"All right, you go ahead," Jennie muttered, forebodingly. "If it was me, I wouldn't give no time to 'em."

But Wallace determined that he would tell Miss Nettie. He would even go a little farther, and ask her not to suggest that he had said anything about it.

Miss Tessie, little by little, shook off the feeling of confusion that had overpowered her. She changed her clothing slowly, and washed her face in cold water; and then, somewhat shaken but stronger, she sat in the piazza rocker.

And then, like a burst of light, making her almost dizzy, the truth swept over her.

She had had a vision of the Blessed Mother! Hadn't she said, "I, too, am a 'mother of sorrows'?" Her own thought! Who else could have known that? And the wounded Sacred Heart!

"God forgive me, I was rude to her," Miss Tessie thought. "I said, 'What concern of yours is it?' And yet she stayed there and comforted me."

All the frustrations and disappointments of Miss Tessie's bitter life suddenly became trifles to her. They had earned her this rich reward. It was worth it.

She reentered her room, and knelt before the image of the Blessed Mother to thank her and to praise God for the great favor she had been shown; and to ask guidance. For she didn't know what she ought to do next, or what status such a vision gave the person who had experienced it. Not to tell would seem ungrateful, and yet there might be presumption there. And was it proper for her to discuss the vision with Father Schmidt? That was what the saints of whom she knew had done—told their confessors. And how was she to tell him about it?

For a moment she had a doubt. Could it have been a dream? But then she recalled how Wallace had looked at her. The simple, ignorant Negro chauffeur had been awestruck. Something about her must have made him stare at her like that—an effulgence, an aureole.

Miss Tessie became very excited. She walked up and down the piazza. She sat down again. She prayed. She racked her brain for stories of apparitions, of saints, of the Beatific Vision. She could hear people discussing it in hushed voices—how the Blessed Virgin had actually appeared to her, Therese Gerard, in broad daylight, and had spoken words of consolation for her grief!

"Aunt Tessie, are you all right?" Annette asked, coming out onto the piazza. She was still wearing her hat.

"Of course I'm all right. What do you mean?" Miss Tessie snapped.

"Wallace said he thought you looked unwell while you were at the cemetery," Annette explained, breaking her promise to Wallace without even giving it a thought.

Miss Tessie's heart sank. Wallace hadn't been really awestruck or impressed! He had thought she was sick! She looked at her niece's healthy face, and reality overwhelmed her. Tell Annette and the family? She couldn't—they would laugh at her if she did! She made a note to settle the Negro's account at the earliest opportunity and clutched at the first explanation.

"Wallace is a fool," she said sharply. "I was asleep, and it just shocked me to find Wallace standing there when I opened my eyes. I'm perfectly well."

Annette looked closely at her. "You want to take good care of yourself, now that the hot weather is coming on," she said.

"Thank you," her aunt replied.

Annette flushed slightly and went inside.

Miss Tessie remained in her chair, suddenly heartsick. She could never tell them, never. And all her life she had longed for some distinction, some recognition of her worth!

Her stomach growled, and her spiritual mood was dashed. She was hungry. Not a very holy thought. She tried to put it out of her mind, but she smelled meat roasting and couldn't. And as it was just one o'clock, she had another hour before dinner.

To drive such a worldly thing as dinner out of her consciousness, she lay down and tried to take a nap, but it was of no use, she decided after a few minutes of lying wide awake and staring at the ceiling. She got up again and tried to read her prayer book, but she was too distracted between her vision and her longing for dinner.

When, after a troubled three-quarters of an hour, she went down to dinner, she ate in entire abstraction, replying curtly to inquiries about her health. As soon as she decently could, she retreated to her room and wrestled with her new problems.

Should she go to Father Schmidt for advice? or Father Dodd? She concluded that it was her duty to see a confessor immediately; but she had read about confessors who had been very harsh to penitents claiming mystical experience. And she couldn't bear to think of being scolded for presumption.

CHAPTER EIGHT

SEVERAL DAYS PASSED, and Miss Tessie's state of uncertainty had not yet yielded to that delightful feeling of pride and joy she had experienced immediately after her vision. The picture of the delight that would come to her when her secret was revealed, and she received the notice and deference she had longed for all her life, had been considerably dulled.

Of the vision as a vision she had no doubt. She was sure of its authenticity. But she had spoiled the credibility of the story by that fatal admission that she had been asleep. She couldn't very well turn around now and say, "I said I was asleep because I wanted to be sure, but what really happened was . . ." They'd say she was imagining things, was becoming old and foolish. She could just imagine them, Annette and Henry and those they told about it, smiling tolerantly to her face and laughing maliciously behind her back. . . . And if she waited too long to tell them it would be too late. Everyone would say, "Why did she keep this to herself so long?"

So Miss Tessie hugged her secret to herself, without deriving much joy from it. She decided to wait until it occurred again. If God once more sent her such a sign, there would surely be no doubt about revealing it.

This state of indecision made her rather ill-tempered, and even a little contemptuous of George's preparation for making his first communion. That seemed, in the face of her vision, rather like a trifle.

Meanwhile, Henry and Annette had conspired about the cemetery plot. It worried Annette to think of Miss Tessie going there and working in the hot weather, but there was no way to stop her. Therefore, she persuaded Henry to pay to have the graves taken care of—not perfectly, for that would arouse the old lady's suspicions, and she had always forbidden any stranger to touch her plot. But they arranged to have the heavier weeding and raking done, so that there would be little for Miss Tessie to do.

And they hoped she wouldn't notice it.

When Miss Tessie returned to the cemetery for her regular visit—a specially important one, for it would soon be Memorial Day—she was surprised to find the graves so neat. Puzzled, she worked a bit with the clippers and trowel and stripped away a few sprigs of ivy that had turned brown. And then a remarkable thought struck her. It almost stunned her.

This was a miracle, too. She saw it clearly now. God in His infinite goodness, most likely upon the intercession of the

Blessed Mother, had taken pity upon her age and stiffness and had kept the graves clean and neat. It was after all a very small thing for Him to do.

Of course, this second miracle proved the first and removed all doubts from her mind. In the hope that the vision would be repeated, she sat as before on the coping, leaning against the urn. But no beautiful lady in black appeared. She was disappointed, and then she seemed to understand, by some mysterious means, that the vision had not been repeated because she had been ungrateful, and had not glorified God by telling about it. To do that was now very clearly her duty. That day at the dinner table she would tell them all, hard as it might be to convince such unbelievers and scoffers.

When she looked at the well fed, worldly face of her nephew-in-law, and the bright, innocent faces of the children, and what she was pleased to call Annette's empty features, she saw how difficult it was going to be to tell them of the miraculous occurrences. She tried to bring the matter up casually.

"I have just had a most peculiar experience," she said, when everyone had been served and they were busily eating.

Annette looked up and asked politely what it was.

"You know, I have not been to my plot at the cemetery in two weeks," Miss Tessie said. "Well, when I went there today, I was amazed to see that it had not become overgrown or disorderly. I was mystified."

"Very peculiar," Henry murmured, wondering if this might be the prelude to a fuss about his interference.

"I came to a remarkable conclusion about it," Miss Tessie continued. "But first I must tell you something you all are going to think is very strange. You remember the last day I was at the cemetery with the car, and Wallace thought I had been sick? Well, I said that I had been asleep. But I hadn't."

She looked around to see how her story was received, and was satisfied with the attention.

"I was resting for a moment, and I had been feeling very sad about the loss of my dear ones."

Henry sighed, but Miss Tessie did not notice.

"It was very still," she said. "Suddenly I was aware of a tall figure in black beside me. A woman. And she said 'Why do you weep, my daughter?'

" 'You mind your own affairs,' said I, 'and leave me to mourn my dead.' "

Henry repressed a chuckle, and pretended to cough.

"She didn't seem to pay any attention to what I had said. She just smiled at me, and said, 'I can understand your sorrow, my child, for I too am a mother of sorrows.' And then she disappeared.

"Now, who do you suppose it was?" she concluded, looking triumphantly around.

"Wallace," James said.

Miss Tessie looked at him with annihilation in her eye. "Have the goodness to hold your tongue, child," she said loftily. "Wallace, indeed! Do you know what you're saying?"

"James, be quiet," Henry said.

"It was the Blessed Mother," Miss Tessie said, triumphantly.

Henry and Annette looked embarrassed.

"Well, that certainly was a remarkable vision," Annette said. "Or dream."

"Dream! Hoo!" Miss Tessie was indignant. "I tell you it was the Blessed Mother, as real as flesh and blood! She opened the left side of her robe, and I saw the bleeding Sacred Heart. That accounts for the other miracle."

"What was that, Aunt Tessie?"

"Why, don't you see? I haven't taken care of the graves for weeks, and yet they weren't grown over a bit! How do you suppose that happened, if it wasn't by the grace of God Himself?"

Her cheeks were flushed, and her eyes were bright.

Annette was disturbed. "I think you ought to discuss it with Father Schmidt," she said, hoping to bring the painful scene to an end. She was afraid the children would burst out in disastrous laughter at any moment.

Miss Tessie said no more. She was cast down by this calm reception of her great experience, and a trifle angry, too; but, after all, they were worldlings, and could not be expected to believe. Their religion—Henry, of course, had none at all—was just a mere show. She must try to be patient. She was angry, however, when Annette suggested after dinner that she plan to go to the mountains with them.

"No, thank you. You don't catch me going to any godless place with no church within miles and miles! Indeed! Hoo!"

She left the dining room, and Henry raised his eyebrows and looked at Annette.

"I don't feel right about this," Annette said.

"It's rich," Henry said. "Think of the old soul believing that she saw the Blessed Virgin and taking Wallace for her!" He laughed softly. "Why, the thing's plain as day. Black robe—black uniform. Standing right over her, the way Wallace said he was doing. And the miracle of the graves being taken care of!"

"I'm really afraid her mind is affected."

"What do you mean by 'affected'?" he asked. "You'd better watch her. You don't want her trying to fly down from the third floor or anything like that."

But Miss Tessie merely went out on the piazza to sit down and think. She was agitated; a nervous feeling had succeeded the calm she had felt after she had told her remarkable story. She had not expected them to be impressed, really; and yet she was disappointed that not one of the family, not even Betsy, a communicant, had shown the faintest belief in her vision. She sat and thought about it and wondered what to do.

"Of course, it was a test of my own faith," she reasoned. "The Lord wanted to see whether the unbelief of other people would have any effect upon me . . ." But that did not satisfy her.

"I'll go over to church and kneel before the statue of our Blessed Mother," she resolved. "Perhaps God will send me a sign."

She dressed hastily, made sure the gas stove was out, and went downstairs, tiptoeing past her niece's room, for she was overcome by a sudden conviction that if Annette knew where she was going she would ridicule her, or try to keep her from going. She hurried out the front door and up the street, her heart beating violently. It did not quiet down until she had got into church. She knelt and prayed a long while before the little side altar devoted to the Blessed Mother. In that atmosphere she left convinced that her vision had been a true one; but there was no other sign, and she felt that she had been mistaken in thinking that God had wanted her to tell of the wonderful thing that had happened to her. No, indeed! She would wait. For, somehow, she knew that she was being tested.

On Memorial Day, when she placed a fresh Confederate flag on her husband's grave, she had a feeling that something was going to happen; but it did not. She went home badly disappointed, and the tension of not knowing what course to pursue mounted in her, and made her very irritable. A few days later the eruption came.

They were at dinner, and Henry was talking to Annette about getting ready for the trip to the country; and then he turned and said to Miss Tessie:

"Mrs. Fisher, don't you want to reconsider about going away? I'm sure you could get a dispensation, couldn't you?"

She was about to reply when James said:

"Aunt Tessie wants to stay here in town so she can see the Blessed Virgin again."

Miss Tessie's face flamed. She put down her fork with a clang.

"Who has been ridiculing me?" she demanded, her voice rising very high. "Who has been teaching these innocent children to make fun of me?"

"James, leave the table," his father said. "Get down, now, and go outside until you can be a gentleman."

The tears started into the boy's eyes. "I didn't mean any harm," he mumbled.

"Do as I tell you!"

Sobbing, James ran out of the room.

"Now, Mrs. Fisher," Henry said, "you know no one has been ridiculing you. I've punished the boy for being impertinent."

Miss Tessie's face became even redder.

"I wonder God doesn't visit His wrath upon you, Henry O'Donnell!" she stormed. "Aren't you afraid to scandalize innocent children with ridicule of holy things?"

Henry flushed, but that was all. "Mrs. Fisher, I swear the child never heard anything of the kind from me," he protested.

"I wouldn't believe you if you swore from now until the day of judgment," Miss Tessie said. "I'm not as much of a fool as I look."

"Then you are practically calling me a liar. Is that it?"

Henry's eyes narrowed in their characteristic way, and Betsy and Annette put down their forks and waited, breathless. Miss Tessie was about to retort bitterly and tellingly; but Annette, with unusual readiness, changed the course of the discussion:

"Aunt Tessie, I think you are the one who's giving scandal. You pay so much devotion to the Blessed Mother—do you suppose she wants prayers from anyone who has such a temper?"

Miss Tessie took a deep breath. "Why, I never—" Then she subsided, and without a word she left the table and went upstairs; her anger quickly ended.

It was true! It was true! That vision had been a warning to her. She had been so puffed up with pride that she hadn't been able to see the real meaning of it! Why, even during the vision she had been rude to the Blessed Mother. And hadn't She said, "Be gentle and kind"? That was the part she had forgotten.

"God forgive me, and I'll try to do better!" Poor Miss Tessie, full of contrition, descended the stairs and returned to the dining room. She sat down in her place and said: "Henry, I beg your pardon."

Henry was painfully embarrassed. "Why, bless your heart, Mrs. Fisher, these little tiffs don't matter, you know. They happen in every family."

"I wish you would call James in. I don't want him to be punished. I'm sure he didn't mean any harm."

"Very well." Henry motioned to Annette, who rang for Sarah.

"Sarah, tell James he may come back in," Annette said.

James reappeared with a tear-stained face and slid miserably into his chair.

"James"—Miss Tessie carried her humility as far as she possibly could—"I'm sorry I made a fuss and got you into trouble. Don't be angry with your old aunt, now, eh?" And she gave him what she meant for a pleasant smile.

James gulped and looked uneasily from his father to his mother. George stared.

"That's very good of your Aunt Tessie, after you've been so rude to her," Annette said. "Tell her you're sorry you were so impolite."

"I'm sorry." James flushed wretchedly.

"Can he eat now?" George asked.

"I suppose so." Annette smiled.

Miss Tessie tried to smile again, but it was a feeble effort.

Dinner was over, and the children had gone out. Miss Tessie went into the yard, where James was playing baseball with George. She called the boys to her, and when they came wonderingly up, she held out a dime.

"How would you boys like to get some ice cream later when the man comes around?" she asked.

"We'd like that fine," James said, taking the dime. "Thank you, Aunt Tessie."

"Thank you, Aunt Tessie," George echoed.

Miss Tessie was not quite sure that she liked the look on their faces, but she was pleased with herself. She was being gentle and kind and humble. She went back upstairs very happily, leaving two very skeptical small boys.

"You know," James said, "I think she's nutty."

"Sho is a heavy case," George said.

James looked at the dime again.

"Granny always gave us coppers," he remarked, thoughtfully. "Come on, George, le's play ball again."

"My turn to bat," George said.

But that was only the feeble beginning of Miss Tessie's attempts to be humble. She had never in her life, by her own claim, done anything by halves, and this was not a time for moderation.

The first thing she did was to write a long letter to Miss Julie. She was cautious about relating the vision; she was content to say that God had mercifully shown her the error of her ways, and that she was truly penitent and realized that she had been the offender in their quarrel. She quite thoroughly abased herself, but she added a hint that any prolongation of the estrangement would, after all, be Julie's own fault.

Miss Julie did not answer the letter.

"Once bit, twice shy," she commented, after reading the letter to Emma and Josephine. "I never did think Tessie was quite right. Now I'm sure she's not."

Miss Tessie bowed her head when she realized that there was going to be no answer to her plea. She could not expect Julie to forgive so easily; it was for her to humble herself further. She did, and wrote another letter, which Miss Julie did not answer.

"She'll regret it," Miss Tessie said to herself, temporarily forgetting her humility. "She doesn't realize what she's doing, and to whom she's being so haughty. If she did, she'd tremble."

She was not in the least discouraged. She was going to be humble if it was the last thing she ever did. She resolved to visit Joe's wife and to show her, plainly, that she forgave her.

That visit was a test of her humility and required courage, for even Miss Tessie was willing to recognize Ethel Gerard as her match if not her superior in verbal combat; but one day she put on her best things and went to Joseph Gerard's house.

It was not far to Coming Street, and Miss Tessie reached the house long before she would have liked to. She went up the three steps and rang the bell.

The shutters on the front windows rattled, and a grating voice said sharply:

"Who is it?"

"It's me—Therese," Miss Tessie said.

"Who asked you to poke your head in my door?" Ethel shouted.

"I've come to ask you to be friendly." Miss Tessie tried to make her voice sound meek.

"You have, eh? Well, get away from here as fast as your dirty feet will carry you."

"Don't you think you might try to be a little more of a Christian?" Miss Tessie asked. She was becoming angry in spite of everything.

"You can go to hell and take your miserable low-down bastard of a brother with you," Ethel said from behind the blind.

"I'm going to stand here until you give me a decent answer," Miss Tessie said stoutly.

She heard footsteps move away from the window. She said a prayer, asking God to soften the hard heart of this sister-in-law. And then she heard the steps coming down the piazza; or was it the upstairs piazza? She couldn't be sure.

Miss Tessie waited, hopeful. Perhaps Ethel didn't look quite presentable, and wanted to fix herself up a bit before she let her in.

And then it happened. Miss Tessie couldn't realize for an instant what had occurred. She heard a peal of bloodcurdling laughter, and realized that she was drenched.

"God will punish you for this," she shouted, making a feeble attempt to shake the water from her hat and veil and waist.

She was nearly weeping. She hurried off, muttering in wrath, and painfully conscious of witnesses to her humiliation from behind discreet shutters: humiliation to her as a person, humiliation to her poor brother. And, worst of all, she understood that her presence was not sufficiently imposing to move the wicked to repentance.

She hurried to her room, changed her things, and never mentioned the matter. It would never do to admit that she had gone to see Ethel Gerard, and that the woman had flung cold water on her. God knew that if she was seeking humiliation she had got it. Those who had seen the affair would tell about it. She hoped Annette wouldn't hear.

By now, Miss Tessie's delusion had gone too far for her to remain content with a rational explanation of anything. It did not take her long to conclude that this episode was a humiliation sent by the Lord himself, to aid her in her attempt to be meek.

CHAPTER NINE

MISS TESSIE'S BEHAVIOR WAS AMIABILITY ITSELF during the two weeks before Annette and the children went to the mountains. She even bought presents for the little boys to take with them; little books of Bible stories.

She said no more about her mystical experience, and Annette and Henry concluded that she had more or less forgotten about it. She was left alone in the big house with Henry and Jennie and Wallace and Stevens, for Sarah had taken her savings and gone to New York to spend a month with a friend, leaving Stevens a free man. He had recently become converted to religion, and he held long biblical discussions with Jennie during the long, dull day.

Henry was a little uneasy at first with the sole responsibility for supervision of Miss Tessie, but the old lady removed his anxiety by her perfectly calm behavior. She was affable and even chatty at the dinner table and at breakfast; she wrote to Annette and inquired about Joe and Betsy and James and George with actual solicitude. Henry was disarmed.

However, in July he became thoroughly disturbed. He did not move in Miss Tessie's religious circle, and had no knowledge of her religious observances except as he saw her come and go mornings and Sundays; but Annette heard from friends that Miss Tessie had formed the habit of standing on the church steps after Mass and asking everyone, in a loud voice, to pray for her, a miserable sinner.

"Jesus Christ!" Henry exclaimed, not inappropriately. "I might have known something was going on!" It was just as it was with children: if you didn't hear a sound from them, you could be sure that there was mischief afoot.

Henry was panicky. He had always known his wife's aunt was not entirely reasonable, and this was full confirmation. Why, she was as mad as a hatter.

Of course, lunacy was amusing in an outsider. There was something very absurd in the obscene shouting of the old lady next door who was mewed up in a room on the fourth floor, or in that of Mrs. Carroll, who, it was generally said, fancied herself a corpse and had to have candles at her head and feet all the time. When it came home, however, it was no laughing matter.

Then there was the element of purely physical danger. Henry was no coward, but he did not relish the idea of being attacked in his sleep and having his skull laid open or his throat cut or being disemboweled.

Even worse than death, however, in Charleston, was the disgrace of having a family eccentric. Henry had learned to put up with Miss Julie's tinfoil collecting and her viva voce praying—after all, she was old, and Charleston was full of old people who did peculiar but harmless things. But Miss Tessie was going too far. It was not pleasant to be associated in people's minds with an old lady who sold magazine subscriptions, and stood on church porches asking people to pray for her. If she should go violently insane, they would have to shut her up in one of the rooms, and give it out that she was ill. To have her committed to a place of asylum would be a crushing disgrace. It would be the admission of lunacy in the family.

Henry watched Miss Tessie closely at meals, for he had the popular notion that insanity could be detected in the expression of a person's face; but Miss Tessie looked and acted more sensible now than before. She put herself out to be affable and chatty at the dinner table, and she had a calm, peaceful expression that was more normal than her former strained intensity.

"Damn it, she doesn't act crazy," Henry thought, puzzled.

He decided to wait and see what might happen. Meanwhile, just to be on the safe side, he locked his bedroom door at night and fastened the shutters on the window that led to the piazza.

But everything was apparently well. Miss Tessie, it was true, continued to solicit prayers from the church steps; but, as the bishop's sister was known to be a little touched and there were several ladies of the parish whose religious observances bordered on the extreme, Henry decided that he could stand that if it became no worse.

It was in August that he received his second shock.

Miss Tessie had become convinced that the vision would not come again except at the cemetery, and she began going there more and more often. Toward the beginning of August she went daily. Only on her regular biweekly visits did she take the garden tools or permit Wallace to drive her. On the other days she went out as if she were going for a walk, or a visit.

It had occurred to her that the more humble she made herself, the sooner God would grant her another glimpse of the vision. For a person who had always been fiercely independent, asking for something was the deepest possible form of self-abasement. And the humbler the person from whom the favor was asked, the greater the abasement.

Miss Tessie got on the car one day to go to the cemetery, and when the conductor came around she said in a loud, clear voice:

"Please let me ride for nothing. I'm going to the cemetery to visit my dead."

"Madam, I'm not permitted to give free rides," said the plump, red-faced Irishman.

"Please!" she begged.

He was polite but firm. He said he would lose his job if he did such a thing and it were reported to the company.

"I knew Mr. Amabile when he was a little boy," Miss Tessie said. "I'm sure he wouldn't punish you for an act of charity to a poor widow."

"I'm sorry, madam," the conductor said, "but you'll either have to pay your fare or I'll have to ask you to get off."

Miss Tessie took out a nickel and paid without further ado. She had performed the act of humility; it wasn't necessary that the person she entreated grant the request. That had nothing to do with it.

Next day she tried the same tactics, with the same result. She did it several days in succession, and then the conductor, after a talk with the motorman, simply passed her in the car.

Miss Tessie was furious. She took a later car, with a different conductor, and subjected him to the same treatment.

It happened that this conductor knew Henry O'Donnell very well: they had gone to school together. Seeing Henry on the corner of Broad and Meeting streets one hot afternoon, he stopped the car and got down on the steps to tell him about it.

"Mr. O'Donnell," he said, "I don't like to tell you about this, but your aunt is behaving very strange. She takes a ride to the graveyard every afternoon, and she always asks the conductors to let her ride for nothing."

Henry flushed. "Thank you for telling me. I'll see what I can do about it. In the meantime, just jolly her along."

He stood on the corner, stunned by this fresh calamity.

"God Almighty!" he said to himself. "Why, the old lady has gone raving mad now, all right. We'll be the laughingstock of Charleston—if we aren't already."

He felt a bit as he had felt years ago, when he had suddenly found himself alone with his oldest child, faced with the wholly unforeseen necessity of changing its diaper. He decided to consult Cyril Forbes.

He took the afternoon off and went over to Dr. Forbes's office, where he sat for fifteen or twenty minutes vainly trying to interest himself in the *Century Magazine*.

"Damn it, if she'd only taken the notion to lock herself up, like old Miss Mary next door!" he muttered.

Dr. Forbes finally ushered out a nervous woman whom he told, "It will only be a matter of a few weeks." When she had gone he asked: "Well, Henry, what's the matter with you? Prostate gland?"

"I'm doing very well in that respect. How are Lucy and the children?"

"All fine. Are Annette and the family having a good time in the mountains?"

"Very fine. What I've come to see you about"—Henry followed the doctor into the private office—"is the way Annette's old aunt is carrying on."

He told about Miss Tessie's oddities.

"Well," Dr. Forbes said—he was always a tolerant man—"she doesn't seem to be violent. These hallucinations may be perfectly harmless. She's always had a very unhappy existence, and she's getting some consolation out of all this. Why not leave her alone and forget about it?"

"But, God damn it, Cyril, it's mortifying! You know how people talk in Charleston. It affects your business, and your children at school, and everything you do or are connected with."

"There's a lot of people right in Charleston who've endured mortifications of that kind without dying of it," Dr. Forbes said calmly. "Of course, if you want to put the old lady away, and want to sign the commitment, I'll arrange it. But it seems cruel to me, at her age. She won't live very long. She's seventy, isn't she?"

"Just two years younger than Mrs. Sharp."

"Well, she looked feeble to me the last time I saw her. Why don't you put up with her for a while and see how it works out? This thing may pass off by itself."

Henry snorted. "Is that the best you can do?"

"The trouble with you, Henry," Dr. Forbes said jovially, "is that you're too stuck up with all this Charleston self-respect. It's no reflection on you that your wife's aunt is a little off. Most old people are. Why, there's that old lady next door to you, and I could tell you about a dozen more, if you didn't know 'em already. You'll probably be queer yourself when you get to be about seventy, if you live that long, worrying the way you do."

"To hell with you!" Henry stood up and got his hat.

"Call me when she starts to go naked in the street. Then I'll see that she's certified. . . . By the way, Henry, how is Miss Julie?"

"She's all right, as far as I know," Henry said. "Off in Chattanooga! I wish to God the other one was there, too," he added fervently.

"I'll tell you what I would do," Dr. Forbes said. "Send for her. She'll keep a better eye on Miss Tessie than you will."

"What, two of them in the same house? Then we'll all be crazy as bedbugs."

"Then you won't mind it. However, that's an idea for you. It might help."

"I'll see them both in Hell first," Henry said.

He walked away from the doctor's office feeling very gloomy. What could you expect of a man who never even sent a bill?

That night he wrote and told Annette of her aunt's new exploits and of his conversation with Dr. Forbes.

Annette was inclined to agree with Cyril. It would be more mortifying, she wrote, to admit that a relative was insane than to pretend that she was just eccentric. As for sending for Miss Julie—they had better think that over carefully. It might be a good idea, and on the other hand it might make more trouble than they already had. Having Ma around might goad Aunt Tessie to frenzy, they had always quarreled so.

And so Henry did what many another man had had to do; he shut his eyes and pretended not to see what was going on around him.

Completely ignorant of all the fuss about her, Miss Tessie continued on her way. She began to go to Mass every morning, rain or shine, and continued to visit the cemetery daily.

People did nudge one another when she went through her routine of pleading with the conductor to let her ride free on the car, and winks were exchanged when she stood on the church steps and implored those going in and out to include her in their prayers. But Charleston was used to such eccentricities. It already had so many that one more made little difference. The city began to say, "Poor Miss Tessie Gerard was at such and such a place," and "I saw Miss Tessie Gerard today again, begging the conductor on the Meeting Street car to let her ride for nothing," and people had almost ceased to laugh by the end of the summer. They spoke with pity and sympathy and tolerance, and Miss Tessie might have passed quite out of notice as a minor celebrity of the eccentric kind had not her monomania taken a more striking form in the fall.

CHAPTER TEN

HENRY WAS MIGHTILY GLAD when it was time for Annette to come home. He could not carry this burden of uneasiness alone any longer. Letters weren't really satisfactory; he needed somebody to talk to.

Miss Tessie, however, was dismayed when she realized that the summer had drawn to a close, and that the children were coming home again. She had enjoyed the months of virtual solitude in the big house, the quiet and the repose. She had detested Joe ever since he had pasted that picture over the photograph of Theodora, and the thought of having him and Betsy and the two small boys, all underfoot and brawling around the house, was more than she could bear.

Waiting vainly for her vision to return, Miss Tessie had been conscious of a growing tension; and she felt that she needed quiet to think her own thoughts. The children, sunburned, energetic, and noisy, seemed to deny the world she was interested in, where virtue was rewarded by such intangible things as visions.

She kept out of their way as much as she could, appearing only for meals and taking little part in the conversation. Sometimes she murmured prayers while the others were talking.

"She does act demented," Annette admitted.

Henry had a lot to say on the subject. He pointed out what a mortification all this was becoming, and how he was going to suffer by it, and how the children would be embarrassed. Annette tried to persuade him that he was taking it all too seriously.

"Too seriously! Hell, don't you realize what this is doing to me?" Henry fumed.

Back in the kitchen, where the town's news was sifted and assayed, there was much shaking of heads.

"There she go," Jennie said, as Miss Tessie closed the front door and started out. "That her step."

"Off to de graveya'd again," Sarah said. "Do, Lawd! if she don't hurry up and see Gawd mother again—"

She rolled her eyes and threw up her hands.

"You think she really see 'em?" Jennie inquired for the hundredth time. She was a little uneasy about the whole affair.

Tchk! Sarah sucked her teeth. "How many times does I have to tell you 'twas Wallace in 'e black suit? Dat po' ol' soul's trouble gone to 'e head. . . . I lose six children myself, and my Pa and my brothers, and I got Mistuh No'count there on my hands for twenty 'ears, and still I ain't seein' nothin' in graveya'ds."

Stevens, who was munching a piece of cornbread and sipping coffee, looked up at this compliment.

"Tha's all right, ol' lady," he said with patient humor. "You ain' never had to worry about me. You ain' never had to wonder where I is."

"No. Can' lose a bad penny," Sarah retorted. "You always home in time for dinner. All I got to do is to light de stove to fin' you right away."

Stevens chuckled.

"Mis' Fisher make me feel creepy sometime," Jennie said. "She look right t'rough you, like ol' Aunt Rosie, the cunjer 'oman."

"You believe all that foolishness? Jennie, I 'shamed of you. Cunjer 'oman!" Sarah snorted. "Dey ain' no cunjer except to take money from fool niggers."

"Well, 'e look funny at you."

"'E jis peculiar," Sarah said. "Do, Lawd! She nearly run de

captain crazy. Beggin' rides on the Meetin' Street cyar, and standin' on de church step beggin' for prayers."

"Well, now, chil', a little prayin' ain' hurt nobody," Stevens interposed.

"If dat's how you feels, you better git started on some; ol' Satan keepin' de fire hot for you right now." Sarah cackled boisterously. "I can' think o' nothin' funnier, when I is up on one o' dem clouds playin' my harp, dan to see you jumpin' around on de coals like a whitin' in de fryin' pan. You goin' ta move fas' for the first time in your life."

"All right, ol' lady. And you won't be satisfy ontell you gits right down dere alongside," Stevens said. "You know you couldn' do widout me."

Sarah sucked her teeth again. "You foolin' yourself. I goin' to sit right there and watch de debbil stick 'e pitchfork right in your behind."

"Oh, do, Sarah, don't talk dat way," Jennie remonstrated. "'Tain't Christian."

Sarah was slightly abashed. "All right, chil'. But don't you worry none about Mis' Fisher. 'E nicer sence 'e got a little crazy."

"I work for one family on Legare Street," Jennie recalled. "De ol' gramma useta think 'e still in de War. She think General Sherman comin'. ''E miss Charleston last time,' she say, 'but 'e goin' ta git us de next time.' You know what 'e do? One day 'e git a piece of lightwood and light 'em on de stove. 'What you goin' ta do wid dat kindlin', Mis' Robertson?' I say. 'I goin' ta burn dis house down right now befo' de Yankees does,' she say. So I sneak upstairs and call de missus. 'Mis' Robertson say 'e goin' ta set de house afire,' I tell 'em. Lawd! what a to-do they was that day! Dey put 'em in de Roper Hospital and tell everybody 'e gone for treatments. I 'fraid something like that goin' ta happen to Mis' Fisher if 'e crazy like you say."

"My Lawd! I hope I see de smoke," Sarah said. "But she ain' goin' ta set fire to nothin'. 'E mind just weak."

"I can' make up my mind about 'em," Jennie said.

Life in the big house had gone on uneasily for some weeks,

and the first cool days had set in, when Miss Tessie developed her new crotchet.

She had a dream, in which a voice said to her: "Why do you doubt? One vision is enough. You have been glorified."

This was too exciting to be kept secret. Miss Tessie told her niece about it, before the others came down to breakfast.

"Well, that's wonderful, Aunt Tessie." Annette treated her like an imaginative child. "It must make you very happy."

"But I haven't told you the strangest part of it." Miss Tessie's eyes shone. "The most wonderful thing, and the thing that convinces me that it wasn't a mere dream, is that the words were in Latin. I can't remember what they were, but I understood them just as if they were English."

She related the dream again to Henry and the children.

"Very wonderful," Henry said, gazing down at his plate in embarrassment.

Joe giggled, and Annette turned a furious frown in his direction.

"I had a dream," George said. "I dreamed I went down the drain, and Hairbreadth Harry was down there, and Relentless Rudolph was trying to cut his head off with a big ax. Gee! I was scared."

"That will do, George," his father said. "We don't need your dreams told this morning. And you'd better stop looking at those funny papers if they're going to give you nightmares."

George grinned in his usual irrepressible way.

"I does like fuh to dream 'bout 'em," he said in his richest Gullah.

"George! None of that Gullah!"

Miss Tessie waited until there was quiet.

"It worries me about Sister Julie," she said. "I don't think she realizes just what she's doing in refusing my overtures. I think I ought to warn her."

Henry shuddered. These increasing delusions made his blood run cold.

"Perhaps it will just come to her," he suggested.

Miss Tessie looked sharply at him, and was satisfied that he was serious.

"I think you're right, Henry. If I write and she continues to be stubborn, it will just be causing her to sin. You're absolutely right. I'll wait."

She finished a muffin and her coffee.

"If you'll excuse me," she said, getting up, "I'll go up to my room. There's a good deal I want to do today."

Henry stood up until she had left the table. He had determined at the beginning to be ultra-punctilious in his manners, so that Miss Tessie should have no chance to criticize. Joe, however, remained seated.

"Joe's manners don't improve," his father said gruffly.

"All that stuff makes me sick," Joe said.

"I'll talk to you later. Now, all of you get on to school."

"James, you keep an eye on George, now," Annette said, as she did every single school day.

She sat stroking her folded napkin as she waited for them to go. Henry lighted a Murad cigarette and inhaled deeply.

"You see?" he said.

"She certainly acts very peculiar. What do you think we ought to do?"

"I don't know what to do. I suppose we have to indulge her in this business, though, until she gets out of hand. Why don't you send for your mother? She needn't tell Miss Tessie you did. Tell her to say she heard a voice or something like that. Then we'll have her to keep an eye on your aunt. She really needs someone to look after her, you know."

"I'll do it right away."

"Make it strong," Henry urged. "Having the pair of them around is going to be tough, come to think of it."

"It's very hard to be saddled with your in-laws."

He grunted. "That can't be helped. After all, they won't live on forever. They're both pretty old now."

"I wouldn't talk that way," Annette said.

"Why not face the truth—especially if it's cheerful? Tell your mother to answer collect, and I'll wire the money she needs."

He banged the front door—which he hated for anyone else to do—and his light springy footsteps died away. Annette rose from the table and went upstairs to write the necessary letter. After she had finished she read it half aloud to herself, as was her habit:

DEAR MA:

Aunt Tessie is becoming more and more peculiar. I told you about that business of seeing the Blessed Mother in the cemetery and going there every day, and begging free rides on the trolley and prayers on the church steps. Well, it has gone farther now. She has been distressed, I suppose, because the vision hasn't come again. Now she has had a dream. A voice told her that one vision was enough, and that she had been glorified! She is sure the dream is true because it was in Latin and she understood it all perfectly, though she doesn't know more than enough Latin to follow the Mass.

It's very hard to say just how far gone she is mentally, but we think it may be pretty far. It's something about her voice and manner.

She said she thought she ought to "warn you" against what you are doing by refusing her "overtures."

Henry thinks it would be good for Aunt Tessie if you would come and keep her company. I suppose you can't do very much; but it may be just loneliness going to her brain. Maybe you can humor her along. The children will be beside themselves with pleasure at seeing you, and you know how glad I'll be to have you back.

Of course, she is not to know that we asked you to come. Let her think you had a mysterious feeling that you had to come back to see her. We'll all act surprised when you arrive, and the children won't know and really will be surprised.

Henry asked if you would answer by telegram, collect. Send it to his office. He'll wire you the money for the trip.

This is just a note because I'm in such a hurry. I'll have plenty to tell you when you come.

Love,

ANNETTE.

She sent Wallace to the post office, to mail the letter.

"Wallace," she said, "not a word about this to *anyone*. I have a reason."

"No, muh. You know Wallace ain't tell everything 'e see."
("I'm not so sure about that," Annette said to herself.)

After the summons had gone to Miss Julie, her sister went even further in her paranoia. It occurred to her that, if she had been "glorified," as the voice in her dream had said, her duty was to let as many people in the city see her as was possible; and the only way to do this was to pass through all the streets of the city, one by one.

To Miss Tessie, it was perfectly simple. She would just stand on various street corners of the city, one after another, so that the passers-by might see her. She was sure they would understand immediately. God would make them know what was happening.

She began on a brisk November day, taking up her post on the corner of King and Wentworth streets, where she stood, nodding to an occasional acquaintance and buffeted by the cutting wind, until it was time to go home to dinner. She determined to be punctual about that.

"St. Elizabeth was persecuted by unbelievers," she said to herself, "and I don't want that infidel Henry O'Donnell to mock me. If I happened to be late to dinner, it would be just like him to send somebody out to look for me."

She trotted west on Wentworth Street, shivering a bit and conscious of a somewhat unsaintly hunger, and arrived just in time to sit down with the others.

It seemed to her that they were acting with a sort of suppressed excitement: maybe they were beginning to realize what a privilege they were permitted to enjoy. She felt a warm satisfaction as she replied to their polite inquiries about her health.

She ate with relish, not bothering to listen to the worldly talk that went on, only now and then catching a word, as when Betsy told about making popovers, the *pièce de résistance* of what was then called "domestic science" at school. Annette had been listening vaguely and, when the girl had finished, remarked that she had seen old Mrs. Lafitte that morning.

[256]

"Mamma, you never take any interest in what anybody is saying," Betsy said reproachfully.

"Of course I heard what you were saying. You were making popovers. If you want to know what I think about it, it's a lot of foolishness teaching white girls to do cooking. You'd think they were going to grow up to be regular Yankee pot-slingers."

"Now, Annette, don't discourage the child," Henry protested. "She has to do what all the others do, and all of them aren't going to get married to some young fellow who can afford two dollars a week for a cook."

What little things they worried themselves about! Miss Tessie ignored the rest of what they said. It would be a good thing if the children were sent where they might learn a little about God, instead of to Protestant schools where their souls were endangered.

"Aunt Tessie, are you going out this afternoon?" Annette asked.

Miss Tessie started, for she had just been planning to stand on King and Calhoun streets, and wondered whether she ought to stay outdoors in such weather.

"Why, yes, I am. Why?"

"I was going to have Sarah start a fire in your room if you were going to be at home. It's very cold for this time of year."

"Don't bother about me, thank you," Miss Tessie said. "I'm not accustomed to all these luxuries. If I get cold I'll wrap myself up a little more warmly."

A fire would feel good, she thought; but it wouldn't be right for her to indulge herself in such comforts. They were worldly.

"I've got a good mind to have a furnace put in," Henry remarked, as he always did when the winter was approaching.

"Miss Low has a furnace," George said. "It's green, and it's got pipes that run all over the house. I wish we had a furnace."

Annette sniffed. "Furnace! I'd rather have a good fireplace any day, or a nice Franklin stove like ours. A climate like Charleston's doesn't need furnace heat. It's like those stupid fireless cookers they talk about. Fireless! Why, they have to cook the food first. What's fireless about that?"

"Mamma's an old stick-in-the-mud," James said.

"James! Don't be disrespectful," Henry commanded, but his eyes twinkled a little. He had noticed Annette's increasing resemblance to her mother (and her aunt) as the years passed.

"I believe Mrs. Wilson approves of a fireless cooker," he said teasingly. "If the first lady of the land likes them, we all ought to have them, don't you think?"

"First lady of the land!" Annette retorted. "Who made her the first lady of the land, I'd like to know?"

Henry laughed with pleasure at the success of his joke. He finished his coffee and rose to go.

"Have Sarah see that the house is warm," he advised.

Annette was profoundly relieved when she saw Miss Tessie go out the front gate. She expected Miss Julie within an hour, and she had to talk to her mother at length and strictly alone. They would have to carry out the deception they had planned, for otherwise Miss Tessie might think they had sent for Miss Julie as a hint for her to leave. She got out her embroidery frame and set to work on the new bureau scarf she was making. It would help to pass the time. She was impatient to see her mother.

It would be nice to have Ma again; but how the two of them were going to get along, God only knew.

She called for Sarah, who came running up.

"Sarah," she asked the little woman, "how do you think we are going to manage with Mrs. Sharp and Mrs. Fisher in the same house?"

"My Lawd, Miss Nettie, I don't know. Mis' Fisher ain't the way 'e used to be. . . . Maybe they get along fine."

"Do you suppose any other family has these things to contend with?"

"Ol' people is sort of foolish sometimes," Sarah said. "I remember when my friend Queenie pa die. 'E was worryin' about 'e black broadcloth suit, and sayin' he didn't want to go befo' de Lawd wid no old clothes on, or half cladded. Well, Queenie go to the chest to git de suit out, and she can't find de pants, because one o' her brothers steal 'em when 'e pa was sick. So she run over next do' and borrow de neighbor's. And she take 'em back and show 'em to the old soul, and 'e ain't know the difference, and 'e was happy. Maybe Mis' Fisher believe what you tell her. Anyway, 'e ain't going to live very long."

"What makes you say that, Sarah?"

"'E look feeble. 'E walk slower. . . . You know what 'e do this morning?"

"No."

"Stan' out on Wentworth and King Street corner. Tha's all 'e do. Jis' stan' there from early mornin' tell dinnertime."

Annette looked her astonishment.

"In all that wind, too. What do you suppose she was doing it for?"

Sarah shook her head. "Lucy, that work for Mis' Horne, tell me about it," she said.

"You keep an eye on her," Annette said. "Send some little boy after her tomorrow, if you need to, and let me know just how she's acting. I'm really worried about the old soul. Maybe Mrs. Sharp will be able to control her. Well, that's all I wanted to talk to you about. See that Wallace leaves on time for the train —it comes in at four—and see that the children don't annoy Mrs. Fisher. I don't want anything to upset her."

She returned to her embroidery. James and George were shouting in the back yard. She hoped Sarah was keeping them warm, playing outside on such an afternoon. The shouting stopped, and she heard the car start, and knew that Wallace was off to the depot to fetch Miss Julie. She went in to see that her mother's room was properly arranged, and then she sat down to wait.

After an interminable interval, she heard the grinding of the big Rambler's brakes and the slamming of the door and then the excited voices of the boys, amazed to see their grandmother step

[259]

out of the car. Annette rushed downstairs to meet her, and pretended that this was all unexpected.

Miss Julie hallooed at and hugged the children, and kissed Annette, and was so obviously glad to be back that it made her daughter's heart ache just for an instant. James and George were beside themselves with delight.

"Well, boys," Miss Julie said, "and what do you think Granny has in her bag? Something you'll like."

"What is it, Granny?" George asked.

"Is it candy?" James inquired.

"Why, you rascals!" Miss Julie chuckled. "I brought them some real New Orleans pralines," she said. "They were sent to Emma. Wait till I go upstairs to open my luggage. . . . Sarah, you look fine. I'm glad to see you."

"Thank you, muh," Sarah said. "The children sho did miss you."

"They did, eh? Well, maybe they'll appreciate their old Granny more when they haven't had her for a while. Familiarity breeds contempt, you know."

"I'll take you up to your room, Ma," Annette said. "There are a couple of things I have to tell you. You boys stay down here.

"In the first place," she told her mother as they started up the stairs, "I've given you the little extra room for a while. Aunt Tessie has the bigger room, and I wasn't sure you'd want to share it, or that she wouldn't think we were trying to put her out by moving you in with her."

"Lord, child, I don't care!" Miss Julie said cheerfully. "Any port in a storm. . . . So Tessie's been carrying on, eh?"

"It's enough to run you crazy," Annette said. "The latest thing is standing on corners. This morning, in this biting wind, she stood on the corner of Wentworth and King Street for hours, just stood there."

"*Tchk, tchk*. It's too bad. It does sound a little as if she wasn't quite right, doesn't it?"

"Maybe you'll be able to quiet her down a little, or at least keep an eye on her. Sarah thinks she won't live very long. She says Aunt Tessie is getting very feeble."

"Dear me!" Miss Julie murmured. "The poor thing. But I was so mad with her, that last time, that I wouldn't even answer her letters. I'll try to make my peace with her now." She shook her head.

"You think this room will be comfortable, Ma? It's really very small."

"Don't worry about me, child. I'll get along all right if I have to sleep under the steps. Now don't even mention it again. How are all the people I know? Anybody dead lately?"

"Nobody that I know of. Not since I wrote you last, anyway. Well, now, Ma, here you are. Put your hat there for a minute and listen to me."

Miss Julie sat in the rocker and put on her glasses. Annette saw now that her hair had become a little whiter, and that her cheeks had more of a sag.

"Remember, we don't want Aunt Tessie to think that we sent for you," she told her mother. "She's very suspicious of us already. They say it's a way people have when they are a little bit touched."

Miss Julie nodded.

"We are all surprised," Annette explained. "The children were really surprised, of course. But Henry and I hadn't the slightest idea you were coming, remember. You understand? And you can tell Aunt Tessie that you had a presentiment that she wanted you, or something like that, or heard a voice—anything you think she'll believe."

Her mother chuckled, and Annette felt how good it was to have someone who was sane and healthy again. It was like all the lights going on in a house that had been dark.

"I suppose the best thing to do is to indulge poor Tessie in every way possible," Miss Julie said. "Remember when poor Pa was in his last illness and got sort of childish? One thing he did was to get up in the middle of the night and sit on the floor and mix his medicine. We never said a thing about it."

"I wish I knew what to do," Annette said. "Henry asked Cyril Forbes about her, and he said there were lots of peculiar people all over Charleston and to let her alone. Henry is so sensitive, you know."

"Here, lemme give the children this candy." Miss Julie took a package from her valise. "Want one?"

"Yes, I'll take one. It's a dog's age since I've had any New Orleans pralines."

Miss Julie went out to the piazza. "James! George! Come here and see what I've got for you."

The boys left off playing and raced into the house.

"What is it, Granny?" James shouted.

"Is it peppermints?" George asked.

"Here." Miss Julie gave each a frosty circle of sugar. "Eat these. And tomorrow I'll give you another. . . . My, how they grow!" she murmured. "Where are Betsy and Joe?"

"Betsy has gone to a party—some of the children at school are giving it at the Chisholm girl's house. Joe is running around somewhere. He's never in the house except to sleep and eat."

"You know," Miss Julie said, "I've never had a single letter from Francis since I've been away."

"Too bad he forgets his duty so easily."

"What else is in the bag, Granny?" George asked.

"Layovers to catch meddlers. James, when you grow up I hope you'll never forget all your Ma has done for you."

"No, I won't. . . . Have you got any silver paper, Granny?" he demanded.

"I sold it all. But I'm going to begin to save up some more. You and George can help me by picking up any you see and bringing it to me."

"Let's go out and look for some now," James suggested.

"All right," George said.

"Don't stay out too long," Annette counseled. "Remember, it's windy and cold."

"Oh, we don't mind that, do we, George?"

"Do you think they ought to go out in all this wind?" Miss

Julie moved nearer to the little coal grate and warmed her hands.

"Oh, let them go. I don't want them around when Aunt Tessie comes in."

"That's right. Well, let's sit down here by the fire and talk about everything. Tell me all about Tessie."

They were gossiping busily when Miss Tessie entered the house and crept softly upstairs. Something made Miss Julie look up, and there in the doorway stood her sister, looking like a frozen turnip.

"So!" Miss Tessie said. "God has sent you, Julie."

Miss Julie got up and rushed to her sister, and hugged her, and cried, and said yes, something had told her to come, that Tessie wanted her and she ought to be there.

"Did it tell you about my miracle?"

"I understood that something had happened."

Miss Julie wiped her eyes. Really, it was shocking to see how thin and peaky Tessie had become. Why, she was no bigger than a shrimp.

"Annette has just explained."

Miss Tessie's eyes lighted up. "To think that I doubted," she said.

"Do sit by the fire here, Tessie, and warm yourself up. You look frozen."

"I'll get you both a cup of coffee," Annette said.

The two sisters sat by the little fireplace and Miss Tessie removed her hat and stuck the pins carefully through it again.

"Sister," she said, "to think that this should have happened to me, of all unworthy persons."

"It's wonderful," Miss Julie said. Wasn't Tessie going to ask her a thing about Josephine and Emma? She had such wonderful things to tell her about Emma's stroke. But no, the poor thing was so wrapped up in herself now that she couldn't think of anybody else. "Yes, it's wonderful, Tessie," she repeated. "Tell me all about it."

Miss Tessie repeated the story of the vision, with elaborations; and then the story of the voice that spoke to her in her sleep in Latin.

"It's a wonderful thing for Charleston, too," she said, excitedly. "That's why I've started out to go all over the city and let everyone see me at least once before God takes me away."

Miss Julie's blood ran cold at this presumption and at the obvious craziness of it. She shivered and, to cover it up, remarked that it certainly was cold for this time of year, and that she feared a hard winter.

"I hadn't noticed," Miss Tessie said. "Somehow, things like that don't seem to have any effect on me. I suppose it's part of the grace, don't you?"

Miss Julie was beginning to be very uncomfortable. She had led a long life of religious observances, and had her share of belief in miracles that had been accomplished by God's grace. There was, for instance, the woman at Lourdes. Melpomene Richards had seen her, paralyzed in both hands, sit right down and write a letter; and Melpomene had become a convert to Catholicism immediately. But having near at hand a sister who believed that she had been singled out for a vision of the Blessed Virgin made her fidget. There was something frightening about it.

"I don't know, Tessie," she answered. "I've always been plain in my tastes, and tried not to wish for the things of this world too much, but I've always thought God meant us to have simple pleasures and comforts. And being warm is one of them, especially when you're old and your blood is thin."

"Hoo!" said Miss Tessie, but it was not the old "Hoo" of former days. Now the exclamation had something expiring and weary about it. "Pleasures and comforts are the temptations of the Devil."

Miss Julie was relieved when Sarah came up with the coffee and Annette sat with them, sipping. She forced the conversation around to Chattanooga, and told again to her heart's content about Emma's stroke, and how she and Josephine had nursed her, and about her little great-nephew who was becoming very cute. Miss Tessie, for all her condemnation of comforts and luxuries, ate a cookie and drank her coffee with relish; but she did not take any part in the conversation. She simply sat and stared at the fire or out of the window with a rapt expression; and when Annette went out, she said she must be going to her own room to tend to some things.

"Don't treat it as my room," she urged. "Come in whenever you feel like it, Julie. And if you feel you'd be more comfortable in the bigger room—after all, it was really yours—why, you take it, and this little one will be enough for me."

Miss Julie didn't enjoy seeing her sister so humble and self-sacrificing, nor her airs of unworldliness, which almost seemed like a reproach. She had been a sight better Christian than Tessie, she said to herself; and she didn't like her sister's acting as if all the grace in Heaven had come down just for her.

But that was silly. One might as well be indignant at a boy for playing he was General Lee.

"That's very nice of you, Tessie," she said. "But I can be perfectly comfortable here."

"I don't feel as if I ought to have the best of everything," Miss Tessie explained.

"Well, Tessie, neither one of us has had enough luxury to kill us."

Miss Tessie looked as if she would retort in her old way, but she didn't.

"I've always had all I needed," she said, and she walked out into the hall.

Poor thing! Really, it was awful to see such a change come over a person—even if it improved her in some ways.

"She has a stricken look," Miss Julie said to Annette when they were alone. "If she starts that business of going out to let people see her again tomorrow, I'm going to talk to Father Mellon and see if he can't do something to talk her out of it."

But she was so happy to be back that she couldn't worry overmuch about her sister. That night, at supper, Tessie was lively and agreeable, and they both enjoyed Henry's teasing. What a pity she couldn't have been like this all her life!

Miss Tessie did, of course, start out on her pilgrimage the very next day, which was cold and damp, in spite of all her sister's persuasions. After she had gone, Miss Julie got on her best things and started for the Bishop's house.

"Mercy! To think of Tessie out in this weather, standing on street corners!" she muttered, pulling her shawl tighter around her neck. "She'll have pneumonia, as sure as you're born."

She was chilly, but how she enjoyed seeing the familiar houses of Charleston once more! Chattanooga was nice enough, but there was no place like Charleston, where you knew every stone in the streets and every tree and shrub in the yards. The return was made extra pleasant by her gathering two pieces of tinfoil before she reached the Cathedral. She went in to pray for a moment or two and to light a votive candle; and then she proceeded to the episcopal residence.

The ancient Irish housekeeper, Annie, said that Father Mellon had gone out but would be right back, and Miss Julie sat in the little parlor and waited, thumbing through a few numbers of the ecclesiastical reviews. Within a few minutes the cheery plump priest entered, greeted her, and gave her his blessing.

"Now, Mrs. Sharp, what's the trouble?" he inquired, sitting down and absently fingering the biretta he had put on the table.

Suddenly, Miss Julie burst into tears.

"It's my poor old sister, Father Mellon," she sobbed.

"Come, daughter," he said, as if she weren't old enough to be his mother. "Try to control yourself, and perhaps I can help you." He was embarrassed.

Miss Julie made a mighty effort. She dabbed at her eyes.

"Don't forget that God is always ready to aid," Father Mellon said, somewhat helplessly, and smiled.

Miss Julie recovered. "You'll have to pardon an old woman's tears," she apologized.

"Now tell me what's troubling you," said the priest.

She told him the whole pitiful story, and he listened intently and seriously.

"I'm afraid she'll be punished for presumption, if she is in her senses," Miss Julie finished, "or, on the other hand, that I may be for misjudging her."

Father Mellon sighed. He was not the only priest who had been faced with such a dilemma.

"It isn't for us to judge," he said soberly. "Some of the brightest saints in Heaven were misunderstood by their fellow creatures. . . . And if it is just imagination . . . Well, I know Mrs. Fisher pretty well. There's no harm in it. Why not let the poor soul have her way, if it makes her happy?"

"But I'm afraid she'll ruin her health. If you could advise her not to carry the thing so far—if you could tell her that it isn't right for her to risk her life going out in all sorts of weather—"

The priest shook his head. "I'm afraid it wouldn't do any good. If she were to confide in me, that would be different. But I can't interfere, really I can't. I don't think it would be wise to." He reflected for a few moments. "She would fret if you did anything to stop her. That might do her more harm than what she is doing now. That's my advice. But I'll think about it and I'll pray for her."

"I'm sure you know best," Miss Julie said. "Perhaps God will see fit to bring her to her senses."

"He will do what is best for her," Father Mellon said, smiling. "Leave it in His hands."

Miss Julie went home somewhat comforted, but a trifle disappointed.

She realized that Father Mellon had been right, and that nothing short of actual physical restraint would be of any use in Tessie's case. But *something*, she told herself, must be done, and done quickly. She couldn't bear to think of Tessie out in this bitter weather, standing for hours on a corner.

"I'd better go and have a look for her," she said to Annette. "God knows it's too cold for me to be tramping around, when I ought to be sitting in front of a good fire." She hesitated in her mind—the grate and rocking chair were strong temptations; but she got up and went out again. "I was never born to believe I was a saint," she thought with grim jollity. "Satan, behind me!" And she started toward King Street. If Tessie had spent the day before on King and Wentworth streets, today she might be either on King and Broad or King and Calhoun. Those would be the first places to look at.

Tessie was not on the Broad Street corner.

A cutting wind swept down the narrow length of King Street. The temperature must be down near freezing. Miss Julie hustled northward as fast as she could go. She glanced at the stone-cutters' yard and shuddered at the idea of her sister's becoming ill and dying. Poor thing, she was so thin and feeble-looking. Miss Julie was so agitated that she actually forgot to look for silver paper.

Unable to stand the wind any longer, she regretfully boarded the car on the corner of Beaufain Street. Tessie was not on Wentworth Street either. She must have thought that standing there the day before was enough. She was sure to be on Calhoun Street, Miss Julie thought. She watched intently from the car window for the familiar figure.

She got off in front of Marks's department store. There was no sign of Tessie anywhere.

"Well," Miss Julie muttered, "I can't go all over Charleston looking for her." Tessie was sure to have pneumonia. "And that will be the end of her. And if I keep on hunting for her in weather like this, I'll have it myself."

She hurried home through the bitter weather without meeting a soul. Before the fire in her daughter's bedroom, she told what Father Mellon had said and how she had searched for Tessie in vain.

"Of course this cold weather won't keep up," Annette said. "There'll be lots of warm days."

For once, Miss Julie refused to look on the bright side of things.

"That will only put off the end," she said. "And I suppose it's all our fault. If we had done more to put up with Tessie, and tried to make her happy in spite of herself, maybe she wouldn't have lost her mind like this."

"Aunt Tessie would have run herself crazy, no matter what you did for her. And besides, Ma, what could anybody have done? She's always had a disposition like a mad dog."

"Wait till you get old, child, and you'll see that life isn't such a bed of roses as you think. Tessie has had a wretched time. We've all had our troubles, but none like hers."

"No cross, no crown," Annette said.

Miss Julie looked intently at her.

"I don't think I ever really believed that," she said. "I always tried to throw off my troubles. It's the people that take things the way they come that get along best in this world, and probably in the next."

Miss Tessie returned shortly before dinnertime, shivering and pinched and white, but cheerful.

"Where have you been, Tessie?" her sister inquired. "It's too cold for you to be out like this."

"I've been walking around. I thought there wouldn't be enough people on the street corners because it was so bleak and windy, so I went through the street myself. If the mountain won't come to Mahomet, you know."

"But you'll have pneumonia."

Miss Tessie looked at her sister loftily. "You have very little faith, sister," she said.

At dinner she behaved quite rationally but, Miss Julie thought, with a kind of caution. She ate sufficient food, and appeared to enjoy it; but she took no part in the conversation, even when Miss Julie talked about Chattanooga and told of all the things she had seen and heard there.

"This is sodality afternoon, Tessie. Are you coming with me?"

"I have no time for that," Miss Tessie said. "There are more important things for me to do."

Plainly she considered the sodality sisters as rank amateurs in the matter of devotion, and Miss Julie did not insist. She went by herself.

They were all glad to see her, but Miss Julie imagined that their conversation was a bit constrained. She knew that they were trying to avoid talking about Tessie to her; they asked why she hadn't come to the meeting, and that made her uncomfortable. It showed that they all realized Tessie was crazy, and were trying to spare her disgrace.

"It's no reflection on me," Miss Julie thought, annoyed. But she realized that it was in the mind of everyone. Insanity was something of a disgrace; it suggested that your entire family was a little bit off, and that any one of them who had the proper stimulation might go crazy.

She resolved not to go again. It was too humiliating. Joe's wife had been bad enough; now it was Tessie.

She suddenly understood what Henry and Annette had been going through for months.

"Why, the poor children!" she muttered. "They certainly needed me to watch out for them."

CHAPTER ELEVEN

Miss Julie edged her chair nearer to the big Franklin stove in the sitting room, holding her quilting in her lap by a sort of magnetism as she gripped the sides of the chair and jerked it along under her weight.

"Ma, you'd do better to get up and move the chair all at once," Annette said.

Miss Julie grunted. She spread her hands before the open door of the stove and warmed them.

"I'm not going to get up when I have me chair nice and warm," she replied.

The rain was pouring down, whipping against the windows and tearing in sheets down the porch, sometimes drowning out the regular footfalls on the floor above.

"I wonder if it will ever stop raining," Annette said, as she finished counting off her crocheting. "This is the second day of it, and you'd think there was none left."

"I always think of the cemetery when it rains like this," her mother said. "I think about the rain beating down on the graves."

"For goodness' sake, Ma!"

"Well, when you get old, child, you think more and more about such things." Miss Julie looked up at the ceiling. "Is she still at it?"

"She's still walking up and down."

Almost by force, they had persuaded Miss Tessie to stay in the house on the two rainy days; and she had been striding up and down her room nearly all the time, frantic at losing precious time that should have been devoted to her mission of revealing herself to the inhabitants of the city.

"I don't know whether to wish for it to stop raining or not," Miss Julie murmured hoarsely. "If it stops, poor Tessie will insist on going out to parade herself; and, if it don't, we'll have her walking up and down like a caged lion all day. Thank God I can't hear it."

"Ma, you don't suppose she's going to be violent?"

Miss Julie shook her head. "How can I tell? There was old Madame What-you-may-call-it—you know, the people that lived on Calhoun Street."

"Delarue."

"That's it, Delarue. Well, old Madame Delarue was like that. She thought she was being poisoned, and one day she got the idea her son-in-law was a tree and went after him with an ax. They say she smashed the furniture right and left before they finally caught her."

"I'm glad Henry isn't home to listen. It would drive him crazy, too," Annette said. "Poor fellow, he takes it so to heart. He says the humiliation will ruin him in Charleston. He's actually had headaches from it, and he keeps dosing himself with Capudine. And he says he's going to ride to work in the car after this. He says he can't stand people looking at him."

"False pride," Miss Julie pronounced. "You'd think he was the only person in Charleston that had ever had a relative that behaved peculiar. Of course I don't enjoy it myself. I gave up going to sodality meeting on that account. But after all it's not a crime."

"Misfortune is no reflection upon anybody."

"Of course not. If it was, everybody in Charleston would be ashamed to show his face in the street, particularly on the score of craziness. Why, there were the Hudsons, for instance—"

They went through a long list of oddities and maniacs they knew of, and seemed to get considerable comfort from it.

"Poor Tessie's not as bad as that," Miss Julie said finally. "She's just got a delusion, poor soul, and she isn't harming anybody or being common or vulgar about it. Of course, she may get worse, and then we'll really have trouble on our hands."

"If she doesn't die first of exposure or something."

Miss Julie shrugged sadly, and said there was nothing they could do about it.

Annette looked out of the window. "I think it's clearing up."

"Maybe so. It'll be cold if it does."

Tap, tap, tap went the footsteps on the third floor.

Annette crocheted and chatted for a while, and then, unable to stand it longer, she got up and went out to the kitchen. Miss Julie continued to sit placidly by the stove.

She continued with her quilting until it was nearly time for dinner, and then she went upstairs to freshen herself up and to tell Tessie, who seemed to have lost all sense of mealtime.

She was not delicate in her way of going about things. She thumped heartily on the door.

"Nearly dinnertime, Tessie," she roared through the panel.

Miss Tessie opened the door and peered out. She was pale and had an excited look.

"Isn't this rain ever going to let up so I can go out and do my duty?" she demanded, as if Miss Julie were the one causing it to rain.

"You just be patient, child. It'll stop raining sooner or later."

"If it doesn't stop by tomorrow, I'm going out, rain or no rain."

"Well, we'll see when the time comes." Miss Julie tried to be soothing.

"Don't try to put me off. You'd think I didn't know what I was doing, the way you and Annette act."

"We want you to consider your health."

"Health, indeed!" Miss Tessie retorted. "I'd like to know what that's got to do with it."

In spite of her disregard of such fleshly matters, she turned up at the dinner table. She might not have been there, however, for all the part she took in the conversation. She sat regarding them all with a look best described as pitying.

When the table had been cleared and Henry retired to the sitting room for a second cigarette and a few moments' relaxation, Annette went with him and said:

"Henry, I'm really getting worried about her. I don't like this silent sitting and looking at all of us."

He made a gesture of helplessness.

"And if this rain doesn't stop," Annette continued, "God knows what will happen. She's been walking up and down all morning, and I suppose she'll begin it again any minute." She looked at her husband as if hoping for encouragement.

"I think it *is* going to clear up," Henry said hopefully. "But of course that's no real solution. It's this going all over town that's the worst thing."

"Maybe she'll get tired of that."

"If she does, there'll just be something else." He lay back in the Morris chair and shut his eyes.

Annette went to her bedroom, and took up her crocheting; then she went into the boys' room and was satisfied to find James and George innocently coloring a drawing with their crayons.

As she began to crochet once more, she heard the footsteps going up and down, up and down, in Miss Tessie's room.

Gritting her teeth, she continued her crocheting. Then Henry called up the stairs that he was going, and the little boys rushed down to see him off, and the car roared away in the rain.

[273]

After a while Annette realized that the walking had ceased. She glanced out of the window, and saw that the rain had ended. But the wind still swooped around the house, whipping the brown garden and rattling the palmettoes.

"If she goes out in this wind, she'll catch her death of cold," Annette thought.

Miss Julie was no help. "We'll have to let her go," she declared.

And Miss Tessie did go. Bundled up in several shawls, and with her heavy coat and gloves, she tiptoed down the hall, crept down the stairs, and went softly out the front door and to the street.

"I really ought to follow her," Miss Julie said, with a shiver, "but I can't afford to have pneumonia too. As for trying to persuade her to come back home, that's no use. She'll stay out all night if I as much as mention it. And I don't want to have a brawl in the street with her."

"I might go, but she wouldn't listen to me," Annette said. "She thinks I'm a fool, as it is."

"There's nothing to do but wait." Miss Julie turned away from the window. "Poor Tessie! I never thought she'd end up like this."

But Miss Tessie seemed to be none the worse for her exposure when she returned home at dusk. She sat in her room, where Annette had kept the fire going, until it was time for supper, and then she came down and ate a few bites in the same sort of silence as at dinner.

A few days later Betsy came home in tears.

"What's the matter?" Annette inquired frantically. "You're not sick, are you, child? You haven't got a toothache, or anything?"

"I can't stand it any longer," Betsy sobbed.

Annette's heart sank. She knew very well what the girl meant. "Can't stand what?" she asked, pretending innocence.

"Why, you know, Mamma. You know how Aunt Tessie is going on. Everybody in Charleston is laughing at us, and the girls at school have been talking about it. I just can't stand it."

"What do you care?" Annette chid her. "Is that going to hurt you? What does it matter what the girls say? You aren't to blame because Aunt Tessie is old and peculiar, are you?"

"I'm going to ask Papa to send me away to school somewhere."

"Well, you try to put up with it," Annette urged. "Don't pay any attention to them." (How easy it was to say that, and what a meaningless thing it was to say!) "They've got grandmothers, too, and great-aunts, and I could tell you about some of them. Don't you worry about it."

But she told Henry what Betsy had said.

"If this business doesn't stop, I'll do it," he said. "I will send her away."

Joe, meanwhile, had experienced the same treatment as Betsy. The first time Annette knew of his troubles was when Mrs. Barnes called up and complained that her boy had been "brutally attacked" by him.

"They're big boys," Annette said. "I never interfere in children's quarrels."

But she did ask Joe what he had done to Alec Barnes.

"Who wants to know?"

"Joe, don't speak to me like that. Remember, I'm your mother."

"Well, don't pick on me."

"Answer me. Why did you fight with him?"

"I don't like him."

"That's no excuse. Why did you fight with him?"

"He said Aunt Tessie was nutty," Joe replied. "I told him to take it back; and he said he wouldn't, and that, besides, Granny was crazy and so were you. So I blacked his eyes for him, and knocked one of his teeth out, too. That'll teach him."

"Why do you get into fights like this?" Annette scolded. "What do you care what Alec Barnes says, or anybody else?"

"Because I don't take that from anybody. You think it's easy, Mamma, to just walk off when somebody calls you names. But you can't do it. I'm not going to have them calling me yellow."

"Try not to pay any attention to them, son," Annette pleaded. "It's mortifying when boys' mothers call up and complain."

"If he was anything but a sissy he wouldn't have gone home to tell his mother." Joe insisted upon his code.

"You don't care whether it makes your mother unhappy or not?"

"I've got myself to look out for."

"Next time it happens I'll tell your father about it," Annette threatened. "He'll put a stop to it."

"He's the one that taught me never to take anything from anybody."

"Well, I wish for my sake you wouldn't have fights," Annette told him, weakly. "I wish you'd try to be a gentleman."

She was rather glad, on the whole, that Joe had done what he did. She had never liked Sarah Barnes. Once, when old Mr. Barnes had been ill, Annette had sent them a pitcher of fresh milk from her own cow, and they had never so much as sent a message of thanks. She couldn't help feeling that this served them right.

She congratulated herself that James was too small for such affairs. Whereupon James came home some days afterward with his face bruised and his lip cut, and after the truth had been wormed out of him, declared that he didn't want to go to school any more as long as the children were going to tease him about having a crazy aunt.

By this time Henry was talking seriously about leaving Charleston.

"We'll never be able to hold our heads up again," he moaned.

Miss Julie thought this was silly. "False pride will kill Henry yet," she said. But she formed the habit of going to St. Joseph's Church instead of to the Cathedral, and Annette went there with her.

They were thoroughly miserable; and only Miss Tessie was happy. She went to Mass every morning, wandered through the streets of the city, begged free car rides, and spoke to strangers; and there was no one to forbid.

Miss Julie was no help at all. She listened to her sister's extravagant talk about her mission, and her glorification, but she could do nothing to keep her from mortifying all of them.

And then she did a cruel thing.

Miss Tessie, as they had feared she finally would, caught a cold, which began with a sore throat and sniffles and became worse when she insisted upon going out as usual. Finally, when she could scarcely breathe, Miss Julie prevailed upon her to go to bed.

"You'll have pneumonia if you don't," she said.

"God won't let me catch pneumonia."

"He let you catch that cold."

"Don't blaspheme, Julie." Miss Tessie was too miserable to argue. "But I'll go to bed, to show that I'm not too proud to be obedient to those who have my welfare at heart."

Miss Julie rolled her eyes at this lofty speech and began fussing with the hot-water bag and the mustard plaster and hot lemonade. She really was afraid that her sister might contract pneumonia. Why, Tessie was just a bag of bones, she thought, when she saw her undressed and ready for bed.

Miss Tessie was restless the first day, but she contained her impatience and got a little sleep. On the second day, she began to be dissatisfied, and talked at great length of "lost opportunities" and the "sin against the Holy Ghost."

"It's no sin against the Holy Ghost to stay in bed when you're sick," Miss Julie said rather sharply, feeling all at once sick and tired of nonsense.

Miss Tessie did not reply, and her sister, feeling that this was as good a time as any to attempt to discourage her from her course, said:

"I've been thinking about that vision of yours, Tessie, and a peculiar thing has occurred to me. Don't you think it's very strange that the Blessed Mother appeared to you in black? She always appears in blue."

Miss Tessie did not answer at first. She looked steadily at her sister with her nearsighted eyes, and her chin quivered. Then she dropped her hands heavily to the coverlet. When she spoke, it was in a weak voice.

"I have wondered about it," she said, and Miss Julie leaned over to catch the words. "But the other miracles—the cemetery plot and the dream I had . . . No, it must be true." She clutched her sister's hand. "Julie, don't take my vision away," she begged. "It's the only thing I ever had that was really perfect."

("My God," Miss Julie thought, "what have I done to the poor thing? Oh, why did I ever say such a thing? If this is what doubting her has done, I'd rather she'd believe almost anything.")

"Tessie, I didn't mean to doubt you. It was just a question in my mind. I shouldn't have asked it."

"You doubted me," said Miss Tessie, tearfully. "My own sister!"

At her most abusive, she had never had the effect on her sister that she now had with this almost abject gentleness. Miss Julie said to herself that if craziness would make the poor soul happy, why, then she could be just as crazy as she pleased.

"Of course," she said, "considering the cemetery plot keeping itself in order, and the dream in Latin, why, it couldn't be anything but a true vision, could it? I hadn't thought of that."

Miss Tessie brightened a little, and the glow came back into her eyes.

"Julie, I'll tell you what I think is the explanation. I think the Virgin appeared in black to me because I was immodest once."

Miss Julie's eyes opened very wide.

"It wasn't really intentional, but I should have been careful. It was one morning when I got up a little late. The clock didn't go off, or something like that—I forget just what. Anyway, I jumped out of bed in a great hurry and stripped off my nightgown, and when I happened to look out of the corner of my eye, there was Willie with his eyes wide open looking at me.

"I think that's the explanation. But I hope the Blessed Mother is going to appear to me once more, in blue, before I die."

Miss Julie repressed a smile. "Perhaps that's it," she said. "I hope she will."

"I should have been more careful," Miss Tessie repeated.

"Well, it was a very small sin."

"I've said many a prayer to be forgiven for it."

"You will be, I'm sure of that," Miss Julie assured her.

"There were times," Miss Tessie continued, "when I thought God had punished me for that lewdness by taking my children away from me."

"Well, sister, God's ways are inscrutable, you know. But I don't think he did it for that reason." Miss Julie shook her head in further denial.

"I've tried to lead a blameless life," Miss Tessie said calmly. "I know that I've been uncharitable and ill-tempered, but I never meant any harm to a living soul. . . . I've never been able to see why Heaven has punished me so. Maybe it was to try me, and to prepare me for my vision."

That strained and eager look returned to her features. Her eyes were feverishly bright.

"It must have been that. And there's something more. Don't tell anybody this, Julie." She coughed slightly. "It's been conveyed to me that I'm going to have an even bigger vision: something even more glorious than the first vision. I don't know when it will be. I must wait, that's all."

"Wonderful!"

Miss Julie was impressed in spite of herself. After all, miracles did happen. Nevertheless, it was hard to get used to the idea of Tessie as a saint. In fact, there was no one she would have thought less likely to gain a place in the hagiography.

"You hurt my feelings terribly when you said that about the Blessed Mother in black, Julie. And to explain it, I had to tell you something I've never breathed to a soul outside the confessional."

"I apologize, Tessie. It was just stupid of me, that's all. I was like doubting Thomas."

"The Devil has tried to tempt me not to believe, you know—

[279]

over and over again. He's tried to make me think I was crazy, and he's put that into other people's minds, too."

Miss Julie nodded sagely, as if she were quite familiar with the snares of the Evil One.

"I think I'll pray a little if you'll leave me alone."

"Certainly."

Miss Julie was thankful for a chance to get away from this atmosphere of overheated imagination. She closed the door and went down to the kitchen to get a sip of coffee from Jennie, and then she returned to the sitting room, where the boys were playing checkers.

"Well, there you are, you rascals. Playing checkers, eh?"

"I'm winnin'," James said.

"He cheats," George explained.

"I do not!"

"You do!"

"Boys!" Miss Julie expostulated. "Don't quarrel. Why aren't you playing outside? It's a nice day. I see the boys next door playing with their football. Why don't you go play with them?"

"We got cold and came in," James answered. "Besides, Mamma told us not to play with Eddie and his brother. They said Aunt Tessie was crazy, and that their mother told them so. And she don't want me to get into a fight with them."

"Well, you do just as your Ma says," Miss Julie recommended.

She went up to her room and sat by the fire, working on a quilt and saddened more than ever by the turn things had taken. But she felt restless and uneasy.

"I wonder if Tessie really has a cold, or if it's something worse," she muttered.

Laying the quilting aside, she went to the door of Miss Tessie's room, opened it softly, and peered in.

Miss Tessie was sound asleep, her swollen, gnarled fingers relaxed on the coverlet.

"Praying, eh!" Miss Julie murmured. She smiled tenderly, shut the door again, and went back to her sewing.

"It would be better for her and for everybody else if she never woke up," she thought. . . . "But I mustn't think such things, God forgive me."

How, Miss Julie wondered, was all this going to end? With Tessie screaming obscenities in her madness, or attempting violence on herself?

There was just the least bit of a doubt in her mind. She did not believe that Tessie had actually seen a miraculous vision, but she wondered just a little. And if it had been a real vision, why had Tessie been chosen for it and not she?

CHAPTER TWELVE

As soon as Miss Tessie had got over her cold and was able to walk shakily about the house—for she had been, in Miss Julie's phrase, "terribly pulled down"—she began to worry again about what she called, quite unselfconsciously, her mission, and to be impatient at staying in.

"She'll kill herself," Miss Julie moaned to Annette.

"I don't know what to do," Annette replied, helplessly.

"Here it is almost Thanksgiving, and damp and cold. And her just over that terrible cold, and she'll go out and get another one, and then it'll be pneumonia. I wish I knew some way to cope with her, but I don't."

"You know the worst of it, Ma. That's what people will say about us. They'll say we neglect her. It'll be just one more thing for them to criticize. They'll say we had no right to let her go out."

"Oh, never mind what people say."

"I don't mean that I'm not considering Aunt Tessie, too, Ma. But there's that unfortunate side to everything that happens to her, now."

Miss Julie grunted. "If your conscience is clear I wouldn't give a sou marquee for what anybody thinks," she said. "How in

God's name are you going to keep her indoors? That'll only worry her to death, if not something worse than that."

But their concern did not have long to last. One sunny morning Miss Tessie dressed herself warmly and, despite the protests of Miss Julie and Annette, declared firmly that she was going to be about her mission. "And nothing on earth can stop me," she said, her eyes flashing.

Miss Julie cried a little. "I can't help it. To think of my own sister going to her death like this is too much for me."

"But if it makes her happy—" Annette was suddenly weary of considering anything other than keeping Miss Tessie quiet.

"I can't look at it that way," Miss Julie said. "It's my own flesh and blood, and she's just like a child of mine to me now, since she's become silly. I keep thinking of the time that poor little Samuel heard one of the darkies say that if you put salt on a bird's tail you could catch it. And the poor little fellow begged me for a bag of salt, and went out and tried to catch the pigeons with it. That's just the way Tessie is acting now, like a child that will believe anything."

"I wish we could think up some way to make her believe that God has forbidden her to go out and risk her health," Annette said with a wry smile.

"No, she wouldn't believe anything as sensible as that. If you told her that you had a dream that said she was the greatest saint in heaven, she'd believe you. But not that."

"I don't think she'll be able to go out like that much from now on," Annette declared. "Didn't you see how she tottered from side to side as she went down the street?"

"If that's the case, we're certainly going to be in for it," Miss Julie said. "If she finds she isn't able to go out on her mission, as she calls it, she's going to be uncontrollable. I remember old Mrs. Pritchard—"

"Ma, don't tell me about any more crazy people. I can't stand to hear it."

"Well, all right, child. I was just going to give you an example of thwarting them. It's the worst thing you can do."

Miss Tessie's intention was to go and stand in front of the post office, and she went over to Rutledge Avenue and took the car. She made the usual request for free transportation, and the conductor, instructed by Henry's friend Mr. Amabile, who controlled the trolley system, consented. Miss Tessie was profoundly gratified.

When she got off the car at the corner of Meeting Street, she felt quite weak, but decided that she would stay. She had half a mind to stand right in front of St. Michael's, directly across the street, for she felt that for a Catholic saint to stand there would be a good lesson to Protestants. But there were more people on the steps of the post office, and she reluctantly chose that location for her afternoon's stand.

She stood there with her arms folded, the hands crossed at the wrists in the familiar pose of Christian paintings, and surveyed the passers-by, some of whom she knew and some of whom she didn't. She treated them all with the same indulgence, smiling tolerantly at them as poor worldlings. And up Broad Street, not quite a block away, Henry O'Donnell sat in his office, blissfully ignorant of the nearness of his disgraceful relative.

He was standing by the window when he suddenly became aware of a commotion in the street. People were running down toward Meeting Street, and he was about to send the office boy down to see what was going on when a boy burst into the office.

"They said for me to tell Mr. O'Donnell that his aunt fell on the post-office steps," he shouted.

"God Almighty!" Henry moaned, divided between honest concern for poor Miss Tessie and horror at the spectacle she was making of herself and him.

"Call my home and tell them to send the car immediately to the post office and have Dr. Forbes come to the house right away," he directed his secretary, Miss Driscoll, as he hurriedly left.

He found Miss Tessie seated on the steps of the post office in the midst of a crowd of people, black and white. One of the clerks had come out with a glass of water for her.

Henry took command of the situation. "Has anybody sent for a doctor?" he roared.

Someone had, and the doctor summoned was Dr. Snow. Henry groaned again. Dr. Snow was on the St. Cecilia committee, and this was an unfortunate situation indeed in which to meet him. He turned to Miss Tessie, who was quite calm.

"Doctor?" she sniffed, as soon as she could make herself heard. "Doctor? Hoo! I don't need any doctor. When I need one I'll send for him myself. I hate people who can't mind their own business!"

Henry was ashamed. "Mrs. Fisher," he said, "I'm sure we're grateful to these people for being so thoughtful." He frowned furiously at her for this breach of manners.

Miss Tessie was abashed. "Of course," she said. "Here Henry, help me up and let's go home."

Wallace drove up at that moment with the car, to Henry's unutterable relief.

"Someone please call Dr. Snow and tell him never mind," Henry said. "Or if he does come, tell him I'm very much obliged, but Mrs. Fisher was well enough to go home and we are going to call Dr. Forbes."

He lifted Miss Tessie to her feet, and with Wallace's aid put her into the back of the car. Then he got in and they were off.

Henry said not a word, angry as he was; Miss Tessie's face was so white that a much less considerate man would have been deterred.

When the telephone rang, Miss Julie and Annette were still talking about Miss Tessie; Miss Julie had remarked that it was a pity they couldn't think up some way of persuading Father Schmidt to come and exhort her sister to discontinue this embarrassing practice of standing around on street corners.

"But that wouldn't do any good," she admitted. "She's never told any confessor about her vision, and she doesn't know I went to see Father Mellon that time. Besides, she's so far gone in this sainthood idea that she might not even listen to a priest."

They looked at each other with a deep conviction that they were helpless.

"To think of all the times I've laughed at silly old people!" Annette said. "I've laughed at Sarah imitating them, and I've laughed at her stories about the old lady next door that she gets from Hattie. I never thought I'd have to cope with it myself. Maybe it was God's punishment for doing it."

"Well, I told you not to make fun of Tessie," Miss Julie said.

"I'm paying for it now." Annette stared at the fire.

"Maybe it won't last very long."

It was at this moment that the telephone rang.

Annette went in to answer it, and came back wringing her hands. "Ma! Poor Aunt Tessie. She's collapsed on the post-office steps!"

Now it was Miss Julie's turn to wring her hands. "Oh, my poor old sister!" She sat down in the rocker and began to sob.

Annette rushed out to send Wallace with the car; and then she called Dr. Forbes, and they sat down to wait in an agony of apprehension. Sarah got a glass of wine ready, and rushed upstairs to open Miss Tessie's bed.

Five minutes later the car was in front, and Miss Tessie, with Wallace and Henry to lift her up the stairs, came into the house. Annette and Miss Julie fluttered around, crying and muttering snatches of prayers.

They put her into the deep easy-chair by the fire, and gave her the glass of wine.

Miss Tessie shook her head woefully and spoke for the first time.

"I was just weak," she said. "I tried, but, all of a sudden, I just couldn't stand, Julie, I'm very weak."

"Well, you haven't got your strength back after that terrible cold." Miss Julie was relieved that Miss Tessie was not dying after all. "Wait awhile, and you'll be able to go out all you want." Though she doubted that very much.

Henry had finished his account of the disaster to Annette, and they stood around and asked Miss Tessie how she felt.

"I think it must be my heart."

"You've never had any heart trouble," Miss Julie said.

"Do you think an old nurse like me doesn't know?" Miss Tessie retorted. "Hoo!"

"I've sent for Cyril," Annette said. "He'll be here any minute."

Miss Tessie waved airily at her. "This is not a case for the doctor. This is God's doing. He has something else in store for me, and He doesn't want me to go around any longer. His will be done."

"Amen," said Miss Julie.

"I think I'd better go upstairs and lie down. Henry, you go back to work, and don't worry about me."

They helped her up the steps. "You're a whole lot lighter than I am," Miss Julie said. "When I had that sick attack, they had a very devil of a time getting me up the steps—Sarah and Stevens and Jennie too. . . . They almost had to get a derrick."

"There isn't much of this clay left," Miss Tessie said solemnly.

"Now, Tessie, don't talk that way."

"*I know.*"

Miss Julie and Annette got her undressed and into bed, and she submitted with entire willingness; once or twice she winced when they moved her arms too suddenly.

She was almost a cripple from that rheumatism of hers, Miss Julie thought, looking at the knotty fingers.

Soon after Henry had gone, Dr. Forbes came and made his examination.

"It's mostly exhaustion," he said. "But her heart is pretty weak. Keep her as quiet as you can."

When he had gone, Annette went in to see if her aunt wanted anything.

"Just to go to sleep," Miss Tessie said, gently.

Annette lowered the shades. "All right, you go to sleep, then. I'll get Sarah to put the dinner bell right here beside you. If you want anything, you ring for me. We'll be right near by."

For a long time they sat uneasily in Annette's room, talking little and waiting for Miss Tessie to ring the bell; but the summons didn't come. In fact, Miss Tessie was still sleeping soundly at dinnertime.

"The poor old soul is exhausted," Henry said, trying to hide his relief, which he felt was unworthy. He turned gravely to the children. "I don't need to say anything to the big ones about being quiet. But you, James, and George have got to be careful. We don't want your Aunt Tessie to be disturbed. Play outside as much as you can, and be very quiet in the house."

"I've already told them that," Annette said.

Henry frowned. "It won't hurt to impress it upon them. Speaking of quiet, I suppose we'd better not plan any company for Thanksgiving."

They all agreed that this would probably be very wise.

"And I think we'd better make up our minds not to have any fireworks this Christmas, either."

James and George looked at each other.

"If Granny was sick, it wouldn't make any difference," James said. "She wouldn't hear them."

"I hear a whole lot better than you think," Miss Julie retorted. "Just because I'm a little bit hard of hearing, people think I'm deaf. Let me tell you I'm not."

"James," said his father, "don't make remarks about people."

"I'm glad Aunt Tessie won't be able to go around for a while like she has been," Joe declared, in the low growl he was using to disguise the change of his voice.

This frankness, however well it expressed the relief of everyone, was not well received.

"You ought to be ashamed of yourself to say such a thing," Henry told him.

Joe flushed. "I meant—"

"Never mind what you meant," Annette interrupted sharply. "Don't say anything like that again."

"You'd better make a good act of contrition," said Miss Julie, whose hearing certainly did appear to be rather keen that day.

"No matter how trying Miss Tessie's actions may have been," Henry said, "we mustn't feel that way. We all ought to wish for her to get better right away."

But after dinner, when he and Annette were alone together, he confessed that this had been the greatest relief he had felt in years: "It's a shame to say it, but I feel like a new man."

"I know, Henry," Annette agreed.

She was thinking of how they could say to everyone now that Miss Tessie had had a breakdown: "She had begun to act a little peculiarly, you know, for some time—" She even rehearsed, mentally, the tone of voice and the deprecating smile she would use with the words. It would be possible to discuss the matter now as a weakness of old age; the stigma of insanity could be forgotten.

Miss Julie's thoughts were of a different order. She foresaw trouble. Tessie might be ill like this a long time (for she knew now that Tessie would never recover) and the burden of nursing would devolve upon her. Annette was of no use in a sickroom, and she would be sure to rub Tessie the wrong way. As for having a trained nurse— Well, Tessie's feelings toward everybody else in that profession were well known.

"I only hope I'll have a little peace," Miss Julie murmured. She hadn't had much since that day, three and a half years ago, when Tessie had come into the garden on Tradd Street and put an end to their years of estrangement.

CHAPTER THIRTEEN

FORTUNATELY, MISS TESSIE WAS QUITE PHILOSOPHICAL about her illness. She kept saying that it was the will of God, and that she would accept it, and that He had something greater in store for her.

For the first two weeks or so, when she lay in bed, no better and no worse, her mind was fairly lucid. She talked on and on to

Miss Julie about events of their childhood and young womanhood, and even remembered to speak in a tone Miss Julie could hear clearly, although it tired her and she had to stop every now and then to recover her strength. Some of the sodality ladies came too, and as Miss Tessie spoke comparatively little of her vision and of her expectations they went away gratified and certain that Miss Tessie was "much better," meaning, of course, that the unfortunate "nervousness" she had shown for some time was apparently on the wane.

Father Mellon came to see her, too, and was very discreet. She told him of the vision, and of the reasons she had for not consulting her confessor concerning it; and he explained kindly that such doubts always assailed those who were so fortunate as to receive marks of divine favor, and merely indicated proper humility.

His visit caused a distinct disturbance in Miss Tessie's behavior.

"Did you hear what he said, Julie?" she asked excitedly. "He said my feelings about the vision proved that it was a true one."

Miss Julie thought this was putting rather a broad interpretation on Father Mellon's politely evasive comments, but did not say so.

"Of course, I knew it all along," Miss Tessie said. "I never had the slightest doubt, except the kind he talked about—that I wasn't worthy of such a thing."

"Naturally."

"You know, it's very odd," Miss Tessie continued. "That vision has made me humbler than I ever was in my life. I've been a different person, I know it. I suppose the kind of pride we've all had comes from our not having anything else."

"I suppose you're right, Tessie."

"I think I ought to get up. Not to walk around, but just to sit up in a Morris chair, or something like that. It shows a lack of faith to lie here on my back like this."

"If you think you're able, Tessie—"

"Of course I'm able, Julie. Go get Annette to help you."

But Miss Tessie was no sooner settled in the big armchair than she wanted to return to bed. Sitting up made her back hurt and her head swim.

"God knows it's swimming enough as it is," Miss Julie thought grimly, as they eased the small body into bed again.

Within a week, however, Miss Tessie was able to sit up for an hour, and within two weeks she could sit up morning and afternoon. Visitors began to come: Miss Georgie Peters, out of deference to Miss Julie, and the various sodality sisters, and Mr. Beauchamp, and Colonel Calvert—"Eddie" Calvert, who had once been a beau of Miss Julie's and then of Miss Tessie's—and many others. They brought flowers, and small treats, and Miss Tessie received them all graciously, with that Gerard air, and seemed to be putting herself out to be pleasant.

Her amiability impressed Miss Julie strangely.

"Sometimes I almost believe in that vision," she told Annette one afternoon after the visitors of the day had departed. "Something must have happened to Tessie to make her behave so pleasantly."

"You'll be having a vision yourself next."

"I guess I'm entitled to it just as much as Tessie."

Miss Julie hadn't realized it, but she was just a little jealous. If the vision had been a true one—well, hadn't she led a more Christian life than Tessie? been more charitable and good-tempered? And if it were only a delusion of an aged and sorely tried brain, she more or less envied her sister the pleasure she got out of it.

Miss Tessie was more wrapped up than ever in her miracle; and she looked positively delighted whenever people came.

"You see?" she said to Miss Julie. "First I had to reveal myself to *them*. But God takes care of everything. He saw that I was tired, and that it wasn't good for me, and He made me sick so that people could come to see *me*."

Miss Julie nodded sagely. She wanted to laugh, and when she went out of the room she did; but it was short-lived laughter. There was something terribly convincing about Tessie's certainty. And thus her resentment increased, and she could not help being just a little cross to her sister when the latter demanded some small service right on top of another.

Even when she snapped, as she did once or twice, Miss Tessie was patient. She would look up like a wounded doe, and Miss Julie would be ashamed and beg her forgiveness.

At times Miss Tessie's mind still appeared to be lucid. She discussed her past life calmly, like a saint repenting of his earlier misdeeds.

"I wanted too much, Julie," she said once. "And when I didn't get it, and was poor and had trouble, my heart got hard and I became proud. That was foolish, but it's trouble that makes us proud. That's what Charleston pride is—it's shame, that's the word for it."

That was terribly sensible, Miss Julie felt. And by Christmas week she really almost did believe in that vision. It made her a little more cross. She was morose at mealtimes, and even the children felt that a change had come over her.

"Ma's tired with all that waiting on Aunt Tessie," was Annette's explanation.

But Christmas Day ended Miss Julie's uncertainty. It had been Henry's idea at first that, because of Miss Tessie's poor health, they should have no noisy fireworks. But when she seemed so much better, he relented, and purchased the usual caseful of firecrackers and aerial bombs.

Somehow, though, Miss Tessie did not seem to take in the fact that it was Christmas. She was in a sort of haze that day. Once or twice she remarked about the noise, and Miss Julie explained. But it was as though the invalid were already living in another world.

She was glad to see all the Christmas guests, who came into her room and chatted with her, and was actually radiant when they left.

"You see?" she said to Miss Julie. "They all know about it, now."

Miss Julie belched irreverently. She was very full of good

Christmas cheer and was in no mood for mysticism of any kind. However, Miss Tessie didn't notice her rudeness. She said she was tired and wanted to take a nap.

She was still asleep after supper when it came time for the fireworks. Miss Julie took a look at her to see that she was all right, and then went down to see the fun.

It began in the usual way, with a balloon or two, and continued through skyrockets and aerial bombs and pinwheels and fountains and Roman candles. Then there were more balloons; and with one of these there was a slight contretemps. It did not rise as rapidly as it should have; perhaps there was a pinhole in the paper. It went up very slowly and uncertainly, lurching as it rose, and a passing puff of wind drove it against the side of the house, up which it crawled, right past the window of Miss Tessie's room, while everyone watched and worried lest the kerosene Stevens had poured on the excelsior might set fire to some of the wooden trimming of the building. But it finally made its way up over the roof and sailed away toward the river; and with the launching of the big balloon shaped like a whale and the shooting off of a few more Roman candles, the festivities ended. It was all quite as usual, even to Henry's unfailing remark that it was a good way to burn up money.

Miss Julie pulled her shawl a little tighter around her shoulders. "I'll run up and see how Tessie is," she remarked. "Maybe the noise has upset her."

She pushed open the door softly lest Miss Tessie should still be asleep. But Miss Tessie was half sitting up in bed, her hands clasped, with a look of wild excitement on her face.

"What's the matter, Tessie?" Miss Julie shouted, for she was alarmed.

Miss Tessie swung her joined hands from side to side. She was almost too agitated to speak.

"Julie! Julie!" she called hoarsely. "Julie!"

"What is it, Tessie? Tell me, for God's sake!"

"I've seen"—Miss Tessie's eyes were wide—"the Holy Ghost!"

Miss Julie started. If Miss Tessie had said that their dead

father was standing beside them, her flesh would not have prickled more.

"Tongues of fire," Miss Tessie said. "Like the disciples saw. Right outside my window. It lingered there for a moment, and I thought it was coming right in to light on the top of my head—you remember the picture? But it stayed outside, and then rose up to heaven again."

Miss Julie sat down in a chair, heavily, as though she had been pushed into it.

"Mercy, Tessie, you gave me a fright!"

"I was awed myself." Miss Tessie lay back. "You must tell them all, Julie. You must tell them what has happened in this house where they all live! Hurry!"

Miss Julie needed no further invitation. She sped down the stairs as rapidly as her age and her stuffed stomach would permit.

Henry and Annette were sitting before the fire in the dining room, Henry leaning on the table, a glass of port before him. They started up.

"What's happened, Ma?" Annette cried.

Miss Julie wrung her hands. "That poor thing is entirely out of her mind—raving crazy!" she sputtered. "My poor sister!" Her voice changed to a wail. "She's got the idea that that balloon that passed by her window was the Holy Ghost in the shape of a tongue of fire, and she wants you all to know about the miracle that's happened in this house!"

"Oh, Lord! I thought she must be dying, by the way you tore downstairs, Ma."

Henry chuckled. "I suppose she's talking in divers tongues," he said.

But Miss Julie was not amused. She turned upon him, suddenly indignant.

"You ought to be ashamed, laughing at an old sick woman's notions. You don't know how pitiful it all is. And on Christmas Day, too!" She wiped her eyes.

"There, Miss Julie, I'm sorry," Henry said. "I didn't mean to be inconsiderate. Sit down and have a glass of wine."

He took a glass from the sideboard and poured the port for her. "That'll make you feel better."

Miss Julie drank it. "She gave me a terrible shock, you know. It made my skin crawl. I'm afraid I'm not a good subject for miracles." She rose. "I'll have to go back and tell her how impressed you are. And you'd better come up, too."

They followed her and entered Miss Tessie's room. Miss Tessie was exhausted. She lay with her eyes half closed, and merely smiled beatifically when she saw them.

"Wonderful," she said. "Wonderful. In this house. Get down on your knees and thank God for what He has done."

They remained standing, but Miss Tessie didn't notice that.

"I suppose when I'm gone this room will be a shrine," she said. "That will sort of upset things. Maybe you could have it taken down and put somewhere else."

"That's what we'll do," Henry promised glibly. "We'll give it to the Cathedral."

Miss Tessie smiled. "You've been a good man, Henry. God will let you prosper."

Henry patted her hand. "I'm only His humble instrument," he said, smiling.

"He will take that into account," Miss Tessie said. "He will bless you for it."

"Try to sleep, Aunt Tessie," Annette said. "Good night."

"Tell the children," Miss Tessie said.

"I will."

Henry walked out after her, shaking his head. "Poor old thing!" he said.

Miss Julie, after seeing that her sister was comfortable, gave her a sedative in her drinking water and went into her own room to think.

"Poor thing!" she muttered. She shook a peppermint out of the glass jar on her dresser. "Poor thing! Well, it wasn't a miracle after all, that vision."

She couldn't help feeling strangely contented at the thought.

"But I'm glad it's made her happy," she said to herself. "Poor thing!"

She smiled. She felt a whole lot more charitable toward Tessie, now that she was certain.

"God forgive me, I'm a jealous old fool."

And she smiled again, at the absurdity of the whole business, and in her own satisfaction.

CHAPTER FOURTEEN

AFTER THAT EVENTFUL CHRISTMAS DAY illusions came thick and fast to Miss Tessie, as if the door had been opened to them. Every day she confided to Miss Julie such experiences as having seen her daughter Theodora, "one of the brightest saints," and having talked to her about the life after death.

"I wonder that she hasn't been canonized," she said on one of these occasions. "When I'm better I'll have to do something about it."

"Oh, that can be arranged," Miss Julie replied. "You wait until the weather is better and you can go out."

Another of her delusions was that old Colonel Calvert was secretly trying to persuade her to marry him. Julie had been present on the two occasions when the old gentleman had visited her sister, and had never heard anything to suggest such a romantic intention, but Miss Tessie was certain of it.

"I think it would be foolish, though," she declared. "Of course, it's better to marry than to burn—but I don't think Willie would like it. In fact, I'm sure he wouldn't. Willie was always terribly jealous of me. He used to say he couldn't bear to have other men look at me in the street."

"I guess it's a long time since Tessie did any burning," Miss Julie said to Annette. "Or Eddie Calvert either." She chuckled at the absurdity of it, though the chuckle was a bit sad.

But the notion persisted in Miss Tessie's mind.

"I don't think it would be proper, do you, Julie?" she asked. "Considering the honor I've received, I don't think such a worldly thing as marriage would be right."

"I'm afraid it would be rather improper," said Miss Julie.

"I must ask Willie about it."

And, very obligingly, Willie appeared. They had a long talk, and he settled the matter for Miss Tessie. It wouldn't do at all, he said. He was waiting for her, and it would be very embarrassing for her to have two husbands in heaven, considering her devotion to the Blessed Virgin.

"I think Willie is quite right about it," Miss Julie agreed.

This world of make-believe was becoming very tiresome and trying to her. It made her rather nervous, too. "Sometimes I almost begin to think myself that I'm about to see somebody that's dead and gone come and talk to me," she told Annette in one of their numerous discussions.

"It's so bad for the children," Annette wailed. "I try to keep them away from her, but I'm afraid it will hurt her feelings. But, even so, knowing there's somebody in the house that's not quite right is bad for them. I can't tell you how it worries me."

"Tessie don't pay any attention to them when they do come in," Miss Julie said. "She called Betsy by some name or other the other day—some name I didn't recognize. I don't think they need to go up and see her at all. It isn't as if she was the same Tessie." She sighed deeply. "What worries me is that I wonder if I'm ever going to have any peace. Ever since the day she came to see me, almost four years ago, something has happened to upset my life. And I'm getting nearer to the grave myself. I wouldn't be surprised if I was to collapse after Tessie goes."

"Oh, you've got plenty of time, Ma."

"I don't mean I'm wishing for her death. That wouldn't be Christian."

However, there is in everybody a natural impatience about the course of a long and incurable illness. Miss Julie could not help feeling that it would really be better for all concerned if Miss Tessie should pass away in her sleep some night. There was nothing much wrong with her, bodily, except for the weakness of her heart and her extreme feebleness. That, at least, was a blessing, when her mind was so entirely out of control.

"At least, she's happy about it all," Miss Julie comforted herself.

But these were hard days for her. She couldn't just sit around and amuse herself, and watch the children. Miss Tessie wanted her every few minutes, for some foolishness or other. And George was now a big boy of eight, and James was ten, and what was left of their childhood was running out very fast. Tessie was the only child left now, and a troublesome one.

"And if she really gets helpless, I'm not going to be able to stand taking care of her.

"Of course they don't want a nurse. Nurses talk, Annette says, and Henry would worry about that.

"As if everybody that comes to see Tessie don't talk, too.

"Henry and his pride. Sometimes he makes me sick.

"Pride goeth before a fall.

"He that exalteth himself shall be humbled.

"Pride will kill some people one of these days.

"*Tchk.*"

When Lent approached, Miss Julie threshed out the question of fasting and abstinence.

"I'm a working woman," she said to herself. "Tessie keeps me on the go all the time. I don't think I'm called on to fast. And I don't think it would be good for my health. After all, I'll be seventy-four next month, and I need all the nourishment I can get."

Her final decision was that she would not fast and abstain. To avoid giving bad example to the children, she was careful to explain her position; and, to make up for her indulgence at the table, she went with great regularity to every Lenten service—stations, vespers, and evening sermons. In Holy Week she doubled her zeal. She attended Tenebrae and visited all the churches and went to the Mass of the presanctified on Good Friday.

Miss Tessie received communion on Easter Sunday from the

hands of Father Mellon, and for that day seemed quite rational by contrast. But this improvement did not endure—the worst of it being that her delusions took an unhappy turn. She imagined that the Devil was talking to her, trying to make her doubt her visions.

"You get right out of here," she said to him. "Don't try to tempt me. I know your tricks. Begone!"

It terrified Miss Julie to hear her sister talking to this imaginary Satan, and it made Miss Tessie much more difficult to pacify. For the Devil had planted in her mind a doubt about that first vision of the Blessed Mother. He was trying to convince her that the apparition in black was not, so to speak, a vision of the first magnitude. Sometimes he tried to persuade her that it was he who had sent the vision.

"If She would only appear once more in blue," said poor Miss Tessie, after one of the Devil's visits, "I'd be rid of that fiend. I saw Her just as plainly as I see you, there. She stood very straight, and She looked very sad, and when She opened Her robe I saw the Bleeding Sacred Heart, just like it is in the pictures."

The tempter tried to persuade her that it was he who had sent the vision of the Holy Ghost, too, and those of Willie Fisher and Theodora. Happily, Miss Tessie was able to talk this over with Willie and Theodora, and they both denied flatly that the Devil had had anything to do with their appearance. But the Virgin never had appeared again, although Miss Tessie had calls from St. Peter, and St. Theresa, and an angel brought her a message from St. Joseph.

One balmy afternoon of late spring, Miss Julie was sitting out on the piazza, quite close to the side windows of Tessie's room, watching the clouds pass by and enjoying melancholy memories of other springs. She had been a little worried about her sister that day, and she kept one ear cocked for a possible ring. Suddenly she had a peculiar sensation; it was as if the flowers in the garden—the honeysuckle, and the early roses, and the pinks—all combined to smell just like a room in which someone was laid out. At least, that was the way she told it afterwards.

Miss Julie leapt up, giving herself a crick in the back as she did so, and rushed in.

She found Miss Tessie with her eyes closed and her face as white as milk. She felt her pulse. It was almost imperceptible.

She ran to her daughter who was taking a nap.

"Annette!" she shouted. "Get up, right away! I think Tessie's dying!"

Annette sat up wide awake, and swung her feet over the side of the bed. She seized a blue kimono and followed.

Miss Tessie had opened her eyes. They had a flat, glazed, and sunken look, and Miss Julie looked at Annette and nodded ominously.

Annette took her aunt's cold, flaccid hand. Miss Tessie's eyes lighted up a little, and she smiled faintly.

"Thank God!" she murmured. "At last." Her fingers feebly grasped the edge of her niece's kimono. "At last," she repeated, "in blue."

"What does she say?" Miss Julie asked.

"She said 'in blue.'"

Miss Julie shook her head and smiled tenderly.

And thus, with the fulfillment of her dearest dream, Miss Tessie's bitter life was ended.

CHAPTER FIFTEEN

JOSEPHINE, MISS JULIE'S SPINSTER SISTER, came from Chattanooga to look her last upon Miss Tessie.

Miss Tessie looked very pretty, everyone said, lying there in the great parlor with tall candles at her head and feet, and a smile on her face, and with her white hair neatly coiffed, and a rosary and the daguerreotype of her father and mother clasped in her hands. "That was good of you, Julie," Josephine said. And

all those who knew the history of the daguerreotype were lauda-
tory of Miss Julie's generosity and thought putting it in Miss
Tessie's hands like that, was a fine gesture. Miss Julie didn't
seem to enjoy hearing that mentioned. She flushed each time.

In the fullness of her emotion, when Tessie was newly dead,
she had resolved to bury the daguerreotype with her. This was a
tug for Miss Julie, and she had quite a struggle with herself. In
the end she had succumbed to what she felt was a duty and a last
kindness to the dead. She had polished the worn leather case and
had been on the way to the parlor to place it in Miss Tessie's
hands when the thought occurred to her that this would be
foolish.

"After all, she won't care," Miss Julie reasoned. "It'll be no
good to her down there in the ground. Tessie was always generous. She'd rather have me enjoy keeping it, I'm sure."

She hesitated there in the hallway; and then, turning abruptly,
she went upstairs to her room again. She removed the faded
images from the frame, opened her old trunk, and put them deep
under layers of clothing—Pa's uniform, and her wedding dress,
and infant clothes she had kept all these years. Then, closing
the daguerreotype cover carefully, she returned to the parlor and
placed it in Miss Tessie's hands. "That will show that my feelings about it were the right kind," she said to herself, and was
quite satisfied with the compromise.

Miss Julie's emotions about Tessie were oddly mixed. She felt
decent sorrow, certainly, for her sister's death, and regretted too
late, as we all do, the things undone that might have made her
life a bit more bright. Still, she thought, what could I have done?
Tessie couldn't get along with anyone. It didn't matter what you
did.

But somehow, too, she sensed that Tessie had, even in dying,
put them all subtly in the wrong. Her very death was a sort of
reproach to those she left behind. And the conventional remarks
people made were a bit annoying.

And how they all came! Friends, neighbors, relatives, Mr.
Beauchamp and Eddie Calvert and the Soubereaus and all the

O'Donnells, and all the sodality ladies, and Annette's friends, and Henry's business associates, and some of Betsy's school friends and their mothers. And all of them said something like "Poor thing," and "What a saint she was, when you think of what her life was on earth!" and "If the cross wins the crown, poor Miss Therese ought to be one of the brightest angels."

"God knows I don't want to speak ill of the dead," she said to Josephine, "but all that palaver makes me tired. If they talk all that rubbish about me after I'm gone, I'm going to turn right over in my coffin."

"Why, Julie!" Josephine said, shocked.

Only Brother Joe, Miss Julie thought, was sensible about the matter, although he went too far. They had been sitting in the dining room, having cake and coffee, and relaxing a little under the strain. There was a sort of timorous gayety about the conversation. Miss Julie had been telling about Miss Tessie's visit from the Holy Ghost in the form of a paper Christmas balloon, and her talks with St. Peter and the Devil, and they had laughed, as they could not help laughing, about it.

"Julie," Joe Gerard said, "I'll bet Tessie's setting heaven to rights this very minute. I'll bet there hasn't been such a to-do there since Bismarck died. You know that story, how he said 'Get up, Christ'?"

Annette protested, but feebly. Her Uncle Joe always made her laugh.

"I can just see Tessie," Joe went on. "Here's St. Peter at the gates, and here's Tessie knocking. St. Peter finally opens the gates. 'Hoo!' Tessie says. 'They take long enough to come to the door here.' 'Who are you?' says St. Peter. 'Hoo!' says Tessie. 'You know perfectly well who I am. I'm one of the Gerards. Don't put on airs. We had our carriage when you were pulling up fish out of the Sea of Galilee.'"

"Uncle Joe!" Annette remonstrated, half laughing.

Miss Julie chuckled in spite of herself and remarked for the ten-thousandth time that Joe was a blackguard; and Josephine looked prim.

"And if poor Willie Fisher has got to heaven yet, I'll bet you she's got him scurrying around right now. 'Willie, see what that child is crying about! . . . Her mother? What right has her mother got to be here? I didn't think heaven was full of all kinds of poor buckras!' "

"Tessie was always exclusive," Miss Julie said. "Dear me! Think of her standing on Wentworth and King Street to let people see her, and begging the streetcyar conductor for free rides to humble herself."

"Well, it's a wonder Henry isn't lying right there with her," Joe said. "It was all a terrible blow to Henry's social standing. It's a wonder to me he didn't bust when she took to selling magazine subscriptions that time."

"You leave Henry alone," Annette said. "He stood it very well."

Miss Julie came to Henry's rescue too. "Henry is always good," she said. "He's got a heart as big as the ocean."

"Different from his brother," Joe said. "Edmund O'Donnell wouldn't have given you his sweat to wash the almshouse windows."

"Joe! This is a very serious occasion," Miss Julie said sternly.

"You know what I am, sister," Joe said, and he put his hand on her arm. "I didn't mean any harm. I'll miss poor Tessie as much as you will, and I'm not being sarcastic, either. It's horrible what life does to us, Julie. Think of Tessie, when she was young and hopeful and thought she was going to have the world. And look at her now."

"If we only knew that when we were young, brother," Miss Julie said, "what a lot of trouble we could save ourselves!"

"But you've always been cheerful, Julie. I never knew anything to make you feel real low."

Miss Julie shook her head. "I've had my share of heartache as well as everybody else. I'm what poor Tante Eloise used to call a cheerful idiot. If I'd wanted to feel sorry for myself—well, there's Francis. He's not a bad boy, but he's just thoughtless. I don't blame him. My sons had a hard life from the time they were little fellows."

"Yes. Francis is peculiar. That is"—Joe realized that he must tread warily—"there's something about him that isn't like the rest of us."

"Oh, he's enough like the rest of us. But he's like the Sharps, too. Do you think I've forgotten how they treated me when I married Pa? 'The little French girl' was what they called me." Her voice sounded so bitter that Joe was startled. "As if the Gerards weren't twice as good as they were, with all their New England tombstones! Although Pa was as fine a gentleman as you could find in the South or anywhere else. He was the pick of the lot. . . . There's a lot of Sharp in Francis. And a lot of Gerard. Unforgiving, like poor Tessie there. And he hasn't got her generosity, either. Poor thing, she would give you the shirt off her back. And proud. It's that Southern pride that we all have that's made so much trouble. And now it's too late. We're all divided up, like North and South; Henry don't speak to his brother, and Francis hasn't been near me for ages, even when his aunt's been lying at death's door."

"I've never quarreled with any of you," Joe said. "The only reason we've stayed apart is— Well, you know. I wasn't the one to blame for that."

"No one's ever blamed you for taking your own wife's part," Miss Julie said. "And that was only for a while." It was what life had done to Joe that was so terrible, she thought. It grieved her to the heart every time she thought of it.

"It's too late, as you say, sister. I'm seventy now, or I will be in a few months. A short life and a merry one. And now I must be going along. I'll see you tonight."

"God bless you, Joe."

Miss Julie put her arms around him. They walked out to the front door together, and she watched him go down the street.

How long life was! She could remember the day he was born, almost. She was four years old. At least, she remembered the time he fell out of his high chair. And that was almost seventy years ago.

John Gerard came late that afternoon, and the family was almost complete.

John was rather a disappointment to Miss Julie. She had not seen him in years, despite the fact that Savannah was so near, and she was shocked at the change in him. He had aged. It showed how old they were all getting, she thought; you didn't realize it until you saw somebody of your own age after a long time. There were heavy lines in his face, and his hair was snow-white and wispy, and he stooped. His eyes were sunken, and his big ears looked like something made of wax. Anybody could see that he had been very ill and had escaped death by the flutter of an eyelid. Miss Julie shook her head forebodingly.

"He looks stricken," she whispered to Josephine in her rumbling way.

Fortunately John was talking to Henry and didn't hear this encouraging remark.

As was natural, the conversation was subdued. They all ate supper with good appetite, but the presence of a stranger made the children uneasy, and Brother John was not talkative. He discussed banks and freight and a few business affairs with Henry, in a complaining tone, and was skeptical about everything. His voice was weak, too, and Miss Julie could never understand without asking him to repeat.

She pretended politely to be listening, but she was thinking he looked like the picture of a miser. That's what he was. She doubted if he ever gave anything away in his life unless it was no further good to him or anybody. Why should he be rich, and Joe poor? Sometimes she felt there was a terrible lot of injustice in the world. . . . She was even surprised he had come. It must have been just to please them. And yet he wasn't paying them the least attention. He was talking about business to Henry in the hope that he would find out something he could make some money out of. Her thoughts ran on and on in this direction, and she felt more and more indignant, only smiling when one of the little boys spoke to her and she turned to answer.

"Yes, Bubber, Uncle Joe is coming tonight again. He's coming to see Uncle John."

Hearing his name mentioned, John looked in her direction, nodded and smiled vaguely, and went on talking to Henry. He didn't trust this Mr. Wilson. The man was a visionary.

Joe came in about half-past eight, and the atmosphere lightened.

"Well, John, you old rascal!" he said, pumping his foster brother's hand and grinning at him. "Haven't seen you in a dog's age. You're looking fine."

"Yes, Joe, my health is very good now," John said in his quavering weak voice. "I was a little under the weather for quite a bit, but I'm as well as ever now."

Now that he was talking about himself, there was almost a trace of enthusiasm in his tone.

"That's good," Joe said. "I suppose you've given up hitting the high spots there in Savannah for a while."

John laughed weakly. "I lead a very quiet life. That's the only way I can keep myself fit for business. I'm not much interested in anything else now. When a man gets on into middle age, he has to concentrate on keeping what he's got before somebody comes up and takes it away from him."

"Go on, Johnnie. Do you suppose I don't know people from Savannah? I've heard how you carry on. Everybody there talks about it."

"You were always a great joker, Joe," John Gerard said, without the faintest trace of a laugh or smile.

Why, he was just a solemn old fool, Miss Julie thought. Joe was worth a hundred of him, with all his money. She wished he'd stayed in Savannah. She would have felt better, not seeing what he was like now. But that was unfair to John. People did what they could, and became what life made them. And she herself—for a moment she saw it clearly, as something apart from herself—was just a foolish old woman, passing her time as pleasantly as she could, trying to get along with those about her, completely unimportant to anybody, even to the children who were growing up so fast and took her for granted.

And when she died it wouldn't make any more difference to anybody than Tessie's death now. People would come, and they would say she was a pleasant old soul, and that maybe she was better off. . . . And her kind were dying off, the people that remembered the war and the good times before it. . . . And the Yankees and the Navy-Yard people would live in their houses, and . . . But what did it matter? All that was left was just pretense. There was Tessie. Poor, and quarrelsome, and proud, and always imagining things, and finally so addled in her poor brain that she couldn't tell fact from fiction. And that was Charleston all over—touchy, and poor, and proud, and full of ideas.

She went in for a last look at Tessie before going to bed, and immediately she became for a moment the practical, matter-of-fact old lady she usually was.

"It's a good thing she's going to be buried tomorrow," she murmured. "She's beginning to look a bit waxy already. I wonder what she thinks now about her visions. I dare say she doesn't care one way or the other."

Miss Julie looked fixedly at the thin face there on the pillow in the flickering light of the great candles. Why, she thought, that was the way her sister used to look when she was younger, when she was asleep. Death must have been a relief to her, poor soul. She supposed it was for everybody.

She went into the sitting room and said good night to John and Henry and Annette and Josephine.

"I want to be rested for the morning," she said. "It's always something of an ordeal, even when death is a merciful relief like this one."

"Do you feel all right, Ma?"

"Never better," Miss Julie replied. She looked at Henry, and it seemed to her that he looked like a man from whose shoulders a load has been lifted. "I'll be around for a long time to plague all of you," she said with cheerful malice, and went up to bed.

CHAPTER SIXTEEN

FOR A WHILE, AFTER MISS TESSIE WAS LAID TO REST under the whispering oaks in the cemetery, Miss Julie felt a little lost. Except for that brief period when she had returned to Henry's house, she had been through four difficult years, and it was very hard to adjust herself to the fact that there was now virtually nothing to worry her. She had no quarrels with anyone, she had no worries about herself. The only things that troubled her calm were regret that Charlie was so far away and that Francis was no more dutiful. Her conscience, which had nipped her at first about her deceit concerning the daguerreotype, was completely at rest again, and the bodily lassitude which had bothered her after Tessie's death had disappeared. She felt full of energy, despite her seventy-four years.

But there was little to do. The children were too big to be dressed now; she had only to superintend their prayers. She had resumed her collection of tinfoil, neglected while Tessie was such a close care, and had begun a new quilt. But that was not enough.

"I've got to make myself of some use in the world," Miss Julie said to herself; and she contemplated various charitable enterprises, and found none that was feasible.

While this matter was still unsettled Miss Julie was ambling down King Street one day, on the way to Mr. Leduc's store to buy some broken peppermint sticks, when she saw Miss Susan Williams hobbling toward her.

They said good day, and wasn't the weather lovely, even for this time of the year; and Miss Susan reported on the progress of her rheumatism. She was obliged to talk quite loud, and Miss Julie explained that she was getting a bit hard of hearing.

"But otherwise I'm fine, thank God," she added.

Miss Susan said that it was generally believed that Mordecai

Levy's wife was going to leave him, and that he was carrying on with some woman "up the road."

"*Tchk, tchk.* I never would have believed that of Mr. Levy. He was one of the ——." Miss Julie mentioned the name of a famous Jewish family.

"Charleston is a wicked city," said Miss Susan.

Miss Julie agreed that times were not what they had been.

"I heard an interesting thing about Eddie Calvert," Miss Susan said. "He was your poor sister's beau once, wasn't he? Well, I've just found out that he had colored children."

"Eddie Calvert? I don't believe it. If Tessie had heard anyone say that— Well, poor thing, she's dead and gone."

"Miss Tessie was just a trifle off, wasn't she?" Miss Susan inquired, bluntly.

Miss Julie colored. She had never thought that anyone would have the unmitigated gall to ask her that question.

"She was worried," she replied, with dignity. "She'd had a lot to worry her in her last years, her health and so on. It made her very nervous. Like your grandmother, Miss Susan. I remember how she used to think the Chinaman who ran the laundry on Hasell Street was a fiend, and tried to have him run out of town. Good morning."

"I guess that cut her comb," Miss Julie said to herself with vast satisfaction. "The idea of that old backbiter having the unmitigated gall to ask me if Tessie was crazy! Unmitigated gall," she repeated. "Unmitigated gall."

But her own remark about the Chinaman had reminded her of something that Josephine had talked about when she was with them, and that she had completely forgotten: saving stamps to buy Chinese children from their heathen masters. Miss Julie wasn't very clear about it; but she resolved to write to Josephine immediately to ask and, in the meantime, to begin to save the stamps. It would go very nicely as a kind of side line to her tinfoil and pin collection.

She bought ten cents' worth of the broken peppermint sticks

from Mr. Leduc, whom she found poorly and inclined to complain, and then went home to write that letter to Josephine.

At dinner she tackled Henry on the subject.

"Do you have a lot of mail at your office?" she asked him.

"Oh, yes, a tremendous amount," he replied, falling into the trap. "We get a great many circulars, and letters, and publications."

"Well, that's fine. Would you do me a favor?"

Henry was feeling expansive that day. He beamed.

"Certainly, Miss Julie. You have only to ask it."

"Well, then, I'd like to have the stamps from all that mail."

Henry's expression changed to one of chagrin. He had hoped his mother-in-law was going to ask him to do something that would make him feel generous in doing it.

"Why, I think it can be arranged, Miss Julie," he said. "What do you want them for, if you don't mind my asking?"

"To buy back Chinese orphans from their heathen owners. Josephine told me about it. She knows where to send them."

"That's a swindle, Miss Julie."

"What do you mean, a swindle?" Miss Julie asked, somewhat haughtily. "My sister Josephine is not in the habit of engaging in swindles, I'm sure."

"I mean—" Henry said, and then he stopped. "Very well, Miss Julie. You shall have the stamps, to do what you please with."

"Thank you," she said, satisfied.

"It's nonsense, but after what I've been through lately, it seems almost sensible by contrast," he told his wife. "As long as she doesn't get the idea she's a saint, or some other nervous affliction like that—"

"Henry," Annette said, "why don't you be honest about it? Aunt Tessie was as crazy as a loon."

"I've just got into the habit of referring to it as nervousness," he explained. There was no pleasing his wife's family. They were a strange lot.

"Well, this is another fancy for Ma to be taking up. Besides pins and silver paper."

"She can pick up all the pins and silver paper she damned pleases," Henry said. "I don't even give a damn if she buys fried fish at the cookshop and brings it home. I've been through the mill."

Miss Julie, charged with her new enthusiasm, set about her new mission in a businesslike way. She begged all her friends to save used stamps, soaked off all those Henry brought home to her, and made them into little piles, which she sent to Josephine, who was to forward them to the organization that was to save the Chinese infants from their horrible fate and restore them to the kindly Christian missionaries. She even neglected her quilting for this. She was very happy; and the receipt of two new prayers which Josephine sent her added immeasurably to her content. She said them faithfully many times a day, adding the total of indulgences gained to her little book, which was now nearly filled.

Life seemed very rewarding again.

The children's departure for the country made her feel a bit melancholy for the first few days, and she went over to visit her cousin Clara on the Island for a week. But she was glad to get back to the big house, lonely as it was. When she arrived, she went immediately to the kitchen to have a talk with Sarah, to whom she imparted a new recipe for a crab stew.

"When Mr. Henry goes, I'll get you to make it for me," she said.

"Yessum, I will," Sarah said.

"There was a great fuss once about a dish of chowder," Miss Julie said, unbending considerably.

"Yessum, I remembers," Sarah said deferentially.

"It was all my fault. Mr. Henry is the kindest man in the world, Sarah. There never was a better."

"Ain't it the truth!"

"He's taken care of me, and he took care of my poor nervous sister. God will bless him, even if he has a bad temper sometimes and doesn't go to church." Miss Julie accepted with a nod the cup of coffee Sarah poured out for her. "You know, Sarah, there are times when I think too much religion may be bad for people. It upset my poor sister. That and her foolish pride that she allowed to rule her."

"Well, she had a lot of trouble on earth."

"She made a lot of it herself," said Miss Julie.

"We all does."

"I wish Mr. Henry would go to church, at least at Easter time. But at my age you begin to realize that you can't force people to heaven. There was my husband. He was a Protestant, you know, until just before he died. . . . That was all right," she added quickly, remembering that Sarah was a Baptist. "But he didn't go to his own church. He said it made him damn' good and tired."

"Do, Lawd," Sarah said.

But that Sunday, as Miss Julie was about to start out for eleven o'clock Mass at a quarter past ten, she looked at Henry, who sat on the piazza reading the *News and Courier,* and she could not resist saying:

"Henry, why don't you put on your hat and come to Mass with me? It would do you good."

He looked up. "I'm afraid I might get the habit," he said. "I was zealous as a boy, you know, and it affected my health. I just couldn't risk it again."

"Oh, pshaw!"

Henry tensed himself for the banging of the door, and relaxed after the crash.

Miss Julie ambled along to the Cathedral in the peace of that summer morning. Father Mellon was the preacher, and he spoke feelingly on the virtue of humility. Miss Julie did not hear the sermon very well, however; she reflected that the acoustics of the Cathedral were very bad. But she did not mind. She said her rosary persistently during the sermon, and once or twice her murmur rose to such a pitch that Father Mellon was forced to pause in the face of this competition from the front pew. Then he saw her, and as he was a kindly man he smiled faintly and raised his voice a bit, and Miss Julie looked up, quite unmindful of the disturbance she was creating, or of the titters behind her.

She walked home reflectively. The city was so quiet, with such an air of peace brooding over it.

"It's as if God was blessing the world," she murmured to herself. "The idea of people with no religion! If they could see a day like this."

She expressed this notion to Henry: "It's wonderful, isn't it, how peaceful God made Sunday."

"Remarkable," he said.

"Peace is the greatest thing in the world," Miss Julie said. "That's all I've ever asked for, and what I wish for everybody else in the whole creation."

Henry was silent. He was thinking of the recent trouble in Mexico, and of his dread of war, now that Joe was almost a man. But Miss Julie had paid scant attention to any world affairs since the inauguration of the Pope and knew nothing about them.

In the afternoon she took a trolley ride up past the Schuetzen-platz, returned in time for Vespers, ate a good supper, and went to bed happy.

When she came to breakfast she found Henry in a state of great excitement.

"Good morning, Miss Julie," he said. "Well, I'm afraid your hope for peace may be in for a bit of a jolt. The Archduke of Austria has been assassinated."

She caught only the word "assassinated."

"Who?" she inquired.

"The Archduke of Austria."

"He probably deserved it," Miss Julie said. "Hurry up with that paper. I want to look at the obituaries."